He Had It Made

ALSO BY SIDNEY OFFIT

Novel
The Other Side of the Street

Memoir
Memoir of the Bookie's Son

For Young Readers
The Boy Who Won the World Series
Topsy Turvy
The Boy Who Made A Million
The Adventures of Homer Fink
Soupbone

Young Adult Novels
Only A Girl Like You
What Kind of Guy Do You Think I Am?

Collection of Short Stories
Not All Girls Have Million Dollar Smiles

Sports Series
Cadet Quarterback
Cadet Command
Cadet Attack

He Had It Made

Sidney Offit

Beckham Classic Reprints

Beckham Publications Group
Silver Spring

To Avodah

Copyright © 1999, Sidney Offit

All rights reserved. Printed in the U.S.A.

No part of this publication may be reproduced or transmitted in any form or by any means, electronic or mechanical, including photocopy, recording or any information storage and retrieval system now known or to be invented, without permission in writing from the publisher, except by a reviewer who wishes to quote brief passages in connection with a review written for inclusion in a magazine, newspaper or broadcast.

Published in the United States by
The Beckham Publications Group, Inc.
P.O. Box 4066, Silver Spring, MD 20914

ISBN: 0-931761-63-8

Praise for *He Had It Made:*

"Last year Richard Llewellyn parlayed his youthful experience in European hotel management into *Chez Pavan.* Now Sidney Offit, who has spent several recent summers working in the Catskills, tells the behind-the-dining-room-doors story of a Catskill resort hotel... The two novels are as different as an order of crêpes suzette and bowl of borscht, but they have in common a warm and sympathetic awareness of the peculiarly intense living that goes on behind the facade of the world-within-a-world of the hotel business."
—*New York Herald Tribune Book Review*

"It is an impressive example of empathy brought off at fictional level... The author has an excellent ear. In particular, one must note that he may well claim to be the first to capture and exhibit what might be called the future imperative, with causative subjunctive. 'You'll go to his room, you'll talk to Allen. He'll stay. We wouldn't get an experienced waiter this late in the season.'"
— *New York Times.*

"The subject in less sensitive hands might result in meaningless burlesque, but Offit intimately knows the zany world of gonifs, tummlers and nudnicks, and instinctively peoples it with real people confronting real problems... Nimbly weaving his way between pathos and the picaresque with a tray-load of humor, tragedy, sex and psychology, novelist Offit serves up a heaping platter of fine writing and even finer reading."
—Hugh Mulligan, *AP Book Review*

"Chronicled with humor and insight... Mr. Offit obviously knows the place and people well, and writes with tenderness of both."
—Ada Oklahoma *Book Round Up*

INTRODUCTION

When *He Had It Made* was published in 1959, I had no idea it was an historical novel. The Catskill resorts—identified as the borscht belt to celebrate appetite and culture—seemed destined to go on, well, certainly into the next millennium. At my mother-in-law Carrie Komito's Aladdin Hotel in Woodbourne, New York, there was constant talk of expansion. The main house, annex, winter cottage and recently built motel rooms were inadequate for the crowds that filled every bed (and occasionally several cots set up in the office) during the last two weekends in July and first two weekends in August.

Bathing habits, too, demanded new construction. Dips in the Neversink River were already a quaint anachronism, as guests sunbathed on lounge chairs surrounding the outdoor pool and spoke with the majesty of entitlement about the hotel's need for an indoor pool. "It rains, you sit, play cards, read a book, that's value? Better a steam room, a pool, up-to-date, ipsy-pipsy."

As a recent émigré from Baltimore, I was simultaneously enraptured and repulsed, admiring and critical, proud and embarrassed by this unabashedly Jewish resort area, vibrant and uninhibited in its esthetic violation of the countryside. And there seemed to be so much of it, although the greatest concentration of hotels covered only about fifteen square miles.

The Concord was in such a frenzy of expansion, the rumor was that it would soon offer an "indoor mountain." The Nevele's spread of mansions, cottages and golf courses on the route from Woodbourne to Ellenville seemed a feudal estate on its way to embracing hunks of Ulster as well as Sullivan County. Brown's patron saint (A saint in the borscht belt? Why not?) deified on billboards along Route 17—the one and only Jerry Lewis!—seemed to be our ambassador as well as the toast of Paris. Kutscher's entertained and was entertained by Wilt Chamberlain and a growing galaxy of NBA stars.

At the time I was weighing-in the mix for gefilte fish (Easy on the carp, a bissel more white and a shtickle pike, please!) and hanging out at Sitomer's, Kagan's and Kogan's butcher shops to be sure we received a fair count of our prime ribs along with two pieces of flanken. I was also moonlighting as a part-time reporter for *Baseball Magazine.* It was exhilarating to interview Jackie Robinson, Mickey Mantle and Willie Mays, but I was convinced there were masters already covering that beat. The Catskills with all its abundance of theatrical and literary talent, as far as I knew, had inspired no novel like George Orwell's non-fiction *Down and Out in Paris and London,* 1933, focusing on the hustle and bustle, eccentric and universal, of kitchen and dining room life.

As an outsider, I thought I brought the appropriate mix of detachment and wonder. I titled my novel *Five and Three House,* jargon for the expected tips to waiter and busboy at the end of the week, three meals a day, at the Aladdin. My agent Kenneth White, a former *Esquire* editor and resident of Westport, Connecticut, proclaimed it all news to him and expressed delight that nobody had tapped this rich source of character and humor. Herman Wouk's classic, *Marjorie Morningstar,* erroneously claimed by locals to be set at Tamarack Lodge, was a bestseller. But there was sufficient suspicion about the sales potential of a "kitchen novel" that even with Ken White's enthusiasm, it required more than a year—and another "season"—before Arthur Fields, a brilliant but demanding editor, changed the title and signed us up for Crown Publishers.

The reception for *He Had It Made* is suggested by the excerpts from reviews reprinted in this edition. I also had the heady experience of appearing on the Jack Paar show, where I met Moss Hart, as charming and erudite a gent as ever graduated from Oxford, Cambridge or the Flagler Hotel, South Fallsburg. Lewis Nichols, who was writing "In and Out of Books" for the Sunday New York *Times* Book Review, invited me to lunch at the Algonquin, and we talked about the mountains as if I'd just returned from a retreat in Tibet.

After all this, summer in the Catskills became less enchanting for me. I'd written my story. Irony: my wife, the elegant, talented, grace of graces, Avodah, bailed me out. In the summer of 1968 after graduating from medical school, Avi, our sons Ken and Mike and I celebrated with a brief tour of the UK. The following summers, as Avi trained at Lenox Hill and New York Hospitals, we rented a cottage in Water Mill, Long Island, where we've been tenants ever since.

On jaunts to visit the old homestead it became increasingly apparent that the borscht belt was in decline; shells of our proud competitors lined the route to Woodbourne. Is that the Heiden? Looks like they're out of business. What happened to the Olympia? Ambassador? Brookside? Chester's? The streets of South Fallsburg, Woodbourne, Ellenville and Liberty that once reminded me of Western towns in gold rush movies, now resembled the boarded-up deserted village of *High Noon.*

We knew Grossinger's, that great flagship of the Catskills, had gone down when my mother-in-law returned from Liberty with carpeting, bureaus and beds she'd bought for "next to nothing" at—was it a bankruptcy sale? We heard, too, that the full houses for the High Holy Days at Brickman's and the Windsor Hotels were memories; the Syddha Yoga Ashram conducted less operatic rituals on their premises.

Yet, Carrie Komito sailed on though Abe Komito, her husband, died. He had been the deputy chief engineer who built the Brooklyn-Queens connecting highway and applied the same talent to the construction of the Aladdin's bungalows, indoor pool and smooth functioning infrastructure. Her children and grandchildren moved on to "fresh woods and pastures new."

On Monday August 10, 1998, the Metro section of the New York *Times* featured a photograph of Yosi Piamenta, an Israeli-born rock guitarist, performing for an audience of teenagers with yarmulkes secure, fringes flying and fists raised. The headline read: " Rocking All Night in Hebrew—Hasidic Guitarist Mixes Religion and Heavy Metal." The scene of this last hurrah was the Ali Baba Room of the Aladdin.

Later in the year Carrie Komito, at the age of 93, announced to her staff and Floridian guests that she intended to sell the hotel. "Enough is enough." This saga has not gone unremarked. Phil Brown, a Brown University Professor and co-founder of the Catskill Institute, recently published a history and memoir of the area. Among the other wonders of anthropological memorabilia discussed in *Catskill Culture* are photographs of the Aladdin, Carrie Komito presiding at the front desk, and—a summary of the plot of *He Had It Made*. Not exactly an ode to immortality or Library of America edition, but a touching reminder that the borscht belt represented an aspect of our time, a celebration of the good life, American style.

                        Sidney Offit
                        New York City
                        July, 1999

A Catskill comedian was once holding forth on the stage of a large resort. He was running through a routine about a bald-headed fat man, and the audience was having a wonderful time.

There was one exception.

In the second row of the audience, the comedian saw a bald-headed fat man.

The comedian, who was himself on the heavy side, stopped and ran his hand over his own head. "Don't take it so personal," he said and pulled off his toupee.

In the preparation of this book, the names of actual resorts and points of interest in the Catskills have been mentioned, but only in so far as they contribute to the background and color. Beyond that nothing was meant to be—or, it is hoped, will be taken to be—personal. All the characters and situations are fictitious and any similarity to actual persons, places, or events is purely coincidental.

Chapter 1

Spring comes late to the Catskills. In the May sun, the weathered shingles of the old farmhouse were as gray and bare as the rocks on the hillside pasture, where five cows grazed on patches of new soft grass. Near the barbed-wire fence close to the house, two boys dressed in T shirts and blue jeans threw stones at a tin can.

On the porch a thin woman sat in a rusty love seat. One cushion was gone, and in its place was a blanket folded up over the springs so the woman could rest her legs.

The screen door from the house opened and shut quietly, and the woman said without turning her head, "Don't forget the medicine, Tom, and while you're in town you can pick up another sack of potatoes."

The farmer struck a match, cupped his big hands to the butt of a cigarette and lit it. He flicked the match away and leaned an arm against the porch pillar. He looked out beyond the hill to where a thick stream of smoke was rising.

"Them hotel people," he said. "Ain't hardly June and they're going right at the summer." After a moment he said, "I see where they cut down your Aunt Beth's crab-apple tree. The hotel man says they're putting up this new playhouse just for babies."

"They have that other house where the old barn was," the woman said. "What they going to do with that?"

"I reckon that's for the big children."

"My goodness," the woman said. "A house for the big ones and a house for the babies too. Why it weren't so long ago the hotel people's mother, she had just that white house and the apple tree and a few folks up for the summer."

"They done the white house over," the farmer said. "Fixed her up with some redwood."

They both said nothing for a while and then the farmer dropped his arm from the porch pillar. He turned toward his wife. "You're looking better," he said. "Be up and around before you know it."

The woman said, "You ought to be getting on into town, Tom. The boys will be wanting to eat."

The farmer walked down the porch steps to his pickup truck. He waved to his wife and honked his horn at the boys playing by the gate.

His car chugged down the dirt driveway from the farm and onto a narrow, rutted path, thickly bordered with ash and elm and maple trees, which closed together as soon as the car passed through. The fragrance of apple blossoms was in the air. He passed a little stream shaded by white and pink dogwood. Then he reached the state road. Directly facing the intersection there were signs.

KNISHES AND PIZZAS
☞

HYMIE'S DELICATESSEN
FORMERLY OF THE BRONX

THE NEW UTOPIA
(THE <u>BEST</u> THERE IS)
AIR CONDITIONED

WEINBERG'S WIGWAM
STRICTLY KOSHER

"See, lady, it's like this—I need a job."

His name was Al Brodie. He was tall and muscular, with a square face and cropped black hair. When he smiled his teeth flashed even and white and there was a dimple in the left corner of his chin. He smiled and Mrs. Mandheimer said, "Sam, look at that dimple—just like Phillip's. Don't he remind you of Phillip, Sam? Sam, you've got to see this."

Sam Mandheimer was sitting on a swivel chair. A switchboard was to his right and a typewriter was in front of him. On the floor were three open boxes containing letterhead stationery, envelopes, and four-color brochures. On top of each was embossed a figure on a magic carpet engulfed in a billow of smoke which descended on the Old English type announcing SESAME HOTEL. Under the name in an italic script appeared, *The Heart of the Catskills.*

"Sam, this you got to see."

The typewriter pecked briskly a moment. Sam Mandheimer had a small, pleasant face. His nose was short but turned down at the end. It didn't seem to go with the fullness of his cheeks and his bright blue eyes. His hairline was receding and there were flecks of gray at the temples. Sam Mandheimer was considered youthful-looking and attractive.

"Don't bother me when I'm working, Becky," he said to his wife.

"He looks like Phillip, Sam."

"Look, Becky, you want to do the letters?" The typewriter started to go again. "I'll do a few, you wouldn't have to work all night."

Mrs. Mandheimer brushed a speck off her starched white shirt front. "So what kind of job you want?"

"I want to make money, Becky," Al Brodie said. "I'm talking to you like you're my own mother. I don't know—somehow I feel I can be honest with you. I feel right at home, like you're somebody I've known all my life." He leaned over the desk and pushed the registration cards aside. "I'm working my way through college, see, and the only chance I have of making my tuition is right here. Here at the Sesame—that's where my future will be made or lost. Let's be honest, where else can I make a thousand dollars in the summer?"

"We need a waiter, Sam?" Becky Mandheimer called over her shoulder.

No answer.

"You know when you talk so serious you don't look so much like Phillip," she said. "And don't call me Becky."

"Mrs. Mandheimer," Al Brodie said, and he smiled the dimple again, "I'd like to be a waiter."

Mrs. Mandheimer smoothed her blouse down once, twice. She jangled the shower ring that held her house keys. "You should always smile," she said, turning away from the front desk and toward her husband. "Sam, we got a waiter's job open?"

He had stopped typing and was studying the stationery in the typewriter. "How you spell accessible? Two c's and one s or the other way around?"

"Sam, I'm asking you a question."

"Becky, how you spell accessible?"

"A-c-c-e-s-s-i-b-l-e," Al Brodie said. "That's me, Mr. Mandheimer. "I'm accessible. I need a job. I want to be a waiter."

Mr. Mandheimer hit the typewriter keys five times. "That was two s's, too?"

"Yes, sir, two s's."

"Sam, the boy is waiting."

"That's all right, Mrs. Mandheimer." He smiled. "Business comes first."

"You got a nice line," Mr. Mandheimer said. "You wouldn't be a bad waiter."

The switchboard buzzed. Mr. Mandheimer put up the tab and pressed down the key. He picked up the phone, cradled it under his chin and said, "Hotel Sesame." There was a pause and then he said, "Mr. Mandheimer is speaking. I'll hold on."

He went back to the typewriter with one hand, held the mouthpiece of the telephone with the other, and looked up at Al. "You play basketball, boy? This year I'm going in for basketball. My waiters are all basketball."

"I'm a senior lifesaver. I could help the lifeguard."

"A lifeguard I got."

"So he don't play basketball. What's such a big deal, he's got to play basketball? Twenty years we run this hotel without basketball. Now all of a sudden Sam sees a few games on television, he wants Bob Cousy should work a window station."

"Becky, be quiet. You don't know what you're talking about. The biggest, the best, they got basketball. The whole team from New York College is by Rabinowitz's this year. If it's good enough for the Tepee Rendezvous, it wouldn't hurt us."

He went back to the telephone. "Yes . . . yes, this is Mr. Mandheimer . . . For the Fourth of July? Tsh-tsh . . . So late? I don't know, it all depends. What d'you want? I got baths on the floor, adjoining baths and privates. We also got the deluxe bungalows. Wall-to-wall carpeting, magnificent furniture, fan and heater in the room—everything strictly the best . . . No, we don't have deluxe bungalows available for the Fourth . . ."

"See?" Mrs. Mandheimer said. "See why I handle the front?"

"Look!" Mr. Mandheimer's voice bellowed into the phone. "The holiday starts tomorrow. You had to wait until the last minute?"

"Sam," Mrs. Mandheimer tugged his shirt sleeve. "That's no way to handle a customer."

"The main building I could give you," Mr. Mandheimer said to the phone. "I got a nice corner room, cross ventilation . . . Yes . . .Yes, it's private bath . . . Of course we got entertainment . . . For the Fourth? I don't know. It'll be Broadway stars, though . . . No, we get strictly Broadway stars . . . Look, I'll tell you," his voice lowered to a purr.

"My agent Harry, he handles the best. See, we're on the circuit with Label's Fontainebleau. Any entertainment Label's got, we get it too . . . What d'you mean how can I afford it? That's the way it works. The stars are up in the mountains so they work two shows . . . Yes . . . Ah-hah . . . No, we don't have an old crowd. Mostly young and old. You know, all kinds of people . . . Of course, a swimming pool . . . Of course, wonderful food . . . Of course, day camp . . . Of course, night patrol. Why not? . . . Why not? . . . No, you don't have to pull the string. The flush box isn't on the wall . . . What d'you mean? It's a regular handle. It pushes up and down . . . Strictly modern . . . All right, so what's the name . . ."

Mr. Mandheimer made a notation on the envelope of one of the letters he was answering. "And that'll be for how many? Just you? . . . You and your sister? Just over the week end? You're not staying the week . . . That'll be twenty-five dollars a day for the two of you. How can I do better? . . . Ah-hah . . . Ah-hah . . . All right, so you'll come up, we'll see."

He hung up the phone and Mrs. Mandheimer said, "So how come you didn't tell them about the basketball?"

"Looks like it's going to be a good Fourth of July," Mr. Mandheimer said. "Didn't I tell you? Decoration Day means nothing. When did we ever have a good Decoration Day?"

"Excuse me," Al Brodie said. "I was wondering about that waiter's job."

"We got eight waiters already," Mr. Mandheimer said.

"So where'd you work before?" Mrs. Mandheimer asked.

"I want to be an accountant. You got to go to college to be an accountant. My cousin Hesch, he's a jerk but he's an accountant and you know how much money he makes? Well, let's just put it this way—he owns his home, drives a Buick and sends the whole family away for the summer."

"Fine thing?" Mr. Mandheimer was pecking on the typewriter again. "He tells us he wants a job and in the next breath he's bragging his cousin goes to another hotel."

"Hesch wouldn't come up here. The Catskills aren't fancy enough for him. He went in partners with the contractor whose books he was auditing. Now he's strictly Cape Cod."

"Cape Cod yet," Mr. Mandheimer said.

"Be quiet, Sam. It's not his fault."

"We got eight waiters. That's all we need."

Al Brodie stood up to his full six-feet two and a half. He pressed his hands deep into the pockets of his khakis and shrugged. His expression was a real effort to look brave. "O.K.," he said, "if that's the way it is."

But he didn't go away. He just stood there.

Mrs. Mandheimer looked at him for about thirty seconds until, very slowly, he smiled.

"Sam, do me a favor. This you got to see. I'm telling you he looks exactly like Phillip."

The switchboard buzzed and Sam was on it fast. "Sesame Hotel . . . What? Sure we got a few rooms left for the holiday . . . I don't know, that all depends what you mean by cheap . . ."

Mrs. Mandheimer rang a little bell on the side of the desk. A broad-shouldered Negro appeared, dressed in stiffly pressed blue pants with a gold stripe running down each side. He was wearing a shirt with a mandarin collar. It had a pattern of small lamps and genies. The word *Sesame* was emblazoned in gold across the chest.

"Calvin, you'll show him the waiter's shack," Mrs. Mandheimer said.

"Yes, ma'am. You know we got eight waiters already?"

"I know."

"So what you want to do that for? We already got more waiters than guests." Calvin lifted his hands, palms up. He'd worked in the mountains for fifteen summers and spent the winters in Lakewood.

"Thank you," Al Brodie said. "You won't be sorry, Mrs. Mandheimer. I need this job, I really do." He took his hand out of his pocket and touched hers. "Thanks, mom," he said.

"What a line. What a line," Mrs. Mandheimer said, and she was vaguely revolted until he smiled.

Chapter 2

"We're not getting a break on publicity," the client said. "We've got something here to talk about—to shout about. You got to tell 'em."

"I know, I know," said the promotion man from the Sullivan County Resorts Agency. "But you get west of the Hudson and nobody knows or cares about the Catskills. You got to face it."

"Half a million people—over a half million people come up here and spend over sixty million bucks every year. You said so yourself. You think Cape Cod can beat that? Palm Springs? The goddamn Riviera?"

"No doubt about it," the promotion man said. "No place in the world gives so many people so much for so little."

"That's the idea," the client said. "You sold me, now sell Life magazine."

It was the end of June and the temperature was in the eighties. Calvin's mandarin shirt was soaked to his back and thick beads of sweat rolled down his cheek. He was carrying Al Brodie's suitcase in one hand and a handkerchief to wipe his face in the other.

"All this new?" Al motioned toward a row of motel-style buildings.

Calvin didn't answer.

"It looks new," Al said.

"What you so interested in, boy? You gonna buy the place?"

"You've worked here a long time—ten, fifteen years I bet?"

"We gon' to have a hot summer," Calvin said. "The missus done put a lot of *gelt* in here." He moved heavily, leaning over to balance the suitcase. "We gon' to have a big summer—a big summer."

"I hope so," Al said. "They seem to be nice people. I hope so."

They walked across the lawn in front of the motels and then down a dirt road. The hotel was on the side of a thickly wooded mountain. Two apple trees blossomed on the lawn, and in front of two large stucco buildings were planted a line of small pyramid- and globe-shaped arborvitaes, a few Greek junipers, and some golden plume-mosses.

Across the road was a huge swimming pool and next to it was a T-shaped wooden building with a big neon sign in front. The sign said "Fatima Bar."

"This is a damn nice place," Al said.

"Boy, they don't need you. They already got eight waiters."

"She's a nice lady, I really like Mrs. Mandheimer," Al said.

"You're a good talker, boy."

They came to a one-story wooden building. The roof was slanted and half-covered by overhanging trees.

Calvin walked in and Al followed him. The walls were unpainted, but otherwise resembled a public men's room. The word "Mong" appeared frequently and there were Greek initials of fraternities. One sign read, "Mandheimer's Whore House— Hang onto them, Mong."

Calvin put the bag down and threw open the first door. It was a small room crowded with a double and two single beds. The beds extended from the back wall and there was a small aisle in the middle. Suitcases were under each bed, a broomstick was arranged to provide a clothes rod on the wall, but whoever had put it up had set it at an angle. The collection of Ivy League tweeds and cord suits hanging on it were bunched at the low end.

There were three boys in the room. One in shorts and a T shirt was playing cards with a muscular blond boy in a basketball jersey. A third boy lay asleep in the double bed. He had a pillow over his head. Otherwise he was naked.

"O.K., boy," Calvin said. "You find yourself a place to sleep in here."

"Fine," Al said.

He stepped out of the room with Calvin and handed the Negro two dollars.

Calvin smiled and Al said, "What the hell, live and let live, I always say. We're here today, gone tomorrow. Right, Cal?"

"Yes, sir," Calvin said, "right." He folded the two dollars and put it in his pocket. "That's the truth. It don't pay to be cheap."

When Al came back into the room the boy in the shorts and T shirt said, "Gimme two." He threw down two cards and picked up the two the boy in the basketball jersey dealt him. He was looking at the cards when he said, "I'm Mike Long. This is Harry Schlong and that's the Great Mong on the bed."

The one called Harry laughed. "Who you play for?" he asked Al.

"Play what?"

"He don't play," Mike said.

"No, I don't play basketball. I play with girls," Al Brodie said.

They both looked at him.

"What d'you say your name was?" Harry asked.

"Al Brodie. Nice to meet you fellows, and what the hell is a Mong?"

"The old lady—what's her name—Mrs. Mandheimer, she gave us red paint to touch up the woodwork. It was Stan's idea. He's Mong."

"That's Stan?" Al slapped the pillow on top of the face.

"Yeah, ain't he cute?"

"Seems to be a little bit of an exhibitionist."

"He happens to be first string all-city."

Al dumped himself down on the empty bed. There was a roar from the double bed and Stan, the Mong, stretched his long hairy arms. He opened his mouth wide, yawned as loud as he could, and scratched. "Oh, God, send me a woman."

21

"Hey, Stan, we got a boarder," Mike said.

Harry said, "Looks like the great Mong's got a bunkie."

"Who is she?" the Mong asked.

"The name's Al Brodie," Al said. "What the hell, we got to make the best of it."

Stan sat up. He had an enormous body with heavy shoulders and big hands. His face was dry and tight from sleep, and he was angry. "Lemme get this straight. You're moving in here with us?"

"That's the story," Al said.

"The hell you are," Stan shot back. "I ain't sacking out with nobody. What the hell they think this is?" He got up and moved toward the bed where Al was sitting. "You ain't living here, Mac. Just forget it."

"This is where they put me," Al said. He smiled but Stan, the Mong, didn't notice.

"Look, bud, get moving. Tell 'em to put you someplace else. This room's crowded."

"Bye-bye," Mike said.

Harry sang, "We hate to see you go. We hate to see you go."

"So good-by already," Stan said.

Al didn't move. He shoved his hands into his pockets, crossed his legs on the bed, and said, "They tell me you're quite a basketball player, Stan. Old man Mandheimer really goes in for basketball, huh?"

"Look, kid, this room ain't big enough for three, much less four. Be a good boy, will ya? Go tell the old lady there's no room here for you."

"How about putting some pants on?" Al said.

"Are you going to get moving," Stan said. "Or do I have to throw you out?"

"No kidding, put on some pants—a jock strap—something. It's disgusting."

Stan put a hand on Al's shoulder. "You know, I'm the captain. See what I mean?"

"I don't play basketball."

"I mean in the dining room, jerk. Now take a hint and shove."

Mike whistled. Harry said, "Bong. Round two."

Al stood up. He was two inches shorter than the big basketball player. The smallness of the room forced them right on top of each other.

"Get your goddamn shoe off my toe," Stan said.

"I think you have a complex," Al said. "You know, it isn't normal to run around with it hanging out."

"Goddamn, you're a wise son of a bitch," Stan said. He clenched his fist like he was ready to swing.

Al put his hands on his hips. "No athletics, not without a jock strap." He smiled.

The boys on the bed laughed.

A red-haired boy with freckles pushed his head around the door. "There's a meeting in the dining room," he said. "Audrey is going to give out stations."

"You're a lucky bastard," Stan said.

"I know I am, Mong," Al Brodie said.

Chapter 3

"The way it works," the proprietor of the knish stand said, "you got first of all your bungalows. They'll give you a place you'll have where to sleep, the mountain air, maybe a little pool you can swim. Your wife is a good cook, you'll have what to eat. You say you don't want your wife she should schlep? So you'll go by a hotel. They'll give you three meals, a porch, a rocker.

"Not fancy enough for you? Some place famous? You mean they should know where you've been when you tell them about it at home? Why not? So you'll take the family to the Aladdin, a Brickman's, a Laurels, a Nemerson's, a Pines, a Kutcher's, a Windsor. They have everything new, everything modern. You should only live and be well, you'll have a wonderful time.

"You want the best, the best in the world? From Paris I wouldn't know. To London I've never been. But you'll go to Grossinger's, the Concord, the Nevele—you couldn't want for nothing better. They've got night clubs, health clubs, golf courses. It rains, already they got an indoor swimming pool— you wouldn't even get wet."

Audrey Grier didn't wear stockings. It was June but her legs were already tanned. She wore shoes with open toes that displayed her brightly polished red toenails. Every part of her that could be rouged or polished was done up carefully. She had full, thick lips and a heavy-set body that came off as a good figure because her hips and bust were larger than her waist. It was her nose that spoiled her. Broad and flat, it spread out across her face like a young fighter's.

She tried to talk like a drill sergeant but her voice was thin and feminine. "I want my stations spotlessly clean," she said. "Every meal I'll inspect. There's no excuse for dirty goblets, and little things like the sugar bowl and salt and pepper shakers, I expect them to be perfect. Every waiter and busboy that works my room has to be a walking advertisement for the hotel. Polished shoes, clean shirts, and I don't want anybody coming in here needing a shave or a haircut. And another thing, I want the mats by each server picked up and cleaned every day." She liked that point and she dwelt on it for a few minutes. When she was finished she consulted a small pad in her hand.

"Watch yourself in the kitchen," she said. "No busboys pick up anything from the stove, unless it's a special, and then they have to have a note from me."

She wasn't all business. She could be sisterly. "I know the going gets tough when we're busy. I've worked the mountains for ten years. The guests will get under your skin, but don't panic. When you run into a tough one—well, they require a special technique." She bobbed the bun at the back of her head. "That's what I'm here for. I want to help you."

She could be tough, too. "I'm not trying to win any popularity contests. There are twenty boys waiting around the agencies, dying for a job. And I'm not afraid to fire. The boys who've worked with me before know I don't take less than a hundred per cent."

They were sitting in the dining room, a tremendous hall with a huge plate glass window along one side. The tables and chairs were painted coral, and there was a paper that looked like a jungle scene against the far wall. The floor was highly polished, and a thin wall trimmed with redwood and artificial flowers concealed an air-conditioning unit.

For the meeting, the nine waiters and eight busboys were gathered around a small table that acted as a desk for the hostess. It was next to the concealed unit and near the dining-room entrance. Most of the boys were sitting with the chairs swung around backwards. Audrey was the only one standing.

"Audrey"—it was Stan, the Mong—"tell 'em about chasing tips."

"I'm coming to that."

"Nobody chases tips, right? You take what you get and shut up. The good make up for the stiffs, right?"

"Thanks, Stan, that's right. The first boy I catch or hear about chasing the guests for tips—out. No questions—just out."

"Tell 'em about busboys' side jobs," Stan said.

"Wait a minute, Stan. I'm coming to that later."

Stan said, "She puts the list up in the kitchen and that's it. No bitching. You got complaints, see me."

"Two months on the breadbox for Joe," one of the boys said.

Joe, the red-haired boy who had announced the meeting, blushed and said, "Not this year. I'm a waiter, I hope."

"Also, you'll be wearing special shirts this year. No more white jackets. I think they're very attractive and should give the dining room color. Naturally, you'll be expected to buy these shirts. Three for each boy. Mrs. Mandheimer is selling them at cost—two dollars apiece. And that's cheap, believe me."

"Right away money," Mike Heimer said.

"Knock it off," Stan said. "Tell 'em about the stations, Audrey."

"I'm coming to that." She inspected her notes, skipping over the reminders to talk about punctuality, place settings, and how to serve. "Of course, everybody wants a window station. Unfortunately, there just aren't enough to go around. The window stations will go to the most deserving. I like to reward the boys who do a good job, but I go hard on the ones who don't. We'll start off by giving priority to the boys who have worked here the longest. I think that's the fairest way." She was looking at the notes when she said, "Stan Macht will work station one, and I'm putting Mike Heimer on station two . . ."

"Oh, no," Joe said. "You promised me a window station last year, Audrey, remember? I was a waiter before I came here and I only agreed to bus for a season with the understanding—"

"Understanding—hell," Stan Macht said. "You go where you're put and shut up."

"I wasn't talking to you," Joe said.

"But I was talking to you," Macht said. "Don't you go telling the Mong what to do. Not you or anybody else around here is giving this boy any crap."

"Hail the great Mong," Mike Heimer said.

"Long live the Mong's schlong," another waiter said.

"Quiet—all of you." The girl's face flushed. "I don't want any vulgarity—let's get that straight right from the start. If you can't act like gentlemen, get out."

"Let's hear the rest of the stations," Stan said.

"Stop interrupting me." She looked at him angrily and then went back to her notes. "This is a tentative list. If anybody has a complaint, see me after the meeting. I'll check with the office, and the final list will be posted on the bulletin board tonight." Her voice was softer when she said, "You should all know by now that I try to be fair."

After the list was read, the meeting broke up. Joe, Stan Macht, and Al were the only boys who stayed in the room.

"I don't want to gripe," Joe said, "but it cost me a couple hundred dollars bussing instead of waiting last year. I need that window station to make it up."

"Why don't you shut up and give her a chance?" Stan said. "You and your damn crying towel—"

"I wasn't talking to you, Jock Strap."

"Somebody around here is going to get their jaw broken."

"All right. That's enough." Audrey Grier sat down on the chair in front of her small desk. She crossed her legs and was very careful to pull her skirt over her knees. The three boys watched. "Now I fully sympathize with you, Joe, but don't let your red-haired temper get the best of you." She thought that was cute and she smiled. Her teeth were even and white, but widely spaced. "I did promise you a window station, but I thought Mike Heimer might be a little stronger."

"I carried the biggest station in the house last year," Joe said, "and I had an inexperienced waiter. Did you have any trouble, any trouble at all from my station?"

"Why don't you shut up and listen to her?" Stan said.

Al Brodie stood far enough off to the side to be out of the way. He made no effort to look as if he wasn't listening.

"I could be wrong. I'm not perfect," Audrey Grier said. "I'll tell you what—you let Mike have the station for the first two weeks. Then I'll try you. Maybe we'll rotate like that all summer."

Joe's face flushed. He wheeled in his chair and turned away from her. "That won't work, Audrey. What would we do about season guests? I can see right now I'm going to get screwed."

"You won't get screwed," the hostess said. "You have my word for that. You just let Mike Heimer work the window station for two weeks. We'll see after that—O.K.?" She put out her hand as if she was going to touch him, but she quickly drew it back, jangled her loose bracelets, and adjusted the chignon at the back of her head.

Joe shrugged. "All right. There's nothing I can do about it anyway." He looked over at Stan Macht, who was smiling. "But you, you son of a bitch, don't you think you can push me around. Damn basketball players think they own this hotel."

"Why don't you drop dead," Stan said.

Joe left and Audrey said, "Stan, take it easy, will you? I know what I'm doing. You only make it harder for me."

"What about this jerk?" He motioned over his shoulder toward Brodie.

Al stepped closer to the table. "I'm Al Brodie. Did Mrs. Mandheimer tell you about me?"

"You a busboy?"

"No, ma'am, I'm a waiter. Mrs. Mandheimer promised me a job."

"She did? She shouldn't have done that. We already have a full staff. Maybe she wanted you to work in the children's dining room. We might need two waiters in there."

"She said the main dining room."

"That's funny. Well, she has so many things on her mind. I'll tell you what—I'll talk to her and see you later."

"I'd appreciate that. I certainly would," Al said.

"Oh, balls," Stan said.

"Stan, will you stop that! There's nothing wrong with acting like a gentleman." She lifted her chin and seemed to tighten her nostrils. "You say your name's Al Brodie?"

"I don't want this guy working here," Stan said. "He's no good. He's an eight ball. I could see it the first time I looked at him. He's a goddamned phony."

"Suppose you let me decide that," Audrey Grier said.

"O.K., you decide," Stan the Mong said, "but he don't work here."

"Stan, I think you'd better leave," Audrey said.

"Where the hell did you ever work before?" Stan asked Al. "Did you ever work as a waiter? Name the place. Give us a reference."

Al looked at Audrey as if it was all he could do to restrain himself.

"All right, Stan, you've said your little piece, now suppose we leave the rest up to me."

"You don't shift none of the regulars for him," Stan said. "I don't want my boys getting the shaft because of a yes-ma'am-no-ma'am phony like him." He made a loud noise with his chair as he got up. "I'm leaving it up to you, Audrey. The old man wants a basketball team this year. He wants to put this place on the map. You better do what's right."

After Stan left, Audrey touched the bun in back of her head three times in a row. She uncrossed and then recrossed her legs. "He's just about impossible," she said. "But he is strong and he carries his station very well. You see, I never let my personal sentiments interfere with my work. I may like a person very much, but that doesn't mean I'll show him any favoritism. The same thing is true if I don't like a person. I mean if I think they are crude and uncouth. I wouldn't let a thing like that keep me from hiring him or treating him with all the respect due because of his professional competence. I tried to make that very clear to the boys. In my speech, I mean—I thought it came through."

"I got it perfectly," Al said.

"Now, about you, Brodie." She folded her hands on her lap

and got right down to business. "Have you ever worked a house this size?"

"I'll be honest with you. You strike me as the kind of person I can talk to straight. I mean without trying to impress you. Like the way you talked to the boys. It came through. It was right to the point. A person has to be pretty sure of themselves and really know what they're talking about to lay it on the line like that."

"You're not answering my question," she said.

"The fact is there's nobody up here I could call up and get a reference from just like that," he snapped his fingers. "I'd rather tell you that than make up some phony names and back it up with a lot of lies."

"I think you'd do very well in the children's dining room," she said. "Children require a special kind of handling. I've got a hunch you'd do nicely, very nicely—"

"The thing is—" Al said. He paused and let out his breath and then said very gravely, "I've got to make a thousand dollars this summer. If you think I can make it in the children's dining room—well, I have confidence in you. I think you understand people very well. If you think that's the place for me, I'll just tell Mrs. Mandheimer I won't be working the main dining room. After all you're the boss."

"Did Mrs. Mandheimer *promise* you a station in the main dining room?"

"She said something about shifting one of the other boys. But then again I don't think she consulted this fellow they call the Mong."

"Don't worry about Stan. I just let him talk. Half the time I don't even listen to him."

"Well—whatever you say—"

"Let me tell you this, Al." She uncrossed her legs, set both her feet firmly on the floor and leaned forward in the chair. She balanced her weight forward on her toes. "This is a five-and-three house—the toughest kind of house in the mountains. You really have to know the ropes to work a house like this. In the height of the season you have to carry a station of thirty or maybe more. We have a menu, but anything that's off the menu that a guest asks for we try to get for them. In that respect our service is à la carte, like it is at the best hotels. But our people are all over you. They keep you running like it's a hash house. There's no sense in our trying to kid ourselves. If I see you can't do it, I'll save you a lot of aggravation and the house a lot of embarrassment. I can be tough when I have to be. I'd fire you like that." She snapped her fingers, just the way he had a few moments before.

"I'll take my chances," Al said. "And thanks."

"Hold on a minute. It's not settled. You haven't got the job yet, not by a long shot. I have a lot of thinking to do."

"I have confidence in you," Al said. "I just hope you have some in me." It didn't come off the way he wanted, and he smiled.

"You'll know tonight," Audrey said. "I'll post the final station assignments on the bulletin board in the kitchen."

"Gee, I don't believe I know where that is," Al said.

"Here, I'll show you," she said. She stood up slowly, and was careful to hold herself straight and tall as she walked across the room toward the entrance to the kitchen. To be a good hostess, she'd often thought, you have to possess the grace and aloofness of a professional model. But there had to be just enough action in the back to keep the men's minds off the food.

Al Brodie was right behind her.

The coffee urns and the glass-washing section were in the passageway leading from the dining room into the kitchen. The kitchen itself was large, divided down the center by long stoves, back to back. On either side of the stoves were serving counters. One side was used for lunch and dinner, the other for breakfast. At intervals along the walls were doors leading to the pantry, bakery, pot-washing tubs and dishwashing machine.

There was a twenty-by-twenty bulletin board nailed to the wall beside the coffee urns. It had a redwood border and the name *Hotel Edgemoore* in black script across the front. Mrs. Mandheimer had bought it at an auction three years ago. She was very persistent about having her hostess use it. The Workmen's Compensation laws were posted along one side, and there was a notice to all the help that said, "This is Your Kitchen. Keep it Clean." The headwaiter who had preceded Audrey Grier had written and posted it the first day the bulletin board was put up. It had hung through summer and winter for three years. There was seldom a day during the season when some waiter or busboy didn't pass it and say, "Yeah, my kitchen!"

"Isn't this a mess!" Audrey Grier said. The table beneath the coffee urns was wet with hot water and leaking coffee. She pulled out a dish towel from under the urns and wiped up the puddles. Her voice lowered. "You know the kind of help we have in the kitchen."

"Let me do that," Al said.

"No, it's all right." She concentrated on the table. "I hate filth. I don't know why. That's just the way I am."

"I don't blame you, Miss Grier. Especially where food is concerned."

"Sometimes it takes a woman. We're naturally more concerned with neatness." She held the wet towel out in front of her, away from her dress.

"Here, let me take that," Al said. "Where can I wring it out?"

She gave up the towel easily. "Over there, where the boys do their trays." She pointed to a big washbasin on one side of the wall.

Al Brodie wrung the towel out carefully. Then he rinsed it and wrung it out again. "Any place in particular you want this?"

"Just put it under the urns. The next person who notices a mess can wipe it up. Big joke." She tightened the handles of the urns and said, "Well, there's the bulletin board. You can get the feel of the rest of the kitchen from here."

"Oh yeah," Al said. "I'm beginning to feel at home already."

"The children's dining room is over on the other side," she said. "You better take a look at it. You'll probably be working in there."

"I hope not," he said. "I'm counting on that job in the main. Maybe I shouldn't say this, Miss Grier. I know it sounds like polishing and all, but I knew right off that I could work with you. Really. I'm not kidding. You put everything so nice and clear, right to the point. I know I can work a station the way you'd want it worked."

She winced. "Come on now, Brodie, you're laying it on a little thick."

"No, really. I'm telling the truth."

"We'll see."

Mr. Mandheimer came in. He was with a portly man in a sport shirt and a roomy blue jacket. The man was carrying a wooden clipboard in one hand and a pencil in the other.

"Nobody keeps this place clean. I have to do everything myself," Audrey Grier said so that Mr. Mandheimer could hear. She pulled the towel out from under the urn and started wiping the table again.

"The local wholesalers can't compete with us," the man with Mr. Mandheimer was saying. "They're trying to get rich in ten weeks. How can they meet our prices?"

"So what d'you want for number-ten fruit cocktail?" Mr. Mandheimer said.

"Right now it's seven ninety-five. Later in the season, I can't guarantee."

"You'll give me six cases." They were in front of the coffee urn. Mr. Mandheimer saw Al Brodie. "Boy, come with me."

"Remember what I was saying," Al said to the hostess. "I'm counting on you, Miss Grier." He followed the two men.

"What d'you get for oil?" Mr. Mandheimer asked.

The salesman walked quickly to get in front of Mr. Mandheimer. There was an expression on his face that it was important for Mr. Mandheimer to see. "We could give you a cheap oil, sure, and steal it back on the rest of the order. We don't do business that way. I got a pure soybean oil, it's right for you."

"You'll give me six cases prune juice, three cases apricot nectar, three cases pineapple juice," Mr. Mandheimer said.

The man made a quick notation on his clipboard. "And the oil?"

They walked through a swinging door that led out of the kitchen past the outside refrigerator and the garbage room. They came to a small graveled area where a station wagon was parked. "Boy, you'll take the eggs out from the car and put them in the cellar," Mr. Mandheimer said to Al Brodie. "Be careful you don't break any."

"Where you get your eggs?" the salesman asked socially. "Pick them up from a local farmer? That's a good idea. What do they get for eggs when you deliver them yourself?"

"Prices fluctuate," Mr. Mandheimer said.

Al Brodie latched his hands into the holders on both sides of the egg crate. He rested the weight on his thighs and carried the first one over to a door leading down a flight of stairs. "Where did you say you wanted these, Mr. Mandheimer?"

Mr. Mandheimer came over, followed by the salesman. There was a light switch on the wall and he snapped it on. "Here, go back, get another case," he said to Al. "Follow me."

"Let me help you," the salesman said. He put his clipboard down on the ledge beside the stairs.

"You want to help, go get a case," Mr. Mandheimer said.

"You think I won't?" the salesman said. "When we're rushed, you think I don't load the trucks at our warehouse?"

"Something's got to be done right, you do it yourself," Mr. Mandheimer said.

They each carried down two cases before the salesman asked, "Did you decide about that oil?"

Mr. Mandheimer looked around the cellar. "This place is a mess. I got to get a man down here to clean it up."

"I was wondering," the salesman said. "I didn't see many outside men—"

"This morning," Mr. Mandheimer said. "Two of the boys who helped open the house, three weeks they worked good as gold. This morning one's drunk and the other's carrying him down the road."

"Gets worse each year," the salesman said.

Al brought the last case down to the cellar. "Is there anything else I can do, sir?"

Mr. Mandheimer wiped his hands on his handkerchief. As they started up the steps, he said, "An unusual busboy. In August he wouldn't be so courteous."

"Beg pardon, sir?" Al Brodie said.

The salesman picked up his clipboard. "What'll it be on that oil, now?"

"Don't rush me," Mr. Mandheimer said. "I can get the same oil a quarter a can cheaper, why shouldn't I?"

"You'd be a fool not to," the salesman said. "I want you to. Why shouldn't you save a quarter a can? It adds up. Look, Sam, you know me long enough. How long has it been? Ten years?"

"Are you through with me, sir?" Al asked. He shifted his weight from foot to foot and rubbed his back.

"Back hurt, boy?" Mr. Mandheimer asked.

"No, sir. It's nothing. Glad to have been of help."

"Look, your back hurts, tell me. The season isn't even started, more or less I should have a compensation case."

"You're covered for that," the salesman said.

"That don't mean they can't increase the premiums."

"I'm perfectly all right," Al Brodie said. He made a muscle. "Strong as an ox, see?"

Mr. Mandheimer laughed. "Crazy college kids we get up here," he said to the salesman.

Al started back into the kitchen.

"Look, Sam, you know me. I don't believe in high pressure," the salesman said. "If you've got the right product, they'll come to you. And needless to say . . ."

Mr. Mandheimer was nodding his head. It was funny he couldn't remember ever having seen that boy before. And he had a good memory for faces.

Chapter 4

Dear Sir [the inquiry began],

I have seen your ad in the newspaper and your place sounds pretty nice to me. Is this the same Sesame where a certain Sam Cohen stopped last year? I know Sam and his wife Ida had a wonderful time where they stopped but I haven't seen them since they moved and I don't know whether or not it was your place or some other place that sounds like yours but isn't where they stopped. Anyhow I'd like for you to quote me a rate for a woman and two children, a girl of thirteen and a boy of six for three weeks with the husband week ends only. My husband is in the electrical supplying business which is a six days a week proposition and he can not come up until after dinner on Saturday and he leaves before breakfast Monday mornings besides which he is a very light eater. Maybe you could put the girl in a room with a fellow girl her age as she is at that age where she is beginning to ask questions and would be better not sleeping in a room with my husband and me. We would like to be in the main house if the price is right and don't mind sharing a bath with another family if they are nice. Please do not put us in a room near old people who snore at night. That is what happened at the hotel where we stopped last year. To be frank about it my little one is a light sleeper anyway and the snoring kept him up and ruined our vacation which we don't want to happen this year. Write us soon with the rates as we are also waiting to hear from another place.

Sincerely yours,

Bessie (Mrs. Hank) Gold

Al was walking through the lobby when Calvin, the bellhop, stopped him. He made a gesture with his hand and Al followed him out the side door and onto a small staircase. This was Calvin's summer perch. From it he had a clear view of any cars coming in or out. He could see the front lawns where, once the guests arrived, there would be clusters of card players. He could half sit, half stand on the thick banister of the staircase and rest without looking as if he were resting.

"I got a room for you," Calvin said.

"I know. I'm in it," Al said.

Calvin shook his head. "I got a special room." He winked.

"It's too bad, Cal, but I haven't got any money."

"Hell, money," Calvin said. "You're all right." He bounced down the five steps. "Come on with me."

"This here's the Annex," Calvin said as they passed a large building that was styled like the main. "Your room is back of the Annex. We got a little house there for special help. We puts the chef and the master of ceremonies, the baker and some of them counselors back there. Use to be all them counselors slept 'cross the road. That's where the day camp is for d'guests' children. They takes them in the morning and keeps them busy all day and then they gives them back to the parents. Man, there ain't nothing we ain't got here. The missus done put everything into this here hotel."

"You really know this place," Al said. "Hell, Calvin, you're a walking advertisement."

"I know my rooms," Calvin said. "Next to the missus and him, nobody knows them no better. I knows my guests' rooms and I knows my help's rooms too. That's what I'm showing you, man. I got this here extra special room for you. Real quiet and private—know what I mean?"

"Thanks, Cal, I won't forget this," Al said.

"Most of the waiters, 'tween you and me, they's schnooks. Know what I mean?"

"I get you."

They walked up a narrow rocky path. They had to duck to protect themselves from low-hanging branches. "'Course you can come up and around the front way," Calvin said. "But best to do it quiet like, right?"

"Right," Al said. "You say something about counselors?"

"You goin' to be right next to them counselors," the bellhop said. "The head counselor, he sleeps down in the camp house 'cross the road. He got a racket, brung his family up and everything. Took all the counselors' rooms for his wife and his two children. That's why we has to put the other counselors up here. They is what you might say on their own. And that head counselor, he got nothing to do with you or them when they is off duty."

"These girls counselors?"

"You see for yourself."

It was another small, white wooden building. There was a stairway leading up to a row of rooms, and over on the side, hardly visible, was a small doorway.

Calvin led Al to the door on the side. "Only two rooms here," he said. "Real private. Them that knows about it all want this here room. That big boy—the one plays basketball—he asks me 'bout it right off. I tell him the missus give it to somebody already. Screw him."

When they walked in the door, Al heard the sound of female voices coming from the room on the left. "Counselors are here already, huh?"

"They come this morning." Calvin knocked on the other door. "The red-head boy he lives here, too. Just you and him—real private." He opened the door. The room was small but there were two beds and a chest of drawers and a closet.

"This is great," Al said. "I'll see you right after the week end."

The Negro shrugged. "Forget it. I know you's a sport. Season really starts big tomorrow, we got a full house. You make plenty money in tips. This is a good house. Boys make a thousand dollars here a summer. We all in it to make money, right? I like you, boy. You're all right. The missus likes you, too. I can tell."

"My name is Al. I mean in case you want me or anything.

And I won't forget you, Cal. You'll get the first five I make."

"Any time. Just take your time. Any time," Calvin said and waved good-by.

As soon as the bellhop left, Al went outside to look around. He swung the door and it slammed.

A sandy blonde in shorts and a halter opened the door to the room next to his. She was barefoot and smoking a cigarette. She wasn't wearing make-up, and she didn't need it. She had high cheekbones and bright eyes. The whole of her face had the sophisticated look of a fashion model, except for her lips which were too full. Her legs tapered beautifully and the halter had trouble concealing her abundance.

"Oh, I thought it was Joe," she said.

"I'll let him know you're looking for him."

"No, I mean when I heard the door slam, I thought it was him." She smiled and stepped out of her doorway and toward his room. "I'm Roz Silvers. Are you going to be living here?"

"I guess so," he said.

"What's your name?"

"Al Brodie," he said.

She smiled and took his hand briefly. "Come on over and I'll introduce you to the gang."

"I don't know if I can handle more than one woman at a time," Al said.

"Stop it. You'll scare us," she said.

They walked across the hall and into the girls' room. A short-haired brunette in horn-rimmed glasses was sitting on one bed reading *Doctor Zhivago*. She was thin and there was a looseness about her blouse where her bosom should have been. She was wearing slacks. The other girl was small and plump. Her eyebrows were penciled in and she wore mascara in the daytime.

"For gosh sake, sweetie, can't you knock before you bring people in?" the plump girl said.

"Where do you think you are?" Rosalyn said. "This is the mountains. Everything's informal up here."

"That's right," Al said. "This is a way of life all its own."

"Now what could the man mean by that?" the plump girl smiled.

"Ellie and I are from Paterson," Roz said. "Linda's from Passaic. Uncle Charlie Roth, the head counselor, brought us up with him. He's from Jersey too. He used to be our teacher at Central High."

She motioned toward the plump girl. "That's Ellie. She's got a car. And Linda's the brain. She's always reading."

Linda looked up from her book. "Roz, I wish you wouldn't say that."

"Well it's true, you are always reading."

"Roz, please."

"Nice to meet you, Linda. Nice to meet you too, Ellie." Al turned toward the door. "I've got to go get my suitcase and get settled." He paused a moment and then said casually, "Maybe you'd like to take a walk, Roz. It's just down the road."

"Good idea," she said. "I want to meet everybody."

She pushed her feet into a pair of loafers. The heel collapsed and she tried to balance on one foot and fix it. Al came over and supported her arm.

When they left the room Al said, "This is your first year in the mountains, isn't it?"

"It's the first time I've been away from home. I mean without my parents. They wouldn't have let me go if it wasn't for Uncle Charlie. He's swell."

"I'll bet he is swell," Al mimicked.

"What's that, a cliché or something?"

They cut across the lawn in front of the Annex. Al saw two cars pull up the driveway to the main building. Calvin was right there on the baggage.

"Looks like the summer is starting," Al said.

"Is it a cliché to say somebody is swell?"

"How do I know? I'm not an English major."

"Well, I mean the way you said it as if it was childish and silly and all. Are you cynical?"

"I'm Al Brodie."

"That's so old it is a cliché."

"So you're from Paterson." He looked down a moment at the deep cleavage of her bosom. "What brings you up here?"

"I'm a counselor, remember? Really, I think you are cynical."

"Maybe I am." He smiled. "There wasn't any Uncle Charlie looking out for my job. I've been banging around the agencies all week. I spent everything but my last two bucks coming up here. I've spent that too."

"But you got the job?"

"I think so."

"You mean you don't even know yet? You must have. They've given you a room."

"That's logical. But the Catskills aren't logical."

"I don't understand you at all. I think you're crazy."

He took her hand in his. "Maybe that's why we strike it off so well, huh? Aren't you a little crazy too?"

"Well, Linda thinks so and so does Ellie. Maybe I am."

"We're going to have a lot of fun this summer, Miss Crazy."

"I hope so. I love fun, Mr. Crazy."

They were on the road and he could see quickly that no one was watching. He slid his arm around the bareness of her waist and pulled her close to him. He could feel the warm strength of her thigh against his as they walked arm in arm.

"There's one thing I ought to tell you though," she said. "I mean, just because I'm up here without my family and we live next door to each other and all. Don't get any ideas."

"How old are you?" he said, "Eighteen?"

"Guess again," she said.

"You must be eighteen or younger. If you were older, you wouldn't talk that way."

"I don't like people who beat around the bush," she said. "I think it's much better to be frank and sincere."

He pulled her in a little closer to him, cupping his hand on her waist and lightly squeezing the flesh.

"Look, I don't like that." She pulled away from him. "That's exactly what I'm talking about. I was trying to tell you that just because we live next door to each other—well, I've heard stories about the mountains and summer romances and stuff like that. And I'm not the type. I mean I *don't*. And I'm not a teaser either. Do you understand me? I don't think you hear a word I'm saying."

"Of course I do," he said. "And I agree with you perfectly."

He pointed toward the shack where his suitcase was. "I have to go in here for a minute. When I come out, we'll finish our discussion, all right?"

"All right," she said. "I'll wait." She bent down and started gathering some stones. "I'll see how many times I can hit the tree before you get back," she said. Al looked down at her appreciatively. Then he started toward the shack.

"Well, look who's back," Mike Heimer said. "It's bunkie."

"You son of a bitch, I thought I got rid of you," Stan said.

"Why in the hell don't you put on some pants?" Al said. "Every spare chance you get, you got your drawers off. You know, I think you got crotch itch."

"It's hot, you dumb bastard," Stan said. He flexed his arms. "Oh God, send me a woman."

Harry came in with a handful of wire hangers and the evening papers. "Honest to God, boys. I'm walking down the road, headed right for the room, and what do I see—the biggest boobs you ever saw in your life, hanging right over the goddamned road."

Stan whooped. "Lemme at 'em."

"Why don't you shut your filthy mouth," Al said to Harry. He pulled his suitcase out from under the bed, wiped off his hands, and looked as if he was ready to fight. "The next time I hear you open your mouth about my girl, you'll regret the day you were born." He stood in the doorway with his bag a moment and said, "She's my girl and don't any of you guys forget it."

Then he walked out.

"That guy's sure got it made," Harry said. "Even brings his own babe up here with him."

"That's why he's so damn cocky," Stan said. "He's getting it regularly."

When he got out to the road, Al Brodie looked around for a few minutes and then gave up. Roz was gone.

Chapter 5

"I don't understand our Allen," Al Brodie's mother said. "What was so bad about Penchansky and Levy's? A trimming company is a good beginning in the garment trade. He had to quit?"

The father kept looking at the newspaper. "He came to me. He told me he wasn't getting anywhere with the job, he wanted to leave and go to college. So I told him. I explained to him education is a wonderful thing. If I had an education, I'm not driving a taxicab today."

The mother said, "You mean you told him he should quit the job?"

"Me? I told him? I should say not," Al Brodie's father said. "To go to college you got to have money. Tuition, books—things like that they cost a good dollar. A working boy wants an education he can go to night school."

"Is that what you told him? He should go to night school?"

The father looked up quickly and then returned to the paper. "I just explained to him," he said. "I told him nothing."

"Your son comes to you for advice," the mother said. "And this is what you tell him—nothing."

"What do you make such a big thing out of it for?" the father said. "He's not a baby. He's a man. All I'd have to do is give him advice. If it doesn't work out, I'm responsible."

"A lot you know your Allen," Al Brodie's mother said.

There were eighteen names on the list under the heading "Main Dining Room," but Al Brodie was only looking at one. Next to station eight was his name.

"Wouldn't you guess it," Joe said. "They got me working the children's dining room. I'll bet the Mong had a hand in this."

"It'd be just like that bastard," Al said, "but what the hell, you might be able to really rack it in. With your personality and all—what's it take to con some kids?"

"Kids? Are you crazy? The parents are all over that place. I started bussing for kids in a schlock house in Fallsburg three years ago. I must have run twenty specials for each meal, and you know what I made—a lousy six hundred bucks for the summer."

"That's why they put you there," Al said. "You got the experience."

Joe looked worried. "This is goin' to hurt. I mean it. I'm counting on that money—"

"So," Al Brodie said, "try another hotel. Hell, this isn't the only place in the mountains."

Joe didn't seem to be listening to him. "I've got a job, at least. I guess I'm lucky at that."

"Sure," Al said, "that's the way to look at it. What the hell, you can't tell what might break during the season."

"That Mong—if I could only—honest to God, I'd like to get that big slob alone in some deserted alley."

Al said, "Come on, forget it. What's done is done. Let's get some chow."

They walked back to the stove where the Chinese second cook was dishing out chicken and mashed potatoes.

"Velly good," the cook said. "Chicky velly good." He put a wing on Al's plate and fished through the thick gravy for a leg.

"Looks good," Al said. "How about giving me a breast?"

The cook shook his head. "Take wat you git. This no gawdahm resrant."

"It's just that it looks so good."

The cook gestured with his thumb. "Beat it, boy. Vamoose. Amscray."

Al picked up two pieces of dry white bread. He waited while Joe's plate was filled.

The second cook put a breast and a bottom quarter on Joe's plate, and plenty of potatoes.

"See, so you don't rate with the Mong," Al said. "You go over great with the cooks. At least you'll eat regular."

"I know him from last year," Joe said. "The food is pretty good around here. Guys like the Mong, they're always bitching, but I'll bet they don't have it half so good at home."

"Doesn't look too bad," Al said. "What the hell, who cares as long as we don't get poisoned."

"It's the garlic," Joe said. "I could eat crap if there was enough garlic on it."

"Come on," Al said. "We'll take a table together in the dining room."

"I might as well start in the kids' room. What the hell, it's probably got to be scrubbed and waxed and every other damn thing."

"Be seeing you," Al said. He left Joe and started through the swinging doors that led into the main dining room.

At the station there was a large aluminum tray on a canvas stand. Each waiter sat and ate with his busboy as though the tray were a table. Most of them were already having supper when Al arrived.

"Station eight is back there in the far corner, near the wall," Audrey Grier told him. "As soon as you're through eating, Brodie, I'd like to talk to you."

"Yes, ma'am," Al said.

His busboy's name was Danny Rose. He was short and round-backed, but his arms and hands were strong. His hair was flat against his head. He ate slowly and silently. There was a peculiar grace about his movements.

While they were eating, Audrey Grier announced that there were fourteen check-ins for the evening meal. She was opening up two stations. She warned them all to get down to breakfast at seven-thirty the next morning. By noon they expected a full house.

Danny Rose said, "Don't forget to draw linen," and Al nodded.

She was sitting at the desk. One of her legs was wrapped over the other and swinging back and forth. She was doodling on the back of an old menu. She told him to sit down next to her.

"I suppose you're surprised that I gave you a station," she said. "You should be. You really don't deserve it. There are other boys who've been here longer and you haven't proved yourself. Well, I talked to Mrs. Mandheimer. She said she didn't have any objections. She wants to be fair, too . . ."

She went on and on like that, but he couldn't hear her. He was uncomfortably aware of her leg, moving steadily back and forth.

She put her foot on the floor suddenly and pulled the skirt down over her knees. "Don't let us down," she said. "We're taking a big chance on you. Also—I'm putting the Erlangs at your station. They're season guests, and from what I can tell they're going to require a great deal of attention. You know what I mean?"

He nodded.

"You have to understand human nature in this business. It's a necessity. I think you'll find I'm a pretty good judge. So tomorrow you'll start to work and you'll have the Erlangs. I've given you a strong busboy. Danny doesn't say much but he's terrific."

"Thanks a lot." He started to get up but he knew there was something more. He took a stab. "Say, if you're not doing anything tonight—maybe you'd like to go into town and catch a movie or something like that."

She'd wanted him to say it, and now he'd said it and she had her answer ready. "I don't like to get too close to the boys. I think it's better for all of us—all around."

"O.K."

"It's not that I have anything against you personally. As a matter of fact, I think you're a very interesting character. I mean that as a compliment. You're a gentleman and I like the way you handle yourself. It's just that not dating the waiters is a policy of mine."

"Oh, sure, I understand." And he was very relieved. Hell, he didn't have a buck to his name. He wondered how far he could get with Roz without spending a dime.

When he got back to his room, Joe was sitting on the bed with Ellie. She was wearing a sweater and a skirt, and her face was made up as if she were playing the wife of Fu Manchu.

He saw Joe's hand on Ellie's knee and Ellie's hand on Joe's, and they were in a deep conversation.

Joe said he was glad to see him and they were going for a drive in Ellie's car and would he like to come along. He asked Ellie where Roz was and she said next door and he said he didn't think he'd particularly care for a drive.

Linda was still reading *Doctor Zhivago* when he came in. Roz was hanging up clothes and her hair was tied up in a towel. She kept hanging up the clothes and didn't look at him. When he asked her if she'd like to take a walk, she said her hair was wet and he had no choice—he had to let it go at that.

He didn't know what time it was when Joe woke him up. He heard one of the drawers slam and Joe humming. For a minute he was afraid it was time to get up.

"This you got to hear," Joe said. "This will absolutely kill you."

"Yeah," Al said. "I'm half dead already."

"There's this beautiful babe coming down the main drag. Orchard Street, maybe. Well, anyway, headed toward her is this guy. He is absolutely the tallest, pimpliest, skinniest, ugliest man in the world."

"What the hell is this, a joke?"

"Live a little," Joe said. "I'm telling you—this one is a riot. Anyway—this beautiful girl—she walks right up to the skinniest, ugliest man in the world. 'Come home with me,' she says, sultry and sexy-like. The skinniest, ugliest man in the world, he just about drops over dead. So home they go. Get this now—she's beautiful. Built, with a pair out to here—" He held his hands out, cupped, in front of him.

"Tell me more," Al said. "That's what I go for—the descriptions."

"So home they go," Joe continued. "Right up to this broad's apartment. She tells him, 'Slip into the bathroom and get undressed—pl-e-ease.' Now he's the skinniest, ugliest guy in the world. You got that?"

"I got it, I got it," Al said.

"He's standing there. He's all bones and sores and he's standing there naked waiting for this beautiful broad, this sure thing that picked him up. The next thing he knows, there's a knock on the door. 'Come in,' says the skinniest, ugliest man in the world. Well, she opens the door and what do you know—there's this little kid, her son, standing right next to her. She takes a long look at the skinniest, ugliest, pimpliest, tallest man in the world and what do you think she says? 'Honey,' she says to the kid, 'take a good look, because this is exactly what you are going to look like if you don't start eating better.' "

"Oh, no," Al said. "For this you woke me up."

Joe was laughing. " 'You'll look like this if you don't start eating better,' " he repeated. "Jerry Furman, the social director, was mixing it up with the check-ins down at the bar. I'm telling you, that guy is a riot. Ellie and me, we split our sides laughing."

"That's wonderful," Al said. "So you're laughing your troubles away."

"Hell with the Mong and the damn main dining room," Joe said. "I'm not going to worry about it. What d'you think of that Ellie—she's some chick, huh?"

"Stacked," Al said.

"She's classy all right. And you know something—she's got a sense of humor, too. The way she makes up, like a regular model or something, you'd think she'd be high hat. But she's not. A guy can be very natural with her."

"How far'd you get?" Al said.

"Never mind. I like her. I really do—"

"Great, so sack out with her and let me sleep in peace," Al Brodie said, and he rolled over and pulled the pillow over his ears.

Chapter 6

Sullivan County's 143rd Regiment always stood "courageously by their places," according to General Joe Hooker, the Civil War hero. The regiment fought with distinction at the battles of Wauhatchie, Kennesaw Mountain, Chattanooga, and Missionary Ridge, and took part in Sherman's march to the sea.

The regiment was organized at Pleasant Lake, later renamed Kiamesha. The site was called Camp Holley in honor of Colonel John C. Holley, the regiment's first commanding officer. The troops were quartered, drilled, and fed on land near what is now the Concord Hotel. There seem to have been no complaints about the accommodations, but there was an incident of rebellion over the food. Troops were reported to have thrown their mess gear into the air and "called down the curses of heaven" on the food supplier from Fallsburg. The new man must have been an improvement, because the food has been getting better ever since.

Audrey Grier's hips swayed in a tight linen skirt. She weaved through the tables, nodding here and there to guests. When she got to the first table at station eight, she stopped and signaled Al to come over. She gestured with a handful of place cards, "This is Al Brodie, Mr. and Mrs. Erlang. He's your waiter."

The man had a small mustache and heavy lips. He was wearing a fish-patterned sport shirt and gabardine pants with suspenders. His wife was a thin woman, with a dissatisfied twist to her mouth. Her hair was wrapped on the top of her head in a bun and when she extended her hand she bent her wrist as if she expected it to be kissed.

"So nice to make your acquaintance, Mr. Brodberg," she said.

"What d'ya say, Al boy?" the man said. "Run quick and get us some borscht." He thought that was funny and laughed hard.

Al shook the lady's hand. "The pleasure is mine."

"Al will take good care of you," Audrey said. "And remember, I'm here to help you too. Let me know if there's anything special you want."

"I'll tell you what I want right now," the man said and made eyes.

Audrey Grier opened her mouth but nothing came out. "I've got to run along," she said. "Three hundred people and all hungry."

Al helped them with their seats and introduced them to the other people at the table. There was a very sad-faced bald-headed man and his wife, Mr. and Mrs. Gerson, and a drab middle-aged woman, Miss Mantell.

Mrs. Erlang started in on her pineapple juice. Mr. Erlang started in on Miss Mantell.

"All alone. My, my, I'll bet the boys are happy."

Al said he was and wondered if the lady wanted potato soup. The gentleman, he knew, wanted borscht.

Mrs. Erlang said she didn't care for soup and Mr. Erlang said, "Bring the borscht on the double, boy. Before I die of thirst."

Everybody laughed at this, even Mr. Gerson, who seemed to find it very painful.

Al had three other tables and he had to move fast.

It turned out that there was a long line in front of the soup station. The kitchen man who was working with the Chinese cook had placed the soup pot in a bad position and the cook had to move it in order to set up two stations.

The chef was checking the baby flounders in the oven and the pan with the potato pancakes, but he found time to curse and threaten everyone.

When Al got back to the dining room with the soups, it turned out that Mr. Erlang didn't care for borscht after all. It was a joke and now would Al mind bringing him some mushroom and barley soup. It looked good.

Danny Rose picked up the mushroom and barley soup. The chef knew he was not a waiter and shouted loud enough for everybody to hear, "I'll cut the hands off of the next busboy I see picking up on this side of the stove."

Al was thinking, "Three baby flounders, two potato pancakes, a chef's delight, and a flounder with pancakes on the side." He was also thinking, "One Fiftieth State pineapple surprise and a salmon salad."

The line in front of the pantry was long so he shot right over to the stove. The chef was dishing out the flounders, using his spatula with a technique that enabled him to steal just enough juice from the bottom of the pan. With the other hand he was scooping up mashed potatoes. A kitchen man was putting on the broccoli, and the waiters put a slice of lemon on top of each piece of fish themselves. The Chinese cook was on the potato pancakes and omelets. Mr. Mandheimer himself was taking care of the chef's delight, an intricate dish that involved a square of pudding, hot fruit, and a hot rum sauce.

Waiters were dashing back and forth from the hot stove to the salad department. The busboys, bussing the soup plates and juice glasses, made a loud noise as their trays landed on the dishwashing machine.

Al got his order off and stacked his plates carefully. He was on his way to the salad department when he heard Mr. Mandheimer's voice shout across the room, "Get those hot plates into the dining room. Who is that boy? I want that boy fired."

He didn't see who it was and Al kept going without looking back. When he got into the dining room, Miss Mantell wanted to know where her salmon salad was. Al said he was going back for the cold dishes, but she said she didn't understand why he served half the table and kept the others waiting.

He gave her the fruit delight he'd intended for someone at another table and promised to bring the salmon salad on the next trip.

The meal was about half through when Mrs. Mandheimer came into the kitchen. She noticed immediately that nobody was working on milk. She pulled up a small table, filled two pitchers with milk and lined up two glass racks. She had twenty glasses filled just in time. One busboy picked up eight and another twelve.

There were Danish for dessert. The baker had them lined out on big plates—prune, cheese, almond, and custard.

Mr. Erlang liked custard. He told Al to bring him two more. "Also, a pitcher of milk. I'm a growing boy, remember?"

"Sorry," Al said. "We're not allowed to bring out pitchers. I can bring you a glass."

"Ridiculous! Bring me a pitcher of milk," Mr. Erlang said.

By this time the sweat was pouring across Al's forehead. His back was drenched and his arms were trembling. When he was back in the kitchen he picked up a milk pitcher that was used for breakfast cereals. Mrs. Mandheimer was busy, so he filled the pitcher himself.

Audrey Grier was on her way to pick up a sliced sturgeon special when she saw him.

"No pitchers in my dining room. What d'you think this is, a hash house?" She took the pitcher, poured the milk back, and then went chasing after the sturgeon.

"What's the matter with you, boy?" Mrs. Mandheimer said. She looked up for the first time and saw Al standing with the empty pitcher. "Oh, so it's you. You never were a waiter before?"

"I know, Mrs. Mandheimer, but it's that Mr. Erlang. He demanded—"

"Demanded. He should demand. Sixty dollars a week and he's demanding." She filled the pitcher. "He should choke on it."

Calvin, the bellhop, came over, picked a glass of milk out of the tray, and swigged it in one gulp. "Dey sure is a pack of gonifs we got this year. Ain't it the truth?"

"What's the matter, you can't eat with the help?" Mrs. Mandheimer said.

Calvin threw his hands out in front of him, palms up. "Check-ins. When the help eat, I'm busy with check-ins. What am I supposed to do?"

Al put the milk pitcher on his tray and started toward the bakery. The platters of Danish, laid out carefully—one for each table—were all gone.

The baker was sitting at his work-table, fork in hand, ready to dive into two baby flounders with potato pancakes and chef's delight on the side.

"I need five more custard Danish," Al called at the door.

"What d'you mean more? I put out one for each table."

"They like your baking. Can I help it?"

"I don't have any more Danish. Get the hell out."

"Look—listen—please—they'll kill me."

The baker got up angrily, went over to the racks that ran from the floor to the ceiling. He pulled out a tray that was half filled with custard Danish. "Three more. That's all you get. Damn if I'm going to kill myself baking for these pigs."

Al was on his way back to the dining room when Danny Rose passed him. "Pick up two chef's delights for table twenty-four, Al."

"I just gave them flounder."

Danny shrugged. "Dessert."

Al reversed and ran back to the hot stove.

"Walk," Mrs. Mandheimer called after him. "You want to break a leg?" She caught a busboy throwing butter into the garbage and she went to get him.

"You still serving mains?" the chef demanded. He cut in front of Mr. Mandheimer. "What d'you have out there, half of Brooklyn?"

"They just came in. I can't help it," Al said.

Mr. Mandheimer lifted a pudding onto a plate. He cut it in half and spooned some hot fruit on top. He bathed it in rum sauce. "Dessert. They're eating main dishes for dessert. Here, take this. My help got to eat too."

"They don't fool you, boss," the chef said, and Mr. Mandheimer was delighted.

Mr. Erlang was strong until the last Danish. He managed

only half of that, lit a big Bering cigar, and poured half a pitcher of pure cream in his coffee. Al was standing near the server, wiping his forehead with his side towel, when Mr. Erlang said, "Quick, boy—the borscht. I'm thirsty." Then he laughed and gestured for Al to come over.

Al trudged across the room and forced a smile. "Anything else, sir?"

Mr. Erlang's after-dinner joke was over. He was serious. "Every morning, you'll make sure there's a glass of prune juice at my place. I don't want to ask for it. When I come in, it'll be waiting."

And it was that way, too, during the months of July and August while Mr. Erlang stayed at the Sesame.

Miss Mantell was the last one left at the table. Only a few guests remained in the dining room. The waiters who weren't busy bringing in their livestock were gulping milk and Danish.

From his server Al watched Miss Mantell smoking a cigarette and sipping coffee. She moved in a slow precise manner. She would take a puff on the cigarette, then place it on the edge of the ashtray, careful to brush off the burning ash. She sipped her coffee, placed the cup down carefully, and each time wiped her thin lips with her napkin.

Al hadn't really looked at her during the meal. He had a fleeting impression of her as being ugly, but now that he looked at her more carefully, he thought it wasn't that she was particularly ugly, just sexless. Her features were even, but small. Her hair was tinted red—it went naturally with her fair complexion. She was wearing a bright strapless print dress. Over her shoulders was a matching stole.

"Three and two," Danny Rose said. "Mike Heimer had her last year. But she's no trouble."

"We can do better than that," Al said. "Five and three or bust."

"Never," the busboy said. "You're wasting your time."

"We'll see," Al Brodie said. He left the server and walked over to Miss Mantell's table. She was just putting the napkin down and reaching for the cigarette when he said, "Is there anything else I can bring you, Miss Mantell? Another cup of coffee maybe?"

"No, thank you," she said, without looking at him.

Al leaned forward and put his hands on the table near her. "Up here for the summer?"

"I take five weeks in July and two weeks again in December."

"That's a good idea, breaks it up. Where you go in December, Miami?"

She sipped her coffee, wiped her lips and said, "No, Lakewood. I don't like to spend too much of my vacation time traveling."

"That's practical," Al said. "Mind my asking what you do? It's none of my business, but I'm a psychology major. I'm interested in people."

"Really?" She held her cigarette to the side of her face with a flexed wrist, and faced him without saying anything else.

"Now I'd figure you for something in fashions. Say a dress designer or a buyer or something like that. Am I close?"

"What makes you think I'd be a designer?" She blushed.

"I don't know." He looked her over carefully as if he was sure of the impression but wanted to find the exact reasons for it. "I guess it's because you dress with flair. That's the word, flair. You look different from most of the guests here."

Miss Mantell didn't smoke the cigarette. She held it in the same pose and asked, "Is that a compliment?"

"Any way you want to take it," Al said. "We psychologists just make objective observations. Of course I could be altogether wrong."

"I'm afraid you are," Miss Mantell said. "I'm in millinery. I'm a salesgirl. I'm only working part time now, but I've been in it all my life."

"But you must be interested in designing. The way you dress and all—well, maybe I'm not being objective."

"You're very complimentary, young man," Miss Mantell said. The ash on her cigarette had grown long and she had to crush it. That done, she wiped her lips again and started to rise.

Al sprang behind her and helped her from her chair.

"Thank you very much," Miss Mantell said. "The Sesame must be improving. I've been coming here for many years and I never received such service."

"It's all new," Al said, quoting from one of the hotel's ads, "and better than ever."

"It seems so," Miss Mantell said. She readjusted her stole. "By the way, whatever did happen to that salmon salad?"

"Oh—that. I'm really sorry about that," Al said. "Matter of fact that's what I started out to tell you about until we got sidetracked."

"Don't bother," Miss Mantell said. "Food is really not that important to me. That pudding you brought me—what do you call it—chef's delight? It was quite good."

"Between you and me," Al Brodie said, "we're very lucky this year. We've got a great chef. It makes it a lot easier on us waiters. You know, the more satisfied the guests are—the better the tips."

"That's interesting," she said.

"Well, we've all got to face it," Al said. His voice was level as if he was talking to an old friend. "That's what we're in it for—the money. Take me—no money, no college. It's as simple as that."

"I'm sure you're going to do very well," Miss Mantell said.

She started toward the door and Al said. "Nice talking to you. See you at dinner."

Miss Mantell looked back over her shoulder and smiled.

When Al was back in the kitchen, bringing in what was left of the livestock—butter, cream, milk, a platter of untouched lettuce and tomatoes—Mike Heimer said, "That Mantell is the nuts, isn't she? The way she puts on—a regular Duchess of Windsor or something. You know what I think she needs?" He made a gesture. "Those old maids begin getting buggy when they get old."

"She's all right," Al said.

"All right?" Mike Heimer said. "You better have your eyes examined or your head examined or something."

Al didn't answer. There was no use explaining to Mike Heimer that they both weren't exactly after the same thing.

Chapter 7

"The place has certainly changed," the guest told the hotelkeeper. "I haven't been here since I was a kid—it must be at least twenty, thirty years. The family used to run it then, I think their name was Lefhauser."

"My wife's family," the hotel owner said. "It was just a farm then."

"The thing I can still remember was the food. They put these big pitchers of sour cream and sweet cream and milk on the table. And there were bowls filled with butter and cottage cheese. They gave us fresh bread and homemade cake—all we could eat. We ate enough to last us all winter."

"Your family came to be fixed," the hotel owner said.

"That's right," the guest agreed. "Gaen to the mountains ziech zu fixin."

"We've got three cooks now and a professional baker on the premises," the hotel owner said.

"Nothing like those good old days," the guest said. "I liked it better when the country was really the country. So what have you got for me? I need a big room for the wife and me and the two kids. Something nice with wall-to-wall carpeting, maybe."

The Fourth of July week end passed, and the house count was reduced to one hundred and eighty. Al Brodie collected forty-eight dollars in tips, which was good considering the fact that one table hadn't tipped yet. The Erlangs, the Gersons, and Miss Mantell were still there, and he would be hearing from them at the end of the week.

He hadn't been able to date Roz over the week end. She'd been hanging out with her roommate, Linda, which was just as well. It saved him money, and his time wasn't being beat by any of the other boys.

The day after the week end, Al put his forty-eight dollars in an envelope and brought it up to the main desk to be put in the safe.

Mrs. Mandheimer handled the safe herself. She made him sign, gave him a slip, and then ducked back into a little room next to the main desk where Al could see her bending down to open the safe.

When she came back, Al said, "You know you ought to have a wall safe. A woman like you shouldn't have to bend down that much. It's bad for your heart."

"A doctor, yet?" Mrs. Mandheimer said.

"No, I'm going to be an accountant, remember?"

"Sure, I remember, the boy with a smile like Phillip."

"Oh, yeah. Gee, that seems like it was a long time ago."

"You make a few dollars, it's a world of difference." She smiled gently.

"It was a pretty good week end. But that Mr. Erlang—"

"Don't let him kill you," she said. "Him I don't need."

"What makes a man like that?"

"You meet all types in the hotel business."

"It only takes one guest like that to ruin a station."

"And bargain—Tsh, tsh, tsh. And you know, he's got money."

"No kidding."

"Don't let him fool you. He's got a store on Long Island. They tell me he does a half a million dollars a year."

"A bum like that succeeds."

"I should only have his money."

"You're not doing so bad. This is a terrific hotel. I mean it. You're growing."

"I'd take money out for myself, we wouldn't grow."

"What d'you mean?"

"I built eight new rooms and fixed the children's dining room. You know what that cost me? Thirty thousand dollars. You think I'll ever see it?"

"Well, now you don't have to do anything for a while. Now the money will start coming in."

"A lot you know. You got to give them something new all the time. You don't give them something new, you don't have guests."

"So what d'you do it for? You mean you're knocking yourself out for nothing?"

"I'm stuck with it, that's why. You try to sell one of these places, you're lucky you get the price of your last improvement."

"No kidding. You know, that interests me. I'm interested in anything concerning business. An accountant has to be."

Mr. Mandheimer came out of the rear office. "Becky, you got to tell everybody your business? Maybe he doesn't want to know your business. Maybe you ought to learn to keep your mouth shut."

"Right away he's a spy. Sam, that's what's the matter with you, you don't trust anybody."

"Becky, do me a favor please and don't tell the waiters your business." He slapped his hand on the front desk. "Please don't tell the waiters your business."

"All right, so I won't tell him. Don't get excited. You wouldn't get excited all the time and lose your temper, your daughter would be here. She wouldn't run away to Arizona."

A kitchen man walked tentatively toward the desk. "Mr. Mandheimer, there's a man out here looking for you. Got a grocery order to sign in."

"All right," Mr. Mandheimer said. "Tell him I'm coming." He turned back to his wife, genuinely pained. "What d'you mean my daughter would be here? Kindly tell me what you mean."

"You think a college girl likes to hear her father lose his temper and beat on tables? You lose your temper, your daughter moves to Arizona." She shrugged and shook her head.

"Maybe if you wouldn't tell everybody your business, I wouldn't lose my temper."

"You got an order to check in. Go already."

He slapped the desk again before he left and said, "Look at yourself. You're so perfect. *I drove my daughter to Arizona?*" he repeated it three times, once again as a question and twice more with exclamations, before he went to check the order.

"I didn't know you had a daughter," Al said. "That's nice."

"Sure I got a daughter, a lovely daughter. I'd show you her picture but she's married. A very smart girl. Got a head like her father's, everything she learns fast. I sent her by Barnard College. You think she graduated? Two years she's on the dean's list. Then she gets married, and runs away to Arizona."

"That's funny. I mean you'd think her husband or her, one of them at least, would want to take over the place someday. You're still young and all that, but just the same—it's only natural."

"My Marsha take over the hotel?" She smiled bitterly. "She hates it. Oh, I can't say I blame her. It's our fault too. In this business you got no time for family. I brought her up here a little girl. I thought it'd be good for her. The fresh air, the sunshine—what's bad about it? She was twelve years old, she wanted I should send her to a camp in Maine. Who knows a camp in Maine? Her girl friends went there. At least she was in high school, she helped me. She goes to college, she changed. I don't know—my mother ran the hotel, I was glad to help her, carry wood, cook. No, she doesn't have to do that, but a college girl—you'd think at least she'd want to help at the desk, keep the books, be a hostess."

"That's the way it goes," Al said. "The grass is always greener on the other side."

"She went to college, so in the summer she wants to go to Europe. She comes up here, all she does is read. All right she's a smart girl, but the business is so bad? What's perfect? Nothing's perfect."

"It's a shame," Al said, "really a shame."

"A hundred boys I introduce her to—none's good enough. This one is ugly. This one is dumb. This one don't talk so good.

This one is dull. So what does she marry? A painter. He makes a living? Every month I send her money, she should have what to eat. Him, he don't know from money. He's painting the desert."

"A bohemian," Al said. "I run into guys like that in college. They're just not realistic."

"It's a fine life for my grandchild. He should be up here, eating good, getting the fresh air, the sunshine. For who else do I live?"

"It's a damn shame," Al said.

"She got married, she eloped. No wedding party. No ring. No nothing. A telegram—that's the way to do things? That's what they teach you in college?"

"Don't worry," Al said, "she'll change. I'll bet she comes back someday and loves this place. No kidding—it happens all the time. My cousin Marcus ran away from home to be a writer once. This is the truth. He went down to Mexico, but he ate something bad and the next thing you know my aunt and uncle had to go down after him to bring him back. He had dysentery. He'd have died if they didn't go down there and get him. So now he's home and last year—you know what?—he graduated from a pharmaceutical school. He's a full-fledged druggist."

"That's nice," Mrs. Mandheimer said. "You're a nice boy, Allen. Only please, in the future don't pick up your salads when you have hot plates on the tray. All right?"

"All right," Al said, and he smiled.

"Just like Phillip," Mrs. Mandheimer said, and there was a look of such pure delight on her face that Al wasn't ready yet to ask her who in the hell this Phillip was.

Chapter 8

The cream-colored Cadillac pulled out of the exit of the Red Apple Rest and waited for a break in the traffic headed toward the mountains on Route 17.

An olive-skinned girl turned toward the driver, who was wearing a white-on-white shirt. "The thing I love about the place is you never can tell who you're going to be rubbing shoulders with. The last time I was there, Eddie Fisher was there and he was with her."

It was the night of the basketball game. Danny Rose was on the team and Al let him go early. He took his time clearing the table. Miss Mantell was there. It was the first time she'd idled after a meal since their first conversation.

She was wearing a navy-blue dress that was high at the collar. Around her neck was a string of pearls. It was unusually formal for the middle of the week and Al noticed it immediately.

Between the appetizer and the soup course, he'd told her again she looked like a dress designer.

She'd passed up the soup and only nibbled at the fruit course. He'd noticed that Mr. Erlang had finished off more than half of her boiled beef and potatoes. Mr. Erlang was always talking to her half-jokingly about things he thought were sophisticated. Sophistication for Mr. Erlang was always food or sex.

"Mr. Erlang ought to pay your bill for you," Al said to her as he cleared the table. "He eats half of what's on your plate."

Miss Mantell was sipping Sanka. The cigarette was in the ashtray. "I don't mind," she said. "He means well. And it is a shame to let good food go to waste."

"All depends upon your definition of waste," Al said. He stacked his tray and was ready to go back to the kitchen. "Want me to bring you something from the kitchen?" he said. "If you're feeling sick I could get you toast and butter or something like that."

"Butter with a meat meal!" Miss Mantell winced.

"Oh, yes—that's right. I guess it slipped my mind. Well, would you want anything else?"

"No, thank you," Miss Mantell said. "Just the Sanka. I'm not feeling very hungry tonight."

Al carried his tray to the kitchen and came back. "The reason I suggested bread and butter," he said, "was because I notice that's about the only thing you really eat."

"You're very observant," Miss Mantell said. "As a matter of fact, I do like bread and butter." She reached for her cigarette and said, "People who live alone and cook just for themselves don't go in for very elaborate dishes."

"I guess that's true," Al said.

He had started back to his stand when he heard her say, "I did a lot of fancy cooking when my father was alive. No, fancy isn't the right word. He liked his boiled chicken and his meats. He didn't eat fish. I made meat for him and hot soups, twice a day."

Al returned to the table. Miss Mantell was staring at the ashtray. He emptied it into a saucer and held it in his hand. Her eyes didn't leave the spot.

"My father died two years ago. He was a wonderful man. In the old country he'd have been a scholar. My brother Sam, he's very much like Dad. He's a professor of economics at California University. Mother was always the breadwinner. Papa was lost without her."

"You sort of kept house for him after she died," Al said.

Miss Mantell looked at him. Her hand arched with the cigarette near the side of her face and she held her elbow with the free hand. "There was no one else," she said. "Sam was in California and Rachel was already married with a home of her own. He couldn't live alone." She looked at Al desperately. "He was too fine a man. His mind was so alive. You know what he did on my last birthday? I mean the last one he spent with me. We were up here together. Papa always liked the Mandheimers. He knew Mrs. Mandheimer's mother, Mrs. Bittleman. The hotel was once called Bittleman's. It was my birthday so he had the baker make us a cake and right in the middle he had a beautiful red rose. He'd picked it himself from one of the rose bushes that grew near the lawn. It wasn't much. I mean it might not impress you. But it was just so typical—poetic and a little romantic, I think, for a man who was nearly eighty."

"Quite a guy," Al said. "Sorry I never got a chance to meet him."

Miss Mantell looked back toward the ashtray again. She caught the ash before it fell and put the cigarette down. "I guess in a way it was wrong. Papa said himself, there's no place in the Bible where you can find a good excuse for a young girl dedicating her life to the care of her father. Procreation is really a part of our religion."

"I'm going to take theology next year," Al said. "I think every good psychologist should have a little theology. I mean religion is a big influence on what makes people tick."

Miss Mantell's head jerked as if she'd been struck. She rose from her chair before Al could help her. "I've really been most unfair to you," she said. "You were just being polite, working toward your tip, and here I am telling you my troubles. I'm sorry."

"No, you're all wrong. I enjoy listening," Al said. "People are my hobby. I'm a psychology major, remember? People are more or less what you might call my business."

"It's just that tonight is my birthday. I wanted to tell someone. You know Mr. Erlang—it wouldn't have been right. Not him, or anyone else at the table without his knowing. I just couldn't have taken his jokes about my being 'sweet sixteen.'"

"You know people pretty good yourself," Al said.

"Good night," Miss Mantell said. "And thanks for offering me the bread and butter."

"Happy birthday," Al said. After she left he was sorry he hadn't argued with her about that thing she said regarding him working toward his tip. What the hell, she'd started the conversation in the first place. Letting her get away with that might cost him money.

Al was the last one to leave the dining room. He had a piece of nut cake wrapped in a napkin, and he was walking toward the back path that led to his room.

Calvin the bellhop came up to him from nowhere.

"Hey, Al, stay away from the missus tonight." There was the faint smell of liquor on his breath. "She's all futummelt. Marsha coming back."

"What the hell you talking about, Cal?"

"Ssh—I don't tell everybody. Just you, 'cause you my friend. Son-in-law died. The missus' son-in-law done up an' died and Marsha she is coming up here." The bellhop squeezed Al's arm. "The missus already been into the city and seen her. I hear her telling Mandheimer all about it. She seen her grandson and everything. Now Marsha an' the kid is both coming up here. Man, that girl got no right runnin' away in the first place. A person leave a beautiful business like this, you know they has got to be meshuga." He laughed. "Marsha always a little meshuga. Anyway she coming back and I tell you, 'cause you is my friend."

"Thanks, Cal, that's a real help. I'll have the band meet her. I'm glad you told me." He started to walk away when he remembered suddenly. "By the way, I still owe you that five. I didn't forget it. My money is in the safe, but I'll pay you first thing tomorrow."

"I know you good for it. You a sport. I knew right off you was a sport," Calvin said.

On nights when she didn't have counselor patrol, Roz was off around seven. Al decided to knock on the door to her room.

She was dressed to go out when she answered. She had on a white summer dress with a low-cut sailor collar. The skirt flared, showing off her legs. Her shoes were also white, cheap, with frayed eyelets on the straps. She had a red sweater over her shoulders.

Al whistled when he saw her. "My girl got a date tonight?"

"Oh, hi, Al. I was just going down to the game."

"All alone?"

"I was sort of going to meet Ellie and Joe."

He smiled. "Here, I brought you a present." He shoved the nut cake toward her and she took it in both hands, carefully. "It's nut cake like the rich people eat."

"That's awfully nice of you. What made you think of me?"

He took her by the arm and led her toward his room. "Come on, I want to have a talk with you."

She followed him, trying to eat the nut cake at the same time. She tasted a mouthful and said, "This is good."

"What I want to know is, what's wrong? How come you been avoiding me?"

She had another mouthful of nut cake. He waited until she swallowed. "There's nothing wrong with you," she said.

"O.K., then you and I are going out tonight. Any place you want—the tennis courts, in back of the casino, behind the swimming pool—you name it."

"Oh stop. I wish you wouldn't talk like that."

"Do we have a date?"

"We can go to the game together."

"I'll tell you what—I'll shave and shower and meet you down there in about twenty minutes. You go down and save us a couple of good seats. How's that?"

"O.K. Fine," she said.

He went to his drawer and pulled out a sweater. "Here, you put this on my seat for me—sort of like putting my name on it. At least you won't have to use your sweater. It's chilly out."

"You know," she said. "I can't figure you out at all."

He went to her and put his hands on her arms. His face moved closer to hers and he gently pecked the tip of her nose. "You're only eighteen," he said. "It'll take you longer but you'll get there."

She said, "Maybe I will." Then they both moved away from each other and she left.

Stan, the Mong, racked up sixteen points in the first half against the team from Shechter's Shangri-La. But the Shangri-La had two forwards and a guard who were first string all-Midwest. By the end of the half, the Sesame was on the short end of 24—22.

Al and Roz were sitting in the second row of a group of seats pulled out from the casino. They were holding hands and neither of them spoke much during the game.

At the half Al said, "Want a drink?"

Roz said, "Sure."

"You just sit here. I'll get it for you."

"Never mind. I can walk."

They got up and went over to the bar on the side of the casino. He put his arm around her waist and whispered in her ear, "Don't worry. I won't get fresh." He cupped his hand on her waist to remind her.

When they got to the bar, Al ordered a beer.

"I thought you were going to get a soft drink," she said.

"Let's splurge," he said. "You have to live sometimes."

"O.K., I think I'll have an orange blossom."

"Orange blossom? You don't like to drink, do you?"

"I don't mind orange blossoms. They're about the only liquor that doesn't make me sick."

"A social drinker, huh?" They were sitting up on the bar stools and he turned sideways to face her. His knees were buckled up in front of him, almost touching her. "Well, you just try a screwdriver. I'll bet you like it."

"Are you sure? Really, I've never had much luck with drinking."

"Leave it to me," Al said.

From behind the bar a man with short-cropped gray hair and a mustache opened a bottle of beer and poured it in front of Al. "And what'll it be for the lady, Al," the man said.

"A screwdriver," Al Brodie said. "Say, T. J., did you ever meet Roz? Roz, this is T. J. Boone, former softshoe artist, multimillionaire and man about town. Currently T. J. is in retirement—that is, he rented the concession here at the Sesame."

T. J. put two pieces of ice into a small glass, poured a jigger of vodka into it and brought a bottle of orange juice from beneath the counter. "Retirement is right," he said to Al. "You know how much I've taken in all night? Honest to God, you come back here and look at the register. A lousy seven-fifty. I don't know how those Mandheimers figure I can live under it."

"What's that he poured in the glass?" Roz asked.

"Vodka," Al explained. "Don't worry, you'll never taste it. The only thing that matters is the orange juice."

T. J. smiled at Roz. "This is a wonderful drink, sweetheart. I use fresh oranges. Maybe I'm crazy. Frozen would be cheaper, but that's me. I got to use the best or I'm not happy."

Al took a long drink of his beer. "T. J. used to be a hoofer. He played all the best clubs. Then he got rheumatism."

T. J. Boone dropped a cherry in the screwdriver, put a cardboard coaster under the glass and set it in front of Roz. He tried to look modest. "Hell, I worked the best club dates in the country. You think I'd be doing this if it wasn't for the back?" He rubbed his back. "Jerry 'Fisherman' Trout from the Big Club called me yesterday. 'T. J.,' he said, 'I got a great spot for you. We're doing a revue. You're the only talent in the country can handle it.' Pays a G a week. But what am I going to do? I got this back."

"That's a shame," Roz said. "Maybe you should see a chiropractor. I know a lot of people don't believe in them, but the lady next door to us, she strained her back lifting up her grandchild. I mean he's only two years old, but he's a bruiser. I'll bet he weighs forty pounds. Well, anyway she strained her back and she went to a chiropractor and he fixed her up good as new."

"I seen them, sweetheart," T. J. said. "I seen the best in the country. When this happened, I was out on the coast. Right after I got out of the service. Personally I always thought I picked it up in the service. But go ahead sue the Uncle. This fellow, he's the biggest bone man on the coast. He's done work for some of your biggest stars. I mean he gets fifty bucks a visit, but it's worth every cent. I bet this back has cost me a good five G's." He shrugged his shoulders and winced. "But it's no good. I'm throwing my money down the drain. The best of them can't help me."

"That's really a shame," Roz said.

"How about another brew?" Al said.

"You finished so quickly?" Roz said. "I've hardly even tasted mine."

"While you were busy talking," Al said, "I was working."

T. J. opened another bottle and set it in front of Al. "Don't discourage him, sweetheart," he said to Roz. "If it wasn't for the help around here, I'd starve to death."

"It's really that bad," Al said.

"Worse." T. J. pulled a cloth from behind the bar and started to wipe glasses. "My soda and coffee business keeps me going. In a spot like this you figure to take in fifty, seventy-five a night during the week. You get a break on the week ends, you make yourself a nice dollar. Look what I'm doing! Seven-fifty for the night. You think they're going to come in here and drink after the game? I won't take in five dollars."

Al said, "Tell me something, T. J. What d'you have to pay for a concession like this?"

T. J. threw the towel under the bar. He picked up a plastic mixer and used it as a pencil. He scratched against the bar. "They ask me twenty-five hundred for this spot." He said it again slowly, enunciating it very carefully. "Twenty-five hundred dollars." He shifted his weight, facing Al, so as almost to exclude Roz. "I got a liquor bill of four hundred dollars already." He scratched that figure on the bar, in the general direction of the first figure. "I got to have stock. There's no sense even putting the lights on without stock. Somebody asks for liqueurs. I got all your best liqueurs. You got to have it. I got a dozen bottles of Piper-Heidsieck champagne. It's your best import. They told me they have birthdays, anniversaries, people buy a bottle of champagne. That's what they told me. I'm lucky I sell one bottle all season. One bottle." He dropped the mixer on the bar. "No, Mandheimer stuck me up. What's the sense in kidding ourselves? He put a gun to my back."

Al's glass was empty. There was still some beer left in the bottle and he poured it. "How about your room and board, T. J. How do you figure that?"

T. J. picked up the mixer again. "All right, so I've got a room over here by the side of the casino. I'm not knocking it. It's all right. Me and the kid works my fountain, we eat in the main dining room. So what do we eat?" He scratched on the table. "I'm up working the bar till one, two in the morning—not that there's so much business. But people come in, you can't kick them out. You got to be here. Breakfast I miss altogether. Lunch, nine out of ten times I catch down here. A cup of coffee, a sandwich, that's my lunch. Who can eat all that stuff they throw at you in the dining room? So what are we eating? What are we costing her in food? Figure big. Figure between the kid and me five meals a day. It stands them a dollar a meal—if it's that high. You go to college. Work it out for yourself. They're sticking me up."

A man in a torn leather jacket and old khakis came in and sat at the far end of the bar, rubbing his hands.

"Here comes my bread and butter—the help," T. J. said. He winked to Roz and squeezed her hand. "How do you like that screwdriver?"

"Very good," Roz said. "I hardly know I'm drinking liquor."

"I'll let you in on a little secret," T. J. said. "They're a lot stronger than you think." He patted her hand and smiled, "Next thing you know you'll be drunk and doing things you shouldn't ought to."

"And I thought you were a friend of mine," Al said.

T. J. moved quickly down the bar toward the man who was rubbing his hands. "What'll it be for you tonight, Jackson? The usual?" he asked the man.

"Set 'em up," the man said.

T. J. poured a shot of whiskey and a glass of beer for the man. Then he made a notation on a small pad.

The man drank the shot of whiskey quickly. He sipped the beer. "What does that make it?" he asked T. J.

"It isn't a million dollars yet, don't worry," T. J. said.

The man laughed. "Let me know when it gets up around a hundred thousand. I'll want to call my bank and check the balance."

"I think they're starting the second half," Roz said to Al. "Shouldn't we be getting back?"

"One more," Al said. "How about you?"

"I can hardly finish this," Roz said.

"I thought you liked it. Or is it that you don't trust me?"

"When I get drunk, I get sleepy," Roz said. "And nothing can wake me up."

"And how many times has that been?"

She crinkled up her nose and smiled. "Twice. Once at my sister's wedding and the other time—" She paused a moment and then said, "I was on a date with a boy I used to go around with."

"Oh-ho. So the truth comes out," Al said. "I'm not your one and only."

"I never said you were," Roz said seriously.

"Say, T. J., give me a refill," Al called down the bar.

T. J. was talking with the man who was drinking whiskey and beer. He held up one finger to Al, but stayed with the man.

"So tell me all about this other guy," Al said to Roz.

"It's nothing. It's all over now." She played with her straw and finally sipped her drink.

"Let me tell you," Al said. "The boy next door. Known him all your life. Suddenly you looked at him one day, real close, and said to yourself—this is a drip. Not for me." He made a gesture as if he was shaking hands. "So long, old boy. Lots of luck. Top of the day. Get out of my life forever."

"Are you drunk or something?" Roz asked. "Really, Al, I think you're drinking too fast and too much."

"It takes a lot more than three beers to flatten me," Al said. "Tell me, is it true or not? Wasn't he the boy next door?"

"Not at all. You're altogether wrong. The thing was—well, Freddie wanted to get married right away. And I didn't think it would be fair to him or me. He's only a sophomore in college. True, he has his father's furniture store to go into, but in the long run I'm sure he'll be better off graduating. A college degree is a good thing to have behind you."

"Very sensible," Al said. "I'm glad you did what was right for dear old Freddie." He called down the bar again. "Hey, T. J., I'm going to take my business next door."

A kitchen man had joined the man called Jackson and was drinking whiskey and beer. T. J. was in the process of refilling both glasses. "One second," he said. "I didn't forget you, sweetheart."

"I didn't mean for it to sound like that," Roz said. "I had my selfish reason too." There was some of her drink left at the bottom of her glass, but she bent the straw, rolled it up and dropped it into the glass. "I want to go to business school next year. There's a nine-month course that teaches you how to type and take shorthand. With something practical like that, I'll be able to get a job as a receptionist and model."

"Whoa—" Al said. "You lost me."

"I might as well tell you," Roz said. "My Dad's brother, Uncle Dave, he's a manufacturer. Well, he has this showroom and he promised me a job. See, modeling is what I really want to do and Uncle Dave says that if I can be a secretary-receptionist, he'll give me a chance to do some modeling. I think it's a wonderful opportunity. A chance to get real experience."

Al looked down at her blouse. "So you want to be a model. I know one department at least where you'll outpoint the competition."

"Why do you have to say things like that? Do you think that's smart?" She pushed her drink across the bar and turned away from him. "Here I am talking to you seriously, and you say a disgusting thing like that."

"Those boilermakers are keeping me in business," T. J. said, moving toward them. "Between you and me, I don't know what keeps those guys standing up." He poured a glass of beer for Al and left the bottle on the bar.

Al drained off the top of the glass, emptied the bottle and told T. J. to mark it down. "Come on," he said to Roz, "let's get back to that game."

She sat with her back to him and didn't answer.

"You still sore? Boy, are you sensitive."

"I'm not accustomed to being talked to like that."

"All right, so I'm sorry. What d'you want me to do?"

She got off her chair and turned halfway toward him. "You talk that way all the time. We'll be going along real nice, getting to know each other. Then, all of a sudden—boom—you say something vulgar."

"All right, so let's forget it. We'll start over again. You're going to be a model." She let him put his hand under her arm and lead her to the door.

"I think it would be interesting work. Not that I think I'm particularly beautiful or have a conceited opinion of myself, but I think I'd be good in it. I think I might really get somewhere. Some of the girls who worked for Uncle Dave are freelancers now. They make big money. Nora Watts, ever hear of her? She used to work for Uncle Dave in the same job I'd be doing. She gets twenty dollars an hour today."

"Sounds very good," Al said. They were at the door and he sipped his beer.

"Do you have to take that outside?" Roz said. "The glass might break."

"You're absolutely right," Al said. He drained the glass in one long swallow, wiped his sleeve across his lips, and said, "See what I'll do for you? No sacrifice is too great, if it makes you happy."

She waited for him as he returned the glass to the bar. Outside the air was cold and the night bright with stars. The second half had started. From the sounds of the Sesame fans, it was obvious that the game wasn't going so well for the home team.

Danny Rose didn't look like an athlete. He was dwarfed by the players on the court. In his basketball jersey it was apparent that he had a hump. It was a small swell at the top of his back, but his shoulders were heavy and his arms long and thick. In its own way the construction of his body had a harmony, and he moved swiftly and rhythmically.

He was playing guard and he brought the ball down court in total command. He would set up the plays deftly, always aware of any shifts in the opposition that should change the attack. Twice he drew out the Shangri-La forward and went in to take a midcourt jump shot by himself. He hit the first time on a perfect swish, and it looked as if he could do it any time he wanted and never miss. But the second time the ball rolled around the rim and fell out. That was in the first quarter and Danny Rose didn't shoot again.

Stan Macht had no such inhibitions against shooting. He played the pivot. The attack called for the ball to be fed in to him. His back was to the basket and he could either pass off or make the wide pivot and shoot. The Shangri-La guard played him close, but he forced his shots. His eye was good and he was aggressive in following up the rebounds. Once he thought he was fouled under the basket and he made life miserable for Jerry Furman, the social director, who had volunteered to referee the game.

That was in the closing minutes of the game and Sesame was trailing by three points. Shangri-La took the ball on and Stan was still arguing. He argued even as Danny Rose stole the ball and tried to set up a play.

Danny called time out. He got the team in a huddle, tried to calm them and had them stack hands in the traditional team vow for victory. He took the ball on himself, passed it in to Mike Heimer who returned the pass and slid by the man who was guarding him. Danny had a shot but he passed it to Mike who cut off and was clear in the corner. Mike made a set shot that brought them within one point.

There was less than a minute left and the Shangri-La team tried to freeze the ball. Danny Rose came from nowhere to steal it again. He was small and lithe as a cat. His movements looked slow and that helped his deception.

He dribbled downcourt, deliberately stalling for the one shot that could tie and win the game. He was trying to set up the play but Stan, the Mong, was calling for the ball. From the sidelines the Sesame fans called for the pass. "Give it to Stan. Let the Mong shoot."

Danny Rose was inside the half-court line. He measured the distance to the basket and there was a second when it looked for sure as if he would shoot. He passed the ball in to Stan, and the Mong pivoted wildly and shot. The ball went on a line, smacked against the inside rim and bounced out. Shangri-La picked up the rebound and the game was over.

Furman, the social director, cupped his hands to his mouth and whistled. He was of medium height, but fat. His face had a plump boyishness about it. There was still talking but the crowd was quiet enough to hear his booming voice announce that there would be square dancing in the casino.

"What d'you say?" Al asked Roz.

"Sounds like fun."

Furman was whistling again, but the crowd had broken up and he couldn't get attention.

As they walked across the court, Al and Roz heard Furman say to Stan Macht, "Listen, Mong, you're supposed to arrange for taking the chairs back into the casino."

The Mong was dripping sweat. A towel was over his shoulder and he had a Coke in his hand. "You know where you can put the chairs," he said to Furman. "Who the hell ever told you that you were a referee?"

"Next time you can get somebody else. But in the meantime I've got square dancing for tonight. How about getting some of the boys together and pulling in the chairs. It'll only take a minute." Furman's voice was friendly even as he tried to be tough.

"That guy was all over me. He was hacking me all night—"

"Give me a hand with the chairs, will you—"

"Get off my back. I'm stinking wet. I'm going to take a shower."

"There won't be any more basketball if you don't help with the chairs. I've got enough to do without this."

"Make with the jokes." Macht started to walk away. "You're

the social director. You're lucky I give you half the night off."

"Let's help him," Roz said to Al.

He held her hand, restraining her. "How about minding our own business."

"This is our business. I want to square dance." She broke away from him and went over to a group of four chairs that were latched together in the back. "Come on, lazy, get the other side."

He liked the way she bent over and the sureness of her movements. "What d'you say we take a walk?"

She was already dragging the bench. "Shake a leg, will you? This isn't easy in high heels."

He walked over beside her and took a hold. The two of them pulled the rack of chairs together.

When the last chairs were inside, Jerry Furman motioned for them to join him. "You'll appreciate this," he said softly. "Isaac Kaplan retired at sixty-five. What do you do when you retire—collect stamps, sit in a rocking chair? Not Isaac Kaplan. A trip around the world, maybe? That's for Isaac.

"So, by Paris Isaac sees the Eiffel Tower. By London, Bucking-kosherham Palace. And always—always Isaac manages, wherever he is, to see a little bit of home.

"Finally, it's the last week of his trip, and Isaac is in Tokyo. Why not Tokyo? Moishe Pippick, his boy, wasn't in Tokyo? So Isaac goes by the geisha girls, sees the shops, buys some silk—wholesale, naturally. But comes Friday night—Shabbos—Isaac Kaplan is homesick."

"Hey, Furman, how about the show?" a guest called from across the room.

"One minute. Halt dein horse," Jerry Furman called back. He returned to Roz and Al. "So anyway, to make a long story short, he sees a crowd of people all headed toward this big building in the center of the street. What does Isaac do? He follows them. Sure enough, inside there's an altar, a Torah, and on the platform a little Japanese man with a yarmelke. Such a Shabbos service Isaac Kaplan never heard before. In Tokyo, yet. The service was over, Isaac got in line to meet the rabbi.

" 'Rabbi,' Isaac says, 'such a wonderful service I never heard in my life. You'll come to America, you'll stop by the Brooklyn Jewish Center, you wouldn't hear better.'

"The Japanese rabbi looks at him, amazed. 'You say you Jewiss?' Isaac says, 'Of course. All my life I'm Isaac Kaplan. By Brooklyn I'm living.'

"The Japanese rabbi nods his head. 'Dat funny. Velly funny. You know something?' Kaplan says, 'What?'

" 'You no lookie Jewiss!' the Japanese rabbi says."

Roz laughed and said, "Very good, Jerry. And so true."

Al didn't say anything until Jerry Furman patted his shoulder. "You put that over real good," Al said. "I like the way you do those dialects."

Jerry said, "I've got to run along. My public is clamoring for me."

"He really is very talented," Roz said. "He could be another Jerry Lewis or Danny Kaye. You know they got started in places just like this."

"Not Furman," Al said. "I can take one look at him and see he doesn't have it."

"Why not? I think he has a very nice look. Not glamorous or anything, but very pleasant."

Al didn't answer. There was a circle with Joe and Ellie, an older couple, Jean Furman, and Andy, the Furmans' son. "Come on," Al said, "let's go over there and spin around a little."

Roz took his hand as they walked over to join the group.

Jerry Furman said into the microphone on the stage, "It's easy. Let's have everybody dance. Even you, bubbela."

People laughed and the band started playing. From the stage, Jerry Furman called the first dance. "You put your right foot in. You put your right foot out. You give yourself a shake, shake, shake, and turn yourself about." It wasn't a real square dance, but he liked to start off with it. Everybody relaxed.

Roz clenched her fist at her waist and shook herself lightly. Al noticed she wasn't wearing a girdle.

Ellie shook herself furiously and put each foot out as

though she were posing for a stocking ad. Joe caught Al's eye once and winked.

When the real dancing started, Jean Furman was very patient in reviewing the steps for the older couple. When they couldn't get the idea of the do-si-do, she took them over to the side and helped them.

Her son said, "Can't we dance without always being interrupted, mom?"

Jean Furman's answer was too quiet for the others to hear, but her son calmed down immediately.

Joe and Ellie invited them for a ride after the first two rounds, but Al said he wanted to get to bed early and Roz said she'd had enough.

They walked together arm in arm across the lawn and up the pathway that led to their rooms.

The sky was brilliant, filled with stars and a three-quarter moon. The air was cool but dry. Al took a deep breath and exhaled slowly. "What a night," he said. "It makes you glad to be alive."

"It is lovely," Roz said.

"It's a shame to waste it. I'm going to take a walk." He said it with a burst of inspiration. "What d'you say? Are you with me?"

"I don't know, Al. It's getting late."

He dropped his arm from her waist and held her fingers in his hand, very loosely. "Come on, Roz. It wouldn't be any fun without you."

They started down the path the way they'd come. Slowly he slid his arm back around her. He brushed his lips against the side of her head. "You make it perfect," he said softly and it came out as a very deep compliment.

"The trouble in this world," he said, "is that people are too pent-in. They don't live enough, really live. They're trapped in their little cages, always worried about what other people will think." His arm exerted a very soft pressure.

"You're so right," Roz said.

They started down the road and neither of them spoke

again until they were well past the help's quarters and the rooms where most of the waiters stayed.

"I remember being ditched here by a girl once," Al said, as if it was a sad memory.

Roz's hand pinched the flesh of his side. "Now you have a reason to ditch me."

"Maybe I should. Maybe you'd be happier that way. So long—" he said. He let her go and pretended to walk away. He took a few steps and then came back to her. He put his arms around her and pulled her to him. For just a moment he held her close, feeling the warm full pressure of her body. She sighed and stirred once in his arms and he kissed her.

It was a long time before he moved his mouth away from hers. "See," he said softly, "I didn't jilt you the way you jilted me."

She ran her hand along the back of his head and down his neck. She seemed very serious. "I didn't know you then, the way I do now."

He held his face away from hers and looked into her eyes. "It takes some people longer," he said.

"I won't jilt you again, Al. Never." She pressed her cheek hard against his face and then kissed his lips.

There was a small ditch by the road and when she stepped in and slipped, he thought the spell was broken. It wasn't. She pressed close to him and he guided her into the woods. There seemed to be no clear space.

She sat down at the base of a big tree. He knew she was sitting on twigs and small stones and there was hardly room for the two of them, but her arms were lifted up toward him.

He pressed her against the tree and kissed her again.

"God, Al," she whispered. "I never felt like this. Never in my life."

He touched her face gently with his hands and kissed her lightly on the ear. By the time his hands had moved to her waist, he knew that she was waiting for him.

She cried afterwards.

He held her head against his shoulder and smoothed her

hair. The first words he said were, "We can't stay here all night, Roz. If we get back now, nobody will know."

She stopped for a moment and dried her eyes and then started again. "If it makes you feel any better," he said, "I didn't lose respect for you or anything like that."

"I never did it before, Al," she sobbed. "Honest to God, I never did it before. I don't know what happened to me. I'm ashamed. I'm so ashamed—"

"It happens all the time, Roz. To better people than us. It's the night," he said, "and the summer and the Catskills. It happens to everybody—everybody who's not dead."

She lifted her head and pressed her mouth hard against his. They were still kissing as slowly he moved his hands beneath her elbows and brought her to her feet.

She pressed fiercely against him. "I love you, Al. I really do. Do you know that? I could never have done a thing like this—never, if I didn't love you."

On the way back to the bungalow she said, "Al, what are you studying in college? What are you going to do when you leave school?"

"I'm going to be an accountant," he said. "There's a lot of dough in accounting, if you play it right."

"I think that's terrific," Roz said. "You're going to be a wonderful accountant, darling."

He kissed her again in front of her door and she clung to him as if she'd never let him go. "I'm not ashamed any more, Al. I love you. I can't be ashamed of that."

He cupped his hand on her side and pinched her lightly.

"I have a lot to give, Al. A lot more to give. I hope you know that."

He lifted a finger to his lips, said, "Sshh," and pointed toward the door of her room.

He kissed her once more and as he turned away, she asked, "Do you love me, Al? Tell me you love me."

He kissed her and said good night.

It was several hours later when Joe came back. Al was suspended between dreams and sleep.

"You up? You awake, Al?"

"I am now."

"I heard a good one. You're really going to like this. There was this little Jewish man whose name was Isaac Kaplan—"

"I know," Al said. "He retired. I was looking over his social security file."

"You heard it?"

"I made it up. Furman steals my stuff."

"I thought it was funny as hell," Joe said. "So did Ellie."

"Good," Al said.

"I mean that part about the Jap being Jewish—Jews are all over, huh?"

"Yeah," Al said. "You might even find a few around here."

"What d'you have to do to be Jewish—be bar-mitzvahed or something?"

"You just got to be born rich," Al said.

"I'm serious," Joe said.

"Some other time, please," Al Brodie said. "I'm sleepy."

"I really like that Ellie," Joe said. "I never met anybody like her in my life."

Chapter 9

Al Brodie's mother said, "It's been almost three weeks and still not a word. At least he could drop us a post card."

"It's better that he's on his own," the father said.

"And when wasn't he on his own? When was Allen not altogether on his own? Does that mean he's not supposed to write—at least tell us how he's feeling?"

The father said, "Don't worry so much. When I was twelve years old, I already had a job. My mother didn't worry so much about me."

"Your mother had eight children."

"It was better that way. You knew at least if you wanted something, you had to work for it. Nobody handed you anything on a silver platter."

"Look who's talking. We're lucky we have what to eat—a silver platter yet. Since when did you ever give Al anything?"

From the desk, the big black-faced clock in the lobby indicated that it was seven-forty. The hour hand was several inches out of line. The right time was six-forty.

Mrs. Mandheimer was in the inner office trying to get out the dinner menus. At the switchboard, Mr. Mandheimer was checking some of the phone calls he'd picked up from his New York answering service. It had been a busy day—lots of calls with heavy reservations for the last two weeks in July.

Six-thirty was the time Calvin usually took his break. But

tonight he was at the desk, stacking his copies of the *Post* and *Journal-American*. He sold the papers for fifteen cents a copy. On a good night he'd sell twenty and clear a dollar. But it wasn't his investment that was keeping him at the desk. There was the possibility of a check-in, and check-ins were a bellhop's business.

"Mrs. Leiderkopf, she's supposed to come this evenin', ain't she, boss?" he asked Mr. Mandheimer.

Mr. Mandheimer was inserting a brochure in an envelope. He wiped a rubber sponge across the top and sealed it. "Becky," he called toward the inner office, "what's the matter Leiderkopf's not here yet?"

"Who's worried about Leiderkopf?" Mrs. Mandheimer said. "Sam, you know how to fix this machine?"

"You had to buy a new machine," Mr. Mandheimer said. "A mimeographer isn't good enough for you. You have to have a multigrapher. All right, so you'll call the salesman. He says it works so easy, he'll make the menus for you."

"Sam, don't be so smart. Come here. Make the menus."

Mr. Mandheimer left the switchboard and started toward the inner office.

"Leiderkopf'll be here," Calvin said. "She be in on the six-forty bus. She come up that way every year."

"I'm giving her room twenty-two in the main," Mrs. Mandheimer called. "She comes, you check her in, Calvin. She shouldn't aggravate me about the rooms on the second floor."

"Becky, what are you doing? You know what you're doing? Here, get away from the machine. Next thing you know you'll break it, we'll have to buy a new mimeographer."

"Right away a manager. So make the menus."

"It's the feeder," Mr. Mandheimer said. "You didn't adjust the feeder."

"So I'll fix it."

"Becky, will you get away from this machine. Two people should never work on a machine at the same time. Arms are lost that way."

"Sam, what's the matter you're so nervous. Keep this up, you'll never make the season."

"Just do me a favor, let me fix the machine. Go outside, watch the phone, ten minutes I'll give you your menus."

"All of a sudden I make him nervous."

Mr. Mandheimer's voice rose. "Yes, you make me nervous. So you want me to do the menus or not?"

Mrs. Mandheimer didn't answer. She left the inner office and walked out to the switchboard. "Which ones of the inquiries didn't you answer? I'm waiting for the menus, I'll start on them."

"Becky, one thing at a time, *please*," Mr. Mandheimer said.

"I'm telling you, he's worse than an old woman. Who'd believe he's been twenty-seven years in this business?"

Calvin laughed, not at anybody or anything. He just laughed.

"You've got to watch your papers?" Mrs. Mandheimer said. "You're afraid somebody will steal your nickels?"

"No, ma'am," Calvin said. "Mrs. Leiderkopf, she suppose' to come today?"

"You're worried she'll check in herself, she wouldn't tip you."

Calvin laughed again. "Bellhop's got to look out for his check-in. No check-ins, no gelt."

"Everybody for himself," Mrs. Mandheimer said. There was an expression of bitterness about her face.

"What you pickin' on me for, missus?" Calvin opened his hands and shrugged. "The lobby's done. I done the floor, cleaned all the ashtrays—"

The switchboard buzzed. Mr. Mandheimer rushed out of the inner office. He was by his wife's side as she picked up the phone.

"Sesame Hotel," Mrs. Mandheimer said. "This is Mrs. Mandheimer speaking. Who? Marsha!" She moved the receiver away from her and said to her husband. "It's Marsha, Sam. Marsha."

"Where is she? She's at the station? The baby's with her?"

"Keep quiet, Sam, I can't hear her. What's that you say, Marsha? . . . You're at the station. And the baby, he's with you?" She nodded her head and held both hands to the receiver. "The baby's well. No cold or anything . . . Fine . . . Fine . . . Stay right where you are. Daddy will call for you. Don't move around, go any place or do anything . . . I mean the baby shouldn't get a cold . . . Daddy will call for you. He'll be there in five minutes . . ." She moved the mouthpiece to the side.

"What are you waiting for, Sam, go already. She's waiting for you by Godleb's." She turned back to the phone. "So how come you took the bus? I left you money, I thought you'd hire a hack . . . Everything was all right in the city? . . . That's good. That you've got to be thankful for . . . Daddy's coming right away . . . All right. All right . . . Good-by. Marsha! Marsha! Don't eat anything. They'll set up for you in the main dining room, you'll have a good meal . . . All right . . . Yes . . . Yes . . . You're in for a big surprise. You wouldn't know the place."

After Mrs. Mandheimer hung up, she went back to the multigrapher. There were fifteen minutes until the dining room opened. Sam had gone to pick up Marsha, and now she had to do the menus again.

Marsha Cooper was a tall, thin girl with black hair that she wore loose over her shoulders. Her eyes were small with slight circles beneath. The skin of her face was dark olive and drawn tight. She had a very small chin but a full mouth and large white teeth.

She was dressed in a black turtle-neck sweater, Black-Watch plaid slacks, and sandals the evening she arrived at the Sesame. In her arms she held her son, a two-and-a-half-year old who was wearing short pants, a white T shirt, and tennis shoes without stockings. Like his mother the boy was thin, but Marsha had to hold him tight with both arms.

An old gray-haired woman came up the steps to the lobby behind them. Mr. Mandheimer was by her side, propping her at the elbow. The gray-haired woman had a large straw shopping bag over one arm. She clung to it tenaciously.

"Becky, somebody here to see you," Mr. Mandheimer called across the lobby.

The little boy was pointing to one of the potted plants and saying, "Cac-tus. Cac-tus. That cac-tus, Mommy."

Mrs. Mandheimer came out of the office, wiping her hands on her apron. She headed straight for her grandson and tried to take him from her daughter's arms.

The little boy took a short look at her and buried his head in his mother's shoulder.

"Let him get used to you again, Mother," Marsha said. "He only saw you for that short time in the city. It's best to ignore him for a while."

"Ignore him?" Mrs. Mandheimer said. "Ignore him," she repeated. "We've ignored enough for a lifetime. Come to your grandma, Phillip darling. Such a nice baby. Such a nice big boy." She stroked his leg and he lurched away from her, kicking his mother.

"Give him a chance, Becky," Mr. Mandheimer said. "He'll warm up."

"So thin," Mrs. Mandheimer said. "We'll put some meat on him. Yes, indeed, we'll fatten him up." She patted his leg again and then said to her daughter. "What's the matter, Marsha, he doesn't wear socks? Shoes like this, you know they can ruin his feet."

Mr. Mandheimer forced a little laugh. "Right away you're home, Marsha. See, nothing changes."

Calvin, the bellhop, came up to the gray-haired woman and said, "Nice to see you, Mrs. Leiderkopf. I get your bags from the car, check you in."

"No hurry. No hurry," Mrs. Leiderkopf said. "Mrs. Mandheimer has a minute, she'll give me a room."

"Calvin knows the room," Mrs. Mandheimer said. She turned away from her grandchild briefly and nodded to Mrs. Leiderkopf. "So how are you?"

"Umbeshre'in," Mrs. Leiderkopf said. She made a fist and tapped the air as if she was knocking on wood.

"And the family?" Mrs. Mandheimer said.

"We've got a lovely room for you, Marsha," Mr. Mandheimer said. "Fourteen. It's a corner room on the first floor of the main building. Mommy thought it'd give the baby plenty of fresh air."

Marsha nodded and shifted her son as she walked to one of the lobby chairs.

"Every Friday mine boys come by me," Mrs. Leiderkopf said. "Mine four boys, and I make for them. You know how a mother makes. Fish, soup, chicken . . ." she recited in a sing-song voice. "Their wives wouldn't cook so good for them. At mine house they eat chicken—chicken like it's bread."

"Marsha, maybe you'd like to go see your room," Mrs. Mandheimer said. "Sam, you have to stand there, you can't show her the room?"

"Here for the boychick," Mrs. Leiderkopf said. She put her hand into her shopping bag and dug around. "Something nice. A toy maybe." She brought out a small, plastic water-gun and handed it to Marsha. "He'll be in his room. He wouldn't be so nervous, you'll give it to him."

Marsha made no gesture to take it. "Thank you very much, Mrs. Leiderkopf, but we've made it a point— If it's all the same to you, we'd rather he didn't play with toy guns."

Mrs. Leiderkopf didn't quite understand. "You want maybe a plastic baby doll? Mine son comes up from Long Island next week, I'll tell him." She turned to Mrs. Mandheimer. "Such things they're making. Mine husband was alive, he wouldn't know the business." She put the toy gun back in her shopping bag, and dug around again. She brought out a plastic whistle. "This would be better?"

Marsha took it and thanked her very much.

Calvin came up the steps with Mrs. Leiderkopf's luggage, two worn, heavy, leather bags and a bird cage.

"Becky," Mr. Mandheimer said. "I meant to tell you, Mrs. Leiderkopf brought a what they call a parakeet."

"Bir-dee. Bir-dee. See the bir-dee," the little boy screamed, and pointed to the parakeet.

"Oh, he talks so nice," Mrs. Mandheimer said. She squeezed her grandson's cheek and the boy's face contorted in an angry cry.

"Mother, you shouldn't do that," Marsha said. She started rocking Phillip in her arms to calm him.

Mrs. Leiderkopf had taken some birdseed out of her shopping bag and was feeding the parakeet. "Tsch, tsch, fagela. Tsch, tsch . . ."

Mrs. Mandheimer took her grandson's thumb in her hand. "Tendala," she said, "tendala, tendala." One by one she took each of his fingers until she reached the little finger. Then she ran her hand up the baby's arm, over his chest and to his tummy. She tickled him and he cried all the harder.

Mr. Mandheimer said, "Mrs. Leiderkopf was saying she expects to keep the bird in her room, Becky."

"He talks," Mrs. Leiderkopf said. "Listen, you'll hear. He says 'Goot Yuntef.'"

"Remember, Marsha, tendala you used to love?" Mrs. Mandheimer said. "You'd laugh so. How could you remember, you were a baby?"

"You want I should check Mrs. Leiderkopf into twenty-two?" Calvin asked. He was still holding the bags and the cage.

"For the time being," Mrs. Mandheimer said.

"You want to come with me, Marsha? I'll show you your room," Mr. Mandheimer said. "Don't bother with Marsha's luggage, Calvin. I'll bring it up myself."

Audrey Grier had a stack of menus in her hands, with two little white cards on top of them. She was looking at the cards. "Marsha Cooper is your daughter. How nice. I know you must be thrilled to have her with you."

Mrs. Mandheimer shrugged. "She just lost her husband."

"Oh, I'm sorry to hear that. The poor girl must be all broken up."

Mrs. Mandheimer said, "I wouldn't know."

"Come on now, Mrs. Mandheimer, I'm sure you're very close. Listen, we have friction in the best of families."

"You'll give her a good table. Maybe that young group at number eight. That might be best for her."

"She'll love the Schusters and the Levines. They're a lot of fun. Perfect for her. I was thinking the same thing myself. They'll do her a world of good."

"We'll see," Mrs. Mandheimer said.

Audrey Grier smiled. "Don't worry, Mrs. Mandheimer, we'll cheer Marsha up. Before you know it, she'll be laughing and forgetting all about her tragedy."

"She wouldn't forget so fast."

Audrey Grier looked at the other card. "And this Mrs. Leiderkopf. She's an older woman. I have the perfect place for her on table thirty-one. With the Erlangs and Mantell—I think we even have a dummy setting there."

"You think she didn't bring a parakeet with her?"

"Beg your pardon?"

"Leiderkopf, she brought a parakeet with her. She'll only share her room with the parakeet. No other guests. Not even when we're busy the last two weeks. She wants to pay the children's rate for the parakeet, that's her business."

"You mean she's actually paying for the parakeet? I never heard of such a thing."

"What do you mean?" Mrs. Mandheimer said belligerently. "There are two beds in that room. I could get good money during the height of the season."

"Of course," Audrey Grier said. "I meant that I can't imagine a parakeet meaning so much to her that she'd actually be willing to pay a children's rate to keep him with her."

"Listen, she's a lonely woman. Her husband's dead now, let's see—five years at least. So she sees her sons once a week. She's an old woman. She needs company."

"People grow very fond of their pets," Audrey Grier said.

Stan Macht came out of the dining room and called toward the desk. "Hey, Audrey, you goin' to open? It's a quarter after seven. The chef is blowing his top."

"Here, take the menus and distribute them," Audrey said to him. "And set up on table eight for one more. Mrs. Mandheimer's daughter is going to be with you. Tell Al Brodie to make that dummy on thirty-one alive."

Stan Macht took the menus and grinned at Mrs. Mandheimer. "Don't worry, coach," he said. "We'll take good care of your daughter."

"Don't take such good care," Mrs. Mandheimer said. "She's a widow. You'll be looking for another job."

"Just kidding, coach," Stan Macht said. "Anybody gets near her, I'll break his back."

"Such talk," Mrs. Mandheimer said. "Basketball players, athletes yet. That Sam—"

Audrey Grier went over to the switchboard and adjusted the microphone. She turned on the master switch and set the buttons that would carry the announcement to all parts of the hotel. "Testing, one, two, three . . ." she said. When she reached "three" her voice came into the lobby.

Mrs. Mandheimer squeezed in beside her and turned off the lobby switch. Audrey Grier put her hand over the microphone and whispered. "I like to leave that on, so I can see how I'm coming across."

"Don't worry, a Steve Allen you'll never be. Make the announcement already."

"Good evening, guests of the Sesame," Audrey Grier said into the microphone. She held the microphone in both hands and leaned close to the speaker. Mrs. Mandheimer pushed her back. "The main dining room is open and dinner is being served." Audrey repeated it twice.

When she was through, she reached over to turn off the switch, Mrs. Mandheimer blocked her hand and moved in front of her.

"We want to welcome Mrs. Leiderkopf to the hotel tonight," Mrs. Mandheimer said into the microphone, very slowly and clearly. "Soup's on. Don't eat too much."

After Mrs. Mandheimer turned off the microphone, Audrey Grier said, "That was very cute."

"You have to put a little personality into it," Mrs. Mandheimer said. "And don't lean too close to the microphone. You'll ruin it."

"I didn't know that," the hostess said. "I'll remember in the future."

"How many years you've been here now, how many announcements you've made? You should know that."

"We can always learn," Audrey Grier said and she went to the dining room to greet the first rush of guests.

When Mr. Mandheimer came back to the desk, Mrs. Mandheimer was busy with the mail. "You think they'll need us in the kitchen?" he asked.

"We're late tonight. They wouldn't be serving the main course yet."

Mr. Mandheimer slapped his hands together. "Well, we've got Marsha settled. Such luggage! Only two suitcases, but pictures—she must have fifty of them. Some are not framed. Others're in a black cardboard thing tied up with strings. Me, she wouldn't even let see them. Like a regular treasure."

Mrs. Mandheimer said, "Her husband was an artist, remember?"

"So you'd think she'd be proud of the pictures. They were good, she'd show them to me."

"She likes the room?"

"You know Marsha."

"Well, it's a nice room. Sunlight and cross ventilation and she'll have her privacy. She wouldn't be near us."

"He's a very cute little boy. Such a mouth. You should hear him talk. He only wanted I should let him carry the suitcases—"

Mrs. Mandheimer's face lit up. "You hear the way he said birdy—so plain."

"Well, he's almost three years old. That's not exactly a baby, you know."

"It'll be good for him up here. We'll put a little weight on him. He'll get fresh air and sunshine in the day camp."

"She say anything more to you about the husband?"

"You think I've even had time to talk to her? Leiderkopf took twenty-two on the second floor."

"She didn't say anything to me."

"Marsha wants to talk to us, she'll do it. I wouldn't bring it up."

"That's best," Mr. Mandheimer said. "I was thinking. Maybe she'd like one of those new motel rooms better. With the wall-to-wall carpeting and the heater in the room—"

"You think I don't know what a motel room looks like? You've got to explain it to me?" Mrs. Mandheimer's voice rose. She nodded her head. "The motel rooms are rented. That corner room is very nice."

"What d'you think he'll call us?" Mr. Mandheimer said. "I don't know, 'Zeide' doesn't sound right. It's old fashioned. Besides, I don't feel like a zeide."

"Stop it, will you, Sam? They just came. Give them a chance."

"There's a law against thinking?"

"You thought ten years ago, she wouldn't have left. She wouldn't run away."

"*I* thought. *I* thought. That's right, blame everything on me. I don't know, you get like this I can't even talk to you, Becky."

"So you won't talk, you'll cover the desk, I'll go up and take a peek at him." She started past the desk and then called over her shoulder, "Better call answering service and get the messages before you go to the kitchen. The chef, he don't know from your being a zeide."

Table eight was empty when Marsha Cooper came in to supper. Audrey Grier led her across the room to her seat and assured her that the waiter wouldn't mind taking care of her even though she was late. She beckoned to Stan Macht, who was serving desserts at another table, and introduced him to his new guest.

Stan Macht said, "Nice to meet you. Be with you in a flash."

Marsha said, "Hello," and lit a cigarette.

Audrey Grier said, "Stan's the basketball star around here. He was all-American, I think. Your dad's going in for basketball. I feel it's a wonderful idea—give us good publicity and attract a younger crowd."

Marsha didn't answer.

"Have much trouble putting the baby to sleep?" Audrey asked.

"Mother's with him," Marsha said.

"Isn't that nice," Audrey Grier said. "It's a wonderful thing for her. She's so excited about having him here. It'll do her good, take her away from the desk a little bit. Honestly, the aggravation that woman goes through."

Marsha's hands were thin and delicate. Her fingernails were unpolished but they grew to long thin points. She flicked an ash from her cigarette and drummed her fingernails against the glass ashtray.

"I suppose you're tired after such a long trip, taking care of the baby and all," Audrey Grier said. "Well, you'll be feeling better soon. Really, you couldn't have picked a better place to rest up."

Marsha turned her face up to Audrey very slowly. "I've been at the hotel before, Miss Grier," she said.

"You're absolutely right," Audrey Grier said. "Look at me giving you a sales talk. Just the same, I do want you to know if there's anything I can do for you, call on me. I mean it sincerely. I'm even a good baby-sitter."

She stood over the table looking down at Marsha Cooper for several long seconds. She expected something, a thank-you or even a brush-off, but Marsha Cooper said nothing. Audrey felt very uncomfortable. For a moment she was tempted to say something about the unpainted fingernails, the adolescent hairstyle, the slacks and turtle-neck sweater for dinner. She could be cold, too, when she wanted. But this was Mrs. Mandheimer's daughter. And—grief does strange things to people, she reminded herself.

"Well, I'll be running along," she said. "Got to check the servers. Make sure the boys aren't stealing too many desserts."

She'd turned away expecting nothing else when Marsha Cooper said, "You do that."

At table thirty-one, Al Brodie was serving a second cup of coffee to Miss Mantell. He had to be careful as he put it down because the table in front of her was covered with candid photographs that belonged to Mrs. Leiderkopf.

"This is mine son Harold's children," Mrs. Leiderkopf was saying. "Such a beautiful house they have in Long Island. This one, the little one here, she's named Deborah for mine husband who was a Dovid. Mine Harold, he's mine oldest, he runs the business. Mine husband he makes a will, I'm the president. Me a president? No. They should come to me? No. Mine son Berle, he says to me, 'Mama, Papa wanted it this way, why not?' Berle, he's what you call a manager. He's mine youngest. Mine husband he lufs Berle. Harold, he's mine oldest. They come by me, I tell them, 'Harold, he's the oldest, he's the president.'"

Miss Mantell motioned to Al Brodie and asked him if he'd mind bringing her a small piece of dessert cake. She ate the cake and sipped her coffee as Mrs. Leiderkopf continued.

"A hundred times they tell me, 'Mama, you done the right thing.'" Miss Mantell decided not to smoke after she finished her coffee, and she sat quietly with her hands folded in her lap. Mrs. Leiderkopf finally noticed that they were holding up the waiter. They left the dining room together. Somehow the conversation had shifted, and Al Brodie heard Miss Mantell saying something about her father's opinions on the Biblical story of Jacob and Esau.

The waiter who'd served Mrs. Leiderkopf last year passed the word on that she was a regular five-and-three, and Al wasn't as worried as he'd been when Mrs. Leiderkopf gave him a plastic key case.

Stan Macht said, "You sure you don't want any dessert?"

"No, thank you," Marsha Cooper said. "I've had quite enough."

"We got plenty of cake left over."

"I'm sure you have."

"I was just kidding. Hell, you're the boss's daughter, you can have anything you damn well please around here."

"I've heard that before," Marsha Cooper said.

"It's true, isn't it?" Stan Macht said. "This place will be yours some day."

"Do you usually talk to guests so straightforwardly?" Marsha Cooper asked.

"Me, talk to guests? I don't open my mouth. I'm too busy running back and forth. Over there"—he jutted a finger toward Al Brodie's station—"we got an eight ball, he's the biggest bucker in the house. He thinks somebody might stiff him, he's got a three-act routine."

"Things haven't changed much, I see," Marsha Cooper said.

"We got a team this year," Stan Macht said. "We dropped a crusher the other night. This guy Furman, the so-called social director, what he don't know about basketball—I could write a book."

"You're just the type to write a book."

"What d'you mean by that? I don't claim to know everything, but I know a little bit about basketball, and the business I was getting the other night—you don't have to be a genius to see that. I was going to say something to your old man. What the hell, he brings the boys up here, don't he? He's interested in putting the place on the map. Well, the first thing he ought to do is can that Furman and get himself a guy who knows a little something about the game." Stan Macht pulled a chair out from the table and sat on it backwards, folding his arms on the back of the chair. "Look, he spends maybe fifty G's on this place, fixing up the front, so who knows about it? You get yourself a basketball team. I mean you knock off some of the big places, the next thing you know everybody in the mountains is talking about you."

Marsha Cooper sipped her coffee. "What are they saying?"

"What d'you mean, what are they saying? They're saying how good you are."

"So how does that help the business?"

"It's publicity. Publicity," Stan Macht said angrily. "What d'you think it is? Why do you figure them Hollywood producers spend so much dough getting the stars mixed up in scandal? It's for publicity."

"That's interesting."

"It's the truth. Look, you can have the greatest hotel in the mountains, in the whole world. You don't have publicity, nobody knows about you. And basketball—a hot basketball team is the best way to get publicity."

"How come the Hollywood producers never thought of basketball?" Marsha Cooper said.

"Stop horsing around. I'm serious. Look, I'm telling you this for your own good. I had this on my mind for a long time. I figure you're goin' to be the boss some day. This'll make your place."

Marsha Cooper left a half-filled coffee cup and got up. She didn't say anything and Stan Macht followed her as she left the table.

"I hope you're not sore or nothing. I was telling you for your own good."

"I'm sure you were." Marsha looked at him quickly and smiled very faintly. "See you around."

"You're all right," Stan Macht said. "I'm going to like you."

From the other side of the room Al Brodie saw Marsha go to the door. He asked Danny Rose if he knew who she was.

Chapter 10

"The trouble with our place is they don't have a golf course," the waiter said. "Everybody plays golf today. A hotel with even nine holes has got to be good for ten and five..."

Al was burnishing his silver. He put his knives, spoons, and forks into the machine, together with the BB's and burnishing cream. Then he locked the machine. The other waiters had set up and were taking off for the night.

Mike Heimer asked how come he didn't wait until Friday the way all the other waiters did so that his silver would be at its best for the week end. Al said he worked when he was inspired.

There was only one machine, and with eight waiters using it, there was a rush on Friday. By burnishing in the middle of the week, he avoided the crowd. Besides, there was a special effect created by working when the rest of the crew wasn't. Audrey Grier had seen him the first week and told him he was very conscientious. Mrs. Mandheimer, on her nightly check-up of the kitchen, had insisted upon helping him. It meant drying each piece of silver individually instead of wrapping them in a table cloth and throwing them into a bucket. Mrs. Mandheimer had been very pleased. She had the impression that he was the only waiter who cared about his silver at all.

The rolling of the machine was the only sound in the

kitchen, until the back door opened and closed. It was Rosalyn Silvers.

She was wearing knee-length shorts, high woolen stockings, and a lumberjacket.

"Look what came out of the night," Al said. He had his hands up to his face in mock horror.

"I'm just too lazy to change," Roz said. She came and stood by his side, watching the machine. "What are you doing?" she asked.

"I thought you had patrol tonight. Who's watching the kiddies?"

"I switched with Ellie. What does that machine do?"

"What did you do that for? She got a heavy date or something?"

"As a matter of fact it was me who asked her. What *is* going on there?"

"It's a burnishing machine. It polishes silver."

"That's interesting."

"It's dull as hell. What d'you mean you asked her? How come you wanted the night off?"

"Oh, I have a date," she said.

He wasn't at all belligerent. "You do? Well, good for you."

"Yes, indeed, a very handsome boy. He has a convertible and he's taking me up to Grossinger's for a late supper and dancing."

"You don't say."

"Why not? Nothing but the best for Roz Silvers."

"You're going to make quite a hit in that outfit. Those pants are the latest."

"He doesn't care how I dress. He loves me for myself," Roz said.

Al didn't play any more. The machine had stopped and he unlocked it. "You have to be very careful with these machines," he said. "One mistake and you've got about a hundred thousand BB's on the floor."

"Want me to help you?"

"No, you run along on your date."

"I think I will."

"So long."

"Boy, are you independent. Aren't you even glad to see me? After all, I haven't seen you all day."

Al took his silver from the machine. He started piling it into his bucket.

"Well aren't you? Aren't you glad to see me?" Roz asked.

"I thought you had a date for Grossinger's."

"Stop it. You know as well as I do that I was just pulling your leg."

"So what did you take tonight off for? Why did you switch with Ellie?"

"Because I thought it was important for us to be together tonight," she said. "There are so many things I want to talk over with you."

"Such as—"

"Not here. You're doing your silver, aren't you? We'll talk later."

All of his silver was piled in the bucket. Al reached down with one hand and picked it up. It was heavy and the large swell of muscles along his arm bulged. Roz reached over suddenly and ran her hand along his arm.

"I love you, Al," she whispered. "Honest to God, I do."

Al put the bucket into a large washbasin that was by the side of the burnisher. He turned on the faucet. As the water rushed into the bucket, he held the handle in both hands and shook the silver.

"Isn't there anything I can do to help?" Roz asked.

"After I'm through. You can help me set up."

"Fine. I'd like that. You know I hardly know what your job consists of. I want to know all about it."

After he'd finished rinsing, Al dumped his silver into an old table top. He tied the top and shook it vigorously.

"I suppose that dries it," Roz said.

"You might say that," Al said. "There's a school of thought that says each piece should be done individually."

"You men, you're always looking for shortcuts."

"You try wiping a hundred and seventy-four pieces of silver individually."

"I don't plan on that big a family."

She followed him as he carried the bucket of silver into the dining room. All the other tables were set up. Only the dishes and glasses were set on his station.

"You know how it goes?" he asked her. "Forks on the left, knives and spoons on the right."

"Come on now," she said. "Don't you think I ever set a table at home?"

"I guess women know more about this sort of thing. I never even noticed until I got this job."

"Isn't that just like you," she said. There was admiration in her voice.

After the tables were set, they left the kitchen through the back door. He put his arm around her and she cuddled up on his shoulder.

"Let's go someplace where we can talk, darling," she said. "Where we can be alone."

"How about my room. I can kick Joe out."

"No, not a place like that."

"I found out today there's a place on top of a hill down the road with a path leading to it. Not too many people know about it. How about that?"

"I'd rather not," she said. "That's a little too private."

His voice was impatient. "There's always the bar."

"You don't seem to understand. I don't want a place where we'll be interrupted."

"Well, goddamn it, then you tell me. What's the matter with you, Roz? You're acting as if you're off your rocker or something."

She snuggled up closer to him and squeezed her arm around his waist. "Don't raise your voice so loud. People will hear you."

"I don't like walking aimlessly. Where should we head for?" He looked down at her and he could see she'd closed her eyes. She was leaning very heavily against him.

"Any place you say. You're the boss."

"It's not a matter of being the boss," he said.

He led her down the road away from the hotel in the opposite direction from the way they'd walked before.

"We're not going to that hotel down the road—that place called Harley's? It has an awful reputation," she said.

"Stop worrying," he said. "We're not going to any place with any reputation. We're just going to sit on the grass and look at the sky—and both of them have terrific reputations."

After he'd gone about a quarter of a mile, he saw a path and they followed it. They came to a small hill with a clearing on the top. There was a campfire site and several large rocks in a wide circle around it.

"What's bad about this?" he said. He let her go and gestured to the area around him.

"Al," she said. "Do you really love me?"

"How many times are you going to ask me that?" he said. He pressed his hands into his pockets and turned away from her. She came up behind him, put her hands on his arms and leaned her head against his back. "Am I rushing you, darling? I don't want to rush you. I really don't. I know we hardly know each other. How long has it been? It seems to me it's been forever. I never felt this way before. I never did, Al." When she paused he didn't say anything, and then she said. "Are you very angry with me?"

"I don't know what's gotten into you," he said. "If you ask me, you think too much. Would I be with you if I didn't go for you?"

"Maybe I do think too much," she said. "Kiss me, Al. Kiss me and make me stop thinking."

It was very easy after that. And she didn't cry afterwards or talk about the things she'd wanted to discuss, and they walked the whole way home silently.

Mrs. Mandheimer was lying across the foot of the bed where her grandson slept, when Marsha tiptoed in. There were two beds and a crib in the room, together with a black mahogany chest of drawers. Against one wall was a sink.

Marsha covered her son with a blanket and started to tiptoe out. She heard the sound of her mother rising from the bed. Mrs. Mandheimer followed her out of the door and closed it quietly.

There were lines across the side of her face imprinted from the blanket; her eyes were bleary and her hair disheveled.

"I must have fallen off to sleep," she said with a sound of gladness in her voice. "I should have been doing my mail."

"I'll stay with him," Marsha said. "It'll take him a while to get used to the change."

"How come he doesn't sleep in the crib?" Mrs. Mandheimer said. "I had the crib set up special for him. I thought sure he'd sleep in a crib."

"We never had a crib," Marsha said. "When he was an infant we had a cradle. He's been in bed for more than a year now."

"Doesn't he get up?"

"Not often. When he does, I put him back in bed."

"Sounds like you make extra work for yourself."

Marsha didn't answer.

"There's a champagne hour at the casino tonight." Mrs. Mandheimer said. "You always liked to dance. I'll watch him."

"Not tonight," Marsha said. "I'd like to get to bed early."

"Suit yourself. But I'm downstairs, if you want me." She rubbed her eyes. "So how do you like the place? Looks different doesn't it?"

"You've done quite a lot," Marsha said.

"We're getting a younger crowd, too. In a few years we'll have only young married people."

"I suppose you'll get a better rate."

"We should. It takes a few years, but we're weeding out the old crowd. I do a lot better with the new people."

"Well, I'll be going to bed," Marsha said.

"Suit yourself. You know we've got a counselor on patrol and I'll just be downstairs."

"You do your letters," Marsha said.

"He's very bright," Mrs. Mandheimer said. "You were too at three years old. You knew all the nursery rhymes. I guess he takes after you."

"He looks very much like Lawrence," Marsha said. Her voice choked and she turned away from her mother.

Mrs. Mandheimer said, "I'm sorry I never met him. I might have liked him very much. You never gave us a chance."

"Good night, Mother," Marsha said and she went into her room.

Chapter 11

"*I adore ocean swimming, but with three kids I get sick of that damn sand between the toes. We had them in Atlantic City last summer. It didn't work out.*"

"*We put ours in a car and just went. So you see the Grand Canyon and Yellowstone, but when you've seen it you've seen it.*"

After lunch the next afternoon, Stan Macht stopped Marsha on her way out of the dining room.

"We're playing a game over at the Buckingham Hotel tonight. I figure maybe you'd like to come. I'll show you what I mean about what I was saying last night."

"No, thanks," Marsha said.

"Have it your way," Stan said. "But if you're figuring on staying in this business, it wouldn't hurt you to see how a big place like the Buckingham handles a game. It'd do you a lot of good."

"I'm sure it would," Marsha said and she walked away from him.

As she was passing the main desk, Mr. Mandheimer beckoned to her. "So how's it going?" he said. "Feel right at home?"

Marsha squeezed out a very weak smile.

"Who's with the baby?"

"He's taking his nap. Mother is with him."

"It's good for her," Mr. Mandheimer said. "You know how

hard Mommy works. Day and night. How many more years can she keep it up? Remember when you were in the office? When was it—six, seven years ago? You were a big help. You still know how to type?"

"I haven't done much lately," Marsha said.

"I guess not," Mr. Mandheimer said. "So how does the place look to you? You recognize it?"

"You've done a lot of building," Marsha said.

"We're growing," Mr. Mandheimer said. "Such a Mommy you have. All the mail we do ourselves. The family, that's all she trusts. I'd like to do more. But nights, I've got to do my buying. When else I have time to go to the butcher?"

A guest came to the desk to complain about the fish used for lunch. He thought it had been frozen and was raw in the middle. Mr. Mandhemier had to leave Marsha to reassure him.

In her room Marsha found her son standing on a chair by the sink with his grandmother behind him. Several of his foam rubber blocks were in the sink and the baby was trying to wash them. Water was spraying everywhere and the sleeves of the baby's shirt were soaked.

"Mother, really," Marsha said. "He's supposed to be napping."

"What am I going to do?" Mrs. Mandheimer laughed. "He wouldn't nap. He had to wash the blocks."

Marsha turned the water off and Phillip screamed. His grandmother lifted him in her arms and hugged him to her, rocking back and forth and kissing his forehead.

"I'll take him," Marsha said. She lifted her arms for the baby but her mother held fast.

"Wait a minute, he'll stop crying. There, there, baby—tsch . . . tsch . . ."

There was a knock on the door and Marsha opened it. Calvin, the bellhop, said, "Mrs. Mandheimer, there's a woman wants to know about a reservation on the phone and some people at the desk want to see a room."

She kissed the baby hard, rocked him once more and said, "Just a minute, I'm coming."

When she handed the baby to Marsha, he was still screaming.

A little after seven that night, Mrs. Mandheimer came to the room and told Marsha she'd stay with the baby while Marsha had her supper. Marsha said not to bother, she'd rather put the baby to sleep herself.

It was eight o'clock when Marsha came down to the main dining room for dinner.

Mrs. Mandheimer stopped her as she passed the desk.

"He's sleeping?"

"Yes, he is," Marsha said.

"What was I going to do?" Mrs. Mandheimer asked. "He had to play with the water. Such a mind of his own. You were his age, you were exactly the same way." She still found it amusing and smiled.

"It's a help," Marsha said, "having a mind of your own around here." She tried to be biting.

"I'll peek in on him now," her mother said. "You want to go out after supper, I'll keep an eye on him. You know he's not exactly what you'd call handsome. But when he smiles, his whole face lights up. There's a waiter here, he's got the same kind of dimple."

"I will go out," Marsha said.

"We have a guest night at the casino. You might do one of those modern dances. You know you always won first prize."

"I may be leaving the grounds," Marsha said. "If he starts crying you can give him a bottle. He still likes it."

"Furman runs a nice guest night," Mrs. Mandheimer said. "You know the people always like to see you dance."

"Whatever you do, don't sleep in the bed with him. I don't want him to get into that habit."

"Don't worry. I'll take good care of him."

As he served her coffee, Marsha said to Stan Macht, "What time do we leave for the game?"

The Buckingham wasn't going in for basketball—not in a big way. They had a team of regular waiters who varied in size from five-ten to the team center, who was a wiry six-feet-two. Stan Macht racked up twenty points in the first half and twenty-two in the second. The final score was: the Sesame—57, Buckingham—42. At the end of the game the management treated all the players to soda and hamburger sandwiches.

It was a big hotel, larger than the Sesame, and it had a spacious night club. There was a show after the game. The Sesame players, showered and dressed, knocked off the free soda and hamburgers and sat around the bar for the show and dancing.

Stan Macht had rye and ginger ale to keep Marsha company. She was drinking straight Scotch.

"See what I mean?" Stan Macht said. "See what basketball can do for a place? Look at this place. It's fabulous."

"They didn't do so well in the game," Marsha said.

They were sitting at a small table in front of the bar. It was a cushioned seat that faced a large plate-glass window affording a view of the stage show.

"So they don't win them all," Stan Macht said. "Next year, the Sesame isn't careful, the Buckingham picks me up. Forty-two points. That's more than the difference."

"What do they mean when they call you the Mong?" Marsha asked.

"It's a nickname," Stan Macht said. "Who knows what it means? I guess it don't mean nothing. I like it. I'm the Mong."

"I'm sure you are," Marsha said.

"So what d'you think?" Stan Macht said. "You goin' to tell your old man about this?"

"I didn't notice too many of our guests at the game."

"We got nothing but a bunch of stiffs at the Sesame. Look at this bar. You ever see this much action at the Sesame?"

"Even if they did come, I don't know if it's such a good idea to show off a competitive hotel."

"You're worse than your old man," Stan Macht said. "You don't get the idea at all."

One of the waiters from the Buckingham came over to the table and told Stan Macht he was a great basketball player. "You ought to try out for the Knicks," the boy said.

Stan Macht said he wasn't ready yet. He needed a couple of good years of college ball under his belt.

The boy said if they couldn't pick up a couple of tall guys for their squad, he didn't see much sense in their playing a return engagement at the Sesame. He started to tell him about their star forward who was sick.

Stan Macht told the Buckingham waiter to run along. They'd discuss it later. He didn't want to bore the lady.

"That was very considerate," Marsha said. "I didn't know you could be so thoughtful."

"What d'you figure, I have muscles in my brain? You know something, I think you got me figured all wrong."

"Really," Marsha said. "How *do* I have you figured?"

"Muscles in the brain."

"You said that before," Marsha said. "It wasn't funny the first time."

"If a guy was touchy, he might get sore as hell at you," Stan said.

"But you're not touchy."

"Hell no."

"Three cheers for the Mong," Marsha said. "And buy me another drink."

Stan Macht called the waiter over and Marsha said make it a double.

"This is really something," he said. "Here I am, out with the boss's daughter, and she's breaking me."

"I'd pay for myself," Marsha said. "But I'm broke."

"I should be so broke," Stan Macht said.

The waiter brought her drink and Marsha drank it quickly.

Mike Heimer came over to the table and said the boys were leaving. There wasn't much around to dance with, so they were going back to the Sesame.

Stan Macht said, "You got your car. You stay a little longer. Marsha and me are going to dance."

Mike Heimer said, "Don't make it too long, Mong."

The band was playing a tango. There weren't many dancers on the floor and they moved freely. Stan Macht had a strong lead. He was an excellent dancer who restrained himself from complicated breaks because his partners were seldom equal to him. But Marsha followed him easily. They swept across the floor, breaking and coming together to the sensuous rhythms of the dance.

Gradually the other couples on the floor moved to the side. People at the bar crowded close to watch. Marsha weaved about Stan, gyrating her hips, throwing herself completely into a primitive interpretation of the Latin rhythms.

When it was over people applauded for more. They did a rhumba and a cha-cha. Marsha was exhausted. She draped her arm over Stan Macht's shoulder and he helped her from the floor.

"I haven't danced like that in years," she said.

He was still holding her, pulling her closer to him. "You're a hell of a dancer," he said. "I like the way you throw yourself into it."

She tried to push his arm away from her, and when he didn't let go she said, "It's over. The music has stopped, remember?"

"That's funny," he said, "I didn't notice." He thought that was romantic and he tried to kiss her.

Marsha broke away and slapped him. It made a loud noise, louder than she'd expected. "Stop acting like a barbarian," she said. "And don't look so damn hurt. You had it coming."

"I got half a mind to—"

"Come on buy me a drink," she said.

He rubbed his cheek. "What the hell gets into you? I wish the hell I could figure you out—"

He followed her to the bar and bought her another shot.

Mike Heimer had a small convertible, but the night was too cool to put the top down. Mike was in the front with Danny Rose. Stan sat in the back with Marsha. The radio was on and Stan tried to talk quietly so that the boys in front wouldn't hear him.

"That was a hell of a corny move. That slap I mean."

"Forget it," Marsha said. She huddled into the opposite corner and looked through the small clouded window.

"I still say you're a hell of a dancer," Stan Macht said.

"Forget that too," Marsha said.

"Forget that, forget this. Just because you own the damn hotel don't mean you can treat me like I'm dirt or something."

Marsha said, "Humpf."

"I mean it," Stan Macht said. "You want to play rough. You picked the right guy."

When they got to the hotel, they parked in a small lot to the side of the waiter's shack. Mike and Danny got out without saying a word. They didn't wait for Marsha and Stan.

"You sure have them trained," Marsha said. "What a Mong you are."

"Don't call me Mong. I don't like the way you say it."

"All right, Stanley."

"You don't say that so good either."

"So what do you want me to call you? I tried barbarian before."

Stan Macht got as serious as he could. His face grew very tight. "Maybe I don't talk so good. I'm no forty-pointer with the books. So what? I can pick up the play as fast as the next guy, and the way I figure it your play is pretty easy to figure."

"And just what is my play?"

"You're cruising, looking over the field. You find the right guy around here, there's no telling how far you go. I mean you got a reputation. Your old man owns the hotel and all. Just the same, you're not kidding me. Maybe I don't know how to say it so nice but it adds up to the same thing—you need it. You want it real bad. Hell, you need it as bad as I do."

"Need what?" Marsha asked.

"Stop playing so god damn dumb, will you," Stan Macht said. "You've been married. You know the score."

"You figure any woman who's lived with a man and lost him can't live without sex, is that right?"

"You said it. Not me."

"Is that what you think?"

"Yeah, that's what I think. And you know it's true. Go ahead deny it."

Marsha looked at him very squarely. "Only a stupid barbarian like you could believe that."

"You like that word, do you?" He took her wrists and pulled her up close to him. "Go ahead, call me that again. Tell me I'm wrong."

Her eyes were unyielding.

Stan Macht said, "I want you. I got to have you real bad, Marsha—that's the only way I know how to say it. What the hell have you got to lose?"

She pulled her hands from him and shook her head wildly. Her hair swished from side to side and her thin body shivered. He was ready to leave when she threw herself at him. Her long nails dug deep into his neck.

"It doesn't make any difference any more," she whispered. "No damn difference at all."

The lobby was dark when Marsha started back to her room. The only light was that coming through the door of the office behind the desk. She could hear the steady beat of the typewriter.

She was at the foot of the steps when she heard a sound that made her turn back. It was a thin happy squeal coming from the direction of the office. There was no mistaking the voice of her son.

She walked angrily through the narrow entrance that led from the lobby to the area behind the desk. Her shoulder hit the mailbox cubicles that extended from the wall. She was still smarting from the pain when she opened the office door and saw her son sitting on his grandmother's lap in front of the typewriter.

"Do you know what time it is?" Marsha said. "That's all I want to know, do you realize what time it is?"

Mrs. Mandheimer's arms were wrapped around the child, her fingers barely reaching the typewriter. As soon as she stopped typing the little boy imitated her, banging all the keys at once. They were entangled before they struck the ribbon.

"He wouldn't sleep," Mrs. Mandheimer said. "What could I do with him? He wasn't sleepy."

"How can he be sleepy when he's keeping *you* company?"

"I put him back in bed twice. A child his age, he should sleep in a crib."

"You mind your own business," Marsha said. She reached over and pulled the child from her mother's lap. Phillip squirmed in her arms and tried to reach the typewriter.

"I want typewriter," he said. "Typewriter."

"They paged you," Mrs. Mandheimer said. "Getting excited isn't going to help. You shouldn't argue in front of a baby."

Phillip stretched and yawned. He squirmed and reached toward Mrs. Mandheimer. "I want you," he said. "I want you."

"Tsch, tsch," Mrs. Mandheimer said. "Grandma will play with you in the morning. Mommy has to put you to bed now."

"I wanna a bottle," Phillip said. He kicked and cried. "I wanna bottle."

"Did you give him a bottle before like I told you?" Marsha asked impatiently.

"Sure he had a bottle." Mrs. Mandheimer motioned toward an empty bottle on the floor by her chair. "You want I should heat him more milk?"

"I'll take him back to bed," Marsha said. "You can fix him another bottle."

Mrs. Mandheimer picked the bottle off the floor. Phillip saw it and screamed. "I want it," he said. "I want my bottle."

His grandmother handed it to him.

"Mother are you going to fix him a bottle or not? How much longer do you want this baby to stay up?"

"Let him see for himself it's empty, he won't cry for it," Mrs. Mandheimer said. "See it's empty, Phillip," she said softly to the baby. "Grandma is going to heat you some more milk. I'll fill the bottle all up again."

Phillip stopped crying and laughed, then his laugh turned back into a cry.

"He's restless and irritable," Marsha said. "You waste your time talking to him when he's like this."

Mrs. Mandheimer hurried out of the office and toward the kitchen. Marsha took Phillip back to her room.

Phillip lay on his bed and kicked and screamed. He wanted

a blanket. He didn't want a blanket. He wanted his pet tiger. He wanted his blocks. He wanted his fire engine. He wanted to get out of bed altogether.

Marsha brought him one toy and then another. "Ssh, ssh," she said. The baby kept screaming and finally she picked him up and tried to rock him in her arms. He resisted her strongly.

She put him down in her bed and lay down beside him. He wanted to lie across the pillow. She got up and gave him room. By the time Mrs. Mandheimer came in with the bottle, Phillip was pinned to his bed, his mother's arms holding him down. He was screaming.

"He's waking up the whole building," Mrs. Mandheimer said. "Mrs. Leiderkopf is standing on the first-floor landing in her nightgown. She thought maybe there was a robbery."

"I can't help it," Marsha said. "You shouldn't stimulate him in the middle of the night. You'd no right to take him to the office."

Mrs. Mandheimer went over to Phillip and picked him up. She held him in her arms and gave him his bottle.

"He can hold it himself," Marsha said.

"Go ahead, go to sleep," Mrs. Mandheimer said. There was a note of anger in her voice for the first time. "What's the matter I can't give my grandchild a little affection?"

Phillip finally fell off to sleep with his grandmother resting across the foot of his bed. Marsha lay still on her bed. Her clothes were on and her eyes open. After Mrs. Mandheimer got up and left the room, Marsha opened the window wide and let the cool night air in. She took off all her clothes and lay naked on top of the blankets, looking up at the ceiling—crying.

Chapter 12

"How come we never have a mock wedding?" the woman asked the social director. "I don't know, last year I went to a place was half this size, things were always going on. The tumler, he was dressed up in my skirt, with pillows and everything. He married the bass player from the band— it was a riot."

It was the third week of July and the hotel was filled to capacity. Mr. Mandheimer had to call the agency for another second cook. The chef claimed the Chinese cook was all right on breakfast, but no help to him for lunch and dinner. It was a rough crowd. They were always calling for specials, and if the Mandheimers wanted everybody to be happy, they'd better get him another second.

The chef was getting four hundred dollars a week. In their winter conference he'd told them he could handle a house of three hundred by himself. He had said he didn't trust anybody else to cook for him. He didn't want any griddle man ruining his works of art and he asked a big price, but he assured the Mandheimers he was worth every cent of it.

Now it was the height of the season. You couldn't get a decent chef for any price, and he was threatening to quit if he didn't get help. The agency sent over a colored man who wore a tall white chef's hat and worked at a New York steak house in the winter. He was very flashy on the griddle. When he put the Sunday steaks on to sear, he bathed them in so much grease they let up spouts of flame. He was a fast man with the spatula, turning them over flames and all.

The chef didn't like that.

He seared the steaks himself. He did all the cooking for the children as well as the main dining room, and the day he caught the colored cook pouring asparagus into a pot instead of spreading it in a pan, he told him to stand around and watch until he got the feel of it.

The colored cook stood around and watched, kidded with the chambermaids, and collected a hundred and fifty dollars a week, which was a cheap price, at that, for an experienced second.

Calvin told Mrs. Mandheimer she was throwing her gelt away, but Mrs. Mandheimer was too busy showing rooms and checking people in to hear him. Calvin was smoking a pure Havana cigar in a plastic holder Mrs. Leiderkopf had given him. Mrs. Mandheimer told him to stop smoking cigars in the lobby and trying to look like a big shot.

Al Brodie deposited a hundred and seventy dollars in the safe at the end of the second week of July. He hadn't received anything from the Erlangs. They would tip later in a lump sum. The Gersons and Miss Mantell had each come through with five and three.

On the third Saturday night in July, Audrey Grier asked the chef for chicken livers. She had a table of old people who had been coming to the hotel for years, and they couldn't eat spicy appetizers. They had to have chicken livers.

The chef was turning his roast chickens at the time. He was down on the floor in front of the oven and he didn't stand up when he asked, "What's spicy about my gefilte fish?"

"I think it's perfect," Audrey said, "but what am I going to do with them?"

"That's your problem," the chef said and there were no chicken livers that night.

On Sunday, Audrey Grier made a note on the blackboard near the stove. She printed the word *Specials*, and next to it wrote, *four orders of chicken livers.*

Mr. Mandhemier was dishing out French fried potatoes when Audrey came in for the chicken livers. The chef had them in a small pan on the warming shelf and he gave them to her.

They were hot and she burned her fingers putting them on serving dishes, but she was happy.

Before she left the chef said, "Go ahead, make money. You run the specials and I break my back." He was sweaty and tired, and there wasn't a soul in the kitchen who would have argued with him.

Mr. Mandheimer had been with the electrician all morning, tracking down a short circuit in one of the cottages. He had a date with a produce man for right after lunch, and he had been up until three o'clock the night before, answering inquiries for the first two weeks of August, while his wife put their grandchild to sleep. He put six big French fries on a plate and said nothing.

The steaks were going out smoothly. The colored second with the big hat was fast, and the Chinese cook kept up with him. The chef was pulling them out of the oven, calling "Rare, medium, and well done," and blessing the days they served steak. It was a popular dish, after all, and gave him a breather from worrying about whether or not he would run out of the alternate choices on the menu. (He'd had veal cutlets, hamburgers, and breast of beef on Thursday, and the pain was still fresh. There'd been a rush on the breast of beef. He'd run out, and ten angry guests had stomped to the main desk to know why.)

Each of the waiters had been around twice when Al Brodie came back with a steak in his hand. It was the filet of the rib, cut two inches thick and then sliced in half. Each portion weighed as close to fourteen ounces as the chef's eye could judge. This one looked a little smaller than the rest. It had been hacked into by an angry fork and was coming back.

Al had ten more mains to pick up. He put this one on the counter as quietly as possible and told the colored second he wanted an exchange.

The second was slicing and dishing out. He tried to exchange it but the chef saw.

"What's the matter with that steak?" He left the oven doors open, broke the rhythmical flow of steaks from the ovens to the dining room, and picked up the piece of meat.

Mr. Mandheimer was working with the Chinese second, and he told him to keep dishing out on his station before the steaks got cold.

"It looks good to me," Al said, "but it is a little small."

"You get steak like this at home?" the chef asked. He held the piece of meat up in front of Al's face. The blood dripped down his arm.

"It looks delicious," Al said. "I'll be glad to eat it right now."

"You goddamn wise guy," the chef yelled. "You take this steak back and make 'em eat it."

Al tried to be reasonable. "I can't do that." He looked toward Mr. Mandheimer. "They want another piece of steak. What am I supposed to do?"

"What are you talking to him for? I'm the boss in here," the chef said.

"You're right, goddamn it," Al said. "I'll ram it down their filthy throats." He reached for the steak and the chef handed it to him.

Al plunked it down on a plate and put on his own French frieds and vegetables. "They'll eat it and like it, the dirty bastards."

The chef went back to the oven. "How do you like that, boss," he said to Mr. Mandheimer. "He thinks he gives them a big steak, he gets a big tip. Costs you a dollar a pound, and he wants a quarter tip."

Mr. Mandheimer nodded and went back to the French frieds.

Al Brodie picked up eleven mains in addition to the one with the small steak. Audrey had come in for a side order of French frieds and had seen the whole thing. It was her rule that the boys were only supposed to take out ten mains at a time but she let it go.

When the chef saw Audrey, he said, "Look at her in her fancy dress, making all the money, while I sweat my balls off. Get the hell out of here, bitch."

Audrey tried to laugh. She picked up the French frieds, cleaned off the corner of the plate where some steak juice had spilled, and left.

Mr. Mandheimer told the chef to "Take it easy. You got half a summer to go yet. You'll have high blood pressure."

"I don't like no bitch to put it over on me," the chef said. "The guests tell me about her. She's the one put them up to that breast of beef. Who ever heard of a headwaiter couldn't sell veal cutlets and hamburgers?"

"Those things happen," Mr. Mandheimer said softly.

"Sure they happen," the chef said. He put the final tray of steaks on the table, and the two cooks dished them out. "But they don't have to happen. Listen to me, boss, I been in this business all my life. You get yourself a good headwaiter, get a man in the dining room, and you'll see your food costs drop. I'll bet you my salary, you'll save ten thousand dollars in a season."

"That's a lot of money," Mr. Mandheimer said.

One of the waiters came over to the stove and asked if there were seconds on steaks.

"No seconds. Seconds, yet," the chef said. "Get out."

"Come back later," Mr. Mandheimer said eying the tray of steaks, "if there's any left, we'll give you."

"What d'you think that veal cutlet cost you?" the chef said. "She don't serve them. That's a total waste. Ain't a chef in the world can do anything with cold veal cutlet. I had to give them to the help."

"You couldn't give them to the kids?"

"Ah, now boss, you think I'd give the children what's left over?"

"There's nothing wrong with putting it in the refrigerator. They don't eat frozen food at home?"

"So what did you tell me at the beginning of the season? The best for the kids. That's your very words."

"Veal cutlets, the best."

"All right, so tomorrow I'll give them what's left over from the chicken à la king appetizer today."

"No. Please, forget it," Mr. Mandheimer said.

Audrey Grier came in and stood through the last part of their conversation. When they were finished, she spoke to Mr. Mandheimer. Her voice was as soft and controlled as she could manage. "All the firsts have been served, Mr. Mandheimer. Do you think I could have a second for Mr. Golden on table one?" Her eyes dropped to the tray of steaks. There were four left.

"What d'you mean, seconds?" the chef roared. "What'd he give you, a dollar? Give me the dollar. Give me the dollar. I'll give you the steak."

"Look, I haven't seen a penny from him," Audrey Grier said. She was getting bold. "Do I get the second or don't I? I'm sick and tired of all this aggravation—aggravation in the kitchen, aggravation in the dining room—"

"You're aggravated. You're aggravated," the chef screamed. His head jutted forward and he beat his fists hard against his breast. "I sweat my goddamn balls off. I kill myself behind this goddamn stove, and *she's* aggravated. Goddamn you, get out of here! Get out of here before I kill you."

Audrey Grier's face paled. She trembled and rubbed her hands together. Al Brodie was on his way to pick up desserts when he saw her. For a moment it looked as if she were going to faint. He came over to her and took her by the arm.

"I got some trouble on table thirty. I need you," he said.

He could feel her body shaking as he led her back to the dining room.

Mr. Mandheimer gave a busboy a steak two minutes later, with instructions to give it to Audrey.

Chapter 13

"You saw the post card," Al Brodie's mother said. "It looks like a very swanky place."

"Didn't I tell you not to worry," the father said. "Al can take care of himself."

"We should answer him," she said. "I'm going to write him a letter."

The father didn't say anything, and she went to the sideboard and took out a writing tablet and a pencil. "Anything you want me to say for you?" she asked.

"Just tell him to keep his nose clean," the father said.

She wrote for a few minutes and then he said, "I've got an idea—let's drop in on him. About the middle of August when there's not much doing in the city, we'll just pack up our kit and caboodle and surprise him."

"That'd be wonderful," the mother said. "We haven't taken a vacation in years. I'll tell him to send us the brochure and rate list."

"Who needs that?" Al Brodie's father said. "When we go, we'll go right. First class—that's the only way to travel. Just bust right in and take their best room."

"Can you imagine Al's face when he sees us?" the mother said. "What a wonderful surprise."

Al Brodie's father said, "Well, we've got plenty of time. Nothing lost from thinking about it."

It was so hot during the fourth week of July that the day camp spent all the afternoons at the pool. Jerry Furman had his band decked out in bright Miami sport shirts over their bathing suits. They played Latin American music, and those who wanted to, danced.

Al would come down right after he got out of the dining room. He'd lay a house towel on the grass by the side of the pool and sunbathe. Most of the waiters and busboys congregated near the band, which played at the area near the diving board. But the children's wading pool was at the shallow end, and that's where Roz was.

When she was off duty, Roz would curl her legs up and sit down near him. They'd hum to the music and talk about his tips and her kids.

It was on an afternoon near the end of the month when she asked him if he noticed her roommate Linda. He said he didn't and she pointed Linda out. She was sitting erect in a beach chair near the orchestra and reading.

"She reads slow," Al said.

"That's not what I mean." Roz tickled his chin with a blade of grass. "She sits there every day. Get it?"

"Maybe the music puts her in the mood."

Roz said, "Don't be silly. You don't know anything about women."

He pulled her down next to him and she touched his toes with hers. "I don't know a thing about women. Teach me." He put his arm around her and pulled her toward him.

She said, "Now stop. Be serious."

He let her go and sat up. Then he spun around and rested his head on her stomach. She played with his hair. "O.K.," he said. "Now tell me about Linda and her affair with old Zhivago."

"I didn't think you'd read the book," she said.

"Now about Linda—"

Roz was very serious. "Linda is a very sensitive girl," she said. "She's not like Ellie and me."

"You can say that again. You've got hide thick as an elephant." He pinched the smooth calf of her leg.

"Stop it. Let me finish." She looked away from him toward

Linda as she spoke. "Linda finds younger men boring. You know, they're not serious enough for her. She's pretty. She could have lots of dates with the waiters. But she just doesn't like younger men."

"How old's Pasternak?"

She ignored him. "I'm afraid she's going to get hurt."

"Boris won't hurt her. He's stuck behind the iron curtain."

"Seriously, Al, this means a lot to me. Linda is one of my best friends."

"I'll talk to the State Department about old Boris first thing in the morning."

"Really, Al—"

"All right, so she's shacking up. What d'you want from me? Damn it, Roz, when are you going to grow up?"

She pulled his hair. "Will you shut up and listen to me?" She bounced his head gently on her stomach. "Now will you listen?"

"Give up."

"This is a *married* man. Now, do you understand?"

"Oh my, you don't say." He tickled her chin.

"I think it's serious," Roz said. "Linda can get hurt. And so can he and his wife."

"What are you telling me for? Tell Linda."

"I can't tell her. She doesn't know I know."

"Then tell him. What have I got to do with it?"

"If Linda knew I knew, much less told you about it, she'd never speak to me again. I'm only telling you because I want your advice. Be serious, now, and tell me."

"Forget it."

"That's all? Just forget it?" She moved away from him and his head hit the ground. "Sometimes I don't think you care about anybody but yourself."

He sat up. "This kind of thing happens all the time. They'll have their fun for two months, teach each other a couple new tricks and then kiss and cry good-by, and never see each other again."

"Not Linda. She's different. You don't know her, Al. She's really very sensitive and serious. This could ruin her."

"You really are worried."

"Of course I'm worried. She's one of my best friends."

"Haven't I told you before—you think too much. Thinking makes problems."

"Boy, have you got a philosophy."

"What d'you know about philosophy? Come on—what d'you know?"

"I only know that Linda's my friend and she's going to get hurt and if there's anything I can do to help her, I'll do it."

"Well, I'll tell you what to do. I'm lending you this from my philosophy, you understand. That means it's guaranteed. If it doesn't work, you can sue me." He looked at the grass and pulled a handful. When he looked up he squinted into the sun. "This is my honest opinion." She was looking at him eagerly. "It's hot as hell. You only have another ten minutes off. Let's take a dip. I'll hold you under the water for five minutes and you'll forget all about it."

"Oh, you—honestly, Al, you never take anything seriously."

"Sit at my station for two weeks and stiff me. You'll see how serious I can be."

"Is money the only thing in the world that matters to you?" Her voice cracked and he knew it had been on her mind.

"No, swimming matters and beautiful women. Come on—" She followed him to the edge of the pool. He was wearing an old tattered pair of nylon trunks that were much too big for him. They dived into the pool together. When they came up, her hair was wet and the water streaked across her face.

"You know what I'd like to see you in," she said, treading water beside him. "A pair of those nice plaid trunks—Ivy League. It's the latest. I bet you'd look real good in them."

"See—I told you you'd forget all about Linda," he said.

Roz was assigned the area at the shallow end of the big pool where the adults and older children swam. There was another pool separated from the main pool, where the toddlers and younger children played in the water.

Roz had to go back on duty. Al walked her over to her station and left her. He was on his way back to his room to rest up and get into his uniform for dinner. As he passed the children's wading pool he saw Marsha Cooper. She was hard to recognize at first because she was wearing dark glasses, a large straw hat and a heavy terry-cloth robe. She was standing in the wading pool, holding Phillip's hand.

The little boy was fair skinned. He had on a pair of cotton training pants that hung low on his stomach, but there was no line of suntan. He splashed the water with one hand and when it flew up and hit his face he clutched at his mother's leg. Al noticed that Marsha Cooper's thighs were surprisingly wide for such a thin girl.

He walked to the side of the pool directly in back of her and said, "Is that the handsome fellow that's supposed to have a smile just like mine?"

Marsha Cooper turned around and looked at him quickly over her shoulder. Her son slipped and she needed both hands to keep him out of the water.

"I'm Al Brodie," he said. "Your mother—Mrs. Mandheimer —she thinks your son and I look alike."

Marsha looked at him again quickly and said, "I don't think so."

"You haven't seen me smile," Al said. "Say something funny." He stepped off the side of the pool and came into the water beside her. It reached a few inches above his ankle. "What d'you think, fellow?" he said to Phillip. "You think I look like you?"

Phillip buried his head in his mother's leg.

"I guess I scare him," Al said. "And I don't think we look alike either. Do we, Phillip?" He put his thumbs in his ears and stuck out his tongue.

"Are you a counselor?" Marsha Cooper asked.

"Think I'm acting like one?" he said. "Matter of fact I'm a waiter. But I've got six nephews and three nieces and I've had a lot of practice making a monkey of myself."

Phillip snuck his head out from behind his mother's leg and put his thumbs in his ears and stuck out his tongue.

"See," Al said. "I'm his pal."

"I don't think that's a very nice habit. Put your tongue in, Phillip. That's very naughty."

The little boy pulled his tongue in, stuck it out again, and laughed.

"That's what we call negative psychology," Al said. "Matter of fact I'm taking a course in children's psych in college."

"Going to be a teacher?" Marsha asked.

"No. No, I'm just interested in kids."

"Well, tell him to put his tongue back in. We'll see how much you've learned."

Al bent down beside the boy. He held his hands toward Phillip and said, "Come on, Phillip, want to swim?"

"No swim," Phillip said and buried his head in his mother's leg again.

"Sure you can swim," Al said. "But I can't. Teach me." He sat down in the water and waddled around. Phillip thought it was very funny. He laughed and splashed water at him.

Al stood up and whispered to Marsha Cooper. "Stuck his tongue back in, didn't he?"

She laughed. "You make the dean's list. And what do you call that? The diverting technique à la Spock?"

He said, "Yeah." And then quickly he bent down again. "Come on, Phillip, let's you and me take a swim." The little boy came to him hesitantly. Al splashed at the water and Phillip did the same. "See, now we're swimming."

"I can swim," Phillip said. "I can swim."

They did that for several minutes. Marsha Cooper sat down on the side of the pool, rummaged through a heavy leather bag and came out with a cigarette. She lit it and smoked.

"Want to play kick-swimming now?" Al Brodie said to Phillip. "It's a lot of fun." He lay down in the water and kicked his feet. "Look at the big splash."

"Big splash," Phillip said and he ran around to the place where Al's feet were kicking and splashed water with his hands.

Marsha Cooper picked up a loose Consolidated Laundry towel and put it over her thighs.

Al Brodie swung around in the water on his hands and sat down in front of Phillip. "How about you—want to kick-swim, Phillip?"

"I can kick-swim," the boy said.

"Sure you can," Al Brodie said. He took the boy's hands in his and gently pulled him into the water. He shifted his arms so as to cradle Phillip's stomach. He was barely touching the water.

Phillip screamed and Marsha crushed her cigarette against the edge of the pool.

"Make a big splash," Al Brodie said. "Kick your feet Phillip and make a big splash."

The little boy continued screaming but he kicked his feet and flailed his arms. In a few seconds he was laughing.

Marsha Cooper was standing over them. Al looked up at her and said, "You give up too easily. See, he's swimming."

"That's a very good course you're taking," Marsha said. "I wasted my time in college."

Al picked Phillip out of the water, swung him up high over his head and put him back down in the water on his two feet. "That's enough for today, pal," he said. "You wear me out."

"What else are you studying in college?" Marsha Cooper asked.

Al said, "Art—I'm interested in lots of things."

"History of art and child psychology, that's quite a combination. Very unusual college you go to."

"I'm an unusual guy," Al said. "You just haven't found out yet."

Phillip said, "I want to kick-swim, Mommy. Mommy, hold me. I want to kick-swim."

"See what you've started," she said. "I don't know whether to thank you or not."

"Think it over," Al said. "I'm available any time you make up your mind."

She turned back to Phillip and Al started away from the pool. When he got to the gate, Roz was there. She had on her rubber bathing slippers and a towel over her shoulder.

"I thought you had to be on duty," he said.

"One of the girls is covering for me," she said. Her face was flushed very red and he thought he could see tiny goose-pimples along her chest.

"I think you got a little too much sun, today."

"Really, I'm surprised you care."

He started to walk in the direction of his room. She followed by his side. "All right, what is it? Let's have it."

"I didn't know you were a friend of Marsha Cooper's," she said. "I didn't even know you knew her."

"Everybody knows Marsha Cooper," he said. "The Mong is her press agent."

She stopped walking and gave the edges of her towel a little jerk. "And just what does that mean? I'm tired of you talking in riddles and making jokes out of everything I say. I don't know just who you think you are."

For a moment he was tempted to tell her, but his eyes fell on that part of her that was barely visible above the top of her bathing suit and he said, "Come on, sweetheart. You're getting yourself all excited for nothing."

On the way back he told her how much he liked kids and how there was no harm in having a little pull with the boss's daughter.

Chapter 14

"*Of course I heard of Rip Van Winkle, but that was the other side of the mountains.*"

The voice on the loud speaker was soft. It was nearly midnight and except for a handful of people at the bar the guests were in bed.

"Baby crying in room fourteen," the voice said. "Will the mother of the baby in room fourteen go to your room please."

Mrs. Mandheimer switched off the mike. "Hold him another minute," she said to her husband. "I'll call the casino again."

"I don't understand her," Mr. Mandheimer said. "Different she always was, but like this—"

Mrs. Mandheimer went to the switchboard and pushed down the button for the canteen. She rang twice. "Hello, T. J. . . . My daughter's there maybe. . . . No, it's nothing. . . . The baby is up, that's all. . . ."

"Becky please, you have to announce it to everybody?" Mr. Mandheimer said.

She put her hand over the mouthpiece. "Will you be quiet, Sam. We want to find her, don't we?" She talked back into the phone. "Tell me something, maybe she was there earlier in the evening. She saw the movie, maybe. Ask around, maybe somebody saw her. . . . Nobody there but a few of the help . . . It wouldn't hurt if you threw them out. We'd have a kitchen

133

staff in the morning. I don't know what's the matter with you, T. J. I never had such a concession in all my days. All you do is get my staff drunk . . . Yes . . . Uh-uh . . . So let them buy it in town . . . How much can one man carry back by himself? . . . That's what you say. Meantime I never had so many drunk. . . . Who says you make them drink? . . . Yes . . . Yes . . . You're supposed to work with the house. Getting my staff drunk isn't working with the house. You send them to bed. Hear me? . . . Listen, I'm going to send Mr. Mandheimer down there. He'll throw them out . . . All right." She hung up.

"Such a concession. I wouldn't have that louse back for a million dollars next year."

"You think he's paid me what he's supposed to this year? Two weeks I been chasing him for another five hundred dollars."

"He doesn't pay you, throw him out," Mrs. Mandheimer said.

"It's not so easy to get a concession man in the middle of the season," Mr. Mandheimer said. "Whatever we get, it'll have to be enough. You want we should run the concession ourselves?"

"I got two thousand last year and I didn't have a new front," Mrs. Mandheimer said. "He doesn't pay you, I'll get Sey Hertz back."

"You think Sey's not working? You think he's waiting for you?"

"For two thousand I can get all the concessions I need."

"So get them."

Phillip started to cry. "Here, take him," Mr. Mandheimer said. "I think he's wet."

Mrs. Mandheimer took Phillip from her husband. She rocked the baby in her arms and caressed his head with her lips.

"Such a thing. Such a thing," Mr. Mandheimer said. "We'll be up all night answering the mail."

"Go ahead, you work. I'll put him back to sleep," Mrs. Mandheimer said.

"A lot of good that does. He gets up, he walks the halls like a lost sheep. Mrs. Leiderkopf didn't see him, he'd fall down the steps. That's all we need."

"You always have to see the worst."

"I don't know what we need this for. We sold the hotel, we'd be better off. We working ourselves to death. Our only grandchild walking the halls. And Marsha—I don't know what's got into her."

"Always the worst. You always got to see the worst, Sam."

"So what's good about it? You tell me what's good about it. You think we run this hotel? You think we're bosses? Every lousy concession man can stick you up. A chef you've got, I'm afraid to open my mouth to him."

"Do the letters, Sam. I'll put him back to sleep."

Phillip was sucking his thumb. His head was on his grandmother's shoulders and his eyes were half closed.

"I should have a talk with Marsha. She's our daughter. If we can't talk to her, who can?"

"And what would you say?"

"You think this is right?" Mr. Mandheimer stormed at his wife. "Where is she? You tell me where is she?"

"Where she is, she is," Mrs. Mandheimer said. "You're talking to her won't help. She lost her husband. Maybe she's trying to forget."

"Forgetting her child, that's helping her forget her husband? I don't know. To me it doesn't make sense."

"Do me a favor, Sam, you'll start on the mail," Mrs. Mandheimer said.

Mr. Mandheimer started to work on the typewriter that was near the switchboard. He put a piece of Sesame stationery into the typewriter. It got caught in the guide and ripped. He pulled it out angrily.

"You can't work in the office? You got to ruin your eyes out here?" his wife said.

Mr. Mandheimer said, "Go ahead, you're putting the baby to bed, aren't you?"

Mike Heimer knocked on the door of his room. There was no answer. He opened the door up a crack and said softly, "It's Mike, Mong. I'm going to come in."

"Wait a minute will you," Stan Macht said. "Another minute."

Mike turned away and walked to the door. He sat outside on the grass in front of the shack. The other roommate, Harry, was waiting there.

"I've never seen anybody like her," Mike said to Harry.

"It's hard to figure," Harry said. "Looking at her, you'd never figure her for this."

"Her old man owns the hotel yet," Mike said.

"It doesn't seem to bother her," Harry said. "You'd think she'd worry about what people say. You'd think she'd be real careful with her reputation."

"She's a hard number, all right," Mike said. "A woman has to be really tough to take an announcement like that—them calling her for her kid, and her in there with him."

"Who do the Mandheimer's think they're fooling with that room fourteen stuff?" Harry said. "They might just as well call her by name. Everybody knows it's her."

"Yeah, you'd think they'd be self-conscious."

"But what else can they do? They can't exactly come down here and pull her out of his bed."

"I figure they don't know."

"Are you kidding? That old lady knows everything that goes on around here."

Mike shook his head. "You're wrong. If she knew, then he'd know, and hell, if old man Mandheimer had the slightest idea what was going on, he'd sure as hell do something."

"What, for example?"

"You think for Chris' sake that the Mong has got the first mortgage on this place or something? They'd fire him, that's what. Give him his walking papers."

"Never," Harry said. "That would really start a stink. No, you don't figure the Mandheimers right. They're business people—they got to figure what's best for the business. And firing the Mong, that's bad business. First thing you know everybody in the hotel'd be talking about it and—what's worse—feeling sorry for the Mong."

"So what do you figure—"

"They know she's this way. I mean this daughter of theirs, she can't be normal. Did you ever think of that? Something must be wrong with her. Look at it like this—here's the Mong. All right so he's the best hoopster this place will ever see—so what! This Marsha she's not what you'd call exactly sports-minded. And you throw out sports, and let's face it—what have you got? The Mong isn't much."

"You better not let him hear you say that."

"Which is point number two—he isn't exactly the answer to a maiden's dreams. I mean a woman has to be either stupid or not normal to crawl into a lousy-looking shack like this to be with a bum like him."

"You sure got it in for the Mong," Mike said. "You know something, I think you got the hots for this girl yourself."

"Who me? Are you kidding. I wouldn't touch her. A girl like that is nothing but trouble. The Mong can keep her. They deserve each other."

"I wish to hell he'd keep her a little less and we could get some sleep," Mike said. "I've had about enough of this waiting outside and sleeping in the car."

Harry was thinking very hard. "Yeah. In order for an intelligent girl like that to go for the Mong something would have to be wrong. You know how I figure her, Mike?"

Mike yawned. "How you figure, Harry?"

"She must be a nympho," Harry said. "That's why the Mandheimers don't do anything about it. They must know it's a sickness and if it wasn't him it'd be somebody else."

"Maybe," Mike said and yawned again.

"A girl like her sleeping with the Mong," Harry said. "It's the only reason."

They heard the door behind them open and they both jumped up. Marsha Cooper walked by them without saying a word.

Chapter 15

The county got its name Sullivan in 1809. It was named for one of Washington's generals, John Sullivan, who chased the Indians out of the northern section of New York state. However, there is no record that Sullivan actually ever was in the county.

The Dutch were the first people to settle the area, and one of their colonial governors picked up the land for only "ninety pounds of wampum, cloth, cider, and strong beer."

Later, in 1708, when they still had the land-grant system, a Kingston landowner named Johannes Hardenbergh did even better. He bought a couple of counties, including all of Sullivan, for less than a hundred dollars.

So far as is known, George Washington never slept here. But Sid Caesar did, and so did Milton Berle and Eddie Cantor.

Mr. Erlang was beginning to get bored by the end of July. On the afternoon of August second, he prodded Jerry Furman into organizing a softball game, the waiters versus the guests.

He came out to the field wearing a straw baseball cap, sunglasses, and a baseball glove autographed by Robin Roberts. He wanted to pitch.

His wife was sitting over to the side. She had put on weight and she didn't look so thin, but her face was covered with Coppertone and she had a piece of wet raw cotton over her nose. Al Brodie was playing first base for the waiters. He had on tennis shoes and his swimming trunks so he could take a dip right afterwards.

In the first inning the waiters brought sixteen men to bat. Al doubled his first time up and blasted a home run into the bushes his second trip. The ball was lost and the game delayed while Jerry Furman's son ran up to the office to get a new one.

While he was gone, Mr. Erlang said it was a disgrace a hotel the size of the Sesame made you run after a softball every time you needed one. They should give you three or four for a game.

Jerry Furman asked Mr. Erlang if maybe he wouldn't like to give one of the other guests a chance to pitch awhile, but Mr. Erlang said he was just getting warmed up.

When the guests came to bat, Mr. Erlang insisted on batting second. He said he was a great man with a bunt and he could sacrifice the guest who'd got to first on a single to second.

The first pitch was low and outside, but Mr. Erlang lunged for it. His hands were spread on the bat just like a major leaguer. He caught the ball and it rolled toward first. Al Brodie picked it up and chased him down the base path. When he put the ball on Mr. Erlang, Mr. Erlang's knee buckled. He fell, rolled over on the ground, and got up at last—holding his knee.

He pointed to a spot on the base path and said, "See, a stone. That's what tripped me, a stone. You should know better than that, Jerry. Before a game you owe it to the guests to check the field. A person could break a leg." He limped off the field and insisted that he be taken immediately to a doctor.

That evening Mr. Erlang limped into the lobby. He carried his leg stiffly and supported himself with a cane. He stopped off at the desk to show it to Mr. Mandheimer.

"I tore a cartilage." He pulled up his trouser leg so that Mr. Mandheimer could see the bandage. "The doctor says it might heal by itself. Then again, it might need an operation."

"That's too bad," Mr. Mandheimer said. "So how'd it happen?"

"I was playing ball," Mr. Erlang said. "Really, Sam, you should have your boy pick up the stones on the field. I'm lucky I didn't break a leg."

"A man your age shouldn't be playing like a boy," Mr. Mandheimer interrupted.

"Oh, it's nothing," Mr. Erlang said. "It'll go away. Don't worry, I wouldn't sue you."

He limped into the dining room and found it a great effort to walk to his seat without getting the attention of everyone between his door and the table. When he sat down, he pushed away the slice of cantaloupe at his setting. He snapped his fingers for Al.

"Al, a little prune juice, please. I'm feeling weak."

The salad man said he'd been working in the mountains for fifteen years, but this was the first time he'd heard of prune juice being ordered for supper. It was strictly a dairy item.

During dinner, Al heard Mr. Erlang lecturing his table about the accident. He was explicit about the stone. By the time dessert came around, it sounded as if he'd tripped on Gibraltar.

Mr. Gerson wasn't impressed. He said he was sure the knee would get better, and men their age shouldn't be knocking themselves out on baseball fields.

Miss Mantell ignored him and Mrs. Leiderkopf said he ate too much.

"I spend eight, sometimes ten hours a day on my feet," Mr. Erlang explained over his tea and cigar. "My legs are like iron. When I was a boy, there wasn't a kid in the neighborhood could tackle me. See my legs? Strong as iron."

He showed them his ankle and calf. He couldn't get his pants up high enough to show them the thigh.

"I'll be all right. Fortunately, I keep in condition," Mr. Erlang told them. "It was the shock that threw me."

Mr. Gerson said, "Pardon the suggestion, but with all that shock, maybe it would be better if you didn't smoke."

Mr. Erlang reassured him, "I live on cigars. To me the air isn't pure unless I smell a good cigar."

Just before they left the table Mr. Erlang asked Al to get him a pencil and piece of paper. He wanted to get all of their addresses.

After dinner Audrey Grier came into the kitchen to make a note on the blackboard. She was wearing a V-necked white sweater. Since the Sunday of their argument, she hadn't talked to the chef. It wasn't easy, but the Negro cook was sympathetic and as long as the chef honored her notes, she could avoid him.

She wrote *Specials* and next to it put *three orders of lamb chops.*

The chef was finished at the stove. The kitchen men were cleaning up and he had a bowl filled with coffee. He was pouring in Carnation milk when he saw her.

His voice was low and even. "Do you know the cost of lamb chops?" She tried to leave without answering him.

"I ask you, Great Lady, do you know the cost of lamb chops?"

"I'm not the steward," she said. "I only put down on the board what people ask me."

"All right," the chef said. "You'll write like this—one bitch in heat."

The kitchen men laughed and Audrey started to walk away. She took two steps but the chef cut her off. He stared at her sweater.

"It must be nice to dress up and look so pretty. That's a lovely sweater. You look good in it. Look at me. Don't I look like a dirty pig?"

"Will you please let me go. I have to get back in the dining room."

"You didn't write what I told you. One bitch in heat. Write it down. Or don't you write everything people tell you?"

"Look, I only ask you for the things I can't talk them out of. I can't help it if they want lamb chops."

"Well, I want a bitch in heat. I can't help it if I want a bitch in heat." He mimicked her, and his expression softened. It was the first fun he'd had all summer.

The hostess' lips trembled. Her eyes filled up as if she was ready to cry. "Please let me go. I have to get back in the dining room." It came out so soft it was hardly a whisper. "Please—"

The chef took a step to the side. He tried to bow low and give her a flourish with his hand, but he lost control of the bowl of coffee. It washed from side to side and rolled out. Some of it splashed on her white sweater.

Audrey Grier's high heels stamped across the kitchen floor. She dashed out through the dining room and up to her room.

Al Brodie was cleaning off his tray at the kitchen sink when it happened. "That son of a bitch," he said to the waiter next to him.

"If you aren't tough you don't belong in this racket," the other boy said. "She had it coming." It was Stan Macht.

Mrs. Mandheimer was at the front desk promising a woman in a mink stole an extra blanket, when Al came into the lobby. The woman in the mink had a freckle-faced daughter by her side. After everything was straightened out about the blanket, the woman told Mrs. Mandheimer how nicely her daughter could recite.

The little girl went through the first two verses of "Gunga Din" before she had a lapse of memory. Her mother said that was all right and now would she please sing "Thank Heaven for Little Girls" for Mrs. Mandheimer.

The little girl was halfway through the song when Mrs. Mandheimer saw Al at the far end of the desk. She motioned to him and tried to move away. The woman in the mink said she *must* hear this, interrupted her daughter's singing, and told her to recite the preamble to the Constitution.

Mrs. Mandheimer kept smiling and saying, "How nice, how nice." As soon as the recitation was over, she told the lady in the mink to be sure to enter her daughter in the talent contest the hotel held every Thursday night. She was sure to win first prize.

"So what happened between Audrey and the chef?" she asked Al. "I've been trying to get away."

"He was really rough on her," Al said. "I think the guy is a sadist. They ought to take him away."

"After Labor Day they can take him," Mrs. Mandheimer said. "But in the meantime, how's Audrey?"

"She was crying when she left the kitchen," Al said. "Somebody ought to go up to see her. You know, she's really on a spot. Some of these people are rough, and that chef—he's making it hell for her."

"Look, there are worse chefs," Mrs. Mandheimer said. "It's no soft job behind that stove twelve hours a day."

"Still, he's got no right to talk to her the way he did."

"It's a horrible thing," Mrs. Mandheimer said.

"Go up to her room and try to make her feel better," Al said. "What the hell, she's a human being."

"Sure, I'll go," Mrs. Mandheimer said. "Come around here, you'll cover the phone for me."

He walked around the desk and went to the switchboard.

"When there's an outside call, the bell rings," Mrs. Mandheimer explained. "You'll know because this thing falls." She pointed to a small metal tab. "You'll put it up. You'll push down this key and this key." She pointed to the keys at the far ends of the board. "You're connected. Pick up the phone."

"Let me try it once," Al said. He pushed down both keys and picked up the phone. He heard Mr. Mandheimer's voice saying, "He may not do anything, but you never can tell. I thought you'd want to know." A well-modulated voice answered back, "You did the right thing. Now don't forget that report, and try to keep it as quiet as you can. We don't want to start any rackets."

"Hello, Mr. Mandheimer?" Al asked.

"That you, Sam?"

"Fred, what did you say?"

"Mr. Mandheimer, hello. How'd you get on the phone?" Al turned to Mrs. Mandheimer. "Your husband's on the phone. What do I do now?"

"Here, let me have it." She took the phone from him. "Hello, Sam, hang up. I'm showing the boy he should operate the switchboard."

"Hello, Mrs. Mandheimer. How are you?" the man called Fred said.

"Becky, for God sake hang up," Mr. Mandheimer yelled. "I'm on the telephone. Can't you see I'm on the telephone?"

Mrs. Mandheimer looked down at the board. She checked the first row of keys. "You're on the phone? How can you be on the phone? I just myself saw the boy push the keys down."

"Becky, take my word I'm on the phone. Hang up."

"Sam, it's important I should show him to operate the switchboard."

"Listen, Sam, maybe it'd be better if you called back."

"No, Fred, you stay on. Becky—please—hang—up!"

"So you'll tell me how come the keys are up, you're on the phone."

"The second row, Becky, the second row."

Mrs. Mandheimer hung up immediately. "I should know from a second row," she said.

"So what about Audrey?"

"He'll be off the phone in a few minutes. He'll cover. I'll go."

"Then you don't need me?"

"No, you can go."

Al was on his way out of the lobby when he heard Mr. Mandheimer call after him. The older man beckoned him into the inner office, closed the door, and asked with as much control as he could, "How much did you hear?"

"Don't worry, Mr. Mandheimer, I won't tell anybody about the insurance," Al said.

"Who says it's insurance? I was talking to a man, he should get me a surprise present for my wife. It's our anniversary in August."

"So that was it. Well, forget it," Al said. "I won't say a word to anybody."

"You're a good boy. I knew the first time I saw you." Mr. Mandheimer said. He put his arm on Al's shoulder and sighed. "Next time my wife asks you should operate the switchboard, you'll tell her it's not your job. After all, you're a waiter, you got enough to do."

"O.K.," Al said.

As soon as Mrs. Mandheimer came back from visiting Audrey Grier, her husband told her to be sure—if anybody asked her—to remember their wedding anniversary was in August.

Chapter 16

"So you know how to make an ad dummy," the manager of the resort advertising agency said.

"I took a course in college," the hotel-owner's son said. "Well—what do you think of it? How does it look to you?"

The advertising man studied the dummy carefully, then he said, "You didn't say anything about the day camp, about the new night club. You'll want to let them know you have this special teen-age program."

"I don't want it loaded with copy," the college boy said. "I'm using white space to catch their eye. I just want to get a simple message across."

"I see," the advertising man said. He looked at the ad again. "So you're telling them—it's charming, elegant, and traditional."

"You picked it up right away," the boy said. "I didn't just do this off the top of my head. I've been thinking about it for a long time. I made a little statistical survey of the resort section in the New York Post. This might interest you. The word magnificent *occurs seventeen times in twenty-two different ads.* New *is used to describe fifteen of these same hotels. This is nothing personal, but honest to Pete, the whole section shows an absolute lack of individuality and imagination. It's just one hotel outshouting the other."*

The advertising man smiled. "You know, a person picks up the resort section and looks at the ads, he wants a little information. A place is new, it's magnificent—he knows he'll *get his money's worth. You tell them charming, elegant, traditional—you know what that means to them? You're spending nothing, you're giving them nothing, your place is falling apart."*

"You don't like my ad, do you?" the college boy said.

"If it was up to you, you wouldn't use it."

"What's not to like?" the advertising man said. "If it's all right with your father, it's fine by me."

"I hope it's the right size," Roz said.

"What did you buy me a present for? It's not my birthday or anything. I'm telling you, you're the last of the great splenders," Al said.

"Go ahead, open it up," Roz said.

They were sitting on the bed in her room. Ellie and Linda were out and the door was closed. It was after dinner. He was dressed for the night in a pair of starched khakis and an open-collared white shirt. She had on a sleeveless dress that was high at the collar and buttoned down the back.

He untied the brown twine and started unwrapping the heavy stiff paper.

"I'm sorry I couldn't have it gift-wrapped," she said. "I think it's a lot more fun to open presents that are gift-wrapped."

"Who cares about the wrapping," he said. "Now, what the heck did you do this for? I'm telling you, you're getting crazier by the hour. If the summer isn't over soon they'll have to take you away."

"Does a person have to be crazy to buy you a present?"

"It helps," he said.

"You must have an inferiority complex," Roz said very seriously. "I think your so-called confidence is just a cover-up."

He winced. "Try once more."

"I think it's true," she said.

He opened up the box and under a sheath of tissue paper was a buttoned-down plaid shirt. There was a knitted maroon tie on top.

"Two presents yet," he said, and he seemed more embarrassed than pleased.

"Well, I wanted to buy you those plaid bathing trunks I told you about, but they didn't have them."

"This'll be terrific," he said. "I'll wear this to the pool tomorrow."

"I hope you're a fifteen collar," she said. "If you're not, I'll exchange it."

"I don't know myself," he said. "It looks right."

"Do you like it?"

"Sure, real sharp."

"That isn't the right word and you know it. It isn't sharp. That's just the point. I think it has class." She took the shirt from him and started to take the pins out. "Let's try it on right now. If it doesn't fit you, I'll take it right back. . . ."

He picked up the tie and dangled it.

"And I want you to wear that tie with it, too," she said. "You know I've never seen you wear a tie. Really, you've got a lot to learn about style."

"What brought this on, all of a sudden? Somebody make a crack about how I dress?"

She had the pins out of one of the sleeves and she measured it against his arm. "The sleeve length seems to be right," she said. "Nobody has to say anything. The idea is to get you ready to meet the public before anybody says anything."

"What public?"

"You're going to be an accountant aren't you? Don't you expect to have some clients?"

"Not exactly the whole public," he said.

She took a cardboard brace out of the collar and unfastened the buttons. "I'll bet you'll look wonderful in this. It'll change your whole appearance." She pushed the shirt toward him. "Come on now, try it on."

He flicked a finger at the small button in the back of the collar. "Get this, will you, regular Joe College."

"It's the latest thing," Roz said. "I think it's very smart."

"Hell yeah," he said. "I don't see how I managed to live all these years without it."

"Listen if you don't like it, I can take it back," she said.

"Who said anything about not liking it?" He stood up and took off the shirt he was wearing.

"And another thing," she said. "You should wear T shirts under your shirt. They make your shirts fall better. Everybody wears them."

"What's the matter with my chest?" he said.

"Nothing's the matter," she said.

He reached an arm out toward her but she moved away. "Come on, not now. I want to see how that shirt looks."

"Boy, you are really getting tough," he said. "I can't get anywhere with you any more."

"And that's another thing," she said, very efficiently. "We'll discuss that later. And tonight we *are* going to discuss it."

"Yes, ma'am," he said.

He put the plaid shirt on and started to button it from the bottom up.

"Button the collar first," Roz said. "I want to see if it fits." She got up from the bed and helped him. "It looks right. You know, I think you are a fifteen."

"We discover things about ourselves every day. As a wise man once said, know thyself and thy shirt will always fit."

"I don't think it's funny," she said. "You should know your shirt size. There's nothing wrong with a man looking well groomed. You ought to start thinking about those things."

"I will," he said. "Right after I thank you." He tried to kiss her but she moved away.

"Boy, am I paying for this shirt," he said.

"And just what do you mean by that?"

He plumped down on the bed. The top button was the only one buttoned and the rest of the shirt flared, revealing his stomach. "O.K., what's on your mind? Let's have it."

"Do you want to wear it tonight?" she said. "If you do, button it up and put the tie on."

"Later," he said. His voice was cold.

"Do you like it?" she asked as sweetly as she could.

"It all depends," he said. "What's on your mind?"

"You don't want to talk now," she said. "I'll tell you what. Why don't you button the shirt up and put on the tie and we'll go down to the casino. They're having a show tonight. Wouldn't you like to see it?"

"I feel like staying here," he said. "I want to take the shirt off."

"No," she said. "I'm not going to do that." She turned away from him.

"So, now the truth comes out," he stood up and unbuttoned the top button of the shirt. "Nice to have known you, Roz. I don't have to have a ton of bricks fall on my head to know I'm getting the old brush-off."

She turned back to him. He was still sitting on the bed and she came close enough to look directly down at him without being close enough for him to reach her. "I didn't mean it that way," she said. "You know I love you, Al. That's why I bought you the shirt—because I love you. Because I want you to really be somebody—I mean I think you should start thinking about these things. Appearances are important. They'll mean a lot to you in your work."

"You said that before," he said and he stood up. "So now we've got that settled, let's relax and make ourselves comfortable. We've got three acts before your little friends come home."

"Stop talking to me like that. I don't like it. It makes me feel cheap."

"How the hell do you want me to talk? You don't like the way I dress. You don't like the way I talk. What do you like?"

"I like you, Al. I really do. Honest to God, believe me. It's just that this isn't right. I mean we can't go on this way. We've got to get to know each other—in other ways. I don't even know where you come from or about your home or your family or anything. We don't even talk, we just—"

"I come from New York," he said. "O.K.? Now you happy?"

"I don't mean that."

"Boy, are you mixed up," he said. "Didn't I tell you about

a hundred times before that you think too much? Can't you take things the way they are and stop complicating them?"

"You don't understand," she said.

"Maybe I don't," he said. He left the shirt on the bed and put on his white one. He went to the door without his present.

She came behind him, holding it in her hands. "I want you to have it, Al. Even if you don't understand me. I want you to have the shirt and tie. They're yours."

"Keep 'em," he said. "I hold together all right without a little button in the back."

He left her room and went into his, slamming the door behind him. He dozed off waiting for her. It was less than thirty minutes when he was awakened by her hand brushing gently across his head.

"You shouldn't leave your door unlocked, that's another thing," she said.

He reached up, half asleep, and pulled her down to him.

The door opened and he felt Roz's leg kick against his. It woke him up and he felt his nakedness. Quickly he called toward the door, "Just a minute, Joe. Wait outside, will you?"

"Sure. I'm sorry," Joe said.

The door closed and Roz said, "I must have fallen asleep. What are we going to do now?"

"Turn the light on, will you? I can't see a thing."

"No, please don't do that. I don't have my clothes on."

"Don't worry. Joe won't know who's here. He's a hell of a good guy. He'll mind his own business."

"Everything is so simple for you. But I care—it makes a lot of difference to me. Maybe you don't believe it, but I'm just not this kind of girl."

He swung his feet onto the floor and started across the room toward the light switch.

"Where are you going?" she called. "Al Brodie, if you turn on those lights—"

"How in the hell are you going to get dressed?" he said. "In the dark?"

She was whispering, but her voice screeched. "Just don't turn them on," she said. "Do you hear me—don't."

"All right, have it your way." He went back to his bed and lay down. He could hear the sound of her heels moving across the floor. In a few seconds, she said, "You could help me. You could snap me up in back."

"If you'd put the lights on, you wouldn't have all this trouble."

"Are you going to help me or aren't you?"

"How am I going to help you? For Chris' sake I can't even see you." He reached his hands out in the dark and fumbled until he touched her shoulders.

He felt her bare back and her dress loose and unclasped. "What do I do with this?" he said.

"There are little hinges," she said. "Hook them up."

"What are you trying to prove?"

"It just so happens," Roz said, "that Ellie and Linda and I are old friends—they know my family and everything else and I'm not going back to my room half dressed. What would I say if they're awake?"

"Ask them how they're making out. For all you know, they're getting more than you are."

He felt her wrench away from him. "Take your hands off me," she said. "Just don't you touch me."

"O.K.," he said. "Button up your own dress. You don't want the lights on, not me."

She was busy for a minute more and then she said, "Just hook up one or two of them. At least you can do that."

He said, "I wish you'd make up your mind."

His eyes were better adjusted to the dark. He found the top hook and managed to attach it. Then he fastened two buttons. He ran his hands up her back until he reached her shoulders. He turned her around, held her in his arms and kissed her. She didn't resist.

"You're not wearing your bra," he said softly.

"I rolled it up," she said. "Only you'd notice that."

He kissed her again. "I notice a lot of things about you. There's a lot to notice."

"Al," she said, "why do we always fight about everything?'"

He lifted her chin and pecked at her lips. "You know, I'd like to get you back in bed. We wouldn't fight then."

"I've got to go, Al. I really do. This bothers me a lot more than you think. You'll try to cover with Joe, won't you?"

"Sure," he said. "I'll tell him it was Ellie. Give him something to worry about."

"That'd be just like you," she said.

When she got to the door, she opened it a crack to make sure no one was in the hall. Then she quickly darted to her room.

Joe came in a few minutes later.

"All clear?" he said, opening the door.

It wasn't until Joe was in bed that he said, "Hey, Al, what d'you think of Ellie?"

"Good kid," Al said. "Good sense of humor."

"No, I'm serious," Joe said. "I mean, do you think she's broadminded? What I'm trying to say is what do you think of her intellectually?"

"I never even talk to her," Al said. "How the hell would I know?"

"I guess you wouldn't," Joe said. He was quiet for a while and then he said, "We sure get on great together. I don't mean just physically. We got a lot in common. Like her old man, for example, he runs a grocery store. You know what my dad does? He's a bartender."

"That's great," Al said. "You're made for each other."

"I mean neither one of them has got much money," Joe said. "Ellie's just like me—she wants something better. We both like to dress good and stuff like that—but she likes to work. I mean she isn't just sitting around waiting for somebody to leave her a million dollars."

"So get married," Al said, "and let me sleep."

"Ellie and me, we were talking just tonight. She's like me—she'd like to run a business of her own—a small place, like say a real sporty men's shop or a women's dress store. She's got the personality for it. She's a terrific mixer."

"Fine," Al Brodie said, "I'll look you up if I want some underwear wholesale."

"When I'm with her I just know I got it beat," Joe said. "I never met anybody like that before. And you know something, Al, she was telling me just tonight—I give her the same feeling. She admitted this thing to me—she said right out she was always scared to try things on her own until she met me. Take that car of hers, she'd hardly use it until we started going together. She always figured it'd get scratched up or be in an accident. Now you'd never guess a thing like that just looking at Ellie."

Al said, "No. So get married and make our highways safe."

"I suppose it does sound kind of unimportant," Joe said. "But in a way that's the thing I go for most, this feeling of confidence. Like me, you think I'd ever really try going into business for myself without Ellie? Never. I always figured I wasn't the type. You know—always kidding around too much, too happy-go-lucky. But Ellie brings out this other side of me. She gets me talking and the next thing I know I got all kinds of ideas —and they don't just seem like daydreams either. I just know I can make it work."

"It's all right with me," Al said. "You have my blessings."

"You think it'd be all right then," Joe said. He was quiet for a long time, and then he said, "Hey, Al, did you know I was Irish?"

Al said, "No, I didn't know that. You kidding or something? It's a little late for jokes."

"I'm serious," Joe said. "Why do you think I took that job here in the children's dining room? I know I'm lucky working here in the first place. I never told anybody. Calvin spotted it right off, but nobody else but you and Ellie know."

Al Brodie said, "I've got to hand it to you—you pull it off perfect."

"Well, I lived around Jews all my life," Joe said. "They're my friends and everything. Where I live, downtown on Second Avenue, we're right on top of the Jewish neighborhood. That's how I came to know about the Catskills. I have this friend of mine, Vic Newman. Vic and I have been pals all our lives. Vic is just like me—no money or anything. Neither one of us thought we had a chance of getting to college. Then Vic started coming up here summers, waiting on tables and all. He's in his second year at C.C.N.Y. After he gets out he's going to dental school. Vic is the one who told me about it. 'Joe,' Vic always says, 'the only difference between the poor Irish kids and the poor Jewish kids is the borscht belt.' In a way, you know, he's right. You know what I did summers when I went to high school? Delivery boy. That pays a big twenty-four dollars a week."

"You're all set now," Al said. "What the hell, you're in like Flynn around here."

Joe laughed. "That's pretty good. I'd tell that to Furman, only then he'd know."

"So what do you have to worry about?" Al said. "If Ellie knows and it's all right with her, you don't have to give a damn about anybody else."

"Yeah," Joe said. "Only she didn't tell her folks yet. My folks—I don't have to worry about them. I been going with Jews so long, they're sort of used to it. But Jewish people are funny that way. I lived around them. I know. You take Mandheimer—I'm not so sure he'd have given me this job if he knew I was Irish. Not that he's prejudiced or anything. It's something else. Like they just don't believe anybody but another Jew can handle those coobahs in the dining room."

"Well," Al said, "you just keep it to yourself and I'll keep it to myself."

"I'm not worried about you," Joe said. "I know I can trust you."

"Yeah," Al Brodie said. "And you just don't say anything to Ellie about what went on here when you came in the first time tonight."

" 'Course not," Joe said. "Don't you think I know she and Roz are friends?"

Chapter 17

*E*xcerpt from an address by Judge Arthur C. Butts of New York city, delivered in 1904 on the occasion of Monticello's centennial celebration:

> ... Between 1795 and 1800 a few adventurous spirits had taken up their residence in this region ... On summer eves at twilight, her young nestling 'neath her wings, the robin thrilled her evening prayer to God, and as its sweet notes echoed through the darkening aisles of the forests, it was unheard by man or maid. At night, forth from their lairs came the bear and wolf to roam these solitudes for prey. Sweet forest ferns and flowers grew unseen. The summer sun kissed the oak and ash and maple, and sometimes its golden gleams beneath their branches strayed and lighted their hoary trunks. . . . Grand! Majestic! Beautiful! Such was this spot a century ago, but the grandeur and the majesty and the beauty of primitive nature were destined to yield to the invading and unconquerable forces of civilization.

Audrey Grier didn't come down to breakfast the next morning.

Mr. Mandheimer got the waiters and busboys together before the dining room opened and told them Audrey had the day off. He explained that he'd take care of seating any check-ins and handling specials. Otherwise, the captain was in charge of the floor and the boys were to listen to him the same as they would to Audrey.

As soon as Mr. Mandheimer left the dining room, Stan smashed his fist against his tray and said, "The Mong rules. Long live the Mong!"

Mr. Mandheimer came right back into the dining room and said, "Stop the fooling around. The next noise I hear like that, you're all fired."

Stan said, "Don't worry, Mr. Mandheimer, I'll take care of the guy who did it."

Mr. Mandheimer said, "O.K., Macht, you're the captain. Just like the game. Work like a team and make the points."

"That's the old spirit," Stan Macht said and he made a fist and shook it.

Mr. Mandheimer left feeling satisfied.

The dining room usually stopped serving from the hot stove at ten-thirty. At ten minutes of eleven Mr. Erlang came limping down the aisle. His prune juice was waiting at his setting. He took it down at one gulp and ordered oatmeal, scrambled eggs, and a side order of lox and cream cheese.

Al went out to the kitchen and told the Chinese second he had a late and could he please have two scrambled. The cook cursed, but put out the eggs.

The lox and eggs, oatmeal, and cream cheese were on the table when Stan Macht motioned to Al.

He was far enough away for Mr. Erlang not to hear when he said, "O.K., wise guy, so what's the idea of serving hot stuff? What are rules for, if guys like you are going to break them?"

"This guy is an all-around pain," Al said. "He's goldbricking with his leg, and he'll probably sue the hotel for a million dollars. I got to keep him happy."

"The guys in the kitchen don't count, huh? They break their hump and you got them working overtime. You let one bum like that push you around, they all do it. Next thing you know we'll be serving breakfast at twelve-thirty."

"All right, so he's got his eggs already. The next time I'll tell him. Not that I haven't told him before, but what can we do?"

"I'm going to do nothing," Stan Macht said, "but you're

going over there and grab them eggs right out from under that slob. We'll teach him to come in on time."

"You're crazy," Al said. "He's got them. What's the difference what we do now?"

"You get them eggs," the Mong said. "Pull them right out from under him. When I run this dining room, everybody follows the rules."

"Skip it," Al said. "Next thing we know you'll be cracking up, too."

"I want them eggs," Stan Macht said. "That's an order. The Mong is giving you an order."

"Dry up, Mong," Al Brodie said. "You're wasting my time." He turned to leave, but Macht grabbed him by the shirt. He knotted the shirt up in his hand and pulled Al up close to him.

"I've taken enough crap off of you. This time, you don't do what I say, I'll knock your goddamn face in and then fire you."

Al spoke very softly. "Let go, Stan. You don't let me go right now, I swear to God I'll slit your throat."

The Mong let him go. "You're a real tough guy, huh? We'll see how goddamned tough you are."

Mr. Erlang had his eggs. Before he limped out of the dining room, he asked Al if there were any onion rolls left over from breakfast. He followed that with a comment that six weeks were up and it was time he was tipping. That he found quite amusing and laughed.

Al brought two salt sticks and a twisted roll. It wasn't exactly what Mr. Erlang wanted, and he let him know.

At lunch time, Mr. Mandheimer greeted all the guests at the door. He was wearing a light tweed suit, which was rare for him, and many of the ladies who passed said it was a shame he didn't dress up more often.

Immediately after the soup course, Mr. Mandheimer took off his jacket, put on an apron, and went to the back to help the chef.

Al was carrying out his last full tray of mains when Stan Macht glided by. Stan was holding his tray up with two hands instead of one. As they walked he latched the edge of his tray under Al's and started to lift.

Al had to dart to the side, dropping a dish. When the plate fell, Mr. Mandheimer called from behind the stove, "I want that boy's name. Get me that boy's name. He'll pay for those dishes."

Al served his guests and came back to pick up another main.

"You don't know how to stack, yet," Mr. Mandheimer said.

"Waiters they call them," the chef said. "With a headwaiter in the dining room, they'd all have been dumped three weeks ago."

Al picked up another dish of blintzes and sour cream and said nothing.

He was carrying out his tray of whipped cream puffs for dessert, when Stan Macht glided by with a handful of salt. He threw it on Al's plates. "Explain it to them, wise guy," he said. "You're full of sweet talk."

It was a bad choice. The taste of salt was hardly recognizable. Three guests asked for seconds.

That night at dinner, Stan Macht announced a change in the kitchen line-up. Al had been carrying a heavy station, so he usually picked up second. Tonight, the Mong shifted him to last.

After dinner Al went to the front desk and asked Mrs. Mandheimer how Audrey was doing.

"Not so good," Mrs. Mandheimer said. "One of the boys was up to see her today. That big boy—the basketball what's his name. He said she feels so bad he thinks she won't come back."

"She's just afraid of the goddamn chef, that's what," Al said.

"I'm sorry for her," Mrs. Mandheimer said. "A single girl. No man to take up for her. It's hard on her. What can I do?" She slapped her hands on her thighs.

"She's got to come back. What are we going to do for a hostess?"

"Another week, the rush is over. The middle of August, plenty of people will be looking for jobs." She paused and added. "We should only have guests."

"Yeah, but in the meantime?"

"In the meantime? We lived today without her, we'll live a little longer. What am I going to do? A good hostess you'll never find now."

"You mean Stan Macht—the Mong—is going to take her place? You mean a waiter is substituting for her until she comes back?"

"He wants more money?"

"No, nothing like that." Al Brodie was very serious. "Where did you say her room was? Maybe she'd feel better if I dropped up to talk to her."

"It's a nice idea. You're a good boy, Al." She smiled, the first time she had in a long while. "Fourth floor of the Annex. She's in room forty-six. You know something? With this busy week and a full house and everything, she wouldn't even let me put another girl in with her. What are you going to do?"

"I'll see you," Al said. "And by the way, I dropped a plate. Your husband was kidding me about paying for it."

"You know I was right, just like my Phillip. You saw him? Tell me, you see the resemblance?"

"Never," Al Brodie said. "Your grandson is handsome. It's like comparing black and white."

"Different, yes," Mrs. Mandheimer said. "But the smile, the dimple, there's a definite resemblance. He's my grandson, I should know."

"He's a very bright boy," Al said. "I was playing with him at the pool the other day. You know, he can practically swim."

"You don't say," Mrs. Mandheimer was very interested. "You were playing with him. You know my daughter? You know my Marsha?"

"Only slightly," Al said. "She seems to be a very devoted mother."

Mrs. Mandheimer's eyes opened and closed. "Tell me,

Allen," she said. "Since you brought it up—any of the other boys know my Marsha? They take her out, make appointments with her, maybe?"

"I wouldn't want to say, Mrs. Mandheimer," Al said. "I mean it's definitely none of my business. I don't know anything. I only know what I hear."

"So what d'you hear? I'm her mother, I have a right to know."

"What I hear—I mean, it's not bad. It's just that—well—she has been dating one of the boys."

"Yes," Mrs. Mandheimer said. "You tell me who?"

"You haven't got a thing to worry about, Mrs. Mandheimer," Al said. "I only met Marsha once, but she struck me as being the kind of person who really knows her way around. I mean she's got a good head. She sees right through people."

"So who's this waiter?" Mrs. Mandheimer said.

"Look—this guy—it's nothing. It's not for me to say, Mrs. Mandheimer. It might not be true. I might not even have the name right."

"This one they call the Mong. My headwaiter, he likes my Marsha?"

Al Brodie said, "We don't fool you—not for one minute. You know everything that goes on around here."

"Such a boy for my Marsha," Mrs. Mandheimer was visibly pained.

"It's nothing," Al said. "For gosh sake, I'm sure it's not serious. She probably thinks the stupid boob is a scream."

"Boob, yet. Mong, yet," Mrs. Mandheimer said. "What a Marsha! What a Marsha. Who knows how people try to forget?"

"What was that again?" Al said.

"Nothing," Mrs. Mandheimer said. "Thank you, Allen. You're a good boy. Thank you."

"But I didn't tell you anything," he said. "Nothing. You figured it all out for yourself."

"It makes a difference?" she said. "All right, I won't thank you. You feel better?"

Al Brodie said it was getting late in the season and they were all cracking up and left the desk.

The lights were out on the fourth floor of the Annex, and Al couldn't find the switch. It was dark and the moonlight coming through the window at both ends of the hall gave it an eerie quality. Besides, he'd taken the steps two at a time, and his heart was beating fast.

He walked down the empty hall looking for forty-six. The first door he came to didn't have a number. It was black like all the other doors, but it had a lock which was latched from the outside. There was a piece of hotel stationery sticking out of the crack of the door. He pulled it out and read, "Chambermaid, please don't forget to leave six clean towels in room forty-four. Thank you."

He put the note back and continued down the hall. He came to a bathroom and then a shower and then a room numbered forty-five. The tabs were off the door of the next room but he could see the lighter-shaded wood where they must have been for a long time. It looked like forty-six.

He knocked and there was no answer. He heard scurrying around inside the room and he said, "Audrey, is that you? It's me, Al Brodie. I'd like to talk to you a minute."

The scurrying continued and then Audrey's voice said, "Just a minute, Al."

When she came to the door her hair was up in a kerchief. She had no make-up on, and the line of her face swelled and shone where her penciled eyebrows usually were. She was wearing a terry-cloth robe with a long belt that tied around the waist. The shoulders were padded and they came to an awkward point.

"I look a mess," she said. "But come on in."

Her room was small, but better than the rooms of the other help. She had a double bed and a large chest and a bridge chair. There were shoes lined up all over the floor, under the bed, under the chest along the wall. The closet door was open and he could see it was stuffed with dresses. A small, round pole extended from the door and she had two slips and three bathing suits hanging on that. It wasn't possible to close the closet door.

"This is sloppy," she said. "But what am I going to do? Clothes are part of my bread and butter."

She led him into the room and pulled the bridge chair over to the bed. "Sit wherever you're comfortable," she said. When she sat on the bed and the springs creaked she winced. She leaned against the headpost, tightening the belt of her robe. She tucked the bottom under her knees.

"So how you feeling, Auds?" he asked. He sat down on the bridge chair.

"A lot better. I needed a rest," she said. "Honestly, you don't know how I go at it. It's a tremendous responsibility. I've had harder jobs, believe me, but I don't know—this year I'm just not up to it."

The top of the bureau was crowded with cosmetics. There were powder streaks across it, and a chignon and hair net. She had a small lamp that was designed like a pump. You pushed the handle and the light went on, pushed it again and it went off. He saw a pack of Camels. He reached over, snapped one out of the pack and offered it to her.

"Cigarette?"

"Thanks, I will."

"You're lucky I smoke your brand, huh?" There was a pack of matches stuck between the cellophane. He took them out and struck a match.

She inhaled and blew smoke through her nose. "Go ahead, have one yourself," she said.

"No, thanks. I don't smoke when I'm working." He played with the pack.

"It's a good idea. I smoke entirely too much. I really think it hurts my wind. One of these days I'm going to make up my mind and stop. I'll do it, too. When I make up my mind to do something, I do it."

"I'll bet you do."

"One thing I have is will power. Look, I have to have will power. If I didn't, I'd never be in this racket. You know those people—some of them get under your skin. I have to have self-control." She stopped suddenly.

"Otherwise you'd be breaking water pitchers over their heads, huh?"

She tried to smile. "Not exactly, but there'd be some burning ears, you can bet."

"Anybody who meets the public has to hide his feelings. You take my old man, he's a cab driver. You think he tells people what he thinks of them? Why, one day—it was right in the thick of the pennant race, I think it was '53—anyway, the Giants were playing the Dodgers in the play-off. Well, the old man, he's a real Giant fan. Been one since John McGraw and Christy Mathewson. Anyway, he makes up his mind right off he's doing all his cruising in East Harlem and the Bronx. You know, stay out of the arguments. Sure enough his first call takes him right to the heart of Flatbush. No matter what he does he can't get out of Brooklyn. All day long he's telling people how the Dodgers can't lose. Imagine what this is doing to him. I mean, he's really a die-hard Giant fan. So Thompson hits his home run and the old man's got three Dodger fans with a portable radio in his car. The meter says one and a quarter, and he don't feel like lousing up what should be better than a two bit tip. Did he burn. He's still telling that story. Not that it's funny or anything, but it brings out the point."

Audrey was listening with great interest. She was ready to laugh all along, and when Al came to the end, she laughed anyway. "That's wonderful. And did he get the tip?"

"I think they were so disappointed they stiffed him."

"Isn't that just the way it goes," Audrey said. She wrapped her fingers together and stretched her arms out in front of her. "Thanks for coming up to see me, Al. You know you made me feel better already." She dropped her arms by her side. "I'm going to miss you."

"What d'you mean miss me?" Al said. "You'll be giving me hell for carrying too many mains before the week's over."

She shook her head. She meant it to be dramatic. "No, I won't, Al. No more, Audrey is through."

"No kidding, Auds, I can't believe it."

"I've had enough. I'm up to here." She held her hand up to her throat.

"That goddamn chef. Don't let him beat you, Auds. He's

no more important here than you are. You ought to give it back to him—blow for blow."

"It's not just that—"

"Look, Auds, I heard the whole argument the other day. But you can take it from me—it's nothing personal. That's just the way chefs are. He'd be that way with any headwaiter or hostess. What the hell, I'll bet deep down inside, he really likes you. He's probably got the hots for you, for all I know."

"The tips are bad too, Al. I made more money two years ago when I worked a smaller house and had less work."

"So what? The good always makes up for the bad. For all you know, you'll make more money the next two weeks than you did the whole season so far. It goes like that sometimes."

"You're very nice, Al." She got off the bed and tried to look gay. "But I'm also tired. I need a rest."

He got up and stood beside her. In her slippers she was more than a head shorter and he bent down, trying to look into her face. "We need you, Audrey. I'm not just saying that. We really do need you downstairs. They're never going to get an experienced hostess like you so late in the season. And how the hell are we going to get along without you? It was hell down there today."

She thought she caught him. "Stan Macht told me just a while ago everything went real smooth. He said Mr. Mandheimer took charge and it ran like a clock."

"Who took charge?" Al plumped down on the bed. "That Mong, he'll stoop to anything." He shook his head. "O.K., Auds, it's none of my business. You do what you want."

"What do you mean, he'll stoop to anything?"

"It's nothing—"

"No, I want to know." Her face was flushed. "It's very important."

He'd hoped for a bite but he was getting a whole gulp. He tried to slow down. "It's just that he wants your job. I guess he figures if he could talk you out of it, there'd be nobody else to take charge and he'd be it."

"You're not telling me everything, Al. What did Stan Macht say about me?"

"Nothing—honest to God. I've told you everything, Auds. He wants your job. That's it."

"Did he say anything about me—personally. If he did—I want to know."

"No, he didn't." He was embarrassed, and it made him look as if he were holding something back.

"You're trying to spare me, Al. You're trying to spare me, aren't you?" Her lips trembled and after a second she couldn't catch her breath.

He got up and put his arm around her shoulder. It seemed to be the only thing to do. "Look, Auds, believe me—whatever it was between you and Stan Macht, I don't know anything about it. If it makes you feel better, you can tell me."

She started to sob and she pressed her head against his chest. He put both his arms around her and held her close, swaying back and forth.

"Easy, Audrey, easy," he said. "Don't let that son of a bitch get you like this." He didn't know what else to say. He kept repeating, "Easy . . . easy . . ."

She buried her head in his chest and he could feel her wiping her eyes on his T shirt. When she raised her head, her face was streaked with tears and her eyes were puffed.

"Don't mind me, Al. Don't mind me," she said. "I'm crazy." Then she cried again.

He kept patting her back. "It's all right," he said. "Cry it out." His voice was soft. "That's good for you."

She pressed close and he could feel her legs working against him. She kept moving her head and he freed one hand and stroked her hair.

The next time she raised her head, she wiped her eyes on her sleeves. She looked right at him, still in his arms, and said, "Stan Macht didn't lay me, Al. He tried to. He said I needed it. He said all the boys knew I needed it. He said that's what was wrong with me. That's a horrible thing to say to a woman, isn't it, Al?"

"It's lousy," he said.

"It's always that way. At the last job, it was the boss. In the city it's every guy I go out with. What is it about me, Al? It must be me."

"I don't know, Audrey," he said. "I can't help you. I never felt that way at all."

She pulled away from his arms and looked right at him. "Do you want me, Al? Do you want to sleep with me?"

"If you want me, Audrey. If you think I'm good enough for you. I know you're very proud, very choosy—"

He'd said proud and that was all she could hear. She repeated it once aloud to herself and then lifted her head to be kissed.

Al Brodie didn't close his eyes when he kissed her. He needed the job and he needed that thousand bucks. He had to get her back to work and he had to get the Mong out. There wasn't any other way.

"But where were you?" Roz said. "All I want to know is where were you?"

"Look," he said. "Stop shouting. You'll wake everybody up."

"It's Marsha, isn't it? You lied to me at the pool the other day. It's her, isn't it? Why aren't you man enough to admit it?"

"Look," he said, "if you must know, it was you."

"Oh my God," she said. "Are you a liar. I've heard everything. It was me, yet. What d'you take me for, Al Brodie—a complete fool?"

"All right, don't listen to me. Have it your way. It was Marsha Cooper. Now, leave me alone and I'll go to my room."

"You think I didn't hear the announcements all night? Where were you, up on the hill? Did you take her up to our hill?"

"Are you going to shut up—"

"No, I'm not going to shut up. Not until I've told everybody in the world what a contemptible, selfish, self-centered heel you are."

"O.K., so announce it on the loudspeaker and let me go to sleep."

They were standing in front of the door to the cabin. He had just left Audrey and he was tired. He'd been thinking on the way back how he'd handle Roz, but he hadn't expected to find her sitting in front of his door.

"Answer me," she said. "Admit it."

He was ready to tell her—not the truth exactly, but enough to settle her for good. But the voice on the loudspeaker, distant but distinct, stopped him.

"Room fourteen," the voice on the speaker said. "Marsha, your baby is up. Maybe the basketball team wants to put him to sleep."

Roz said, "Oh my God—" And later, after he'd given her a long silence to let it sink in, "Al, will you ever forgive me?"

He said, "I took a long walk and did a lot of thinking about us. You're right. We ought to give ourselves a little breather to think this over. The best thing would be for you and me to both make it a point to see other people, get out more. That's the only way we'll really know. It'll be hard all right, but it's something we've got to do."

She said no at first, and she swore she'd go anywhere and do anything in the world he wanted, but he convinced her that they had to have self-control. When she went to her room Rosalyn Silvers was persuaded that this little breather would bring them closer together than ever before.

Chapter 18

"His name is Miller," the hostess told the social director. "Nobody suits him. I had to set up a table for two so he could be alone with his wife. He's got a chain of shoe stores—the *real* hoi polloi."

The social director winked and made a small O with his thumb and index finger. When he came to the table he leaned both hands on the tablecloth. Mrs. Miller looked at him.

"Mr. and Mrs. Miller," the social director said. "Nice to have you with us. Staying for a while?"

"Perhaps," Mr. Miller said. "We were at the Concord for two weeks last season. It's my wife's idea to try a smaller place."

The social director said, "Did you hear the one about Ginsberg and the airline? Well, Ginsberg walks into the airline terminal at Forty-Second Street and goes right up to the desk of American Airlines. 'Gimme a ticket,' says Ginsberg. 'Yes, sir,' the clerk says, 'and where to?' Ginsberg says, 'What do I care—anywhere.' The clerk is used to running into all kinds of characters, but this he's never heard before. 'A little pleasure trip?' he says. 'What part of the country did you have in mind?' Ginsberg is annoyed. 'What d'you mean pleasure. A business trip I'm taking. Gimme fast a ticket.' The clerk is patient. You know those clerks—real professional types. 'Sir,' he says to Ginsberg, 'I just can't make out a ticket to anywhere—you must have a destination.' Ginsberg says, 'What do I know from destination. Me, I got stores everywhere.'"

Mrs. Miller said, "Very cute."

Mr. Miller didn't smile, but he said, "Our shoe chain consists of eight stores, located in the metropolitan area."

"Very interesting," the social director said. "Maybe you can help me. I been having trouble with my feet all summer..."

Audrey Grier was in the kitchen at seven o'clock the next morning. She had a cup of coffee and joked with the breakfast cook, who was making the cereal and getting his eggs ready.

The chef was working on the far side of the kitchen, but at seven-thirty he came over with a stuffed cabbage and asked Audrey to taste it. She hated to eat in the morning, but she tried it and smacked her lips and said it was very good.

The chef said, "A lot you know. I put them up in June. They been in the freezer for six weeks. All I did was heat them up."

"You'd never know the difference," Audrey said.

"Make the lady some eggs," the chef hollered at the breakfast cook. "What the hell is the matter with you?"

Audrey asked for a fried egg and she picked at it.

When she started into the dining room, the chef called after her, "Some people are sure lucky. Vacations yet? Where did you go, to Harley's?"

"I went to the Greasy Spoon to get something decent to eat for a change," she fired back. They both laughed.

Most of the boys were coming down for breakfast and before the dining room opened Audrey gave them a talking-to. There was a tendency to slack up and she wanted it stopped.

Miss Mantell told Al she was leaving right after breakfast. Her five weeks were up and she had to get back to work. After she'd finished eating, she went over to the server and handed him two envelopes—one for him and the other for Danny Rose.

"It's been a pleasure having you for a waiter," Miss Mantell said. "When I come back next year, I'm going to ask for you."

"It's been nice having you," Al said. "I really mean that. I wish I had a whole station with guests like you."

Mrs. Leiderkopf joined them. "You want you should get rid of me yet?"

Al laughed. "A station with you and Miss Mantell," he corrected himself. "You're my best guests."

"We wouldn't tip, we wouldn't be best," Mrs. Leiderkopf said.

"That's not true," Al said. "Other people tip—to be frank, some more than you. But you're really nice people. I mean it."

"Hurry, darling. You'll miss your bus," Mrs. Leiderkopf said to Miss Mantell. "Better you should be early than to rush."

"She's right," Miss Mantell said. "Somehow I just can't seem to pull myself away."

Al said, "That's because you've had such a good vacation and made such swell friends."

"I suppose that's it," Miss Mantell said. She turned to Mrs. Leiderkopf and took the older woman's hand in hers. "Really, it has been such a pleasure sitting at the table with you. And our evening conversations, too. I just hope I didn't keep you up too late."

"Sleep I have plenty of time for," Mrs. Leiderkopf said. "Come, you'll miss your bus."

"Now, you take good care of Mrs. Leiderkopf," Miss Mantell said to Al. "Make sure she doesn't eat cake and keep her on her saccharin." She waved a finger reproachfully.

"You can count on it," Al said.

As they walked out of the dining room, Al saw Mrs. Leiderkopf give Miss Mantell a plastic pocketbook. Miss Mantell paused by the door and pecked Mrs. Leiderkopf's cheek.

"Here's your last dividend from Mantell," Al said to Danny Rose. He handed him his envelope.

Danny opened it, counted the bills and put it in his pocket. "True to the end—three bucks. How'd you do?"

Al opened his envelope and saw a ten dollar bill. "The usual five," he said. "I'm going to miss her."

Danny was bussing dishes and cleaning up the tables. Al was doing his goblets. "You ever been up to that place called Harley's?" Al asked.

"You mean the cultural oasis," Danny said. "I've been there

once or twice. Supposed to have free-loving women, but they're highly overrated."

"Yeah," Al said. "What else you know about it?"

"You looking for a woman or something?" Danny said. "I thought you had a girl."

"Well," Al said, "I can always use a spare."

"They're not your type," Danny said. "I mean, it's an arty crowd—writers, advertising guys—you know the type."

"What do they do? I mean outside of what everybody thinks they do?"

"They have lectures and folk dancing and plays—stuff like that," Danny said. "I don't think you'd like it much."

"It's not far from here, is it?" Al asked.

"I'd say it's about a mile," Danny said. "But you're wasting your time, Al. I'm telling you as a friend. You'd be bored stiff."

"They let anybody in? You don't need a ticket or anything."

"Very informal," Danny Rose said. "That's the whole point, they're very informal."

Danny was ready to leave the dining room when Al said, "You wouldn't happen to know what's going on up at Harley's tonight, would you?"

Danny said, "Give them a call. They're usually only too glad to tell you. All for art, you know."

At eleven o'clock that morning, Al Brodie knocked on the door of room fourteen. Marsha Cooper answered, wearing a housecoat and looking bleary-eyed.

Al said, "I'm sorry to bother you, Marsha, but I just heard that Osworth Crewshank the poet is giving a recitation at Harley's tonight. I thought it'd be a hell of an idea for us to go together."

Marsha Cooper looked at him with annoyance. "Is that what you came up here for—to ask me for a date?"

"I guess you'd call it that," Al said. "I thought you'd be interested in it—I mean Crewshank is a poet and it—should be interesting."

"Is this your idea?"

"Of course. Who else?"

She said without very much enthusiasm. "Pick me up here about nine."

It was a wet night. Marsha Cooper was wearing a trench coat and blue sneakers. Al could see her slacks under the coat and her hair was tied up in a kerchief.

Marsha tiptoed out of her room and left the door slightly ajar.

"Let me take a look," Al whispered. He poked his head in the door briefly.

As they were walking down the steps, he said, "You know, I bet you could clear up this night-walking stuff if you'd put him in a youth bed."

"And what's a youth bed?"

"Well, it looks like a regular bed only it's smaller. My cousin Walt has one for his oldest kid. The younger one is in the crib and this youth bed—well, it has sort of bars along the side, they run down about half the length of the bed. It's real good."

"I don't see how," Marsha said. "He can get out of it if he wants to."

"Miriam—that's Walt's wife—she says it gives the kid a sense of security. You know, kids like to sleep in cribs. I mean they don't feel pent in like us."

"Miriam majoring in child psychology, too?"

"Huh? Oh, no," he thought quickly and remembered. "Miriam didn't go to college. Her psychology comes from experience."

"I thought it came from you."

"Is that a dig?"

"Take it any way you like."

They came by the main desk. Mrs. Mandheimer was there talking to some people. She beckoned to Marsha.

Marsha nodded toward her and kept walking.

"I think she wants to talk to you," Al said.

"Marsha, come here a minute," Mrs. Mandheimer called. "You know the Pottses. They knew you when you were a little girl."

Marsha approached the desk with an expression of pained boredom.

Mr. Potts was a graying man with a pipe. "You were going out," he said. "We just wanted to say hello, Marsha."

"Congratulations. I hear you have a wonderful son," Mrs. Potts said. She extended her hand.

"Remember their Solly?" Mrs. Mandheimer said. "You used to go out with Solly."

Marsha said, very tolerantly, "How is Solly?"

"He's a doctor. He's in research. He has two children now," Mrs. Potts said. "They live in Cincinnati."

"That's nice," Marsha said.

"It's wonderful that you're with mother," Mrs. Potts said. "I know I miss my Solly. It's always so much nicer when a family can be together."

"They have to lead their own lives," Mr. Potts said.

"Of course they do, dear," Mrs. Potts said. "And how many times have you said you wished you could be closer to the children?"

"They've got to do what makes them happy," Mrs. Mandheimer said.

"Do you still dance, Marsha?" Mrs. Potts asked. "I remember you were such a fine dancer."

Marsha didn't answer.

"This is one of our waiters," Mrs. Mandheimer said. "You'll be a good boy, Allen, I'll put the Pottses at your station. They're a good tip."

"It'd be a pleasure to wait on them," Al Brodie said. "Tip or no tip."

"A new kind of waiter we're getting now," Mrs. Mandheimer said. "See how the place has changed?"

"It's lovely," Mrs. Potts said. "What do you think of it, Marsha?"

"Marsha doesn't like it," Mrs. Mandheimer said. "You know my Marsha never liked the hotel."

"Let her talk for herself," Mrs. Potts said. "What d'you say, Marsha?"

"Give my regards to Sol," Marsha said. "I think we'd better be going, Al."

Mrs. Potts said it was nice seeing her again and Mr. Potts said she'd grown into a lovely young girl.

Outside the night was muggy and there was a thin trickle of rain. The sky was dark and the ground wet.

"You could write a book on 'How to Give a Brush-off,'" Al said.

"Don't you like it?" she said. "You know you don't have to take me out. We can call it quits right here."

"I rub you, don't I," Al said. "Be honest about it—something about me rubs you the wrong way."

"I don't like phonies," Marsha Cooper said.

"Oh—"

"Don't try looking so damn innocent. Child psychology. Majoring in art. What d'you take people for—fools?"

"O.K., so you got me," Al said. He threw his arms up and slapped them on his sides. "We'll start over again."

"We'd better," she said. "And a good place to start would be with my parents, your ever-loving bosses. Don't start telling me how to treat them."

Al said, "You told me what you think—I'll tell you what I think. If I'm a phony what in the hell are you? You think it's real smart kicking them around, dumping your kid in their laps, killing your reputation, giving them all kinds of hell—What does that prove?"

"Don't you start keeping score for me, Brodie," she said. "That's my business."

"So we're even. You know what I think and I know what you think. We're going up to Harley's. Want to hear what this Osworth character has to say?"

Marsha Cooper smiled, "Boy, is this going to be tough on you. I mean now that you know you can't fake it. I'm going to like this."

"See," Al said, "we're getting along better already. We might even wind up friends."

"'A pleasure to serve you,'" she mimicked. "'Tip or no tip.'"

"What am I going to do?" he said. "I'm a natural phony and you—you're a natural bitch. Come on, we better start walking. On the way up to Harley's I'll tell you all about this child psychology course I took. Chris' knows you need it."

Harley's Salon was located on the top of a big hill. Its buildings were styled along the lines of ranch houses and furnished like a New England inn. The chairs were made of walnut and cherry, and there were large thick tables. There were fireplaces in all the meeting rooms, and old prints and modern paintings on the walls.

Osworth Crewshank was holding forth in the main meeting room, the Bull Session they called it, and there was a plaque over the door that everybody thought was quite funny with a bull on it.

A fire was blazing and the room was sticky, but no one seemed to mind. The place was filled with Harley's guests, young people in their late twenties and early thirties, most of them dressed with fashionable informality. Couples sat on the floor in front of the fire and around the sides of the room. There were a few chairs and benches, and these were occupied by unescorted girls.

The poet stood to one side of the fire. He had a thick face with large lips and small eyes that were hardly visible in the low light of the fire. He was wearing a flannel shirt with a flowered tie, and a tweed jacket that was several sizes too small for him. His hair was crew-cut and his hands, which were large, seemed much larger because the sleeves of his jacket and shirt ended several inches above his wrist.

Al Brodie and Marsha Cooper arrived as Mr. Crewshank was winding up an introductory talk on the background of a series of his shorter poems.

"The most notable tribute of all," the poet was saying, "is that awarded by a legion of publishers, none of whom saw fit to put these verses into print."

For some reason, unaccountable to Al, most of the guests thought that was quite funny.

"So, we have 'Dirge,'" Osworth Crewshank continued. He made a short bow and started to read from a paper he held in his hand. His voice changed as the poetry began. It was much deeper and louder and dramatic:

> "At the seaside of my soul
> The waves wash in a dead gardenia
> Billowing brown, bobbing broadside
> From the wide unawakened hour of my youth.
>
> "In the continent of my soul
> The earth cries up a kiss
> Timid tender, tempestuous torment
> Oh the flower's blood is dead.
> Dead. Dead. Dead, Mother. Dead."

Al looked at Marsha and he saw her leaning forward on her seat, applauding.

"I don't get it," he whispered.

"Ssh, I'll explain later," she said. She put her elbows on her knees and listened.

Osworth Crewshank went on with two more short poems, and then changed to his more philosophic side. He read a long allegory about an alley cat who was the only living creature on earth that knew a great flood was coming. Mr. Crewshank had traveled much, and read many languages. The poem had lengthy descriptions of foreign streets and occasional phrases in other languages. When he finished, the guests at Harley's gave him a standing ovation.

The boy next to Al stretched after he sat down, and Al Brodie saw by his wrist watch that it was ten of eleven.

"Think we better be going," he said to Marsha.

Marsha said, "One minute..."

There was a long silence following Mr. Crewshank's request for questions. Then a dark-haired girl, who was sitting directly in front of the speaker, said, "Do you think there are ample opportunities for serious poets to be published today?"

Mr. Crewshank said he didn't know. He'd been in Europe for the past five years, and although he was well aware of the opportunities abroad, he wasn't up to date on the status of American literary journals and little magazines.

The girl wanted to know if it was easier for a poet in Europe. Mr. Crewshank took his time answering. He defined what he meant by easier and made some general observations on the "intellectual climate" abroad.

Al said, "We better be going. This can keep up all night."

Marsha pulled her raincoat over her shoulders and walked with him to the door. Out in the hall she said, "Before we leave, I'd like to say hello to Frank Harley."

"You mean that's a family name?" Al said.

"A lot of these Catskill hotels use family names," Marsha said. "The Harleys have had this place for years. Frank is an old friend of mine. Come on, we'll probably find him at the bar."

She led him down the hall and through a narrow passageway that led to steps down to the basement. There was a very large lounge room with leather chairs, coffee tables, and another fireplace. Off to the side, along one wall, was a bar. Two men were there. One was wearing a gray flannel suit. He was sitting and drinking. The other, dressed in a plaid sports shirt and khaki pants, was standing.

Marsha said, "See, I told you. That's Frank over there. Same old Frank."

The man in the plaid shirt saw her. He narrowed his eyes, studying her a moment, and then approached smiling and offering his hand. "Marsha! Marsha Mandheimer! Where have you been? It's been years."

"Hasn't it, Frank," Marsha said. "But Harley's hasn't changed, except I see you've put some new furniture in the lounge."

"Over my dead body," Frank Harley said. "And also over my dead body the old man has just put in a stainless-steel kitchen. You say the place hasn't changed? You haven't looked at our mortgage recently."

"How's the book coming, Frank?" Marsha said. "Every time I go in a bookstore I look over the jackets for your picture."

"Stop looking," Frank said. "We're open all year round now. Whenever I get time off, the most creative thing I can do is sleep."

"That's too bad," Marsha said.

"What the hell are we going to do with them?" Frank said, and then, "I hear you ran into some lousy luck. A painter, wasn't he?"

Marsha nodded and her eyes half closed.

"Marsha and I have a pact, you know," Frank Harley said to Al. "We made it years ago, when we were kids having five-hour bull sessions down by the Neversink. We both swore to dedicate ourselves to finding a rich uncle who would buy both hotels."

"I never found him," Marsha said.

Frank laughed. "All the rich uncles are too smart," he said.

"We just dropped in to hear Crewshank. Very good."

"He's schnorring for the week," Frank said. "He used to be good. Frankly, I think this European trip has made him totally incomprehensible."

"Your guests seem to like him," Marsha said.

"We have a jazz pianist—George Choo-Choo Burlington—coming in for the week end. You ought to catch him. If I told you what we're paying him, you'd think we're crazy."

"Marsha, it's getting late," Al said.

"By the way, Frank, I forgot to introduce you. This is Al Brodie, boy psychologist. What a line—he should be selling encyclopedias."

"You think there's bad money in that?" Frank Harley said. "Come on over to the bar. I'll buy you a drink. Make the place look alive."

"No, really, Frank, we have to be going," Marsha said.

"See how bad business is. We can't even give the stuff away," Frank said.

"It's been good seeing you again, Frank. It really has," Marsha said. "Come on down to our place sometime, I'll show you the latest in Miami Beach Renaissance architecture."

"Spare me that, please," Frank Harley said. As they turned to leave, he added, "I didn't hear that line of yours, Brodie. Drop in some night when you're free and we'll have some laughs."

They walked down the hill silently, without touching. Once Al reached for Marsha's hand but she pulled it away, "It's easier alone," she said. She was right. The road from Harley's was narrow and rocky. A car passed and they had to step back behind the tree line to make room for it.

When they were on the road leading to the Sesame, Marsha said, "Well, what did you think of Osworth Crewshank?"

"No good," Al said.

"I thought you didn't understand him."

"Well, not everything. You take that first poem with all that wild stuff about dead mother dead. I bet he thinks that's cute as hell, a real shocker."

"All right, start from the beginning. Tell me what the poem was about."

"Don't start that superior stuff with me."

"Skip it, I thought you wanted to learn."

"Me, learn? Are you kidding. You're the one that should start learning. You and those horny phonies in there getting all worked up over dead mother dead."

"Is that the only thing from the whole recitation that you can remember?"

"Yeah, I think I quit right about there."

"I think you quit before you started."

"That's putting it very well," Al said. "Only you've got the wrong person quitting."

"I didn't know you had such penetrating thoughts," Marsha Cooper said. "Don't tell me you're taking Elements of Philosophy, too?"

"If the poem was so damn good, why didn't somebody publish it?"

"Did you ever hear of a little book called *Ulysses*? Now there's a case where the writer ran into publication trouble. So what does it prove?"

"It proves," said Al, "that the guy isn't playing ball in anybody's league by anybody's rules."

Marsha said, "One more analogy like that and I'll think I'm talking to the Mong."

"Besides," Al said, "the guy doesn't know the first thing about life."

"And you do?"

"You're damn tootin' I do. I know it's here, right here under my foot, and up there, and out there where the hotel is and my station is—and maybe over there where you are too."

"Very simple. Very basic. I'm afraid you'll never make a poet, Brodie."

"Who wants to be a poet? For Chris' sake, dead mother, dead. I mean honest to God, you don't really think that's it, Marsha?"

"I think it expresses a sentiment," Marsha said, "and a situation. How many mothers have you known that crushed a young love affair, destroying something beautiful because it was too young and weak to stand on its own?"

"Is that a question?"

"That's what I think the poem was about. And if you understood, you'd see it had a point."

"If that's all the guy has got to talk about, I feel sorry for him. In the first place, he sure as hell isn't getting his kicks."

"His what?"

"Kicks," Al said, "kicks. Not that I ever thought about it a lot—I mean regarding poets—but you take musicians or actors or guys like my cousin Walt who's studying history in graduate school—if they're not getting their kicks, what the hell are they getting? If you ask me, a guy who gives up making money and raising a family and living like a normal human being to write 'dead, mother dead,' isn't getting his kicks."

Marsha Cooper said. "Brodie, I'll never underestimate your line."

"And you know I'm right," he said. He reached over and put his arm around her.

"You think you talked me onto the floor and now you can pick up my limp body?"

"Who wants your body?" Al Brodie said. "I'm Osworth Crewshank, I want that beautiful seashore of your soul."

"Seaside," Marsha said. "And you can take your hand off because you're not getting either." There was something in her voice that cracked for a moment, and he knew she was enjoying herself.

They walked along quietly until they came to the large neon sign that announced the entrance to the Sesame. Marsha stopped and said, "Well, here you are, Brodie, back in your heaven."

"Oh, yeah, this is such an awful place," he said. "Poor little Marsha, she can't find a rich uncle to give her a million dollars so she can live off the interest. She has to stay here and suffer. You and that Harley pal of yours have got a lot to learn."

"Remind me and we'll enroll in the same class with Crewshank."

"This is really tough to take," he said. "All you got is roast beef twice a week and steak on Sunday, a hundred and ten rooms to choose from, and forty maids, bellhops, and waiters thinking you're a princess or something. And of course the old lady is impossible. She'd just cut her right arm off for you and the left one for your kid. I don't see how you do it, Marsha. All they give you is everything. And if it doesn't sit just right, you can take off. There's always those big fat checks from Mama."

His arm was around her waist when he began, but it wasn't after he'd finished. She threw his hand off and shouted at him, "Shut up. Shut up. Shut up. Do you know what you're talking about? A check from Mama. A check from Mama. That's all there is to life as far as you're concerned. Let me tell you something, Mr. Sharp Guy, Mr. Phony—" She was near tears and Al couldn't understand. There was something there, something deeper that he'd missed, and he was looking for it. "Life isn't just one big check from Mama. You think this is Paradise? Well, to me it's a rotten, dirty, filthy place. It cheated me out of everything. You know how many times my cheeks were pinched, how many thousands of times I heard what a lucky girl I was, how they were doing it all for me? You know what my parents were doing for me? Nothing. When I got the measles, my father's biggest worry was that the guests would find out and all the children would go home and it'd ruin the season. How many times did she sit with me in the children's dining room? Wonderful meals! Three squares a day! All I ever heard day and night for twenty years was the hotel, the hotel—should we build a new casino and how much will it cost. She says yes, he says no. And how about the head counselor, he's got a following but he's such a slob. And the laundry man is robbing us blind and the butcher is cheating us on weight and on and on. Good old Mama and Papa, those poor overworked Mandheimers, killing themselves, dead on their feet and doing it all for me? Well, I think it's ugly and I hate it—I hate it all."

She was crying and she couldn't talk any more. He waited with her on the side of the road under the neon Sesame sign until she stopped. He was quiet until she'd dried her eyes, and then he said very softly, "I think we'd better be getting back."

Both typewriters were working when they returned to the lobby. Mr. Mandheimer was sitting at the typewriter near the switchboard. From the inside office came the sounds of Mrs. Mandheimer doing letters.

They were at the foot of the steps and Mr. Mandheimer looked up at the lobby clock. It was ten after twelve and he smiled. "Have fun, kids?" he called to them.

Al said, "Yes, sir, we had a fine time."

"Marsha, Marsha," Mrs. Mandheimer's voice called from inside the office.

Marsha started up the steps.

"Your mother wants to talk to you," Al said.

"Marsha, Mommy's calling you," Mr. Mandheimer said.

Marsha stopped on the steps. She didn't move, just sighed and waited.

Mrs. Mandheimer came out of the office. She was smiling. "He didn't get up yet tonight, Marsha," she said as she started toward them. "I think he's beginning to feel more at home. Maybe he'll sleep through the night."

"That would be nice," Marsha said.

Mrs. Mandheimer was standing near the steps but Marsha didn't look at her. "Have a nice time?" Mrs. Mandheimer asked Al.

"Fine," Al said. "I think Marsha wants to go up."

"He may need a blanket," Mrs. Mandheimer said. "I notice he didn't have his trundle-bundle on tonight."

"Don't worry about it," Marsha said.

She started up the steps with Al behind her. At her door, Al said, "Maybe we'll go dancing or something tomorrow night. Start getting you your kicks." He squeezed her shoulder.

"I'll think about it," Marsha Cooper said. She went into her room and closed the door.

As he passed through the lobby on his way back to the shack, Al Brodie started to hum. He wanted to make enough noise for Mr. Mandheimer to realize he was leaving. The humming wasn't necessary. Mr. Mandheimer was standing at the desk.

It was late when he got back to his room, but the ceiling light was on, casting a dim yellow reflection. Joe was sitting on the bed. His collar was open and he appeared disheveled. When Al came in he said, "Hi. Through with your date?"

Al said, "Yeah, caught a little poetry up at Harley's. Not even one corny joke."

Joe smiled. "That's not for me."

Al started getting ready for bed. His shirt was off and so were his shoes. Joe said, "What d'you make of this?" He pushed a letter toward Al. It was typed on the letterhead of a wholesale grocer.

DEAR JOSEPH,

    I hope you will read this letter in your confidence. I am Ellie Shafter's father, and as you can see what I am writing herein is strictly between you and me. Ellie has talked with her mother something about wanting to marry a Joseph Miner, whom I believe is you. I do not have to tell you that a thing like this is very upsetting to a mother, especially when she does not know the boy and he is of a different religious faith from Ellie.

    Ellie's mother is very nervous and wants to take the bus right up to the Hotel and take our little girl home but I do not think this is right thing to do and have talked her out of it. That is why I am writing to you man to man. I am older than you and maybe this doesn't all the time mean a person must know better, still I have seen more of life and know that a person has a better chance to be happy if they marry one of their own religious faith. Ellie has never talked this way about marrying any boy before so I think you must have something very different and special on the ball but religious faith has a lot to do with how you live and bring up a family and you have to think about it a very long time before doing a thing like getting married to a person of different religion.

    I am trusting that you have good sense enough not to do anything in a hurry that you will be sorry for later and will only hurt the people who love you. When the summer is over and you are home we can all sit down and get to know each other and talk the whole thing over and do what is best.

    My wife thinks that writing a letter to you can do no good but coming up to the hotel and getting everybody excited and then just hurting and embarrassing Ellie who is very sensitive would be even worse I think. So if you will just wait and not say anything to Ellie about my writing this letter to you because she told her mother she did not want us to interfere as she likes you very much, maybe we can do the thing that is best for everybody.

    Please remember that Ellie is a good Jewish girl with a Jewish upbringing and even if she thinks she can give all this up now because she likes you so much it will hurt her

very much later. Maybe you would like to talk to me and let me know how you feel about this as I am trying to be fair and do what is best for everybody concerned. It would be better if you call me at my store, which is a grocery that I run myself and not the wholesale grocery on this paper who give me the paper because I buy from them. You can call me collect anytime after six as I am there until ten o'clock when I am through for the day.
Waiting to hear from you,
Morris J. Shafter

P.S. The car which Ellie is driving she saved for herself working after school and in the summer because she had to have it.

When Al finished reading the letter he didn't say anything.

Joe said, "Ellie and I, we just want to get married. Hell, we don't want to hurt anybody."

Al looked back at the letter.

"He wants me to call him," Joe said. "I guess I should, but what am I going to say to him? I never even met the guy. What can I tell him?"

Al still didn't say anything and then Joe said, "What would you do? I mean if you were in my place, how would you handle a thing like this, Al?"

"I'd call him," Al said.

"And what would you say?" Joe wanted to know. "I mean I just can't ring him up and start telling him how much I go for Ellie. A thing like that sounds like hell."

"I guess so."

"So what can I say to him then?"

Al said, "Well, he seems all worked up about you running off this summer. You weren't figuring on doing anything like that, were you?"

"Hell, no. I got another year to put in at business school. We plan on going steady and maybe getting engaged next spring. But we want to get married. I mean we talk about it."

"That's what you could tell him. Just explain it to him. He'll understand."

"You think so?"

"Hell, yeah," Al said. "It'll take a little while but this guy will be on your side."

"I wish I could be so sure."

"You'll bust out with a couple of those jokes of yours and they'll think you're their long-lost son."

Joe smiled. "So you really think I should call him?"

"The sooner the better."

"Come to think of it, it does remind me of a story. The one about this Jewish girl who was going to marry this Gentile boy. Well, right away she has to tell her mother and as soon as the mother hears about it, she goes straight to the father. He hits the ceiling, but the mother calms him down. She explains how this is a nice boy, good for their daughter—all that. Then she starts in calling all the aunts and uncles and lines up everything with them. Finally she has to tackle the bubbela—you know, the Jewish grandmother. She explains to the old lady that everybody likes the boy, he fits into the family, they're going to send the kids to Hebrew school, have a bar-mitzvah—the works. Finally the old lady agrees. It's all set and everybody in the family comes to the wedding. At the last minute the bride is in her wedding gown, the band is playing 'Here Comes the Bride,' the mother says to the daughter she's going to take a walk up to the roof. The daughter says, 'The roof? What are you going to do, Mama, pray?' The mother says, 'Pray? Who's going to pray? Everybody is happy you're going to marry this Gentile boy. Me, I'll go up to the roof—I'll jump off.' "

Al laughed and said, "See, so what have you got to lose? Right off you'll get rid of your mother-in-law."

Chapter 19

"Boss," the dishwasher said, "I just can't do this here job alone. Them other boys is drinking. I'm not saying I don't take a drink myself, but when I'm on a job, when I'm working —I do not touch the stuff."

"All right already," the boss said. "So here's your money—go ahead get drunk."

The next day Audrey Grier had to fire Mike Heimer.

One of his guests had given Mike four dollars for two people for a week. They'd given the busboy the same thing and Mike thought they didn't understand. When the man expressed his opinion that "Two dollars a head is enough for a tip," Mike told him about the Sesame being a five-and-three house.

"I never heard of such a thing," the guest said. "Who tells me what to tip?"

"It's the way it works," Mike said.

The man said, "That's too bad."

"You wanted fast service. I gave you specials—this isn't fair," Mike said.

"If you don't want the money, I'll take it," the man said.

Mike Heimer threw the money on the floor and called the man a son of a bitch. He wasn't at all upset when he was fired. He said it was worth it. He would take off right after the evening meal.

While the waiters and busboys were eating at their servers, Audrey announced the firing.

"I don't like to do this," she said, "but we warned you about arguing with the guests." She went on to tell them that Mike's window station was now open and she was giving it to Al Brodie.

It was the first Al heard of it. He felt so good he stole some pineapple juice, put ice in it, and had it with his supper.

"You better tell the people at your station that you're leaving them," Audrey said. "Pick up your tips tonight, because you'll start your new station in the morning."

"Thanks, Audrey," Al said. "Don't think I don't appreciate this."

"You deserved it," she said. "And believe me, Al, it hasn't anything to do with—" She stopped.

He said, "I know, Audrey, this is strictly business."

Al told his people about the change just before he served dessert.

Mr. Erlang bounced the hook of his cane on the table and said, "This is no good. I've just got you broken in. I'll talk to the desk."

Al said, "I wish you wouldn't. It might reflect badly on the boy who's taking my place."

"How can it? I don't even know him yet," Mr. Erlang said.

"You won't say anything, Henry," his wife said. It was the first time Al could remember hearing her address her husband directly. He dropped the subject at once.

Al was putting out desserts and Danny Rose was pouring coffee when Danny said, "There's roughly thirty bucks coming to me from Erlang. You know, he hasn't tipped in six and a half weeks."

"We'll get it," Al said.

"I'd like to bet you," Danny said.

Most of the guests tipped right there. A few promised to see them the next day.

Mr. Erlang was the last one to leave. He lingered a long time over his tea and cigar. All the other tables were bussed when he asked for another cherry tart.

Al brought it to him and after he'd forked a big chunk, Mr. Erlang said, "You know, it's not right to clean up in front of the guests. It makes them feel unwelcome."

Al said, "I guess you're right." He left with a tray of livestock. He was returning it to the pantry when Danny Rose came in.

"Fifteen dollars," Danny said. "That comes to a little more than a dollar a person a week." He was counting the money with disbelief. "I thought it would be bad, but never this bad."

"Did you say anything?"

"I didn't know. I didn't count the money until I was on my way into the kitchen. I didn't say a word to him."

"Don't," Al said. "Leave it to me."

"I was thinking I might mention it," Danny said. "I need the money for books. Another ten makes a lot of difference to me." He paused. "You know he rides you. He might take it a little easier from me."

"Can you cry?" Al said.

"What d'you mean, cry?"

"All right, I'll tell you what you do. You go into the dining room. He's still there, isn't he?"

"Sure, he's waiting for you."

"You don't say a word to him. But you wipe your eyes and blow your nose twice, real hard. Then come right back into the kitchen. Remember now—no matter what, don't say a word."

"That's not for me, Al. I wouldn't give him the satisfaction."

"He's getting the satisfaction right now," Al said. "He's saving himself maybe fifty bucks."

"Look, we're liable to get fired."

"I'm not going to argue with him. Don't worry."

"Forget me. Do it on your own."

"For Chris' sake, Danny. You set up a goddamn play and you let Stan Macht muff it. All I'm asking you is to do the same thing for me. Only this time it's for money and I won't miss."

"What are you talking about?" Danny said.

"The basketball game with Shangri-La. You know damn good and well."

"What's that got to do with it?"

Al jabbed his shoulder. "Stack them up," he said. He held his hands in front of Danny palms down. "Let's get 'em, team."

Danny smiled and said, "You are a crazy guy." He stacked his hands over Al's the way he did on the basketball court, and then went back into the dining room.

Danny came back with a tray full of dirty napkins and leftovers he'd cleaned off the tables.

"I think I made it look real," he said. "He wanted to know if I had something in my eye."

"Good," Al said. "Well, here goes." He started back into the dining room with his silver wrapped in an old tablecloth. He put it on his server and started to shake it dry.

"You're leaving us, tomorrow?" Mr. Erlang called.

"Beg pardon, sir?" Al walked over to the table and bent down. "Is there anything else?"

"I say, you're leaving us tomorrow?"

"Oh, yes sir."

"You did pretty good with this table?"

"I don't know what you mean."

"You got good tips?"

Al made a small sound indicating nothing.

Mr. Erlang leaned far back in his chair. He kept the leg in the bandage stiff. His hands went into his pocket. "This leg, sometimes it kills me," he winced. "It's so bad. I think I'll go up right away and lay down. Some vacation."

"That's a shame," Al said. "Really a shame."

Mr. Erlang's hand lingered in his pocket. He was careful not to take it all out at once.

"It's a bad thing," he said, "to have trouble with your leg on a vacation. No dancing. No ball. No nothing."

He held a small roll of bills in his hand. It was clasped together with a big silver dollar sign. "That's nice, isn't it? Real handy. It's for people with a thin bankroll." He rolled the dollar sign in his hand.

"It's very sporty," Al said.

Mr. Erlang peeled off a few bills. "I like young styles. You're as young as you feel, I always say." He held the money toward Al with his palm down. "Five and a half weeks, right? It would be six weeks this Tuesday." He looked very serious and intent on that point. "Yes, that's right."

Al took the money with a broad smile—his biggest. "Thank you very much," he said. "It was a pleasure having you, Mr. Erlang." He counted the money boldly right in front of Mr. Erlang.

When he finished his expression changed to pain. "Mr. Erlang, I know you're a busy man. I know your leg hurts and all. But this is important. There's something I have to know."

Mr. Erlang was cautious. "What d'you mean, know?"

"I depend upon this job, Mr. Erlang. Without it I don't go to college. It's important that I do it right. What did I do wrong? I want to know. I really do. I want to be a good waiter. I want my guests to be happy with me. There must have been something I did. What was it?"

Mr. Erlang was interested. "You didn't do nothing. You're a good waiter."

"Come on, Mr. Erlang, you're a business man. Let me have it, man to man. You don't tip less than five and three unless there's a reason. A guy like you is a sport. I must have done something wrong."

"Matter of fact—" Mr. Erlang had to think. "I wasn't going to mention it, but—well. Like I said before, cleaning the table off when I'm still eating. That's not right."

"It isn't, Mr. Erlang, and I'm glad you mentioned it."

"I ask you for onion rolls. You remember—when was it, a few days ago? You bring me salt sticks."

"I felt bad about that, Mr. Erlang, but what could I do? We're not even supposed to serve breakfast after ten-thirty. That was ten minutes of eleven."

"I never heard such a rule. Any hotel, you can have breakfast when you want it. On a vacation, a man likes to sleep late. It's such a big deal?"

"I agree with you, Mr. Erlang. I've been raising hell about it."

Al kept the money in front of him; he slapped it against his palm.

Mr. Erlang slid off his chair and stood up. "You're a good waiter. There's nothing wrong with you."

Al dropped his eyes onto the money; he counted it over again. "I wish I knew what it was I did, Mr. Erlang. I really do. If I don't know, I can't keep this from happening again..."

Mr. Erlang opened his mouth, but nothing came out. He pulled his sports jacket up around his collar, bounced his cane on the floor and turned to walk out.

"It must have been pretty bad," Al said. "If you wouldn't even mention it."

Mr. Erlang turned around quickly. He thrust his hand in his pocket and pulled out the roll of bills again. "So how much you expect? You boys think everybody's made of money."

"Whatever you think is fair," Al said.

Mr. Erlang peeled off a twenty. "I never tipped so high in my life."

"Thanks," Al said. "Thank you very much. And, by the way—my busboy, you know, Danny Rose—how was he?"

Mr. Erlang gave him a ten. Before he left he said, "You're looking for a job someday, boy, you come to me. I'll set you up in a branch, and I'll retire."

It came to forty-five dollars for two people for five and a half weeks. Not the best tip of the year. But not bad, not bad considering...

It was nine o'clock when he left the dining room. He was the last boy out, and after he'd turned out the dining-room lights he walked through the lobby entrance. Mr. Mandheimer saw him as he passed the main desk.

"You should know better," he said, and he pointed to the khaki pants and the T shirt. "In the lobby yet."

"It won't happen again," Al said, and he started up the steps to the first floor and room fourteen.

When he knocked on the door, Mrs. Mandheimer came out.

"Oh, gee, I'm sorry. I thought Marsha was in."

"She went out," Mrs. Mandheimer said.

"Think she's down the casino?"

Mrs. Mandheimer shrugged her shoulders. "There's a game by the Tepee, maybe she went."

"With Stan the Mong?"

"Who?"

"You know, Macht, Stan Macht. Did she go with him?"

"You think she tells me?"

"Well, that goes to show you—"

"Did you have an appointment?"

"Sort of," Al smiled and Mrs. Mandheimer involuntarily smiled back. "Don't worry, Mom," Al said. "No Mong is going to beat my time. You just take care of little Phillip. I'll find her."

"It's none of my business," Mrs. Mandheimer said. "She's a grown-up girl. She can go out with whoever fancies her. And don't call me Mom." There was no anger in her voice.

"Be seeing you," Al said.

He went to his room and showered and put on the plaid shirt Roz had given him. On his way out he saw Linda. She was wearing slacks and a light suede jacket and she was holding her copy of *Doctor Zhivago*.

"You're a slow reader," he said.

"At least I read," Linda said.

"Point," Al said. "I'm sorry, it looks like a hell of a good book. I'd like to read it some day."

"You should," Linda said. "It's really in the tradition of the great Russian novels." Her face lit up and she went on to explain how Pasternak studied the effects of the revolution on people at every level of society.

When she'd finished, Al said, "You know there's a lot more to you, Linda, than I guessed. I mean I figured you were just one of these good-looking girls who'd had enough of men and found books more interesting."

It caught her by surprise. Before she had time to analyze it, she was flattered.

"Roz went out with Danny Rose," she blurted out. "In case you'd like to know, they went to that game over at the Tepee."

"Anybody else with them?"

"They're chaperoned. That is if you can call Stanley Macht a chaperone. One of Stanley's guests drove them over. You know Mike Heimer was fired. He took his car into Monticello to check at the agency for another job."

"That's all?"

"I don't know. Maybe some of the other players went with them too." She realized she'd talked too much. "If you're so interested in Rosalyn, you could go to the game yourself and find out."

"No," Al said, "I'll just wander over to the casino and see what's cooking."

"Jerry is running a champagne hour," Linda said.

"Oh, is he?"

"What do you mean by that?"

"Nothing," Al said. "If he's running a champagne hour I'm going over. I think he's a hell of an entertainer."

"I never thought about it," Linda said.

He started toward the door and she stayed with him. "I have a hunch about Jerry Furman," he went on, baiting her. "I think underneath that gay front, he's a very intelligent guy. A lot of people around here don't understand Jerry. They think he's just a clown, but I'll bet if you really got to know him—" He stopped and said. "Want to walk me down? Maybe we'll even dance."

"I don't like formal dancing," Linda said. "What were you saying about Jerry Furman? It's very interesting—psychologically speaking. I mean simply from a clinical standpoint."

"Just that he's a very deep person," Al said.

"Really?" Linda said. "You surprised me. I didn't know you were so interested in people—I mean analyzing them. What you said—it's a very accurate observation. Theoretically a person who is a comedian—or a clown as you called it—can have a very real emotional problem when their private personality is so different from the one they display publicly. They can develop very deep inhibitions." She stopped suddenly. "I hope I'm not boring you. It's just that you did mention it. I thought you might be interested."

"People are a hobby of mine," Al said. "What were you saying about this emotional guy, this comedian?"

"This is theoretical, of course," Linda said. "But discussions like this are good practice. I mean if you are really concerned about people's emotional problems, if you want to help them. Sometimes the very people who are closest to those with problems ignore them—they don't have the slightest idea what it's all about. I don't sympathize with that. I have no patience with people who won't face up to the emotional needs of their friends or family or even their husbands."

"There's nothing worse," he said, "than a misunderstood husband."

Linda was walking slowly. She looked away from Al and spoke determinedly. "A person who can create comedy," she said, "is more than just normally sensitive. The reason why we hear so much about the misunderstood husband is because it's a problem that's so much with us. Some women just don't understand that it takes a little more love, a little more understanding when you're married to a man like that."

"A girl who is really interested in people would be just right for a guy like that," Al said.

Linda didn't seem to hear him and went on. "A woman has to be capable of giving a really great love, a selfless love to help him—I mean to help this type of man we're analyzing."

"You have that type down cold," he said. "You're really great on this psychology."

"Well, I'm interested in it," she said. "I think a woman's psychological adjustment to a man is as important as the physical. As a matter of fact I don't believe the physical is even tolerable unless two people really understand each other—I mean their deep emotional needs."

"You take this married man—this guy we were just talking about—theoretically. Now most people wouldn't take it the way you and I do, Linda. We just got to face it—most people they're just not so concerned about mental health. They'd figure the guy was just getting what he could and the girl—well, you know how people talk about a girl who messes around with a married man."

She said, "Gossips don't interest me in the least. I never concern myself with what gossips think. You can certainly discuss people—types I mean—without gossiping."

"Absolutely," Al said. "I'm all for the scientific approach."

Linda wasn't quite satisfied with that. She started to ask him to explain further but they were already at the casino and they couldn't talk without being overheard.

The casino was crowded. Most of the people were sitting in the long lines of seats in front of the stage and watching a professional dance team entertain. From time to time the dancers would bring guests onto the stage who would pair off so that the team could teach them new steps. The bottle of champagne was in a bucket on a small table to the side of the stage. It was to be awarded to the amateur couple that the other guests thought was the best team of the evening.

There were four people sitting at the bar. Three of the hotel's employees were at one end. Marsha Cooper, on a seat at the farthest end of the bar and hunched over a glass, was the fourth.

Al saw her as soon as he walked in. Linda was still trying to pick up their conversation. "Excuse me a minute," Al said, "I see somebody I know." As he turned to leave he said, "No doubt about it, Jerry Furman is an interesting type—I wouldn't be at all surprised if he's deep enough to go crazy for a book like this." He slapped her copy of *Zhivago*. "Be seeing you, Linda, and by the way, you don't tell anybody my secrets and I won't tell them yours."

He walked directly over to Marsha Cooper. Linda was stunned. She looked toward the stage. The dance team had taken an intermission and Jerry Furman was singing that old favorite, "It Had to Be You." She wondered how Al Brodie had found out.

T. J. Boone opened a bottle of beer and filled a glass when he saw Al coming. "Where you been, sweetheart? I was beginning to worry that I'd be stuck with all these cases of beer."

"I've been working hard," Al said. He slid his glass and bottle down the bar and sat down right next to Marsha.

T. J. said, "You two know each other? Marsh, you got to meet this guy. He's the best thing ever happened to this place."

"He means I'm the only waiter who's run up a bill," Al said.

"Cut it," T. J. said, very hurt. "Your bill means nothing to me. What's a few dollars more or less? Say that again, I'll tear it up."

"What was it I said—?" Al tried to remember. "Oh, yes, he means I'm the only waiter who's run up a bill. Give me the little pieces."

T. J. thought that was hysterical. "I should have known you ten years ago. I'd of gotten you a spot writing material for Benny. A guy like you should make no less than two big ones a week."

"How's the lumbago?" Al asked.

"Rheumatism," T. J. said. "It's killing me, kid. I get a call just yesterday. Georgie Foxie. You heard of him of course. One of your top agents. Does all the biggest joints. They're opening up a place in Vegas—the most tremendous thing yet. Fabulous. He wants me to do a single. Three a week. They throw money away out there. An entertainer is God. What the hell, they can pay. 'Tween you and me"—he leaned over the bar and whispered—"they take it all back from the suckers at the craps table."

"See, Marsha," Al said. "Here's a guy who would rather work here at the Sesame where he's happy than make a million dollars in Las Vegas."

"Well, I mean I got this back," T. J. said. He rubbed it. "Giving me hell this week. I think it's all this goddamn rain."

One of the men at the other end of the bar wanted a refill and T. J. said, "Back in a minute, sweetheart," and hurried down the bar.

"How are you?" Al said to Marsha.

She didn't answer.

"I thought we had a date."

Still nothing.

"Why don't you shut up?" he said. "You're giving me a headache."

That made her smile. "I think you're turning into a professional bringer-outer of people. I have a suspicion—there's a movement under way to elect a new president of the Sesame. Nobody knows about it but you, so you're cornering all the votes. You'll win unanimously—even Mr. and Mrs. Mandheimer."

"Not unanimously," he said. "I wouldn't get your vote."

"And now comes the line about that vote being the only one you *really* want."

"No." He drained his glass and refilled it with what was left in the bottle. "I don't think I'd care if I got your vote or not, if I won anyway."

"Very honest. You're changing."

"You're just looking."

She shuffled her glass on the bar and said, "Do you think you could persuade your good friend and agent to get me another Scotch?"

Al called to T. J. and the bartender came quickly. "You saved me," T. J. said. "Sometimes I think I can't stand another one of these guys. You know, I try to chase them out of here. After all, it does me no good or the house no good having them get drunk all the time. Some concession men don't give a damn. I'm strictly a house man. What the hell am I going to do?" He poured Marsha's Scotch. She took a five-dollar bill out of her purse but T. J. pushed it back. "Never. Never. This one is on the house." After he'd put the bottle of Scotch back on the shelf, he said, "You know, you could do me a hell of a favor if you'd just tell your folks what I'm up against. They never come down here. They don't know."

"I'm paying for her drink," Al said. "Put it on my bill and I insist." There was something in his voice that made T. J. Boone look uneasy.

He said, "Yeah, sure." And when Al said, "Mark it down now," T. J. went to get his pad.

Marsha turned around in her chair and looked at him. "Tell me something about yourself, Brodie," she said. "Start with why you want to go to college." Before he said anything, she said, "And you can drop all that stuff about what you've already studied. I know this is your first year."

"Is it that obvious?"

"No, it wouldn't be obvious at all, except that every time you feel a little unsure, you start that business about the course you're taking. Only a guy who'd never been in a college classroom in his life could think the courses were all that good."

"I'll have to remember that," he said. "You know, you're pretty sharp."

She fluttered her eyes and forced him back to the point. "Come on now, the truth—why are you going to college?"

He ordered another beer from T. J., and after he'd drained off the top of the glass, he said, "I tried it the other way a couple of years. It doesn't work."

"Doing what?"

"Hacking, selling insurance, working as a stock boy in the garment district—all kinds of jobs where you can work your way up. That is, if you're going to live to two hundred and five and everybody else dies first. Or you happen to be standing on the goal line and the boss runs out of wind and throws you the ball."

"Which is your way of saying luck."

"Sure, luck," Al Brodie said. "I don't like to play it counting on luck. I had to kick around awhile to find that out. What I need is something to give me a foot in the door. Something like accounting, so I could walk into a business and right away find out what makes it tick."

Marsha Cooper said, "You've got it all figured. First you'd be the accountant, then the treasurer. If the place is big enough you can wind up comptroller and then president. It can't fail, can it, Brodie? You've got to go right to the top."

"Maybe," Al said. "I'd like to find out."

"And what if you don't make it?" Marsha said. "Have you ever thought about that? Suppose you just climb up that first rung and the ladder stops right there?"

"I might not mind it too much," Al said. "If I liked what I was doing."

"I don't believe you," she said.

"You just don't know me."

Marsha looked at him, and when he didn't look away she turned back to her glass. Slowly she said, "If you don't want to be rich, what do you want?"

"If I have a good job or a spot with some possibilities, all I'd need is enough dough to live right and raise a family," Al said. "That's another thing—you don't have to believe me, but I love kids."

She said, "I believe that." She was quiet again, then she said. "A job, a house, and a family—that's all? That's everything?"

"Now you got it," Al said. "But the trick is to make sure they're right."

"And how are you going to do that?" Marsha Cooper said.

"Easy," Al said. "I'll just take them one at a time and work at it."

Marsha said, "How can you say easy? You can study accounting and get a job. Save your money and buy a house. But when you talk about a family, that's people. How can you be so sure of people? How about Mrs. Al Brodie? Suppose she doesn't go along with all this?"

He smiled at her and sipped his drink. "Mrs. Al Brodie? Now why would she give me any trouble? If there's one person in this world I'll be able to count on, it's Mrs. Al Brodie."

"And what makes you so sure of that?"

"Because she can count on me," Al said. "One hundred per cent, all the way. She's Mrs. Al Brodie, isn't she? Now why would I marry her if it wasn't going to be just like that?"

Marsha Cooper turned back to her drink. She made a small sound in her throat and then she lifted her drink. "Here's to Mrs. Al Brodie," she said, "the job, the house, and all your sitting ducks."

He held her hand before the glass touched her lips. "Stop making wisecracks," he said. "I don't tell everybody what I just told you. If you weren't interested, I wouldn't have told you."

"What makes you so sure I was interested and wasn't just pulling your leg?" Marsha Cooper said.

"I know those things," he said. "I might not have hit college yet, but I know those kinds of things for sure."

"I envy you," Marsha Cooper said. "It must be wonderful to have life all boiled down and be so damn sure of everything."

"Don't kid yourself. There's a lot I can't figure." He let her finish her drink and then he said, "Like you, and that husband of yours. What kind of guy was he? Tell me about him."

Marsha pushed her chair away from the bar. She slid her feet onto the floor. "I don't want to talk about it. It's none of your business."

"You want to know what I think he was?" Al Brodie said, "Would you like for me to tell you how I see him?"

She lifted her feet and edged back onto the chair. Finally, she plumped her hands onto the bar and picked up her glass. "That's a very neat little trick, and the hell of it is—it almost works."

He ordered another drink for her and another for himself, and after he'd shaken off T. J. Boone he said, "You know, of course, that this is all wrong. Why make me make an ass of myself? Why don't you just go ahead and tell me?"

She sat quietly rolling her glass between the palms of her hands.

"You're going to have to tell somebody, sometime," he said. "You'll never be able to pick yourself up until you do."

"Here comes the psych major again," she said.

"Well, it's true, isn't it?"

"Maybe," Marsha Cooper said. "But that doesn't mean I have to tell you."

"Why not? You got a better audience? Besides," he said, "it happens I'm really interested."

"You mean curious," she said. "Lonesome widow spills guts to phony bar fly."

"Something like that."

"Oh, what good would it do?" she said bitterly. "You're no different from the rest. You'd never understand."

"Try me."

She looked at him a long time, and then she said, "O.K.,

O.K. Anyway, the first part's right up your alley. I met Larry my first semester at Barnard—on a subway platform. I guess you'd say he picked me up."

She stopped, waiting for a wisecrack, but Al said, "Go on."

"He was doing a picture of Andromache's farewell to Hector. Do you know the story? Do you know it at all?" Marsha asked him suddenly. Before he could answer, she said, "It's the whole story of war told in a woman's farewell to a husband she knows she'll never see again." She explained that it was right after the war and she thought Lawrence Cooper had a sense of guilt because he'd been 4-F. That's what she believed inspired the picture. It was called 'This Might of Thine Destroys Thee,' which were Andromache's first words to Hector."

She had lost her self-consciousness, now that she had started, but it was as if she were talking to herself. She did not seem to be aware of Al at all.

"Larry was the only boy I ever knew who really loved the classics. As a matter of fact, his very first words to me there in the subway were, 'You are my Andromache.' If it had been anyone else, I would have called a cop."

Her voice became very low then as she told how she had agreed to model for the picture. After the second session Cooper had asked her to live with him. "I would have," she said, "but I knew my parents. Without some papers from the justice of the peace, we'd never have been safe. Three weeks after we met, we got our license, but we really didn't need it. We were married the first second I saw him."

Marsha stopped and Al said matter-of-factly, "How'd you wind up in Arizona?"

She said, "That was Larry—he couldn't live in one place too long. He said it gave him the feeling he was in jail. Larry was totally dedicated to his painting. He lived wherever he thought was best for his work. He didn't care if he never made any money at all. I admired him for that. Coming from a place like this where making money is all anybody ever thinks of, I didn't know there could be a man in this world like Larry."

Al said, "He doesn't sound like a guy it'd be too easy to live with."

"Don't feel sorry for me," Marsha said. "I knew just what it would be like when I married him. I knew he wouldn't be a husband or a father in the usual sense of the word—but it didn't make any difference. He gave me something that meant a lot more. For the first time in my life, I felt a part of something that might be important someday. I was Lawrence Cooper's wife and he was an artist. We weren't just living to make a few more dollars and build a couple more rooms. I had a purpose. I was helping Larry create pictures, things that might someday bring people great pleasure. I got away from this. Larry saved me," she said. "I could never pay him back enough for that."

Al said, "That explains why you wanted to get away from here. But why did you marry him? Was that enough, just beating it away from the hotel?"

"I told you you'd never understand," she said. "He was the first man who'd ever cared for me, who didn't even know about them, about this place. When I described it he just laughed. Who have I ever met like that? He wasn't less successful than them. He wasn't even competing. I was proud of that—damn proud."

Al said, "All right, but what the hell, your mother was sending you money, wasn't she?"

Marsha Cooper said, "If you must know, Brodie, the first time I received a check from her I tore it up and sent the pieces right back. Who wanted her lousy money?"

"But you cashed the checks after that, didn't you?" Al said. "That's where you got the money to live on. If it wasn't for your mother's checks—how would you have lived?"

"Larry wasn't afraid to work," Marsha said belligerently. "When I met him he was working nights in a bookstore and days on his painting. He worked harder than anybody I've ever known. He was always working."

Al said, "O.K., don't get excited."

"I just don't like that superior tone in your voice when you talk about making a living, as if that's the only thing in the world that makes a man a man."

"I didn't say that."

"But you think it. As a matter of fact, it was work that—that killed him. It was very hard after Phillip came. It took all our money for the diapers and the bottles and the formula and the hundred and one other things a baby needs. But Larry never said a word. He didn't complain because I neglected him. He just threw himself into his work all the harder. I was so busy with the baby, I couldn't help him when he fell sick. Larry never knew how to take care of himself."

"What did he die from?" Al asked.

"The doctor told me it was a respiratory infection—pneumonia. It could have been avoided if we caught it in time. If I'd taken him to a doctor—I heard him coughing, I knew he was sick, but I also knew he hated doctors, wouldn't go by himself—" Her voice rose, and Al could see T. J. and the men at the end of the bar looking toward them.

"Come on," he said, "I think it's about time you were getting home. You've had a rough night."

As they left the casino, a car pulled up and Al saw Danny Rose and Roz and Stan Macht get out. There was no way he could avoid their seeing him.

Marsha and Al were standing in front of the door to her room. From inside they could hear the voice of Mrs. Mandheimer.

"Tendala, tendala, tendala," Mrs. Mandheimer was singing.

They both listened for a few seconds and then Al said, "What's going on in there?"

"She takes one finger at a time and says 'tendala.' When she comes to the last finger she tickles the baby," Marsha said. "That's all there is to it. She tells me she played it with me—"

They heard Phillip shriek and then laugh.

"Your son seems to like it," Al said.

"He likes anything with enough repetition," Marsha said.

They could hear Mrs. Mandheimer beginning the game again.

"That'll go on all night," Marsha said to Al. "I'd better go in."

"Why bust up their fun?" he said.

She said, "Thanks, Al—for tonight, I mean. I'm not so sure you understood, but you helped."

He could hear Mrs. Mandheimer reciting "Tendala" again. The baby was repeating the words and he could hear the grandmother laughing. There were lots of things he wanted to tell Marsha, but she was soft for a moment and her defenses were down and he didn't want to fight. Very gently and slowly he took her into his arms and kissed her.

Chapter 20

At the hotel supply store in Liberty, two hotelmen were in the basement searching through the stock. There were three more on the first floor waiting for duplicate keys. On the second floor a group fought to get to the salesman for electrical supplies. In the furnishings department a chauffeur was on his hands and knees measuring a bath mat.

The glassware salesman was saying, "We'd love to give you what you want, but we just haven't got your china in stock."

"So what'll I use for cups?" the hotelman said. "Two hundred cups for two hundred sixty-three people and he tells me he doesn't have stock."

"This is very nice," the salesman said. "It's a heavy duty china in a very neutral shade."

The hotelman said, "I spend forty thousand dollars on my lobby, I have to have a thirty-five cent cup it can't match the saucer."

"Take the saucers too," the salesman said.

"Between my wife and what she buys by auctions, and you and your neutral cups, my dining room looks like a regular schlock house."

"With all you're giving them to eat, who has time to look at the china?" the salesman said and he started to write the order.

Mike Heimer left his station in a mess.

The sugar bowls were black along the edges and the silverware was tarnished. It wasn't deliberate; it was the accumulation of weeks of neglect. One part of the double burner which he used to keep his coffee hot wasn't working, and there was a thin cake of dirt on the bottom of the mat by his server.

Right after breakfast, Al Brodie went to work. He went over all the silver and polished the bowls and scrubbed his mat. He took a damp sponge and went over the server, getting it spotless.

By twelve o'clock, when the other boys were coming in for lunch, he was tired and dirty. He skipped eating and went up to his room to wash and change his shirt. At a quarter of one, fifteen minutes before the main dining room opened, he reported. He noticed immediately that some of his silver bowls were still dirty and there were knives and forks at his settings that hadn't been there when he left.

After he'd served lunch, he went back to work on the dirty silver. His shirt was off and he was sitting at his server working over a tarnished sugar bowl, when Stan Macht dropped by his station. Macht's station was set up for dinner and he was ready to leave. He elbowed Al's shoulder as he started to talk.

"You know we played over at the Tepee last night."

"I'll read about it in the New York *Times*."

"Don't be so damn wise," Macht said. "We dropped her by one lousy point. Mike was there, we would have won."

"That's too bad," Al said with a tone of boredom. "I got my own troubles. Some idiot has been switching silver bowls and dumping his dirty settings on me."

Stan Macht said, "Don't go popping off unless you got proof."

"Just don't do it again," Al said.

"Do what? Where the hell do you come off accusing me?"

"Stick to basketball, Mong. You're a lousy actor. Just don't mess with my station."

"Don't you mess with my girl," Macht said.

"Don't kid yourself, you never had a girl."

"Look, you wise little bastard, I got more off Marsha in one night than you'll get in ten years," Macht said. "And I'm warning you right now, don't move in."

"You're a little late," Brodie said. He was still shining the silver and he didn't look up.

"Her old lady queered it with that damn announcement the other night," Macht said. "It wasn't for that, you wouldn't have a chance."

"All right, Mong, shut up," Al put his silver down and stood up. "And let's get two things straight: One—I'm not interested in your thoughts about Marsha Cooper. That's over, so forget her. Two—lay off my station. Just lay off. Is that clear enough or should I draw you a diagram?"

"You really think you got this place wrapped up," the Mong said. "A window station and the boss's daughter. Have fun, wise guy, 'cause you ain't goin' to have either one of them much longer." He bounced his fist off Al's chest. "And don't talk tough to me. I don't bluff easy."

Al said, "See you around, Mong. Sometime when I'm not so busy." He turned back to his server and his sugar bowls.

"Any time," Stan Macht said. "Any time you want to talk it over in back of the kitchen. I mean man to man, real friendly."

"You see too many movies," Al said, "old ones."

Stan Macht went out and Al finished setting up. He had everything in good shape when he left the kitchen. He started toward his room to rest and change and maybe take a swim, but when he was halfway there he decided suddenly that he wanted to see Marsha. It was a humid afternoon with no sun. There were few people at the pool, so he tried the day camp first.

Roz was at one end of the playground with a group of older children, ranging in age from seven to ten. They were playing snatch-the-bacon. She was in the middle calling out numbers, and when she saw Al she waved. He knew she was getting ready to find Ellie or Linda to take her place so she could talk to him.

There were five other children around Phillip's age. They

were all sitting in the sandbox, digging. Marsha was off to the side with Phillip. He was pulling grass and piling it to make a house. Al went directly to them.

"Hot day," he said. "But no sun."

"Did you read the papers?" Marsha said. "There's a hurricane on the way."

"No kidding?"

"That's what they say."

"See house. See house," Phillip said.

"Pretty good," Al said. He looked at Phillip's small pile of grass and then back to Marsha.

Her face looked clearer than he'd ever seen it before. She wore no make-up and there was a new brightness about her eyes. She was wearing a sleeveless blouse and he could see the strap from her bra or her slip edging out from beneath it. He realized suddenly what a strong, straight body she had. The story she'd told him the night before, and the baby, Phillip, didn't seem as though they could possibly be a part of her. She seemed too young and fresh and unknowing.

"You look good today," he said.

She looked at him directly and her eyes seemed very liquid. "Really," she said. "I can't imagine why."

He said, "You know, you're beginning to get me."

"Where's door?" Phillip said. "Where's door to my house?" It was very important to him and there was anxiety in his voice.

Al bent down and poked a finger into one side of the pile of grass. "It's over here," he said. "Here's your door."

"That's my door?" Phillip said, somewhat relieved. "That's my door. See, Mommy, see my door...."

"I see it, darling," she said. "Very nice." She pulled some grass and put it on top of Phillip's pile. "So I'm beginning to get you," she said to Al. "I wonder why."

"I'm not sure I can figure it yet myself," he said.

"It may be nothing," she said. "Sometimes things happen like that."

"Yeah," he said and he pulled up some grass.

"I enjoyed talking to you last night," she said. "I thought about it today."

"I'm not such a bad guy, huh? Even if I am a phony with a line."

"You're improving," she said.

"Damn it, Marsha, let's take a walk."

"See door," Phillip said. "House got a door," he squealed.

Marsha reached out for some more grass for Phillip's house and Al put his hand on hers. He squeezed her hand lightly.

"You're not very tactful," she said, "but you come through."

"How about tonight? About nine, O.K.?"

"O.K.," Marsha said.

"You know, he should be playing in the sandbox with the other kids," Al said. He changed his expression and his tone and he concentrated on Phillip. "What d'you say, Phillip, want to build a house in the sandbox?"

"I try to keep him away," she said. "It's so frustrating for a child to keep making friends and then they go home. By the time I was ten, I'd given up."

"The sandbox will still be here, though," Al said. "Want to build a house in the sand?" he asked Phillip again.

Phillip stood up. He picked up two handfuls of grass and said, "Build house in sand. I have to build house in sand. I have to."

"See," Al said to Marsha. "It's an emergency."

Al was in the sandbox with Phillip and the five other children. He'd built a mound of sand five inches high with several tunnels and grass piled on top. It wasn't entirely peaceful. One of the little boys who was Phillip's age kept knocking down the top of the house, Phillip would fight to stop him and then try to do the same thing himself. Marsha was sitting on the edge of the box, smoking and watching.

Rosalyn Silvers came over. She was wearing tight shorts and a blouse that revealed too much of her bosom. She'd just put on a cardigan sweater and it was obvious she was trying to hide herself.

"Time for milk and cookies," she said very formally. She saw Al in the sandbox and she looked everywhere to avoid staring at him. "Come on, children. It's time for milk. Let's make a snake line. Who wants to make a snake line?"

None of the children responded. They were too busy throwing sand.

"You shouldn't do that. You know better than that, Roy," Roz said. "You too, Nancy. I'm surprised at you."

"I've turned them all into delinquents," Al said. Just then Phillip let fly a little sand at him.

"Phillip, you mustn't do that." Rosalyn said. She looked at Marsha. "It's the first time I've seen him do that. He's usually not so difficult."

"I'm glad to see it," Marsha said. "Sometimes I think he's a little too shy."

"I don't think so," Roz said. "When you work with a lot of children like I do, you learn that there's nothing wrong with the ones who have good manners."

Al got up and tried to brush himself off. Phillip grabbed his leg and hugged him.

"Where you going?" Phillip said. "Where you going? I want you."

"To get some milk," Al said, and he bent down to pick him up.

"I wouldn't do that," Roz said. "It's not fair to carry one unless you can carry them all."

"O.K.," Al said. "You're the counselor." But he carried Phillip to the steps of the camp house anyway before he put him down.

Ellie was pouring the milk and Uncle Charlie, the head counselor, was dispensing the cookies. He had a mouthful when Marsha, Roz, and Al came in with the children, and he said directly to Marsha, "We have a very good baker this year. You know that?"

Ellie said, "I thought you wanted to go off, Roz. I'll handle the milk today."

"It's all right," Roz said. She was busy taking a sweater off one little boy. She seemed to find no end of things that had to be done. "I'll stay."

Marsha sat Phillip up at a table and he immediately screamed for cookies. Uncle Charlie said, "Only one. Only one for each child." He held up a big chocolate-chip cookie and handed it toward Phillip. "See the big cookie. Want this cookie, Phillip?"

"Two cookies," Phillip said. "I want two cookies." His eyes watered and he began to cry.

"Here, two cookies," the head counselor said and he broke the cookie in half. Phillip thought that was very funny and he laughed. He ate the cookie but wouldn't touch the milk.

Al took a cup of milk and a cookie himself. Roz offered one to Marsha Cooper, but Marsha said she didn't care for any. She sat with Phillip until he'd finished and then got up to leave. She explained that Phillip had skipped his nap and she thought it would be better for him to rest up before his bath and dinner.

Al started to walk her to the door and Roz came up behind him. She tried to be casual but her voice cracked. "Could I see you a minute, Al? I'd like to talk to you a minute."

Al was annoyed, and she could see it.

"If you'd rather not—" she said sharply.

"Go ahead, Al," Marsha said. "I can handle Phillip by myself." Her son wrenched away from her and she had to struggle to pick him up. "See you later," she said and she started out the door.

Al called after her, "I'll just be a minute. Wait for me." When the door closed, he said to Roz. "All right. What is it?"

There was the sound of the children screaming in the background and Uncle Charlie's commanding voice directing them to organize a circle for farmer-in-the-dell.

"Couldn't we go somewhere?" She was begging. Then, very bitter: "If you'd rather not, go ahead. I don't want to stop you."

"Let's get it over with," Al said. "Come on, we'll go up to the room."

When they were a few steps out of the door, she said very sweetly, "I didn't know you were so fond of children. I never saw you in the day camp before."

"Don't be so damn smart," Al Brodie said.

They didn't talk again until they were in front of the cabin and then Roz said, "Al, what happened? What's happened to us?"

He said, "What do you mean, what happened?"

"Let's not fool ourselves," she said. "We're not the same any more."

He said, "Let's have it. You tell me how we were. Tell me what's changed and what's different."

Rosalyn fidgeted nervously and he noticed again that she had beautiful legs. "We'd better go inside," she said. "My room. I've got to get this off my mind."

"Are you sure you want to be alone with me in your room?" he said. "That's not what's on your mind, is it?"

His words cut her and her mouth hung open for a second. All the desirability he'd seen in her body was gone and he didn't care if she was waiting for him any more or not. "Whatever you've got to say," he said, "tell me now, right here. Once we get inside, let's face it—it's bodies again."

"You're the crudest person I've ever known in my life," she said. Her voice choked and he knew she was ready to cry.

There wasn't any other way. "If I'm crude," he said, "what the hell—that's the way it's been with us from the beginning. What are you kidding yourself for, Rosalyn? That's all there ever was between us."

Her tears weren't uncontrolled like the first night he'd had her. She cried evenly with the wetness streaking down her face, and her voice was hoarse but soft and clear. "How can you say that? Do you think I would have ever if I didn't love you? I never did before. You were the first. Doesn't that mean anything to you? Oh, Al—Al—" She couldn't hate him for long and she came to him and tried to put her head on his chest. He caught her by the shoulders and held her gently away from him.

"We could be happy, Al. I know it. We want the same things. We're the same kind of people. I could make you happy. I love you. I can't help it. I love you." She whimpered and she shook her head, and he had to lift her head up by the chin to face him.

He spoke slowly so that she could catch every word. "There's nothing there, Roz. Nothing. It'd be great in bed. That's all. That's all we've had from the beginning and that's all we'd ever have. Maybe we want the same thing but we don't run the same way. You're running scared with those button-down shirts and worried about what people think. We've got nothing to say to each other, Roz, nothing—"

"You haven't given me a chance," she said. "I was too easy. It's my fault. If I hadn't—if I hadn't—" she couldn't make herself say the words. She pressed her head toward the hand that held her shoulder. She wanted to rub her face against him. "Don't let me go, Al. Don't throw me away. I'm right for you. I know I am."

He couldn't reason with her and he knew it. And yet, he felt a desperate need to get rid of her and decisively. When he spoke his voice was soft but his hand on her shoulder tightened, pinching the flesh of her arm. "The only way it can be," he said, "is like this—bodies, that's all. That's all you have to give me. All I'll ever want from you."

"Oh—my God," she said. "My God." She struggled loose from his arms and ran the few feet toward the cabin. When she was at the door, she turned around and shouted at him. "I hate you. I hate you. You lie and you deceive and you make a fool of people. And you don't care about anybody but yourself." The words ran together and finally she turned away from him again. He heard her saying, "How could I ever—" And he knew she meant it.

Chapter 21

The publication was called Summer Homes. *It was issued by the Ontario and Western Railway for the period 1893-1897.*

Monticello is 1500 feet above the ocean with an atmosphere pure and bracing, an air peculiarly favorable to asthmatics and persons afflicted with kindred diseases. The transportation fare is $3.08 for 128 miles.

Heat never interferes with sleep and neither dampness nor fog makes evenings or mornings disagreeable. Favorite retreats near the village are Pleasant Lake [Kiamesha], Katrina Falls, Edwards Island in the Neversink, Strange's Grove. There is unsurpassed fishing and an abundance of partridge.

He finished his setting-up quickly after dinner. It was eight-thirty when he was back in the lobby, showered, dressed, and waiting for nine o'clock when he could knock on Marsha's door.

Mrs. Leiderkopf was in the lobby and Calvin was tuning in the T.V. set for her. She wanted to see "Name That Tune." It was a rerun, but that didn't seem to matter to her.

Calvin managed to get a fair picture just as the orchestra stopped playing and a contestant identified the music. Mrs. Leiderkopf was delighted. She gave Calvin fifty cents and a plastic cigar holder which she pulled out of her shopping bag.

Mr. Erlang came in just as the music was starting again. He made great ceremony of limping on his cane and sprawling out on the love seat in front of the set, blocking Mrs. Leiderkopf's view. Calvin moved Mrs. Leiderkopf's seat for her. But Mr. Erlang said, "Quick, Calvin, get me the game."

"No game tonight. Raining in New York. That's what I hear," Calvin said.

"Quiet. I'll hear maybe the answers," Mrs. Leiderkopf said.

Mr. Erlang said, "Those things are put on. Staged. You don't read the papers?"

"So who cares?" Mrs. Leiderkopf said. "Quiet. I'll hear maybe he wins the money."

"Sure there's no game?" Mr. Erlang asked Calvin. "The Yanks are playing the Sox. Maybe there's no game, there's a fight."

A contestant failed to identify the music and Mrs. Leiderkopf said, "Such a shame. I thought maybe he'd win. Five children he has and such a young man. The money, he could use."

"How much they playing for?" Mr. Erlang wanted to know.

"You were quiet, I could hear," Mrs. Leiderkopf said.

Calvin was emptying ashtrays. He had the plastic cigar holder in his mouth and Mr. Erlang noticed it. "They give those away maybe? Mandheimer gives souvenirs?"

"Sir?" Calvin said.

"The cigar holder. You got another one?"

"No, sir," Calvin said.

Mrs. Leiderkopf struggled out of her chair and moved to a seat directly to the side of the set.

"We're talking, you can't hear," Mr. Erlang said. "That's the trouble today. Everybody is so busy watching television, nobody talks any more."

"That trouble you'll never have," Mrs. Leiderkopf said.

"So where did you get the cigar holder?" Mr. Erlang asked Calvin.

Calvin laughed and shook his head, "Yes, sir. People, they don't talk no more. They either watching them quiz shows or them gelt shows."

Mr. Erlang pulled out a cigar and unwrapped it. He smiled

and said to Mrs. Leiderkopf, "He puts it nice, 'gelt shows.' You know, that's what they are, gelt shows."

He was going to ask Calvin about the cigar holder again, but Calvin had taken his ashtrays and moved away.

"You know, he's smart," Mr. Erlang said to Mrs. Leiderkopf. "Such a head..."

Something was happening on the program that interested Mrs. Leiderkopf. She turned her head to the screen, her face practically touching it.

"You'll ruin your eyes, yet," Mr. Erlang said.

"Quiet. Quiet," Mrs. Leiderkopf said, "I think he wins the money."

Mr. Erlang bit the end off his cigar, lit it, and puffed out a thick circle of smoke. "You know, there's nothing doing here. They say we're having a hurricane. I was staying till Labor Day. I think I'm going home, maybe this week."

Calvin came back with the ashtrays. "Big show coming up. Yes, sir, the boss he givin' you a big show."

"He better," Mr. Erlang said. "He wouldn't have a soul here. People are fed up. The weather and no activity. This is a way to spend an evening? Television I can't watch at home? For this I have to pay?"

"You can't talk someplace else?" Mrs. Leiderkopf said.

"I'm listening," Mr. Erlang said. "The music they just played it goes dum—de dum—de do." He imitated the rhythm, but his pitch was a monotone.

Mrs. Leiderkopf wasn't impressed. "So," she said, "What's the name of it?"

"Who knows from music?" Mr. Erlang said. "Ask me better a question on baseball."

They were quiet for a moment and then Mr. Erlang said, "Maybe you've got another cigar holder in the bag? Just a minute, I'd like to see one. Maybe I could sell it in my store."

Mrs. Leiderkopf said, "I haven't got. The last one I gave away."

"I was thinking," Mr. Erlang said. "You know, I had one, I use it—I'd show it around, maybe I could give your son a big order."

"I haven't got. I haven't got," Mrs. Leiderkopf said.

Mr. Erlang sat a few minutes more, puffing on his cigar. Finally he got up and went to the desk to complain to Mr. Mandheimer about the lack of activity.

After he'd gone, Mrs. Leiderkopf moved to her first seat. When she thought about Mr. Erlang she shook her head from side to side.

Marsha was waiting. She had on a bright print skirt and a pink blouse with a sash that wrapped and tied around her. Her hair was in a pony-tail. There was lipstick on her mouth and the slightest trace of rouge.

"Hey, pretty good," Al said. "I'm beginning to rate."

"Well, I see I've got competition," Marsha said.

"Oh, that—" He shrugged and took her by the arm.

They went down the steps together and through the lobby. Mr. Mandheimer was at the desk talking to Mr. Erlang. He nodded toward Al and Marsha with what seemed to be pleasure. Before they were down the lobby steps, Mr. Mandheimer had brought his wife out of the office to tell Mr. Erlang about the big show they were planning for the week end.

Mrs. Mandheimer said she didn't know why her husband bothered her when that was his department, but she came out of the office and she saw Al and Marsha too.

"Where do you want to go?" Al asked.

"I don't know, what do you think?" she said.

"Let's take a walk. And then drop in at the casino."

"Sounds fine."

"Better than a night of dead, mother, dead?"

"Let's call it different," she said.

They started walking toward the casino. The lights were on and the music was coming from that direction.

"Tell me about your girl friend," Marsha said. "I want to know."

"Why?" he said.

"Feminine curiosity. It's natural. You know, she's in love with you."

"I wouldn't say that."

"The hell you wouldn't. Don't start getting modest all of a sudden. There's not a man alive who isn't tickled pink to have a beautiful girl in love with him—and that's whether he's in love with her or not."

"You think I'm in love with her?"

"What are you asking me for? You ought to know."

"I do know," he said. "I just wondered if you did."

"If I thought you loved her," Marsha said, "I wouldn't be here tonight."

"Wouldn't you?"

"Maybe, I would," she said. "I'm not as noble as all that."

"Me either." He took her hand in his and held it. But somehow after the first seconds it felt awkward. He had to let it go or do more.

"I thought we were going to the casino," she said.

"I'm not in the mood for a lecture on T. J.'s rheumatism yet."

"Go ahead, you encourage him. Besides, I think you like to know all about people. It flatters your ego to think you draw them out. You're a professional character collector."

"You know a hell of a lot about me," he said.

"You're very easy to figure out."

"For you, maybe."

"Maybe," she said.

"So where were we last night? You were telling me about your husband—"

"Let's drop it, shall we?"

"You'd gotten to the point where he died. You didn't go any farther than that."

"Sometimes I don't like the way you say things."

"You rather have me say 'passed away' than died?"

"It's more than that. Everything in the world isn't so goddamned matter-of-fact."

"That's the way I talk," he said. "I can't figure any other way to say it."

"Maybe it is the only way," she said. She was distant for a while.

"O.K. I'll drop it, like you say. If only you'll tell me one thing."

They had reached the road that led to Harley's. "What's that?" she said.

"What happened to you after he died? What the hell could have been so bad that you'd sleep with a guy like the Mong?"

"You do put things crudely."

He said, "Well, that's what I want to know."

"Suppose I can't tell you?"

"Then I don't give a damn," he said. "If it doesn't mean anything to you, it goes the same for me."

She turned around on the road. "Don't go too far, Brodie," she said. "You might not like everything you see."

"Is that right?" Al Brodie said. He looked at her slowly, his eyes moving from her face, down her body, back to her face again. He swaggered but there was softness in his smile. "I like your dress. It's very happy," he said. "And that's a nice way you wear your hair. You know, this is the first time I've ever seen you with lipstick. You keep this up, you're going to spoil me." His fingers touched hers and in another moment his arms were around her waist and he kissed her.

She moved away from him after the kiss and walked on. Their hands touched for a moment and then separated. "I didn't care any more," she said, "not about anything. When they buried Larry, they buried me. Coming back here, facing them again was the end. So it was Stan—it could have been anyone else. I didn't care—"

"And now?" he said. "You feel a little different now?"

"I don't know. I honestly don't know, Al. I still love Larry. He's the only man in the world for me and he's dead. I don't know."

"You didn't feel that way a few minutes ago," he said.

"Don't make a case out of it," she said.

He smiled. "One thing I know all about, that's kissing. I'm a positive genius when it comes to figuring out what a kiss means."

"I'll bet you are," she said and smiled, too. "All I'm trying to do is warn you."

"You? Warning me?" He took her hand and swung it once and let it go. "You fooled me, Marsh. I'd have never guessed I'd bring out the mother in you."

She laughed. "How did we get there?" she said. "You know, Brodie, you have a real gift for twisting things."

"If I can't convince them, I confuse them," he said. "One or the other always works."

"Is that right? So this is all a technique?"

He said, "Uh-huh." And then he said, "You know, I still like your hair." He reached over and gently stroked her head, holding the pony-tail softly in his fingers. "How about that lipstick?" he said. "Should I tell you about that again?"

She said, "You're going to have to do better than that. I've heard that line before."

She moved her head away so he couldn't kiss her, but she held him close to her for a moment. "What am I going to do with you, Brodie?" she whispered.

"You could lie to me a little more," he said. "You're very convincing."

They kissed again and then they started toward the casino.

"Now, if you're a good girl, I'll teach you a few of the latest dance steps."

"Who's going to teach who?" she said.

When they came to the casino the band was playing on stage. The chairs had been moved back to form a large circle around the middle of the floor, which was crowded with dancers. The band was playing a fox trot.

"Come on," Al Brodie said. "You're going to see the finest two-step in the country." He put his arm around her and led her back and forth in time to the music. Marsha said nothing but smiled and moved with him gracefully.

When the fox trot was over there was a roll of the drums and Jerry Furman said from the stage, "It's cha-cha time, everybody. Let's see all those people in our dancing classes. This is your chance to prove what you've learned."

A group of teen-age girls paired off together and joined the dancers on the floor. The band struck up a cha-cha and the dancers started to move. Al made a tentative start and Marsha followed him. He kept time to the music but his eyes were on the floor trying to pick up the step.

He felt Marsha Cooper's hand on his back bringing him lightly forward. He took one step forward and started another, and she said, "Now back in place. Cha. Cha. Cha."

Al followed her. He was slow breaking into the next step and she said, "Now who's going to teach who?"

"Forward, back, cha, cha, cha. Nothing to it," Al said. He tried to take back the lead, but he'd missed a beat and they were moving slowly on a fast beat. He bumped into a gray-haired man who was dancing with his wife.

Al said, "Sorry." He picked up the beat again and Marsha followed him. He shifted his weight quickly to the time of the cha-cha and swept into a forward step. His step was too long and this delayed his back step. He was out of time with the music.

Marsha tapped the time on his shoulder. She took back the lead and he followed her. They stayed with the music for a while and he said, "See how easy it is? Didn't I tell you I'm a natural?"

Marsha didn't answer, but she swept away from him and did an elaborate break. When she returned Al was out of step with the music again.

"Brodie," Marsha Cooper said. "You have two left feet."

"I was just worried about you. I didn't know where you were going."

"Just keep doing that forward-back step," she said. "We'll try it again." She tapped his shoulder, "Now concentrate."

When she returned from the break this time, Al was saying, "Forward. Back. Cha. Cha. Cha."

He kept repeating it, varying in expression from gravity to lightness.

"You're a hell of a conversationalist," Marsha Cooper said. "Now let's talk about side-together—cha, cha, cha."

She showed him the next step and he picked it up quickly.

It was eleven o'clock when they reached the door to Marsha's room. Al said, "You're all wrong—I haven't got two left feet. It's that I have four feet and you never noticed before."

She said, "So that's why you can move in two directions at once."

He laughed and then he said, "You might have at least warned me. How was I supposed to know you're a regular Arthur Murray?"

She said, "You were doing me such a big favor." She mimicked him: " 'Come on down to the casino and I'll teach you the latest steps.' "

"They slipped that cha-cha in on me," he said. "You have to admit I do a smooth fox trot."

"Very smooth," Marsha said. "One, two—forward, back. Your variety is spectacular. Wait until I teach you those breaks—" Her tone changed. "Good night, Al," she said. "It was fun."

He caught her by the shoulders and turned her slowly toward him. "You mean that, don't you?"

Marsha Cooper's eyes were closed and her face flushed. "Yes, Al," she said. "I haven't enjoyed myself—not this way—in a long, long time."

He kissed her cheek and then her eyes and then the corners of her mouth, but she held her hands over his lips. "Don't Al," she said. "It was an evening and it was fun, but it's just an evening."

"Who said it's anything more," he said. "I can wait. I've got lots of patience."

After he'd kissed her lips she said, "I wish I could be as sure as you are about everything."

"You will," Al Brodie said. "It just takes time."

The television set was on and Mrs. Leiderkopf was watching the late late show. There were no other guests in the lobby. Mrs. Mandheimer was banging away at the typewriter in the office and Mr. Mandheimer was standing at the front desk enclosing letters and a special announcement in envelopes.

"Allen," he called as Al Brodie passed. He gestured with his head for Al to come to him. "So how are you?" he asked.

Al said, "Just great."

"That's good," Mr. Mandheimer said. "Next week you won't be so great. None of us will be so great. Between the hurricane and the fifteenth of August, we'll be lucky if we have a hundred people."

"It's that bad," Al said.

"Worse," Mr. Mandhemier said. "In July maybe, a hurricane. We'd have people anyway. They get off from work, they take their vacations. But the middle of August—it couldn't be worse."

"I'm sorry to hear that," Al said. "Well, what the hell, we've had a great season so far."

Mrs. Mandheimer's voice came from the inside office, "Sam, who you talking to?"

"One of the waiters," Mr. Mandheimer said.

"I thought you were mailing the letters. I thought you had to see the butcher," Mrs. Mandheimer said.

"She's nervous," Mr. Mandheimer confided to Al. "I've never seen her so nervous." Louder, to his wife he said, "Just a minute, I'm going."

"Hurry up, you won't be out in the hurricane," Mrs. Mandheimer said.

Mr. Mandheimer nodded his head. "Very nervous," he repeated to Al.

"I wouldn't worry about it," Al said. "Maybe if we give them a sensational show on Saturday night, they'll stay over."

"Saturday night?" Mr. Mandheimer said. He waved a finger at Al. "Not Saturday. That's the gimmick."

"The what?"

"Gimmick, that's what you call it, the gimmick."

"Sounds great. What is it?" Al said.

"You know this business has to be in your blood," Mr. Mandheimer said. "It's a good business, interesting if you like to think." He stacked up the envelopes. "Maybe you're not so tired. You'd like to take a ride into town with me?" He added quickly, "No, you better go to sleep. I'll go myself."

"I'd like to go," Al said. "I want to hear about this gimmick."

"Becky, I'm going," Mr. Mandheimer called into the office. "You want me, I'll be by the butcher's."

Al reached toward a stack of letters, but Mr. Mandheimer stopped him. "These I'll take myself. You'll come along just for the ride."

Mr. Mandheimer was very quiet all the way to the car. It was an old Chevrolet station wagon with a wood body that was coming apart. The front seat was loose and had to be adjusted to keep it in place. The dashboard was chipped, and there was a glass curtain-rod in the back that rolled from side to side as the car started. Mr. Mandheimer stopped as soon as he heard the rod roll. He got out of the car and took the curtain rod out. He put it against the wall of the main building, got halfway back to the car. Then he turned back, picked up the rod, and carried it into an opening under the steps.

When he was back inside he said, "My Becky, she loads this car down like a junk collector. I don't know what's the matter with her sometimes. She ruins this car."

"It's got a good motor," Al said. "They don't have engines this good in the new cars."

"It runs. Who needs a fancy car?" Mr. Mandheimer said. "You go to buy a car, they think every man's a millionaire."

"Some hotels have pretty swanky jobs," Al said. "I guess they figure the guests are impressed when you pick them up in the latest models. You know what I mean—with your name on the side and all."

"You got a new car, the guests think you have so much money they fight you on the rates," Mr. Mandheimer said.

"I guess that's right, too," Al said.

"In this business you have to think of everything," Mr. Mandheimer said.

They were quiet for a while. As they went up a hill, Mr. Mandheimer shifted into second and the car stalled. He stopped, pulled his hand brake and started again. Al watched and waited and then said, "Sometimes, you know, it figures that if you run a business like this—I mean you're knocking yourself out—it wouldn't be so bad if you took the advantages, too. You could buy a new car and charge it to the business. What the hell, you're riding it all the time. You're entitled to that."

He was ready for some argument, but all Mr. Mandheimer

said was, "I guess—well, we never did things that way. Never made things easier for ourselves. This car can't run, we'll buy a new one."

Al looked out the open window. The sky was overcast. It was getting very warm and there didn't seem to be the slightest trace of a breeze. "What was this gimmick?" he asked. "You said you'd tell me about it."

Mr. Mandheimer said, "Maybe next year Becky will buy a new car. Now Marsha is here and we'll be driving the baby back and forth. A car like this is no car for taking a baby."

Al didn't say anything.

"The new casino will cost us a fortune. You got to have it. You must have it. You don't build and give them something new every year, you can close your doors," Mr. Mandheimer said. "I don't know, maybe we're crazy. Five hundred dollars for one act. Where does a place like us come to Myron Blum?"

Somewhere, the older man had lost him. Al wasn't at all sure about the continuity of Mr. Mandheimer's thoughts. He nodded and shrugged and said, "You're so right."

"That's your gimmick," Mr. Mandheimer said. His voice was very critical. "For five hundred dollars, you have a gimmick? For a Thursday night yet—I don't know."

"You mean Myron Blum, the great comedian, he's coming here?" Al asked very slowly.

Mr. Mandheimer nodded. "On a Thursday night. You ever heard of such a thing?"

"Thursday, of course," Al said. "Everybody else runs their big shows on the week end. But we have the people over the week end anyway. So with a Thursday—some people will stay over, and people figuring on the next week-end, they come up early. You get a full house—"

"Maybe. It's not that simple. I don't know you young people—" Mr. Mandheimer was disgusted.

"It could be a bomb," Al said. "A lot of people say Blum isn't what he used to be."

"You know what you're talking about?" Mr. Mandheimer said. "Myron Blum—Five-Hundred-Dollars-a-Night-Blum— everybody in the country knows him. He plays by Ed Sullivan,

television, Broadway, everything. 'Isn't what he used to be—'"
He was angry. "We should only be able to get enough letters out, everybody should know we have him."

"So that's the mail," Al said. He shifted quickly. "I guess you been working pretty hard on the mail."

They came to the intersection where the road met the highway. There was a sign that said, "Woodmere, bungalows and hotels for your pleasure." A movie house was on the corner and there was a large parking lot next to it. Then came a succession of small stores with big signs and plain window displays, merchandising groceries, meats, dairy products, and dry goods. The only lights that were on came from two bars, one called The Paddock, the other The Joker's.

Mr. Mandheimer parked in front of the butcher shop. There were no lights on and Al said, "What do they do, wait in back for you?"

He didn't get any answer. Mr. Mandheimer got out of the car with his bundle of letters. He met Al on the sidewalk and then with an air of great freedom and confidence he said, "First the mail, we'll get rid of these. Then, you're interested, I'll teach you a few things, you'll know how to pick out a good rib."

Al said, "Fine. That's great."

The post office was a small building, one of a row that extended up the street. The door was locked but there was a thin light coming over the transom. The letter slot was at the bottom of the door. Mr. Mandheimer took the letters and carefully put them through the slot.

When he was through, he wiped his hands for no reason and said, "Well, that's done. With a little luck—who knows?"

He was very gay as they walked up the street. He told Al Brodie all about the schedule of mail pick-ups. He was most proud of the fact that by delivering the mail at night he took the pressure off the morning when there were so many other things to do and he didn't like to be bothered with mail. He also made a point of telling Al how Mrs. Mandheimer used a bag they'd received from the bank when she delivered the mail. Mrs. Mandheimer put all the letters in the bag. More efficient, yes—Mr. Mandheimer pointed out. But, he cautioned Al, somebody might be confused and think it was money, with the bank bag and all, and there was no sense in looking for trouble when you could avoid it.

By the time they'd reached the butcher shop, his mood had shifted. "You think I know how many ribs to order? You think I know how many people we'll have?"

The door was open and Mr. Mandheimer walked in. The shop was dark. Only when they were inside was there any sign of light. It came from the back of the shop.

As they approached the place from which the light was coming, a man came out to greet them. He was elderly, with a mass of gray hair. He stood up very straight and tall and walked like a general approaching the reviewing stand. He wiped his hands on his apron and nodded to Mr. Mandheimer.

"We were waiting for you, Sam. We've got your ribs." He made a circle with his thumb and forefinger. "Beauties. In your whole life, you never saw such diamonds."

They walked into a room that had three heavy wooden work tables and a scale. A sawing machine was attached to one table. The other two were empty. Along the ceiling ran a metal track from which hung steel bars. Each bar had a series of a dozen hooks. Two bars were loaded with ribs.

A small man with a bald head and a bloodstained apron was taking the ribs from one rack and loading them on a similar rack that hung from the scale.

"Hello, Max," Mr. Mandheimer said to the small man. "Fleischer was telling me they're such beautiful ribs."

"Very nice," the man named Max said. He was bent under the weight of the two ribs he was carrying, but he nodded and smiled.

Mr. Mandheimer walked over to the scale and turned the rack so he could examine the eye of one of the ribs. He motioned to Al to come over. "See this," he said. "This is the rib. Our steaks, the deckle, a few pieces flanken, chopped meat, we get from this. Understand?"

"This is a relative? You're teaching him the business?" the butcher, Mr. Fleischer, asked. "You're a lucky boy. Nobody knows better than Sam Mandheimer. Him you couldn't fool." He laughed and walked over to Al, throwing a heavy arm across Al's shoulder. The butcher's hand was large and strong, and when he squeezed the shoulder Al winced. "A fine, strong boy," Mr. Fleischer said. "He's your nephew?"

"He works by me," Mr. Mandheimer said casually. "He wants to learn he should be a steward some day."

"Why not?" Mr. Fleischer said. "Let me tell you, they make good money."

"You want I should weigh them all off, Mr. Mandheimer?" Max asked. "Nice ribs. You wouldn't find better."

"This," Mr. Mandheimer said to Al. He fingered a small circle of meat encased in bone and fat. "This we call the eye. This is your steak—"

"Filet." Mr. Fleischer interrupted. "You wouldn't mind, I butt in. Forty years in the business, I know a little something. Not much—a little something." He patted the eye of another rib near the one Mr. Mandheimer was pointing at. "Filets is what you call them, too. Did you ever see such a diamond?" He ran his hand along the meat. "Look at the flower. It doesn't have the fat running through—what we call the flower, I wouldn't sell it to Sam Mandheimer. For the Sesame the finest. Let me tell you, you can learn from Sam Mandheimer, sonny."

"So how come this rib isn't aged?" Mr. Mandheimer said. He pointed to the rib he had been showing Al.

Mr. Fleischer was deeply wounded. "Not aged?" He pointed to the rib he had shown them. "Any older would be rotten. Soft, yes, but such waste you'd have. Sam, your people pay you so much you can afford to throw away so much meat?"

"That rib I'm not talking about," Mr. Mandheimer said. "That's all right."

"All right," Mr. Fleischer smiled to Max. "All right, he tells me. Isn't that a Sam Mandheimer for you? He knows. He knows, he's not so dumb he doesn't know. Such a rib you find maybe one, two in a hundred."

"I should weigh them?" Max asked again.

Mr. Mandheimer looked over the eyes of several more ribs. "So many," he said. "You're so sure I'll have to have twenty?"

Mr. Fleischer looked very worried. "Tell me, Sam, business is bad?" He made a sound with his tongue and nodded his head. "You were doing so good. The weather? What is it?"

"Business is all right," Mr. Mandheimer said. "But twenty ribs—it's not the height of the season any more. Fifteen ribs maybe."

Mr. Fleischer looked pained. "I'm sorry. I'm sorry, business isn't so good by you. I can't understand. You give them such a good table. I know you're buying the finest. Meat like this they don't eat so good at home."

"I should weigh all but five?" Max asked.

"You'll give him what he wants," Mr. Fleischer said, very much the boss. "What's the matter with you, Max? All of sudden you're going to tell the customer what he should take?"

"He says he'll take fifteen ribs," Max said excitedly. "What d'you mean, I told him?" He turned to Mr. Mandheimer. "You said fifteen ribs. I should live so—I heard you say it."

"Don't get excited," Mr. Mandheimer said. "Tell me, Fleischer, the price of meat is down?"

"I'll show you my bills," Mr. Fleischer said. Quickly he started from the room. "I should tell you? We should fight? I'll show you my bills."

Mr. Mandheimer stopped him. "The bills you don't have to show. You'll tell me the price. It's right, I was going to take fifteen ribs, maybe I'll take twenty."

"Smart," Mr. Fleischer said. He directed himself to Al. "You'll be a buyer like Sam Mandheimer, you'll be the best. He thinks he fools me," Mr. Fleischer was smiling and looking as if he wasn't going to be outfoxed. "This week he'll buy diamonds for fifty-five. Next week—the way the market is going—he'll give me fifty-eight, not a penny less and then I won't be making money. And ribs like this we might not see again."

"Fifty-five?" Mr. Mandheimer said. "You can't do better?"

"The bills," Mr. Fleischer said. "My bills, I'll show you." He whispered, "Fifty-two I paid." He held up a finger. "Where's my transportation? It doesn't cost me a cent a pound? I'm not entitled to two cents a pound profit? Max works because he loves me? No, Sam, I wouldn't make a profit. Why lie to you? I wouldn't be in business."

"I thought maybe comes the end of the rush," Mr. Mandheimer said. "Nobody's buying—"

"Let me explain to you, Sam, my friend," Mr. Fleischer said. He went to Mr. Mandheimer and put his big hand on Mr. Mandheimer's shoulder. "The market is in Chicago—in the West. You do business, I do business. They don't know from it. The supermarkets, they're buying ribs, the price is up. Go ahead, you can fight them? I can fight them? I'll show you my bills." He started from the room again.

"Forget the bills already," Mr. Mandheimer said.

"It'll take me a minute, I get them," Mr. Fleischer said.

"You'll get me another one for this," Mr. Mandheimer said. He pointed to the rib he'd shown Al. Mr. Fleischer came over, interested. "Something with a little more age and a bigger eye. And this one too—"

Mr. Mandheimer went through each rib individually. He exchanged four of them. Max, Mr. Fleischer's assistant, went into the refrigerator and Mr. Mandheimer put on a butcher's coat and went in after him. Mr. Fleischer followed and then Al.

It was cold inside and there were rows of meat—huge forequarters and calves and racks of lamb. Mr. Mandheimer went over to the ribs and carefully selected four to take the place of the ones in the original group.

Al was cold and he put his hands in his pockets.

"You'll be in this business forty years, you wouldn't feel the cold," Mr. Fleischer told him. He started to tell Al about the tremendous range in grades of veal and how to recognize the difference, but Mr. Mandheimer said that could wait.

When they stepped out of the box, Mr. Mandheimer told Max to weigh off ten of the ribs and put the other ten away for him. It was late and he didn't want to keep Al out too long.

Mr. Fleischer said, "Why not? You can have it any way you want."

Then Max took the ribs off the hook and laid them out on a table. He ripped the deckles off and then went to work with a small knife, cleaning away the fat, and tearing the forty-pound ribs down into parts. Mr. Fleischer went to work on the machine, cutting the slices of flanken and removing the extensions of the rib bones.

It took them over an hour to bone-out the ribs. Mr. Fleischer talked a lot during his work. Max, his assistant, worked quietly and quickly, but as fast as he worked—conversation, dramatics, and all—he was no match for Mr. Fleischer. The old man was faster and more efficient.

After the meat was wrapped into parts, Max packed it into boxes. One box for the ten deckles, two more boxes with five filets apiece, and another smaller box for the chopped meat and the twenty-five pieces of flanken.

Mr. Mandheimer said the chef wanted the bones for soup and they were loaded, too. The whole order was put into Mr. Mandheimer's station wagon. Mr. Fleischer and Max followed them to the hotel in the butcher's truck, and they unloaded the meat and put it in the Sesame's refrigerator.

Mr. Fleischer said it was nice to have met Al, and he hoped Mr. Mandheimer wouldn't mind him saying it, but when Al was a steward he should be careful like Mr. Mandheimer was.

It was after two o'clock. There was a slight rustling of leaves now; it was beginning to get windy. Before Al left Mr. Mandheimer to go to his room, Mr. Mandheimer said, "Well, now you know a little something about the business. You're in a business like this, you don't always have time for yourself. Fun, taking it easy, families—a hotelkeeper misses all these things. But the season is over—at least now, thank God, we've built the place up—maybe you've got a little money, you can live during the winter."

"It's not so bad," Al said.

"It's in your blood, there's nothing you can do about it," Mr. Mandheimer said.

"Good night," Al said. "It was very interesting."

"You're a good boy, Allen," Mr. Mandheimer said. He cleared his throat and looked away. "Marsha looks better. Who knows about these things?" He looked at the trees and the dark sky and then at his foot where for some unaccountable reason he started to build a little hill of sand.

"Well, it looks like we'll have our hurricane," Al said. "I hope Myron Blum can save the season for us."

"Hurry to your room, you won't get wet," Mr. Mandheimer said.

"See you," Al said. He started walking but when the first burst of rain came, he ran. It was the fastest, heaviest rain he'd ever seen, and by the time he got to his room he was soaked.

Chapter 22

"What d'you mean you never heard of the place?" the theatrical agent said. "It's in the Catskills. That's all you got to know. Was Tamarack the London Palladium when Danny Kaye worked it? You think maybe Brown's was on Channel Seven when Jerry Lewis was busting up the joint? Maybe you didn't hear Sammy Davis Junior got a whole night club named for him at the Raleigh. You know a better place in this racket to break in? You tell me."

The lobby ceiling was leaking in three places. Water rushing down the hill had broken through the cracks in the wall and was flowing across the floor of the children's dining room. There was a series of small break-throughs in the ceiling of the main dining room, too, and it was necessary to move all the window tables.

Mr. Mandheimer was shuttling pots back and forth, measuring off the exact spot of each leak and putting the pots on the floor beneath them. Mrs. Mandheimer was fighting with a kitchen man for using clean linen to soak up the wet floors. Calvin had on a black poncho and a matching fisherman's hat. He was running back and forth from the Annex, bringing the guests to breakfast under the protection of an umbrella.

The radio said that the hurricane had hit the northeast with heavy damage in parts of Pennsylvania, New Jersey, and Connecticut. Ellenville, in the Catskill mountain area, was flooded and was being declared a disaster area. There was also an announcement of cellars flooded on the Long Island coast.

By the time breakfast was over, twenty guests had spoken to Mrs. Mandheimer about leaving.

Mrs. Mandheimer told Jerry Furman to make an announcement on the loudspeaker that Myron Blum had just been signed to appear at the Sesame on Thursday night. She had a big picture of the entertainer placed on the main desk, and on the bulletin board in the main lobby she put up a sign that said, "Ten Per Cent Discount after August fifteenth."

The rains continued all that day and through the night.

After dinner, the lobby was crowded. Jerry Furman organized a bingo game in the dining room for the evening activity, but most of the guests were in the card room or the lobby, complaining about the weather and speculating on what was going on back in the city.

Al and Marsha sat on the steps in the corridor near her room. He told her he hoped the rain would stop before it ruined the season.

She said, "Want to listen to a wise old woman of the mountains?"

He said, "Sure, old craggy face."

"Don't worry," Marsha said. "It's never as bad as it seems. You'll make your thousand bucks. If the last two weeks of August are bad, Labor Day makes up for it."

"I wish I could count on that," Al said.

"Never fails," she said. "I'll guarantee it. Now smile."

But he still looked serious.

"You're sick, Brodie," she said. "Phase one of the Catskill disease. Diagnosis—worryitis."

"And what does that mean?" he said.

"Phase one isn't too dangerous. It's curable if caught in time. The symptom is common. You start worrying when business is bad for fear it's going to get worse. But phase two—that's incurable. Once you've got it—" She snapped her fingers. "That's a very advanced stage. You start worrying when business is good, because you're sure it's going to be worse."

Al smiled. "How about me, Doc? Give it to me straight. Will I pull through?"

"All depends," she said. "Let's see how you respond to treatment." She tickled him with both hands and when he laughed, she said, "You'll live. There's hope."

They were interrupted when Phillip got up and started into the hall. Marsha put him back to bed and after he was quiet she came back and sat with Al.

Mrs. Leiderkopf passed them on the way to her room. She asked Marsha how the baby was and Marsha asked about the parakeet.

"So long he gets from me an egg every day," Mrs. Leiderkopf said, "no trouble. Loves the country. My boys were children, I took them by the hotel, you think they liked it so?"

Al stood up as Mrs. Leiderkopf spoke and the old lady motioned for him to sit down. She spoke a few more minutes about the parakeet and invited them both in to see it. Marsha explained that she had to stay near the room in case Phillip woke up. Mrs. Leiderkopf said she understood and slowly trudged up the rest of the steps toward her room.

When she left Al said, "Can you figure spending good money to keep a bird in your room? I hear she's paying a child's rate for him."

"And why do you think she does that?" Marsha said.

"I guess we all get a little off our rocker when we get to be her age," Al said.

"I don't think it's that at all," Marsha said. "She's just lonely. You should have seen her in the old days. She always came with her whole family. They took up three rooms and had a long table in the dining room. Once a season we used to have Leiderkopf night in the casino. There would be an amateur hour, and she would give out the prizes. I won a doll once. A big Shirley Temple doll with eyes that looked almost human. I only had it for a few minutes. I had to give it back. Daddy didn't think it was right for me to take a prize that should go to a guest. I cried when they took it away from me. Mrs. Leiderkopf sent me one a lot like it. It was larger, and it wet and cried, but to me it wasn't the same. I never liked it."

"Damn nice of her," Al said.

"We get some human beings up here, too," Marsha said. "Law of averages."

"You know something," he said. "I don't think you got it in for this place half as bad as you think."

"Don't start getting sentimental, Brodie," she said. "We weren't going to discuss Mommy and Daddy any more, remember?"

He said, "O.K., have it your way."

A group of guests came up the steps headed toward their rooms. The noise woke Phillip again. Marsha said she'd better call it a night. Al said, Sure, and he kissed her lightly on the cheek and went downstairs.

He stayed a long time, listening to Mr. Mandheimer telling people at the desk about the hurricanes of '53 and '56—and how after they were over, the mountains had the most beautiful weather he'd ever seen.

Chapter 23

In 1663, following the intrusion upon their land by the Dutch, the Esopus tribe of Indians raided the "New Village" of Hurley. Except for one barn they completely destroyed everything. They killed the men and took the women and children prisoners.

Among the women was Catherine Blanchan, the wife of Lewis DuBois. DuBois received word from a friendly Indian that his wife, along with four other females, had been transported to a wigwam on Shawangunk creek, a stream which forms part of the eastern boundary of the town of Mamakating today.

Legend has it that the women were bound while the Indians were piling fagots. Sure that they were to be burned at the stake, the ladies began to sing the 137th Psalm in the Dutch Reformed Church Collect:

> "By Babel's stream the captive sate
> And wept for Zion's hapless fate.
> Useless their harps on willows hung
> While foes required a sacred song.
>
> "If Zion's woes our hearts forget
> Or cease to mourn for Israel's fate
> Let useful skills our hands forsake
> Our hearts with hopeless sorrow break."

James Eldridge Quinlan, who reports this in his History of Sullivan County, written in 1873, tells what happened.

> *"The savages were so charmed with the music, they delayed the execution of the singers while they listened."* He concludes with the assurance that *"Mr. DuBois and his rescuers soon arrived, and the ladies of faith were forthwith in the arms of their loved ones."*

By the time the rain stopped the next morning, eighty-three people had checked out. It was a Saturday and the Mandheimers' big hope rested with Myron Blum.

After breakfast on Sunday, Audrey Grier called a meeting to announce some changes. She had to lay off three waiters and three busboys. The remaining stations were cut down and consolidated. Only Stan Macht and Al Brodie had as many people at their stations as they'd had before the hurricane.

The Mong wasn't satisfied. He put up a fuss because some of his players had been laid off, while waiters who didn't play basketball stayed. When Audrey told him her decision was final, he reminded everybody that he was still the captain in the dining room.

To prove it, he announced that he was personally inspecting stations, and every waiter's and busboy's room. "I been getting hell all season because you guys are slobs," he said. "I want every server shining, every bed made, every room clean. And I don't mean tomorrow."

Al Brodie dropped into his room a few minutes before the main dining room opened for lunch. Macht was leaning on the bureau. He had a letter in his hand and he was reading it.

Al said, "How'd we make out in the inspection, sarge?"

The Mong didn't answer. He was busy reading.

"What d'you have there?" Al said. He looked closer and saw it was the letter Joe had received from Ellie's father. "Lay off, snoop. That's somebody else's mail." He made a grab for the letter but the Mong moved it away, blocking it behind his back.

"Holy smoke!" the Mong said. "You know what the hell is in this letter?"

Al said, "I know whatever it is, it's none of your business."

"Oh, no?" the Mong said. "They fire my whole team and you know what they got working here?" He had the letter in front of him and he slapped it.

"Give me the letter, Mong."

"A good guy like Mike gets the gate and they keep a spook like this around."

Al held his hand out, waiting.

"You been rooming with the guy all summer, I'll bet you don't even know—"

"You trying to tell me you just found out Joe isn't Jewish?"

"Damn right," the Mong said. "They let a guy like him hold a station and then they go and fire my team."

"Heil Hitler!" said Al, making the Nazi salute.

"O.K., wise guy, but maybe it won't be so funny to someone else."

"Mandheimer? You thinking about giving that letter to Mandheimer?"

"Why not? He ought to know."

"And what d'you think Mandheimer will do? Pin a medal on you, make you a goddamn hero—"

The Mong said slowly, "Look, you said it yourself, the guy isn't Jewish."

"So you're going to tell Mandheimer," Al said. "You're going to take Joe's letter right to the boss."

"That's right," the Mong said. "My team's getting the dirty end of the stick long enough."

Al Brodie walked up to Stan Macht. "Look, Mong, up to now there's been no special love lost between us, but I'm talking to you like an old buddy. Only you and I know something. Let's just keep it between us, huh?"

"What d'you mean—?"

Al's voice was soft. "So far, Mong, you been pulling it off very smooth. So you throw your weight around in the dining room—so what? No one really knows for sure how stupid you are. Why don't we just keep that little gem between us?"

"What d'you mean stupid? Where the hell do you come off saying that to me?"

"You're prehistoric, you creep," Al said sharply. "Nobody else but you is going to give a damn what Joe is or what he isn't. That stuff went went out with your friend with the mustache. Only a knucklehead like you wouldn't know that."

"Watch who the hell you're calling names," the Mong said.

"Go ahead," Al said. "Take the letter into Mandheimer— I want to be there. I'd like to see him laugh right in your face."

The Mong said, "I'm warning you for the last time—"

Al stepped away from the Mong leaving him a free path to the door. "There's the door. Go run to the boss."

"I been taking your lip all season, Brodie. You're going too goddamn far."

"Go ahead, creep. Go on. It's your own funeral."

The Mong threw the letter on the bureau. "Drop dead, you son of a bitch," he said.

Al made no effort to pick up the letter. "I'm going up to the dining room. I'd be happy to walk you as far as the desk."

But Stan Macht was already out of the room.

Joe Miner was in his room dressing for a date when Al came in. Joe had one foot up on the baseboard of the bed. He was shining a shoe with a Consolidated Laundry towel.

Al said, "How you doing, lover boy? Where you headed for tonight?"

"We thought we'd take a ride up to the reservoir," Joe said. "It's a terrific view."

Al said, "So what are you shining your shoes for? Business isn't bad enough, you got to louse up the house's towels." He grabbed the towel from Joe and snapped it at his roommate's legs.

"Talk about your company men," Joe said. "You're worse than Mandheimer."

"That's where the money goes," Al said. He flipped the towel back to Joe and started to undress for a shower.

Joe said, "Ellie was telling me she heard you having a brawl with Macht this noon."

Al said, "Who pays any attention to the Mong?"

"He was reading my letter, wasn't he?" Joe said.

"Forget it," Al said. "It didn't amount to a damn."

"You did me a real favor," Joe said. "He could have caused me a lot of trouble."

When Al came back from the shower, Joe was still in the room. He said, "Hey, Al, how about doubling with us tonight?"

"You're already dressed. Why should you wait around for me?"

"We'll be parked by the big tree on the side of the casino," Joe said. "Come on, man, we'll put that top down and live a little."

"If I'm not there in fifteen minutes, take off without me." He put on a pair of starched khakis, an open-necked shirt, and a heavy wool sweater. Before he left he picked up the towel Joe had discarded and brushed it quickly over his moccasins.

The yellow convertible moved slowly down the road past the Sesame Hotel. It cruised past the bungalow colonies and roadside signs announcing rooming houses. At the bend of the Woodmere road where a wooden bridge passed over the Neversink, the car stopped.

"I think we can put the top down, honey," Joe said. "There aren't so many overhanging trees here. We won't get wet."

Ellie unlatched the hinge that fastened the top on the driver's side of the car, and Joe did the same on his side.

"You'll have to push it down in back," Ellie said to Al. "The rain has made the canvas a little stiff." She pushed the button and slowly the top slid back.

Al stood up and started to press the canvas against the cradle above the rear seat.

"I'll get this side," Marsha said.

There was the soft sound of water dripping from the rain-wet trees, but the night air was fresh and clean. The sky was filled with stars and a half-moon was partly hidden behind a cloud.

"Man, what a sky," Joe said.

"Listen to nature boy," Al said. "They really breed them in Central Park."

Ellie said, "You sure you don't want to drive, Joe? You know the way much better than I do."

"You're doing fine," Joe said.

Ellie started the motor and moved the car across the bridge. The planks rattled beneath the weight of the car and Marsha said, "A true wonder of engineering. I'd have sworn ten years ago this bridge wouldn't last another season."

"Look at that river," Joe said. "The Neversink really moves around here."

Ellie glanced quickly down, then back to the bridge and the road ahead. She held the steering wheel with one hand for a moment and touched Joe's arm.

"It's beautiful, sweetheart," she said. "I love it."

Joe turned on the radio and picked up a music program on a local station. He moved closer to Ellie and put one arm around her. She joined Joe as they whistled and sang in time to the radio's music.

In the back seat Al said, "How did you get someone to stay with Phillip? I thought the night patrol had to go out and make rounds."

"All the children left in the hotel now are in the main building," Marsha said.

They sat quietly as the car moved down the country roads. They passed a store with a large sign saying, "Everything for the Family." There were some bungalows set back from the road, with a large swimming pool in front of them. Slowly the signs of the resort area disappeared, giving way to the large hilly farms and acre after acre of woodland.

Marsha Cooper lifted her face toward the sky. Her long hair blew back behind her, whipped by the night air. Al brushed his hand against her cheek and she looked at him, her head thrown back, her eyes bright and warm. She took his hand in hers, squeezed it tight and held it to her side. Neither of them spoke until the car stopped.

They were parked on a wide paved roadway overlooking

the reservoir. On every side were trees and bushes and grass, clipped and groomed. There was a large landscaped hill and a path leading down to a bridge which spanned the water. In the distance were the low rolling mountains of the Catskills. Nowhere was there a sign of people or traffic.

Joe got out of the car first and opened the door for Ellie. "Come on, honey," he said. "Let's show them our private view."

Ellie said, "I don't think we should tonight. The grass is going to be awfully wet. Another time." She got out of the car and stood by his side. "We could take a walk down to the bridge," she said to Al and Marsha. "The water looks really beautiful from there. Want to come?"

Al said, "I think we'll just sit here for a while and take in the sights. Maybe we'll move up into the front seat and make believe we own the car."

Joe said, "I guess you've seen this lots of times, Marsha. But it has special meaning for Ellie and me. This is where we dreamt up the biggest haberdashery in the Bronx."

Ellie smiled. "We rented it, decorated it and even added two new departments without spending a cent," she said. "See you."

As Ellie and Joe walked off together, Marsha Cooper folded her hands in her lap. Her head was bent forward and Al noticed her long black lashes. He was going to tell her about them, but she lifted her head and said, "Didn't you say something about moving up front? I'd like to stretch my legs."

He helped her out of the car and they stood together, his arm around her waist and her head resting on his shoulder. They were looking out toward the water and the mountains and the sky.

Marsha's voice was wistful. "It is lovely, isn't it, Al? The whole country must have looked like this before the resort people came along and ruined it."

"Without the hotels who would ever get up here to see it?" Al said. "We city people just have to take our nature a little bit at a time."

They were quiet a while and then Marsha said, "Looks like it's serious between those two."

"I should hope to tell you," Al said. "They're all set. It wasn't easy, but they worked at it. Next year it will be wedding bells and all the trimmings."

"I hope they're not disappointed," Marsha said. "I've seen a lot of these summer romances."

"Ellie and Joe are going to make it," Al said. "It's obvious."

"What makes it so obvious? How can you ever tell if two people are really right?"

"They go together. They do things for each other. You take Joe—that girl makes him a man. I know. I been living with the guy all summer."

"And what does he do for her?" Marsha said. "She seems like a perfectly adequate girl to me."

"Well, she used to be kind of dizzy. Take this car. Joe tells me Ellie was scared to drive it. Bought it and everything and then didn't want to use it."

"You think that's enough?" Marsha Cooper said. "Is that all marriage is? Just giving a person enough confidence to drive a car?"

"If it's right on the little things," Al Brodie said, "you can make it when it counts. You take Ellie and Joe—you know he's not Jewish."

"I didn't know that," Marsha Cooper said. "Does Ellie know?"

"Sure, she knows," Al said.

"For a girl like her—that could be a very big problem," Marsha Cooper said.

"It is. But what are you going to do? That's the way it breaks sometimes. You meet somebody and you know you're right."

"Not quite. You've also got to be ready," Marsha said. "The right person doesn't mean a thing if you're not ready for him."

"Maybe. Maybe not," Al said. "But you've got to help out, too. Hell, it would have been much easier for those two just to chuck it all because some problems came up."

"I don't know," Marsha said. "Right now anything still would be second best to Larry."

"Sure, Marsha," he said. "But two people don't strike it off right every day, either. You pass up a big chance, it may never come again."

She didn't answer even though she knew he was waiting.

"Maybe we should get in the car, Al," she said finally. He helped her back, and they sat without saying anything until Joe and Ellie came back from the bridge. During the ride home Marsha sat close to him. It wasn't until they reached the bridge over the Neversink that Marsha lifted her face to be kissed. He looked at her silently, then gently clipped her chin with his fist. "You'll learn," Al Brodie said. "One of these days you'll learn."

Chapter 24

Mr. Mandheimer said, "Calvin, you'll put the roast, it's in the tinfoil, on the back seat. The pot of soup, you'll make sure it's covered, put it on the floor."

Calvin said, "Sure is a shame 'bout Mrs. Newell dying like that last week. That farmer lady—she was good goyim."

Mr. Mandheimer drove the old station wagon down the driveway leading from the hotel. When he got to the road a guest stopped him and motioned for Mr. Mandheimer to open up the window.

"Mandheimer, you know you got two beach chairs by the pool, they're broken?"

"I'll be gone a minute," Mr. Mandheimer said. "I'll come back, I'll get the handyman, we'll fix them."

The entrance to the Newell's farm was the first driveway down the road. The boys were playing on the grass while their father painted the gate of the front fence.

"Hello, Newell," Mr. Mandheimer said as he left his car. He made a gesture with his hand as if saluting. "So," he said, "we had a little rain."

"Ain't seen the likes of it since '53," the farmer said. "Lucky we got us a hill."

"At least you have pasture land, it's not flat, your cows have what to eat."

"Bad for you hotel people, weren't it? You slow down a bit last of August."

"A few people more or less," Mr. Mandheimer said. "With the weather you can't make contracts."

The two men stood quietly and then Mr. Mandheimer said, "My wife was saying, now you don't have Mrs. Newell to cook for you the children should have a good home-cooked meal."

"Sister comes up from Ferndale," the farmer said. "Does the cooking."

Mr. Mandheimer folded his arms across his chest. "So you're painting your fence. I was by Billy's hardware. He tells me they have a new paint, an outside white—it has a water base."

The farmer said, "That so? I been planning to do me some work on the house come fall. Maybe I'll get the name of it."

Mr. Mandheimer said, "I'll see Billy, I'll call you."

The farmer didn't say anything.

Mr. Mandheimer gave the farmer the roast and the soup, and then dropped his arms and slapped them against his thighs. "Well, you know my wife. She wouldn't be happy she didn't send you a little something."

Mr. Newell put down the bundles and followed Mr. Mandheimer to the car. Mr. Mandheimer was looking away from the farmer. "We didn't know Mrs. Newell very well," he said. "Neighbors, they should know each other better. Mrs. Newell, she seemed like such a nice lady."

"Thank you," the farmer said. "Thank your missus, thank —Rebeccah—for me, too."

Monday evening before dinner Al Brodie found his silver drawer loaded with coffee grains. His table settings were intact and he borrowed the extra pieces he needed for that meal. After dinner he spoke to Stan Macht.

"Get it cleaned up," he said. "Just get it cleaned up."

Stan Macht said, "What the hell you talking about?"

"Make sure that drawer is cleaned, Mong. That's all I'm telling you."

"What drawer?" Stan Macht said.

"If it's not clean by breakfast tomorrow, you'll be a very sorry little Mong."

"I'm scared," Stan Macht said. "Hold my hand."

Al looked at him evenly. Stan Macht squared away, ready to fight.

"Any time," Macht said. "I'd like nothing better—"

Al didn't say anything else. He set up his station minus the silver that was in the drawer, then left to see Marsha.

He had to wait outside for her while she put Phillip to sleep. It was nearly nine o'clock, but she explained that her son had taken a late nap and wasn't very tired. It was after ten when she came out of her room. Al was sitting on the top step of the stairway, waiting for her.

Marsha's skirt was creased and there was a dryness about her face. Her cheeks were marked with the impressions of the bedspread, and strands of her hair hung loosely across her face.

"Still waiting?" she said. "What time is it?"

"So this is what you look like when you wake up in the morning," Al said.

"I'm a mess," she said in a thin, fresh voice. "How long did I sleep?"

"Not too long," he said. "Come on, there's still time if you want to go out."

She stretched and he noticed the way her blouse rose. "Would you mind very much if we didn't tonight?" she said. "I don't feel like getting dressed. Too damn lazy."

"Any other ideas?" he asked.

She walked over and sat on the stairs next to him. She wasn't wearing shoes and her stocking had a run along the side. Her legs were well shaped and her feet small and thin. "Let's see," she said. She locked her fingers and stretched again. "What is the matter with me? I'm so tired tonight."

"Maybe you'd rather I left and you'd go to sleep," he said.

She considered that for a minute and then said, "I'll tell you what—room sixteen, right next to my room—is empty. The people checked out today. We could sit in there and talk awhile. How about that?"

"O.K.," he said. "Sounds fine to me. What the hell, if you can trust me I can trust you."

She put her hand on his and said a little coquettishly, "You know what you can do for me first? Go down into the kitchen. There's a big urn filled with the most delicious-tasting liquid—bring up a pitcher full."

"I don't know if there's any coffee left," he said.

"Calvin always puts some up for the card-players. It's after the fifteenth, remember, and we have to give service."

He stood up and said, "Sugar and cream?"

She said, "Black. Maybe it'll revive me."

"Before I go," he said, "there's something you can do for me."

She said, "Huh?"

He leaned down and raised her by the elbows. When she was up and leaning against him, he moved his arms around her. He kissed her forehead and her eyes and as he moved his lips to hers, she shifted her head away.

"Not now," she said. "I just woke up. I should brush my teeth or something."

He put one hand under her chin and tipped her face up to his. She screwed up her nose, "You know, I don't think it makes any difference to you."

"Only one way to tell," he said, and kissed her.

His lips were demanding and it was the first time she opened her mouth for him. He wanted to kiss her again, but she moved her face away and kissed his neck.

"Come on," she said. "I want that coffee."

He ran his hand along the firm lines of her back and down along her buttocks.

"Is this what comes of inviting you into a room?" she said lightly. "I expected a little more subtlety from you." She pecked his lips and took his hand away. "Get me that coffee before I die of thirst."

"If that's what gets you drunk, O.K.," he said. "I couldn't make out with Scotch or moonlight, maybe I'll do better with coffee."

"You're making out," she said. "You just don't know it."

He went down the stairs and through the lobby to the kitchen. Calvin was standing by the urn, pouring a gallon pot full of boiling water into the top.

"Bellhop does everything around here, huh?" Al said.
Calvin shrugged. "What you gonna do with them schnorrers? Dis a cheap crowd. Want everything for nothing. D'missus don't give them the tea room, they check out. After the fifteenth, you want people, you got to give the house away."
"I guess so," Al said. "Any chance of me getting a potful?"
Calvin said, "You know, anything for you. You my friend." He went over to the rack by the glass department and took down a big clay pitcher. "You want her filled up?"
"About halfway," Al said. "That should be enough."
"Yes sir, you my friend." Calvin turned the handle of the urn and let the coffee run into the pitcher.
Al said, "How you making out? This been a good season for you?"
Calvin turned the urn off and put the pitcher down. He opened his palms and spread his hands face up in front of him as he shrugged. "Could be better," he said. "What's d'use complaining."
"You're a hell of a bellhop, Calvin," Al said. "Mandheimer is lucky she has you."
Calvin laughed. "Yes sir, thank you very much. You want cream, maybe a little cake with this?"
"Skip the cream," Al said. "Maybe I'll take a piece of that sponge cake."
Calvin had a half-dozen platters of assorted cake ready for his tea room. He took a piece off each and put it on a plate for Al. He took two saucers and two cups and put the whole thing on a tray with two napkins. "Now you and Miss Marsha can have yourselves a ball," the bellhop said. "You good for that girl. I hear the missus say so."
"Yeah, what else did she say?" Al wanted to know.
Calvin concentrated on arranging the tray. "You know they never was much takin' care of her," he said. "Marsha never did like d'hotel business. I mean, ain't just me says it, everybody knew that. Mrs. Mandheimer, she's a business woman—" Quietly he added, "Ain't no time for children, a woman like her. Jus' the same—all dis—it's all Marsha's some day."

"What else did Mrs. Mandheimer say?" Al persisted.

"Dis a bad season," Calvin said. "All dis crowd, nothing but schnorrers. I fix up the tea room and all, I'm lucky I make two dollars in tips. For this work? What am I gonna do, it's my living."

"Here's a buck for the coffee and cake," Al said. He reached into his pocket and pulled out a few bills. He handed one to the bellhop. "What the hell, you only live once. Be a sport, I always say."

Calvin smiled and folded the dollar, putting it carefully in his pocket. "It's the truth. Nothing but the truth," he said. "And you is a sport, one hundred per cent sport. Like I hear the missus say to him jus' today, you brung Marsha out of herself. She ain't running around all night like she used to and she look happy."

"That's all they said?"

"They don't say it right out," Calvin said. "I mean they don't talk about it much. But they did say you is good for her and a lot better than that other gonif."

Al picked up the tray and started out of the kitchen. Calvin came behind him and asked quite casually, "Think there's goin' to be a wedding, boy?"

Al said, "Cut the crap, Calvin. You made your buck off of me."

Calvin laughed and said, "You my friend. I don't tell anybody what I tell you. Yes, sir, I'm gonna like workin' for you some day."

Al carried the tray back to Marsha's room. There was no sign of her in the hall. He pushed the door of her room open with his shoulder and called her name in a whisper. No answer.

He managed to latch his foot around the base of the door and swing it half closed. Room sixteen was next door. He kicked at the door three times and called her.

A key moved in the lock and in a few seconds the door was open. Marsha was standing there. The sleep had worn off her face, but she was dressed the same as when he'd left her.

"Help at last," she said, and took the tray from him.

He followed her into the room. The building was an old one and though the furniture had been modernized and the room painted, there were signs of its age. A wash basin was against one wall and there was a transom over the door. There were two single beds and a cot that was folded. A small rug, more like a bath mat, was on the floor between the two beds. There was a blond-finished bureau and a straight-back black chair.

"Not exactly a palace," Marsha said. "But it pays the bills."

"I've seen the rooms before," Al said. He remembered quickly the one other time he'd been in a guest room—with Audrey Grier. "Those motel rooms are the sellers though. That's where we make the money."

Marsha put the tray on the bureau. She was pouring two cups of coffee. "We?" she said.

He said, "What the hell, you work for a place and it does well, you do well too. It figures."

"Very loyal," she said. "You should get a bonus, but don't worry, you won't." She took her cup of coffee and carried it over to one of the beds where she sat down. "I poured for you. On the table."

Al went to the bureau and picked up the cup. "You *must* be bushed. I thought we got over the sour grapes, but I see you still have it in bad for this place."

"You don't just 'get over' something like that."

He put his cup down and came over to her, kneeling on the floor beside her. "You know, I still don't get what's so bad about this place," he said. "People come here—they bring their kids—they have a million things to do, great food, and the whole family has a ball. What's so awful about that?"

Marsha said, "It may be just wonderful for other people's children but it's no place for my son. Phillip isn't going to be playing second fiddle to everybody who can afford ten dollars a day for a room the way I did. I was considered a walking suggestion box for all the guests' complaints. Oh, they'd smile nicely enough to my folks—they knew what kind of rates they were paying, but they could always get even with me. I was always hearing insulting things about my parents. Guests would tell me how they lied to them, cheated them, overcharged them. 'Tell your mother the casino's not big enough, little girl.' 'Remind your father they need more chairs at the pool.' 'The show was lousy last night.' I heard them all. It got to the point where I couldn't even look at another guest. If somebody said hello, I said excuse me," she said.

Al said, "People raise kids everywhere—a good family clicks no matter where they are. And in a place like this, with all the operations you have in running a hotel, you need a family. You're lucky to have each other."

"This place—need somebody?" she said. "You don't know what you're talking about. Anybody can see this is a two-horse show. I'm not raising my son to fight to get into the act."

"It doesn't have to be that way," he said. "For Chris' sake, you don't even give them a chance."

"I'm giving them the same chance they gave me. What did they ever do for anybody that wasn't strictly business?"

Al said, "Maybe you didn't hear about the food they been sending over to that farmer next door. Calvin was telling me this guy's wife died and your old man has been running a regular carry-out service. What's that for? Don't tell me that guy is ever going to check in—"

"So they gave a poor neighbor a pot of soup," Marsha said. "Some big deal."

"Let me tell you something," Al said. "A lot of people do nothing but talk. You take my old man. He's got a mouthpiece, you'd think he was a regular senator or something. But what does he do? He hacks—runs a little taxi around the city and is scared to open up his mouth to anybody but my old lady because it might cost him a ten-cent tip. Mandheimer doesn't make speeches. They see the right thing to do, they do it."

"Wonderful," she said. "They're the nicest people in the world. You can have them."

Al Brodie was very quiet for awhile. He drank his coffee and finally put the cup and saucer down on the floor. Then he said, "What did you ever do, Marsha? What did you ever do that makes you more important than them?"

"I married Larry," she said.

"You mean that? You really believe that guy was so good—just being married to him and living with him—that was really doing something with your life?"

She didn't answer but she nodded her head and there was a look of conviction in her eyes.

Al Brodie folded his legs up and wrapped his arms around them. "I'd like to see something this Cooper painted," Al said. "I really would. You have anything around?"

She blushed and put her coffee cup down silently.

"You must have something," Al said. "Why don't you get them? I'm not kidding. I'd really like to see them."

She said, "Skip it, will you?"

He touched her leg lightly with his hand and held the calf of her leg in his palm. "Did he ever do any pictures of you? How about showing me one—just that one about the woman and the soldier saying good-by. I'd like to see what you look like in his pictures."

Marsha said, "Well—"

"Go ahead. For gosh sake, what the hell did he paint them for if nobody can see them? I swear I'll just look at them and won't say anything unless you ask me."

She stood up and said, "You better not." She looked at him a moment silently. There was an expression of anger on her face that slowly gave way to amusement. "You know, you're shrewd," she said. "Or is it that I'm just a born sucker? Want to see a picture of me," she mimicked. "They ought to make you our ambassador to Russia."

He ran his hand along her leg very objectively until he came to her ankle. He closed his hand around it. "I don't think I'd like it in Russia," he said. "Too much borscht."

She pulled her foot loose and left the room. A few minutes later she came back with a large black cardboard portfolio and some canvases.

"I haven't shown these to any one since he died," she said. "I don't know—I haven't decided yet what I should do with them. I suppose I should raise the money and give him a one-man show in one of the New York galleries. He would have liked that."

"Let's see," Al said.

She was standing with the big portfolio in front of her. It covered the length of her body and it seemed she was caressing it.

"I couldn't bear to sell them, though," she said. "They mean so much more to me than money."

He said, "I guess they do," and he waited.

She untied one of the black strings that held the backing together. "I don't know whether you're going to understand these at all. I mean Larry was really quite esoteric—he was a modernist, but with a style of his own. The whole thing might just be unintelligible to you."

"How about letting me decide that?"

The string was untied and the front cardboard escaped from her hand and fell. It was as if she were suddenly physically exposed.

"Oh, my God," she said. "I never know the right way to handle this."

"Let me help you," he said. "I won't look at the pictures. Just let me get this thing organized for you." He moved the portfolio over to the wall where he leaned it for support. Then he lined up the canvases, facing the wall. "All you have to do now," he said, "is take the pictures out one by one and pile them on top of the bed. Then, when you're through, I'll put the whole bunch of them back for you. See? Easy. Just don't get so excited."

"I suppose I am nervous," she said. "You see these pictures were such a part of Larry. I mean they were him. More him than me or Phillip or anybody or anything. It's almost—almost—like having him here in front of you."

"Don't worry," Al said very patiently. "I won't make a pass at you—not in front of his pictures."

That put it in perspective for her and she opened the portfolio. The first picture was a great mass of water color. There was no discernible object in the picture, only the very faint trace of what might be a building or the bow of a ship in the right center of the paper.

"He called this 'Poet's Morning,'" Marsha said. "It was supposed to be a pun. You know, morning with a *u-r* and the straight *r*. He wouldn't say much about it, but Larry had been a sort of poet before he found himself in painting. I don't think I told you that, did I? Well, anyway, Fred Rogers—he was a friend of Larry's and a very good critic—Fred said the picture brought out an overpowering sense of darkness and loss with only the vaguest suggestion of form or matter or reality. They were his exact words. I know because—Larry and Fred—they used to discuss this particular painting dozens of times. Fred thought it was typical of a poet's mood, but he said he hoped Larry would do more with it. Fred never considered it a finished work. Oh, he thought it was good and all that—the color, I mean—but he just didn't think as it stood it was what we'd call finished." She paused, as if from a difficult recitation, and when he didn't say anything, she continued, "Would you want to look at it for a while? I guess actually you have to see it in daylight. The damn lighting in here. You can ruin your eyes in these rooms."

"Let's see the next one," Al said.

She put the picture on top of the bed and was very careful to place it where no one would sit.

The next picture was a canvas—a great splurge of chalk-white. It looked like the side of a building. There were lines that resembled the frames of a window, but they overflowed and spread across the picture until they gradually disappeared into the chalk-white.

"I think this idea came to him from Cézanne—or was that another one?" Marsha said. "No, I think this was it. It's been such a long time. Actually, I get confused myself. Anyway, it always reminded me of this hotel. The stucco, you know. That's the dominant construction here—stucco. I suppose you know that." Al nodded and Marsha continued. "Well—Fred didn't like this. I might as well admit it, nobody really did. They thought it showed a talent for color and a very daring experiment in white, but—well— Larry always called this his white period. Actually, the picture only took him a few hours. Very fast for him. I mean he worked fast, but it took him days, weeks sometimes to get his inspiration. Would you want me to go on? There are two other pictures here in this white period."

"If you don't mind," Al said. "I'd like to see that one you told me about. The one with the soldier and his wife—"

"You mean 'This Might of Thine Destroys Thee,'" Marsha said. "Sure, if you'd like to. I'll get directly to that. As a matter of fact, I've often heard it said that you shouldn't look at too many pictures at one time. Larry used to go to a museum and stare and stare at a single picture. Sometimes it would go on like that all afternoon. He said he'd get more out of it that way. It's better to take art a little at a time. You're right."

He was going to tell her that wasn't what he meant, but he didn't. She was quite serious and quite busy about finding the painting, so he waited quietly.

"You'll have to help me," she said. "I think I've got it right here among the water colors. How about holding the rest of these and I'll see if I can get it out."

He held the other paintings while she carefully extracted the one he'd wanted to see. "I really ought to get all of them framed," she said. "It ruins them carrying them around like this."

She put the oil on the floor by the bed. It was a small canvas, no more than twelve by twelve, and after she put it down she thought again and picked it up, holding it in front of her.

"You can't look at this expecting to find me," she said. "If you knew anything at all about moderns, I mean you'd know realistic detail and camera work—that just isn't a part of it. It's the mood—the expression is what they see with their inner eye."

The girl in the picture was dim. There was only one recognizable feature—her breast. It was large and swollen and the nipple was stiff and ripe. There was a small bundle of blanket which she held toward a figure that looked somewhat like a man. The hands of the woman holding the baby had three fingers. The man had huge arms and a muscular chest and his body diminished as it went down. He was standing on small feet and incredibly stubby legs, and he seemed to have no groin.

"When he said I was his Andromache," Marsha said, "he didn't mean it in the sense most people would think of an artist meaning it. It wasn't that he meant to paint me as I actually am—the way you or I would see me. It was sort of—I guess you'd have to call it his inner vision or inner eye again. It doesn't look like me. It isn't supposed to. As a matter of fact—well, I mean it's not me. I hope you're sophisticated enough to understand that." She paused waiting to hear something from him. His silence made her very uneasy and she said, as close to pleading as he'd ever heard her, "It does say something though, don't you think so? War is really ridiculous. Our finest young men going off to be slaughtered and husbands and fathers—"

She was becoming passionate and desperate and Al Brodie interrupted her very gently, "Nobody would argue with that," he said. "It's a hell of a waste."

"That's it—I think that says it as well as anything. It's the waste Larry was trying to express. You see, if a picture does touch truth it can reach any of us. You don't really have to be an artist or a critic to appreciate it."

"No," he said. "It can even reach a boob like me."

"I didn't mean it that way," she said in a tone that was closer to the one he'd known. "But I'm glad you like it." She turned the picture away from him and looked at it herself. She studied it and said, "I wouldn't sell this, not for all the money in the world."

"Well, then that knocks out my bid," he said. "I guess I'll have to live without it."

She was somewhat relieved by his humor. "I wish you wouldn't joke about it. You don't have to be ashamed. I'm rather glad you understand the picture. It goes to prove that Larry wasn't wrong. He did have something. He was a genius—" She caught herself. "That's horrible! Every mother up here who has a son says he's a genius. But that's what Larry was. Honestly, Al, I think I'm going to have that one-man show for him. He's entitled to it. You don't think I'm crazy, do you?"

He didn't answer her directly. "Did he ever sell any of his work? I mean did Larry ever make money from it?"

"He never really tried. Money didn't mean anything to Larry. He had his work and that was enough for him."

"All this time he was painting out in Arizona, you lived just off what your mother sent you?"

"Larry had his savings," she said. And then knowing that wasn't enough, she added, "I didn't want him to hold down a job. He was a painter—an artist. A job would have compromised him."

"Pretty hard raising a kid and all with no money coming in."

"We didn't need money. I know that sounds totally incomprehensible to you, but it's true. Larry had his work and his friends. We had more fun, more activity in our house—people used to come and they didn't leave until three, four o'clock in the morning sometimes. We had more than money can buy."

"Sounds a little rugged," Al said.

"Well, it wasn't," she insisted. "It was wonderful. I could sit for hours and just listen to them talk about art and literature and music. You think money is so important, you can't do anything without it? Well, you're wrong. Our friends had a lot more than these so-called practical people who are worried all the time about where their next dollar is coming from."

"I guess it's O.K.," he said. "If you get your kicks."

"You might not believe it to see me up here, I mean in the middle of this—this—stucco cage, but I liked my life with Larry. I'd have never come back, never, if it wasn't—wasn't—" She stopped talking suddenly and started putting the pictures back in the cardboard folder. "What's the use of talking? He's dead now."

Al said, "Did this Larry ever change a diaper? Take his kid out for a walk? Mix a formula? Make his own breakfast?"

She stopped putting the pictures away and turned toward him. "Now what in the hell does that have to do with it?"

"I'm just trying to figure him," Al said. "That's all."

"You can't judge Larry by the standards of other men, by 'kicks.' I've tried to make that clear to you. He was different. Can't you understand that?"

"Yeah, I guess he was," Al said.

She continued with the pictures until she had them all back in the folder. She was tying the string when she said, "You didn't tell me what you thought of the paintings? I'd really like to know your opinion. I mean, do you think it's worth my having a one-man show for him?"

He didn't answer her at first and she continued. "You liked that one with the mother and the child and the soldier, didn't you? I mean that had something to say to you?" Still no answer, "You were in the army weren't you?"

"Infantry," he said. "Private first class. You can't go by me. I never saw anything like that."

"Stop joking," she said. "This is important to me. You said something when I showed you the picture—something about war being wasteful. That's what the picture said to you, isn't it?"

He didn't answer and she finished tying the string and then said flatly, "Well, I'm going to have that one-man show for him. I don't care what anybody says. These pictures deserve to be seen. Larry's entitled to it."

"That's up to you," he said. They were both quiet. She stood with the folder of pictures in front of her, playing with the string she'd just tied. He sat down on the bed and leaned forward, watching her and studying the soft bewilderment of her face.

"It's a hell of a shame," he said, "that he never did a picture of you. I would have. Honest to God, if I was an artist, sure as hell I'd paint you. Not with just one breast either."

"Stop that. You and Larry are worlds apart."

"Larry and me, maybe we are worlds apart. But not you and me, Marsh. We're nowhere near that far."

"Aren't we?" she said. "I'm not so sure."

He shifted very gently. "You never exactly studied art, did you? Everything you picked up about it was from him and his friends."

"You don't have to study these things. Not when you're married to a man like Larry. He never went to school himself, I mean formally to study art. You don't have to. Take Cézanne or Van Gogh—some of the greatest artists never formally studied art, I'm sure."

"You'd have to know a hell of a lot about it," he said, "to bet your life on it."

"It's better than this," she said. "It's better than this lousy rotten business. Look at my parents—what have they got to show for twenty-four hours a day living and breathing check-ins, dirty laundry, week-end shows, temperamental chefs? At least I've got these." She patted the pictures.

"And Larry had his work," Al said. "And if you can scrape up the dough for a one-man show, you can let the world see." He nodded his head. "I hope you're right. I hope they're real good."

"You don't think so," she said. "You don't think Larry's paintings are any good at all."

She looked at him directly with an expression that he knew could bend either way. She wanted him to be with her—all he had to do was say he liked Larry's paintings. If he said what he really felt, everything he'd done this whole summer might not come to a damn.

He didn't have to tell her anything. What did he know about art? If he ducked she might let it go at that. Or he could hedge it. He tried it in his mind: "Marsha, they're very interesting. He might really have something." That would keep it alive and give him time.

But he couldn't say it. Not to Marsha. He'd compromise a lot of things to get somewhere in this world, but this was different. Marsha Mandheimer was Al Brodie's girl. Who the hell was Lawrence Cooper or anybody else to make him lie to his girl?

He said, "I don't think those pictures are worth a damn, Marsh. For me they don't come through at all. I couldn't put five minutes into talking them up, or five dollars into that show."

"I wasn't asking for your help," she said, and in that moment she knew she had been.

He went to her. She moved her shoulder away as he tried to touch her.

"He's the only man in the world that there ever was for me," she said. "You're wasting your time, Al."

"I'm not wasting a minute," he said. "You are. You can hold them forever, Marsh, and they'll never be as close to you as I am now."

"You're so sure," she said. "Always so goddamn sure."

"I know because you tell me so, Marsh."

The room was pale and dark and the walls seemed suddenly yellow like a cloudy sunset. He squeezed her shoulder even though she tried to shake away.

"I'll see you tomorrow," he said, "about nine. And don't look so dead-mother-dead serious. We used to have a lot of laughs, remember?"

She didn't answer him, but when he got to the door, she said, "I don't want to see you again, Al. Forget me."

Chapter 25

"Table twenty-two," the hostess told the hotel owner. "They say they won't be in for lunch. You know what that usually means."

The hotel owner walked quickly to table twenty-two, where a tanned young man was sitting with his blond wife. "Hearty appetite," the hotel owner said. "You're having a nice breakfast?"

"This lox omelet is wonderful," the young man said.

"Nova Scotia," the hotel owner said. "Lox is a lot more salty."

"I must have put on five pounds with these onion rolls," the blond wife said.

"That's what they're here for," the hotel owner said. He shifted his weight from foot to foot. "My hostess was telling me—you won't be here for lunch? You'd like maybe we should pack for you a little something?"

"If we missed a meal it'd do us good," the wife said.

The hotel owner said. "You're paying for a full day. The lunch is coming to you."

"We'll make up for it at dinner," the man said.

The hotel owner said, "When you registered, I put you down—you said you'd be staying for two weeks."

"That's right," the man said. "It'll be a week tomorrow."

"So—" the hotel owner said. "Everything is all right? You're happy?"

"Couldn't be better," the man said.

273

"This I don't understand," the hotel owner said. "Everything is so good, so why you're looking around?"

"Who's looking around?" the woman said. "We're just going to take the day to do a little sight-seeing."

"Sight-seeing?" the hotel owner said. "There's not enough activity for you here, maybe? We're catering to a young crowd. You'd do me a favor, you'd let me know."

"The hotel is fine," the man said again. "To tell you the truth we've been pleasantly surprised. You keep your grounds so nicely, and the room is first rate."

"If you ask me, I'd say we're not paying enough for what we're getting," the woman said. "I know what it would cost me to serve a breakfast like this at home."

"And don't forget the pool," the man said. "The water's so fresh. Doesn't even taste of chlorine."

"Maybe you've already guessed," the woman said. "This is our first trip to the borscht belt."

"You're telling me," the hotel owner thought to himself.

The silver drawer was clean. It had been washed and scrubbed and lined with glossy paper. The silver was stacked in neat piles. There wasn't a trace or even an odor of coffee grains.

Danny Rose was watching as Al examined the drawer. He was hanging back to the side, concentrating on putting the butter and rolls on the tables before the dining room opened for breakfast.

"What d'you make of this?" Al asked him.

Danny shrugged.

"Doesn't look like the Mong's work, does it? I can't see Stan Macht doing a clean-up job like this."

"What are you worried about? It's clean, isn't it?"

There was something in his voice that made Al say, "You wouldn't be stupid enough to do it yourself, would you? If you're worried about me and the Mong—"

"Hell no," Danny said. "That's your business."

After breakfast Al went over to the table where Audrey Grier was making up a list of side jobs for the busboys. She was biting the top of a pencil, and when Al spoke to her she didn't look up from the list.

"By any chance, did you find some loose coffee grains in my silver drawer?" Al said.

Audrey said, "I don't know what you're talking about."

"Look, Audrey, this is important to me," he said. "I don't like the idea of somebody else covering up for that ape. You did it, didn't you?"

"Why don't you forget it, Al?" she said. "Honestly, he isn't worth it. Your drawer's clean, why not let it go at that?"

"Did you clean out that drawer or didn't you?"

"I didn't," she said, "but what difference does it make?"

"It makes a difference to me," he said. "And I'm going to find out."

Right before lunch Mrs. Mandheimer found it very important to inspect every station in the dining room. She went from table to table, looking at the glasses and the silver, picking up the tops of the sugar bowls and testing the salt and pepper shakers.

She found some dirt under one of the rubber floor-mats and she called Audrey Grier to look at it.

"Filthy," Mrs. Mandheimer said. "All kinds of filth these boys can work in." She told one of the boys to bring her a dustpan and broom.

"I'll have him do it," Audrey said pointing to the waiter. "It's his job."

"It was his job, why didn't he do it before?" Mrs. Mandheimer said. "You got to keep after them, Audrey. You make up the tables, a few announcements, that's not enough. You should be ashamed—such a dirty dining room."

She was down on her knees cleaning up when she said, "You'll give me the mats, I'll have Calvin wash them tonight. We got a few people, a clean dining room is very important."

Audrey said to the waiter, "I've told you a hundred times about that. Now after lunch you can pick up your pay."

"Firing him wouldn't make the dining room any cleaner,"

Mrs. Mandheimer said. "It's your job. You know you have to keep behind them."

In a few minutes all the waiters were busy rewiping their goblets, putting salt in their salt shakers, cleaning up their servers.

The dining room was fifteen minutes late opening and the chef stomped in and said, "What the hell we waiting for—Christmas? Get some people in here before I burn my eggplant Parmesan."

Audrey ordered the boys to stand by their stations. Mrs. Mandheimer said they could work until the people came in. Audrey went out to make the announcement and Mrs. Mandheimer opened Al's silver drawer and borrowed a knife. She helped herself to a piece of pumpernickel and butter, but left the drawer open.

"You put the butter out after the people came in, it wouldn't be so soggy," she said to him.

"Well, you know these people," Al said. "They've got to have something to dig into right away or they start raising hell."

"Why so much butter in the dish?" she said. "You're afraid you'll have to run back for more? You know what butter chips cost me? Seventy-three cents a pound, that's not money?"

He started to take some of the butter off the plate.

"Leave it already, they're coming in," she said.

"Look like much of a crowd for Thursday?" he asked.

"Five hundred dollars for Myron Blum, we shouldn't have a crowd yet?" She ate the pumpernickel in small bites, very daintily. "It doesn't rain again, we'll be all right."

"That's great," he said.

"You want people," she said, "you got to give them something."

"I'm glad to hear we're getting the reservations," he said. "It'll be a good season for you."

"We keep the crowd we have now—who knows?" She shrugged. His silver drawer was still open. Very casually she said, "It's a nice clean drawer. I wish all my servers were so clean."

"Yeah," he said. And then very pointedly, "You know you have better things to do with your time than poke around here, cleaning out my silver drawer."

She didn't try to evade it. "Why not? You think it's better my waiters shouldn't get along?"

"Who told you?"

"That makes a difference? I knew, so now the drawer is clean."

He saw some people coming toward his station and he said, "Back to work."

One of the guests stopped near Mrs. Mandheimer and said, "That's no way for the owner to eat. Come on and sit with us, Becky, we'll treat you to a good meal."

"Who eats here?" Mrs. Mandheimer said. "Such garbage, who can eat it?"

The guests laughed and went on to their table.

Al had taken their soup order and by the time he came back from the kitchen, Mrs. Mandheimer had been called to the telephone.

Mr. Mandheimer came into the dining room during lunch. He went from table to table to make sure each guest was satisfied. To one irritated lady he explained why the chef couldn't stop serving the whole dining room to make a special order of French-fried potatoes. He went on to say that baked potatoes had less calories. With another guest he discussed whipped cream desserts and recited the names of the last three that had been served and on what dates. He explained the advantage of whipped cream made with a stabilizer base as opposed to pure heavy cream. Three times he made trips to the kitchen to pick up extras for guests who weren't getting service fast enough.

The dining room was empty when he came over to Al's station.

Al said, "Can I bring you a plate from the kitchen, Mr. Mandheimer? We've got a dummy setting all ready for you on number four."

"After Labor Day, there'll be plenty of time to eat," Mr. Mandheimer said.

"You got to have some nourishment," Al said. "Your stomach doesn't know about Labor Day."

"Doesn't it?" Mr. Mandheimer said. He laughed weakly. "My stomach could tell you to the last minute how long it is to Labor Day."

"How about some milk and an omelet or something?" Al said. "That's easy to digest."

"I have a free minute, I eat," Mr. Mandheimer said. "To me eating is not such an important thing."

"You know what the doctors say," Al said. "Next thing you know you'll have an ulcer—"

"We'll get a few check-ins," Mr. Mandheimer said, "I wouldn't know from ulcers."

"How's it look?" Al said.

"How can it look? It rains the fifteenth of August, you're in trouble. So it rains. But this I've never seen—we had to have a hurricane yet."

"That was a lousy break," Al said.

"Thank God we have a few people," Mr. Mandheimer said. "It wasn't for them, we could be ruined."

Al said, "I didn't know it was as bad as that. I figured with Myron Blum and all—"

"Myron Blum? You're talking like Becky already. There's a guarantee we'll have a full house with Blum? Don't be silly. What's here we know. Whether for Blum they'll come or not, that nobody knows."

"I guess so," Al said.

Mr. Mandheimer said, "There's no taking it away from Becky. She's some business woman. But—women are always looking on the better side of things. A time like this, you got to face it. We don't keep these guests absolutely happy, we're in trouble, real trouble."

"You're right," Al said. "We have to give them extra special service."

"Let me tell you something," Mr. Mandheimer said. "In a seasonal business like this, you can work twenty-seven years, a hundred and twenty-seven years, but one bad season and you're finished."

"No wonder you're in the dining room," Al said. "I thought something was up when you started running specials."

"Why not?" Mr. Mandheimer said. "You have to do more for the people who are here now than for any guests all season."

"If they want steak every night," Al said, "we have to give it to them."

"The people now, they are the roughest," Mr. Mandheimer said. "They pay you less, they want most. You don't give it to them, there are a hundred hotels in the mountains happy to have their business."

"We'll keep them happy," Al said. "You can be sure of that."

Mr. Mandheimer said, "Everybody should do their best. The smallest trouble, the least disturbance, our season is ruined. You have a small crowd, everybody is very touchy. Maybe because we have Myron Blum, some people will check in Thursday. At least comes the end of the season we'll be able to pay some bills."

"Don't worry," Al said. "Myron Blum will pack them in."

"So—" Mr. Mandheimer said. He cleared his throat and gave a short hitch to his belt. "How's everything with you—personally, I mean? Everything is all right?"

"Fine," Al said. "Couldn't be better."

"That's nice," Mr. Mandheimer said. He nodded his head, looking away from Al. "Well—at least you have your two feet on the ground. Young people today—I don't know—they have some crazy ideas." He jutted his lower lip and thought a moment, then he shrugged and said hurriedly, "A day like this, there's no swimming, my lifeguard could make a volleyball game, calisthenics—something to keep the people busy. If I don't keep after him, he'll be in his room sleeping."

He started away from Al and Al said, "Nice talking to you, Mr. Mandheimer. And don't worry, nobody is going to be checking out on us—"

As soon as Mr. Mandheimer had left, Stan Macht held the back of his hand up to his lips and smacked hard. "How's it taste, Brodie?" he called across the room.

Al said, "You should know, Mong. You've eaten enough yourself."

The Mong came across the room toward Al. He was grinning and he said, "O.K., smart guy, what's it going to be?"

"What's what going to be?"

"The coffee grains," the Mong said. "All of a sudden you don't know from nothing."

Al said. "Why don't you wise up? You stay away from me and I'll stay away from you. For once in your life, use your head."

Macht said, "Look at the feathers, Mama. Ain't he a beautiful chicken?"

Al said, "Scram, creep."

"Why, you phony son of a bitch," Macht said, "I even beat you out of your girl."

"Who are you kidding?" Al said.

"Come around about ten o'clock, I'll let you peek in the keyhole. You might pick up a few pointers."

"You trying to tell me you have a date with Marsha?"

Macht's voice was low. "She don't give it all to you, lover boy. She saves the best for me."

Al Brodie's face flushed. Goddamn Marsha, she had no right to do this to him. Didn't she have enough guts to work it out between them without throwing herself away on the Mong? It meant taking his chances with the job, too—the old man had warned him. But, hell, he'd have to show her.

"Tonight—I'll meet you right after supper," Al said. "You've had it, Mong."

"First good idea you had all summer," Stan Macht said. He thought it was hysterically funny when he walked out of the dining room singing, "There's no tomorrow—there's just tonight."

The chef took off his apron and told the Chinese breakfast cook to make sure the kitchen was clean before he left. "This I got to see," he said.

A small, bony dishwasher with gray hair and no front teeth

poked his head out of the dishwashing room and asked the chef, "Did you catch dat foist Dempsey-Tunney fight? Dat was a honey. I was dere. Right at d'ringside."

"Dempsey should have killed him," the dishwasher next to him said. "There never was, never will be another the likes of Jack Dempsey." He was tall and thin with a balding head and rimless glasses.

"Whadda y' mean? Was you dere?" the short dishwasher said. "I seen it. Anybody'd know, it's me."

"Jack Dempsey," the tall dishwasher said very slowly and very distinctly, "was the foremost pugilist of all time. He was. He is. And he will be. That is final."

"Shut up," the chef said. "Do your dishes and shut up. Dempsey and Tunney both of you."

"Dat chef, he's a card," the small dishwasher said. He laughed.

"Jack Dempsey was without a peer," the tall dishwasher said. I knew him well. He was"—he paused—"a personal friend of mine."

The chef said to Danny Rose, "Well, where are they? I haven't got all night. Tell them the chef needs his rest."

"He sure does," a kitchen man said.

"Al's cleaning up his station," Danny said. "They'll both be out soon."

"This I got to see," the chef repeated.

"Chris', this ought to really be something," the kitchen man agreed. "That character, the Mong, he's got a build on him like a wrestler."

"Think so?" the chef said. "I tell you what—I lay you a box of Berings against a carton of cigarettes and I'll take the other boy."

"Hell, chef, I wouldn't bet you," the kitchen man said.

"Why not? Why not?" the chef said. "You think I wouldn't pay up?"

"I like the same boy," the kitchen man said.

"All right then I'll take the Mong. Suits me," the chef said.

"No, we better not," the kitchen man said.

"Hell, you're goin' to spend the money for Stinky Pete anyway," the chef said.

"I don't touch that stuff," the kitchen man said, very insulted. "All I drink is Four Roses."

"Too bad," the chef said. "I had a bottle of Burgundy I was going to give you."

The kitchen man laughed and said, "Chris', you get me every time."

Stan Macht swung out of the door from the dining room. His shirt was open and he had his tray in his hand. He threw the tray down on the kitchen table and it made a loud clang.

"Cut out that noise," the chef said. "Or you won't make it to the fight."

"So where the hell is he?" Stan Macht said to Danny Rose. "How much longer is he going to set up that station? What's he think, I'll get tired of waiting and go home?"

Danny said, "He's coming. It just takes him a little longer to set up."

"That yellow son of a bitch, I bet he beats it out of the lobby door," Stan Macht said.

"Such language. From a college boy yet," the chef said. "You get too smart, I'll take you both on."

"You'd show them a few tricks, too," the kitchen man said.

The small dishwasher came out of the dishwashing room with a dessert plate in one hand. He'd been wiping it off to feed into the machine. "Cheffy, you catch dat Dempsey-Tunney fight? Tunney was smart. He had the head." He jabbed a thumb at his temple. "September twenty-toid in Philadelphia. I was dere."

The tall dishwasher came over excitedly. "Dempsey was the greatest that ever lived," he said. "I defy any man to defile the name of my good, dear friend Jack Dempsey."

"Get back to those dishes before you have to see your good dear friend about a job in his restaurant," the chef said.

"Don't think Jack wouldn't be only too glad to see me," the dishwasher said. He turned back to the machine and said to the other dishwasher, "They don't have the fights these days the way they did in our day. Know why? People aren't hungry enough today."

The man who had seen the Dempsey-Tunney fight nodded.

"I'm going in to get him," Stan Macht said.

"Don't wet your pants," the chef said. "He's coming. If he doesn't show up, I'll fight you."

"That wouldn't be a fight," the kitchen man said. "That'd be slaughter."

"Come on outside," the chef said. "We'll get the ring ready."

In the dining room, Al Brodie was polishing the last of his goblets and talking to Calvin the bellhop. Calvin was looking out of the small window that overlooked the back of the hotel and the garbage room.

"Man, they out there already," the bellhop said. "Look like they fixin' for a regular crap game or something."

"Let 'em wait," Al Brodie said. "I'm in no hurry."

"What for you going to do this?" the bellhop said. "I was like you, fight every meshuga come along, I'd be dead long ago." He went away from the window and started picking the mats off the dining-room floor.

"Don't worry about it," Al said.

"You know the boss and the missus don't like this at all," Calvin said. "You in good with them. Why you want to mess?"

"I haven't messed yet," Al Brodie said. He jutted a goblet toward the yard where the kitchen men were waiting. "One thing you can be sure of—I'm not going out there."

Calvin stood up with an armful of mats. "You fixin' to walk out?"

"If he wants me," Al said, "he knows just where he can find me."

"What you need it for?" Calvin said. He shrugged and screwed up his face. "You have the right idea the first time. Walk out on 'em. Few days everybody forgets it."

Al said, "You take one back step to a guy like the Mong and you keep right on going all the way down. If I have to—" He stopped suddenly. "You ever fight, Calvin—ever really go over somebody?"

The bellhop said, "Some time you has to. What else you going to do?"

"When I was a kid," Al said, "there was this Red Markham. He thought he was a Milton Berle or something—a regular joker. Well, he was big and strong as an ox and he had this way of pushing you as far as he could go. He got going on me one time, just horsing around. I didn't think he wanted to fight, and I'd never hit anybody in my life. But then he said one thing that hit me where I lived. I even forget what it was now; all I can remember is that it meant more to me than the chance of getting my face pushed in. My knees were shaking like hell and I was practically crying for Chris' sake—but I could have killed him. All I kept thinking was keep hitting him. If you can cut him up in small enough pieces he won't be able to lay a hand on you. You know why I won that fight? Because I had to more than he did."

Calvin adjusted the mats in his arms. "This ain't the bellhop's job," he said. "You know it ain't. That missus—not another bellhop in the country, in the whole world, could make a season up here. I ain't complaining, but it's the truth. Ain't it the truth?"

"No other hotel this size would let one bellhop have the place for himself," Al said.

"She's my friend," Calvin said. "Nothing I wouldn't do for that woman." He started toward the kitchen with the mats. "You ain't going to do nothing—I mean you has got better sense than to— 'Course you has."

Al laughed. "They won't need a paddy wagon for me. You can bet on that, Calvin."

"You all right," Calvin said. "All right."

The door from the kitchen swung open suddenly, forcing Calvin to move aside. The Mong came in alone. He had his shirt off and the cuffs of his khaki pants were rolled up.

"How the hell long you want me to wait?" he called to Al. "Come on for Chris' sake, everybody is waiting."

Al said, "I'm setting up my station. I'll come when I'm good and ready."

"You'll come right now," the Mong said. "Who the hell do you think you're fooling with this stall act?"

Al put the goblet he was cleaning on the table. He tucked in his shirt and came over to the Mong.

"You really mean this? You really want to go through with this?"

The Mong said, "I thought so, you chicken bastard. I thought you'd try to squirm out at the last minute."

"Let's go," Al said. "Let's go."

"That's more like it," the Mong said. "Hell, I got a date. I can't wait all night." He rolled his shoulders and shifted his weight to the toes of his feet. He jogged through the kitchen door with Al following behind him.

Calvin was by the sink. The faucet was on and the bellhop was rubbing soap against a stiff bristled brush. No one else was in the big room.

As they passed the coffee urns Al moved up close to the Mong. He yelled, "Hey, Mong!"

Macht turned, startled. Al's fist lashed out, catching Macht squarely in the face. There was a crack like a hatchet splintering wood, and Macht fell back against the stainless steel table that held the coffee urns. His arms dropped to his sides and Al was on him again. This time it was an open fist and it caught the side of Macht's neck.

The Mong's head rolled back and sprang forward. He stumbled but managed to stand up. Twice he swung wildly from his ankles with a broad sweeping movement that Al avoided. Al stepped in close and his fists splashed into the Mong's midriff.

Macht was still conscious as he went down. He clung to Al Brodie's T shirt, ripping it as he fell. He struck from the floor but his blows had no force. Al dropped to the floor beside him, straddling the Mong's neck, locking his head between his knees. He smashed his fists into the Mong's face, making loud welting noises.

At the washbasin the water was still running. Calvin the bellhop kept scrubbing a mop. He heard the thumping sound of the Mong's head against the floor and then the bellhop turned the faucet off. He came over and pulled at Al's shoulder.

"It's all right, boy," the Negro said. "Come on, 'fore you is in trouble."

Al got up and moved toward the back of the kitchen where the slop pail from the evening's dinner stood. He moved the pail quickly, half pushing, half rolling it toward where the Mong lay.

He called to Calvin. "Out of the way. Leave him alone. He'll live." In the next moment Al dumped the garbage over the Mong. A thick pasty liquid came out full of onion skins and potato peels.

It was then that the back door opened. The chef came in, followed by a group of the men who had been waiting outside.

"When the hell is the fight?" someone called.

A kitchen man saw the Mong first and said, "I'll be damned—we missed it."

The chef came over to the Mong's outstretched body. He poked his foot at the garbage. "Clean it up, goddamn it," he said, "before the boss sees we threw away yesterday's soup."

Chapter 26

The "Poverty Social" held at the Middlefield Center Presbyterian Meeting House on Friday evening, October 2, 1903, was advertised with a handbill stating the following regulations:

> (1) Awl wimmen what comes must ware caliker or plane gowns and apurns or be subject to fines.
> (2) Awl men must ware old cloze and outing shirt or be subject to fines.
> (3) Grumbling at fines, 5 cents.
> (4) Awl pursons what can't pay there fines must sing a song or make a speech.

Dew covered the grass and the bodies of the cars in the parking lot. There was the sound of a bird singing in the woods. Smoke curled out of the big chimney on top of the main building and from the kitchen came the smell of fresh baked bread.

Al Brodie moved quickly along the path from his room toward the main building. When he passed the linen room the housekeeper was standing on the top step with a big bunch of keys held on a curtain hook. She was giving out linen to the chambermaids.

Al heard one of the maids say, "That's him. That's the one."

" 'Morning," the housekeeper said.

All the girls turned around and stared in his direction.

He kept walking and said nothing.

There was no one in the main dining room. He drew a cup of coffee from the urn and drank it at his server. Then he finished cleaning the goblets that he'd left the night before and went over his silver.

He was refilling his sugar bowl when the door to the dining room opened and an elderly guest wearing a golf cap and gray coat-sweater put his head in.

"Excuse me," the guest said. "I heard somebody moving. Katz, I'm Mr. Katz. I sit by table twelve. Maybe you wouldn't mind, you could get my wife a cup of hot water with lemon?"

"Of course," Al said. "I'd be glad to, Mr. Katz."

"It's not too much trouble," Mr. Katz said softly. "You'll bring me maybe a piece toast. First thing in the morning—you know—you get old—"

Al said, "Right away."

"We'll wait for you by the card room," Mr. Katz said. "Please, you wouldn't forget."

"I won't be a minute," Al said.

He went back to the kitchen and lit the gas toaster, took two pieces of white bread from the breadbox and placed them in the wire rack. He spun the handle that brought the bread into contact with the heat. After he had drawn hot water and picked up a slice of lemon from the pantry, he picked up his toast.

Mr. Katz was sitting in the card room with his wife. On the other side of the table, wearing a broad-brimmed, peaked cap and chomping on a cigar, was Mr. Erlang. As soon as Mr. Erlang saw Al he said, "Look who's here—the champ."

Al said, "Good morning, Mr. Erlang. Can I bring you a cup of coffee or something?" He put the hot water and toast on the table for the Katzes.

"You know what you have here?" Mr. Erlang said to Mr. Katz. "You've got probably the next heavyweight champion of the world. That's who's serving you hot water and toast."

Mr. Katz put his hand in the pocket of his sweater, drew out a quarter, handed it to Al and smiled. "Thank you," Mr. Katz said. "This is perfect." He didn't seem to be paying any attention to Mr. Erlang.

From the lobby, two younger guests walked in. Mr. Erlang turned toward them. "You people met the champ?" Mr. Erlang said, swinging around in his chair and gesturing toward Al. "You remember that big boy—he must be two hundred twenty, he's a pound. You know, the one they call the Mong." He turned back to Al and pointed at him with his cigar. "This one knocked him out. One punch and he's unconscious."

"There was a fight?" Mrs. Katz said. "Tsch, tsch." She looked sheepishly at Al. "You was in a fight—"

Al said, "Mr. Erlang, you sure I can't bring you some prune juice or something—anything?"

"Nothing," Mr. Erlang said. His voice boomed across the quiet card room. "So come on, don't be modest. You must have hit him pretty hard. We got a regular Benny Leonard, a Max Baer yet on our hands."

Al said, "Excuse me. I've got to get back to my station. My people will be coming in soon."

"What's the hurry? We're not guests?" Mr. Erlang said. "So you had a fight. You'll tell us what you hit him with. It was a right cross. It's got to be a right cross." He addressed himself to Mr. Katz. "You catch a man when he's moving with a right cross, you can tear his head off."

One of the other guests said from the back of the card room, "I heard something about a fight but I didn't know anybody was hurt as bad as all that."

"It was nothing," Al said. "You know Mr. Erlang. He's the pride of the Sesame, the hotel's biggest humorist."

Mr. Mandheimer came walking in from the direction of the office. He greeted everybody with a very cheerful "Good morning," and then said, "You're all late from supper or you're early for breakfast?"

"We don't give you a chance," one of the younger guests said. "By the time we're through eating, you can't make a profit."

"You should only have a hearty appetite," Mr. Mandheimer said. "I never worry about how much my guests eat, so long as they enjoy it."

"So tell me something, Mandheimer," Mr. Erlang said. "You got free entertainment, you're going to advertise it?"

289

He motioned toward Al, and Al said, "Can I bring any of you other people something? How about some coffee and hot rolls?"

Nobody said anything and Mr. Erlang put in quickly, "He was working for me, I'd put in a ring. I'd advertise everywhere. Grossinger's can have a Marciano and an Ingemar Johansson. Kutcher's can have a Floyd Patterson. Who says the Sesame can't have better? From what they tell me this boy did to the other one—"

"It was nothing," Al said. "A little disagreement. These things have a way of getting exaggerated."

"Disagreement, he calls it," Mr. Erlang said. "I hear he nearly killed him. I'm serious, Mandheimer. I mean it. That's what your place needs—prize fights would put you on the map."

Mr. Katz looked up from his piece of toast. "Somebody was hurt?" he asked Mr. Mandheimer. "One of the boys is in the hospital?"

Mr. Mandheimer said, "You'll listen to my good friend Henry Erlang, he'll have us all in the hospital." Everybody laughed and then Mr. Mandheimer said, "Henry is all right. He's all right. Five years ago, he was telling me I should buy atomic stock. I listen to him, I don't need the hotel business today."

"Why not?" Mr. Erlang said. "You're in the market, you got to keep up with the times."

"You don't say," Mr. Katz said. "You wouldn't mind telling me—"

Mr. Erlang started telling him about his experiences in the market. Mr. Mandheimer continued on his way toward the kitchen. As he came past Al Brodie he said very softly, "After breakfast, Allen, stop by the office. I want to talk to you."

It was eleven o'clock. On the loudspeaker the lifeguard was announcing noon calisthenics on the front lawn. Jerry Furman was standing right behind him.

As soon as the lifeguard was finished, Jerry said, "Pancho Ginsburg talking. Si, si, amigos. Cha-cha lessons beginning pronto in the casino."

In the television room a group of guests were sitting around watching a local program called "Memory Lane." Mrs. Mandheimer was standing at the far corner of the main desk talking to a young couple. The wife was dressed in a tight skirt and sweater. Her husband had on corduroy pants and flannel shirt. They wanted directions for a walk to Old Falls.

When Mrs. Mandheimer had finished giving the directions, Mr. Mandheimer excused himself and explained to the couple that there was a much more scenic walk along the banks of the Neversink River approaching a beautiful old bridge.

Al Brodie was standing at the desk next to the young couple. He heard Mr. Mandheimer say, "Of course, you can suit yourself, but that walk up the Neversink, it's real country. To Old Falls all you see is a public highway."

"Maybe they want to see a public highway," Mrs. Mandheimer said.

"They can suit themselves," Mr. Mandheimer said. "I was just suggesting a little more private walk."

"You don't have to suggest," Mrs. Mandheimer said. "They want to be some place alone, they don't have to walk. They have their room."

The woman laughed and said, "Isn't she frank?"

"What can we do in our room?" the man said. "That mattress—it's like sleeping on the Atlantic Ocean."

"You sure it's my mattress and not your wife," Mrs. Mandheimer said.

The man smiled and said, "You know, you might have something there."

The young wife giggled. "She really is something," she said. "Really, Mrs. Mandheimer, you have some sense of humor."

"That's room twenty-one in the Annex," Mrs. Mandheimer said. "I'll see you get a new mattress. I wouldn't want my mattress to be the cause of you changing your wife."

"You got something nice around here?" the man said. "I could use a little change."

The woman said, "Manny, stop it."

Mrs. Mandheimer didn't say anything for a moment. She lowered her eyes and arranged the check-in cards. Then she said, "It is a nice day. A walk should give you a good appetite."

The man said, "Come on, we'll take a look at the Neversink." He put his arm around his wife's waist and they started off.

"Since when you're making dirty jokes," Mr. Mandheimer said to his wife. "All of a sudden, Becky, you start talking that way."

"You have a younger crowd," Mrs. Mandheimer said. "You loosen up a little."

"That's a way for a hotelkeeper to talk? We've got a few guests, you have to insult them."

"You don't know what you're talking about. They like it," Mrs. Mandheimer shrugged. "So how about you? You have to suggest they should take a walk—it's got to be a lonely road."

"You'd think a minute," Mr. Mandheimer said, "you'd realize I only wanted they shouldn't walk by Old Falls, they shouldn't be on route forty-two. They shouldn't have to see a hundred other hotels."

Mrs. Mandheimer turned to Al. "Everything worries him. You'd think they take a walk, they see another hotel, right away we're out of business."

"Times like this," Mr. Mandheimer said, "you have to be extra careful."

Al said, "He's got a point. We sure want to hold on to every guest we have in the house now."

They were both quiet for a moment and then Mr. Mandheimer said, "Allen, you'll come into the office. I'll talk to you."

Al said, "Sure, any way that's convenient." He swung around the front desk and squeezed past the mailboxes. Mr. Mandheimer led him into the inner office. There were two small black desks in the room. Both were covered with letters, open envelopes, typing paper. A big steel spike was on one desk. At the bottom of it were a few bills and invoices.

"Any place in particular you want me to sit?" Al asked.

"Make yourself comfortable," Mr. Mandheimer said.

Al sat down on a small swivel chair. It had a cushion on it and he had to sit forward to keep the cushion from slipping.

Mr. Mandheimer went to the door that led to the desk. "You coming in, Becky?" he said.

The switchboard buzzed and they could hear Mrs. Mandheimer's voice answering it.

"Well," Mr. Mandheimer said. "I'll talk to you alone. Man to man. We shouldn't bother Mrs. Mandheimer."

He closed the door and stood for a moment with his left arm folded in front of him and the elbow of his right arm resting in his left hand. He stroked his chin.

"So, Allen," he said. "I'll come to the point. From someone else, maybe, there's an excuse. You're boys. You can make mistakes. You're young, you don't know. But you—you're different. Just yesterday I was telling you, myself. You and me, we were talking, I told you this was an extra special bad time for the business. We have to be extra careful."

"You're right," Al said. "You're absolutely right, Mr. Mandheimer."

"What was between you and the Macht boy," Mr. Mandheimer went on, "it has nothing to do with this business. My guests—they don't have to know from it." His voice rose and he nodded his head. "My help are here so the guests should be happy. The guests come first—all the time."

Al said, "You're right, Mr. Mandheimer."

"You're telling me I'm right, that wouldn't help you now," Mr. Mandheimer said. "People are talking already, you heard yourself this morning. A thing like that gives a hotel a bad name. For what? For who? You're working for me. I'm paying a fair salary. I'm feeding you. I ask only that you serve my guests, that's all. A time like this above all else. You admit yourself—you know how important it is." He dropped his hands and slapped them against his thighs. "So Allen, I'll get your payroll card. I'll give you what's coming to you. You'll pack up. You'll go."

Al said, "Mr. Mandheimer, could I—?"

The old man held up his hand. "It wouldn't do you any good to talk, Allen. Personally, I got nothing against you. I'm disappointed yes, but personally there's no bad feeling, at least for my part. Perhaps because I talked to you quiet, like one grown man to another, you thought I didn't mean it. If that's the case, you don't understand me—I tell a help something, I mean what I say."

Al said, "Could I please, Mr. Mandheimer—could I please say this one thing?"

Mr. Mandheimer started into the file after his payroll card. "It's a free country," he said. "You want to talk, nobody is stopping you."

"I admit everything you say is right, Mr. Mandheimer. I'd be the last guy in the world to want to do anything to hurt this hotel. I'm all for the business. You know that—"

Mr. Mandheimer looked up quickly from the filing cabinet. "What you feel, what's in your heart, my guests don't know. There was a fight, a boy's in the hospital, that they know."

"Mr. Mandheimer, listen to me. Just for one minute. I know you've got this whole thing worked out in your mind. You've made your mind up, I can see that. But don't do it, Mr. Mandheimer. Please, I'm asking you not to fire me. Everything you said—it's true. But the thing is—I really go for this place. I like everything about it. I know that sounds like real bull, but it's the truth. This is more than a job to me." Al stopped and stood up. The old man was standing at the filing cabinet with the payroll card in his hand. He looked at Al and nodded, and though there was a long moment of silence, he didn't speak.

Al said, "Mr. Mandheimer, I got the interests of this place at heart. How many waiters you going to find like that? Look at it this way—you think there's another guy on the floor has the feeling for this place that I do?"

Mr. Mandheimer made a small sound with his lips. Then he leaned the payroll card against the top of the file, and with a little book from the Department of Internal Revenue, started to make his computation.

Al took a step to be closer to him, then he said, "Look, Mr. Mandheimer, I'll be honest with you. I don't like to say this, but maybe you'd understand. It wasn't only Macht. Hell, he's been on my back all summer. I could have taken a couple more weeks. It wasn't just that. It was something more—something a hell of a lot more important."

The old man looked up from the payroll card. There was anger in his expression that Al had never seen before. "Yes?" Mr. Mandheimer said. "What are you trying to tell me, Allen? It is something we should talk between you and me?"

Al Brodie swallowed hard. "No—no, I guess it isn't. I'm sorry I started to bring it up." He stood a moment silently and then he said, "Look, suppose I finish the season for nothing. I made a mistake, I have to pay for it. Let me pay for it that way." He pressed toward the payroll card, closer to Mr. Mandheimer. "How about that? I work for nothing. That makes sense, doesn't it, Mr. Mandheimer?"

The old man shook his head. "No. No, Allen, why should you work for nothing? I wouldn't ask you. Anybody should work and not be paid for it—this is a business. I got to do things in a business-like way."

Al Brodie's voice came out choked. "Please," he said. "Please, Mr. Mandheimer—one more chance."

Mr. Mandheimer said, "You'll sign here, Allen, where it says you're healthy, here again for the money. You'll endorse the check, Becky will cash it."

Al Brodie took the pen and moved toward the payroll card. "I didn't think you'd do this to me," he said. "Not you."

Chapter 27

A little man with a mustache motioned with the second finger of his right hand for Jerry Furman, the social director. "This one you got to tell them," he said. "You tell it up there from the stage, it's a riot. I don't tell it so good, but you can put it over. Maybe Friday night, we'll have a full house—that's the perfect time. You heard this one, maybe? The man next door was selling this thing cheaper than the other man but he didn't have it in stock?"

The second cook was ladling out fish, spaghetti, and Brussels sprouts to the help. There was a long line of waiters, outside men, and chambermaids, but Joe cut through the line. The children's dining room opened an hour earlier than the main and he had only a few minutes to eat before the first arrivals.

"Likey sprouts?" the Chinese cook said.

"Sure," Joe said. "Business slow on them?"

"Diney room no eat. Children no eat. Help no eat. But dey velly good. Velly, velly good for blood." He gave Joe an extra heavy portion.

Joe took his plate to the children's dining room and ate quickly. He was halfway through when he heard the sound of a baby squealing.

"Slowly, Phillip. Wait for Mommy," he heard Marsha Cooper's voice say.

"Hi," Joe called over his shoulder. "I'm all set up for you."

Phillip was dressed in overalls and a fleece-lined jacket that bunched up at the chest. Marsha had on slacks and a heavy knit sweater. Her hair was tied in the back with a red ribbon. When she bent down to take the jacket off Phillip he spun away and she had to hold him locked between her knees to keep him still.

"Phillip is a big boy," she said. "Let's show Joe how we take off our own jacket."

Phillip tugged at one sleeve, gave up and tried to escape again. As soon as the jacket was off, Marsha picked him up and put him in the high chair that was his regular seat.

"Oh, look what Joe has for us this evening," Marsha said. "Melon and chicken soup—and if we're a good boy, maybe Joe will bring us some applesauce."

Joe got up quickly. "I better get that jar of Gerber's for you now. There's only one left."

"Sit down," Marsha said. "Finish your supper."

"No trouble," Joe said. "I should have put it aside before. I just forgot."

When he came back with the jar, Marsha said, "I hate bothering you like this, but it's so much easier feeding him early."

"Forget it," Joe said. "By gosh, he's no trouble at all. You should see some of the specials I run for kids."

"I know," Marsha said. "The waste in this place is just fantastic. I don't see why we can't cut all the children's menus in half. Four courses is just too much for any child."

"You know these people," Joe said. "They'd start screaming we're starving them."

He sat down again at his place and ate his supper. When he was through he said, "Let me know when you're ready for the main."

Marsha said, "Listen, Joe, you can save this melon. He didn't touch it. Just a small piece of white chicken and I'm set. And please tell the chef to cut a breast in half. Don't tell him it's for us—that way he won't be so overgenerous."

Joe smiled. "I guess everybody is out to impress the boss, huh."

Phillip said, "Sauce—I want sauce." Marsha had to ease him

back into his chair. He got very absorbed dipping white bread into the applesauce and smearing it over the tray of his high chair.

Joe cut the chicken into small pieces for Marsha before he gave it to her.

"You didn't have to bother doing that," Marsha said. She turned to Phillip. "Look what Joe fixed for us—chicken."

The baby reached over and took a big handful. He stuffed it in his mouth and chewed with his mouth open.

"What manners," Marsha said. "See why he eats early?" She took a paper napkin and wiped off the high-chair tray.

"You should see some of the combinations I've seen this season," Joe said. He whistled. "Steak dipped in ice water. Spinach in milk. And sandwiches made out of everything."

"You wonder how they grow up to be civilized at all," Marsha said. She wiped Phillip's mouth with the napkin and with a fork picked up a piece of chicken and held it for Phillip.

He pointed toward the applesauce and she dipped the chicken in the applesauce. Then he ate it.

Joe said, "It's a shame about Al Brodie, isn't it?"

Marsha fixed another piece of chicken with applesauce for Phillip. He moved his head away from it and she put down the fork. "What happened to him?" she said.

"He got canned," Joe said. "Because of the fight and everything."

"He did?" Marsha Cooper said. "Well, I'm certain he'll be able to take care of himself."

Joe said, "Sure, that Al is on the ball. But he's taking it pretty hard." He pulled up a chair from another table and sat on it backwards. "You never can tell with guys like him. I lived with him all summer, but when you come right down to it, what do I really know about him?"

Marsha said, "I wouldn't worry about it. You know everything he wants you to know."

"I didn't mean it exactly that way," Joe said. "Two guys live together, they bitch a little bit to each other. They've got something on their mind, they get it off. Like I told him about Ellie—our troubles and stuff like that. But Al—he's different."

"He's that, all right," Marsha said. This time Phillip picked up the fork and Marsha tried to help him guide it toward his mouth. He pushed her hand away.

"Take like now," Joe said. "He gets fired and all. I know he's burning inside, but you think he'd say anything to me? Not a word. He just lays on his bed—thinking."

Marsha looked at Joe quickly over her shoulder. "You mean plotting, don't you?" she said.

Very seriously Joe said, "I don't know. Maybe he is, but whatever it is I hope it works out for him." Then he said, "I like Al. He's helped me and I'd like to help him. Only, hell, he's tough to do something for."

"What would you like to do?" Marsha asked.

"I'd like to get him his job back. I think he wants it—real bad."

Phillip started to slap the fork against the table. He laughed as the applesauce flew off to the side. Marsha tapped a spoon against the table, and when Phillip went for that she took the fork from his hand. "If Al Brodie wants his job back," Marsha said, "he'll find a way to get it. Nobody is getting rid of him that fast."

"I don't think so," Joe said. "I hear Mandheimer was really teed off about that fight. Al's been paid off."

"He'll think of something," Marsha said.

"He's packed and everything. There's nothing Al could do to get his job back now."

Marsha picked up Phillip's jacket and started to put her son's arms into it.

Joe pushed his chair back. It scraped against the floor and he stood up. "You know, Marsha, it might help if you talked to the Mandheimers. They are your folks. It's just a couple of weeks, but it means a lot to Al."

Marsha zipped up Phillip's jacket. Then she stood her son up on the high chair, smoothed his hair, and bent down to retie his shoes.

Joe went on. "I figure you're the only one who could talk them into it. A guy like me—if I say something—I'm just butting in."

Marsha tied the lace in a double knot and then stood up. "Why should I go out of my way for Al Brodie?" she said. "What do I have to do with him?"

Joe said, "It was the fight that got him in all this trouble." He looked away from her. "Hell, Marsha, everybody knows they were both going out with you."

Marsha put her son down on the floor. She held both his hands and swayed him gently as she faced Joe. "He told you to talk to me. Brodie put you up to this."

"You're wrong," Joe said. "He'd be sore if he even had an idea I mentioned it."

"Who told you that thing about the fight? What makes you so sure it had anything to do with me?"

"Mandheimer warned him and everything," Joe said. "I mean, just figure it out for yourself."

Marsha looked at him a moment without saying anything. Then, still holding both of Phillip's hands, she gently kicked one of the boy's legs and then the other. Phillip squealed with delight as she walked him in this manner toward the door.

Mr. Mandheimer swung around from the switchboard. He put his hand over the mouthpiece. "Becky, we have two adjoining rooms on a first floor for the week end? Must be corner."

"Corners yet, the end of August," Mrs. Mandheimer said. "It's so hot they need cross ventilation?"

"Two adjoining on the first floor," Mr. Mandheimer said. "They can't walk steps."

Mrs. Mandheimer said, "I can give them in the bungalow."

"You don't have the main house? Already our first floor is all taken?"

"You're so smart," Mrs. Mandheimer said. "I give them all the first-floor rooms now at their price, what'll I have left for my price at the last minute?"

Mr. Mandheimer said, "Please, Becky, no lessons. I have people on the phone."

"The bungalow," Mrs. Mandheimer said.

"Hello," Mr. Mandheimer said into the mouthpiece. "Sorry to keep you waiting. Yes, we do have a lovely pair of adjoining rooms in a cottage . . . No, these cottages you have to see . . . All new furnishings . . . Our deluxe rooms? My dear lady, at that price I wish I could afford to give you the deluxe rooms . . . I'm getting fifteen dollars a day and you think I have one left?"

Mr. Mandheimer was still on the telephone when Marsha came around the desk. She moved past her father and went into the inner office where Mrs. Mandheimer was working at the typewriter. It was the first time that season she had come into the office without her son. As her mother typed, Marsha picked up some yellow second-sheets and looked them over.

"So how's the baby?" Mrs. Mandheimer said. "He's at the camp? Somebody is watching him?"

"He likes the flag-lowering," Marsha said. "And he seems to be very fond of that counselor, Rosalyn Silvers."

"That's nice," Mrs. Mandheimer said. She was still typing. "So," she went on, "he likes the camp. That's nice. It's good he stays with counselor. Gives you some free time."

Marsha took the second-sheets over to the filing cabinet, opened it, and started putting away the letters. "You know you could change these index tabs for correspondence. They were old when I was here."

Mrs. Mandheimer pulled the letter she was typing out of the machine.

From the switchboard Mr. Mandheimer called, "Becky, we have maybe one room on a first floor? Absolutely they can't walk stairs."

"I told you two in the bungalow," Mrs. Mandheimer said.

"They're taking one for themselves by the cottage, but for the mother. She's got a condition."

Mrs. Mandheimer said, "I could give her maybe Katz's room, they're supposed to leave I think Thursday."

"You're sure?" Mr. Mandheimer said. "Becky, look, I got these people still on the phone."

"So tell them yes," Mrs. Mandheimer said. "They'll come, I'll find something for them."

Mr. Mandheimer's voice was pained. "Becky, do you or don't you have something? An old lady—I wouldn't make a fool out of her."

"So I'll give her Feiblebaums' room and move them upstairs with their uncle. They'll save a few dollars, they wouldn't mind."

"That's definite then?" Mr. Mandheimer said.

"Sam, please—what d'you want, a contract?" Mrs. Mandheimer said.

Mr. Mandheimer went back to the phone and Mrs. Mandheimer signed and sealed her letter. She said to Marsha, "You'd listen to your father, who would believe he's twenty-seven years in the business?"

Marsha finished filing the last of the yellow sheets. "You know, you could have a big room-chart on the wall, and when you got a reservation you could mark it down. That way you wouldn't have to carry everything in your head."

"I suppose," Mrs. Mandheimer said.

"The hotel is getting larger," Marsha said. "There wouldn't be anything wrong with hiring a girl to help you out in the office either. Smaller hotels have more help."

"I had a girl," Mrs. Mandheimer said. "When was it, two years ago. Oh yes—it's easy to say have a girl. All she wanted to know was when she had time off, she could go dating with the waiters. She sits here all day, her hands are folded, she has nothing to do."

"You have to organize help. You can't just expect people to know what to do."

"By the time I explain, I can do myself," Mrs. Mandheimer said.

At the switchboard, Mr. Mandheimer had hung up the phone. They could hear the sound of the typewriter going.

"Sam," Mrs. Mandheimer called, "you'll leave me with the typing, you'll take these letters into town, they should get them tomorrow morning."

Mr. Mandheimer said, "Becky, please—"

Marsha reached over to the desk where her mother was

sitting and picked up another pile of second-sheets. She leafed through them. "All of these confirmations for the Myron Blum week end?"

"Some," Mrs. Mandheimer said. "I wouldn't be surprised you'd find July letters there yet."

Marsha started to alphabetize them.

"You know," Mrs. Mandheimer said, "he's put on weight. He's filling out."

Marsha said, "I hope he doesn't get fat. I try to keep him off starches."

"What's wrong with a fat baby?" Mrs. Mandheimer said. "To me a fat baby is healthy."

"Not necessarily," Marsha said.

Mrs. Mandheimer said, "You're putting them by alphabet, you'll see in the corner the letter—"

"Oh, yes," Marsha said. "Why do you put the letter in the right-hand corner after you type them?"

"I mark the letters," Mrs. Mandheimer said. "I get a chance, I file them. At least I save my eyes."

Mr. Mandheimer came in with an envelope in his hand. "Becky, you'll put a brochure in. These people on the phone wanted they should see what the hotel looks like."

"The ones with the adjoining rooms?" Mrs. Mandheimer said. "They're such a bargain. We get some nice weather over the week end, I wouldn't need them they should take my best rooms and bargain for the price."

"Twelve dollars," Mr. Mandheimer said. "You can do better?"

"Two people in a room," Mrs. Mandheimer said.

Mr. Mandheimer said, "So all right, if you got three people, the room brings more. What if there's not such a rush at the last minute for Myron Blum? What if we get bad weather?"

Marsha said, "Myron Blum seems to be bringing them in?"

Mr. Mandheimer turned to her. "Yes," he said gently. "But you know your mother, she sees one bird—how does that go?"

"You mean one swallow doesn't make a summer?" Marsha said.

"That's right. That's your mother," Mr. Mandheimer said.

"We have a few reservations, right away we're going to have a big week end, a full house."

The switchboard buzzed again. Mr. Mandheimer went to answer it. While he was gone, Marsha continued alphabetizing the correspondence. Then she opened another file drawer and started to put the carbons away.

Mrs. Mandheimer went back to her typewriter.

When Mr. Mandheimer came back he said, "You remember Sam Marcus, was here for four weeks in July six, seven years ago? He wants we should hold three private rooms for him Thursday. He's coming up with a family."

"Marcus? Marcus?" Mrs. Mandheimer said.

"That bald fat man who was always bringing his friends to visit from the bungalow colony," Marsha said.

"That's right," Mrs. Mandheimer said. "I forgot, but you remember."

Marsha concentrated on the file drawer. "If you're going to have so many people for the week end," she said, "you're going to need a bigger crew."

"Don't worry," Mr. Mandheimer said. "The agencies will have plenty."

"It's not easy to get experienced help at the last minute," Marsha said.

"All of a sudden you're so interested in the business, Marsha," Mrs. Mandheimer said. "You're afraid maybe we shouldn't have enough waiters?"

Marsha said, "Why don't you take Al Brodie back? He's worked here all summer—God knows he loves the place."

Mrs. Mandheimer said, "You run a business, you have to learn to be hard."

Mr. Mandheimer said, "I warned him, your mommy warned him—he shouldn't fight. It's a bad thing for the business, Marsha. We've got maybe a few people, they don't want to know from fights."

Marsha turned away from the file drawer. The yellow sheets were still in her hand. "Sometimes people come before the business. A person's feelings can be a lot more important."

"Listen, Marsha," Mr. Mandheimer said. "Our help is not

worth it. Between us three speaking, who else cares about your business? To the best of them it don't mean a thing. You got to keep your eyes on them all the time. You want something done right, you have to do it yourself."

"You say something, you have to stick to it," Mrs. Mandheimer said. "He cared so much for us, he wouldn't have to fight."

"This job meant a lot to him," Marsha said. "You never had a waiter who cared so much."

"Next year, we'll all live and be well," Mr. Mandheimer said, "everything will be forgotten, we'll give him a station."

"So what's so bad about that?" Mrs. Mandheimer said. "It's a few weeks, that's all. He's a nice boy. We got nothing against him. He wants next year his job, why not? But he's not so important he should come before the business."

"Exactly," Mr. Mandheimer said.

Marsha slid the file drawer shut. She put the yellow sheets down on the desk. She was standing between her parents when she said, "Who *is* more important than the business? Does anybody ever come before the goddamn business?"

"This business was so bad to you?" Mrs. Mandheimer said. "You got married, you ran off to Arizona, you had a few dollars in your pocket. Your husband died, you have a place your baby can get fresh air, eat good—that's so bad?"

Mr. Mandheimer said, "What did this business ever do to you, Marsha? Why should you hate it?"

"So maybe you don't like all the people," Mrs. Mandheimer said. "So the crowd is a little old. So they eat too much, they talk too loud. It's still yours. You'll go any place in the world, you wouldn't find it perfect."

"Any other place in the world," Marsha Cooper said, "isn't my home." She looked from one to the other. Her voice was even and low. "Where were you when I was growing up? Where were you when I went to Arizona?"

"Marsha, don't be silly," Mr. Mandheimer said. "You ran away from us, so it's our fault."

"I didn't send you checks?" Mrs. Mandheimer said. "So you

tore one up—I made another one. It's the same thing. Did I say one word to you, you came back your husband was dead? A mother learns to forget—"

"When I wanted you—when I needed you—you were always too busy," Marsha said. "I can't forget that."

"You needed?" Mr. Mandheimer said. "What did you need? You should have told us. We're your parents. It costs us our last penny, we would help you."

"My God, we're not even speaking the same language. We're saying the same words but they mean different things."

"So then tell us, Marsha. That's your trouble—always so secretive," Mrs. Mandheimer said. "A girl gets married, she talks it over with her mother. You introduced us? We even met the boy? This is feelings? This is being good to people? Everybody is all right—everybody gets consideration. But your parents —we're made out of stone."

"I was always in your way," Marsha said. "Oh, you gave me plenty of things to do—little things, the kind of jobs you could have hired a numbskull to do in my place. I never felt for one minute as if I was needed around here. I could have been dead for all the difference it made to you." She looked from one to the other. "I did you a favor when I went to Arizona."

The switchboard started to buzz, but neither Mr. nor Mrs. Mandheimer answered it.

Finally Mrs. Mandheimer said, "That you should say such a thing. That such things should cross your mind. It's not all yours anyway?"

"Of course," Mr. Mandheimer said. "For who do you think we're working? For you. The whole thing is for you, you shouldn't have to kill yourself working like we do."

"And suppose I don't want it?" Marsha said. "Suppose I don't want the hotel? Is it for me—is it really for me? Or is that just your excuse for doing what you want?"

Slowly Mrs. Mandheimer said, "This boy—this Al Brodie— he means so much to you? You want—for you—we should keep him, Marsha?"

Marsha said, "Forget it. Forget I ever mentioned it. Run your business your own way."

As she walked out of the office she picked up the switchboard phone. "Hotel Sesame," she said. Then, pushing the receiver toward her parents, she said, "Here, it's for you."

Chapter 28

"I wish the summer would never end," Linda said.
"It always ends," Jerry Furman said. "It's been that way with every good thing that's happened in my life."
"What do we do now?" Linda said. "Should we see each other in the city, darling?"
"I don't know," he said. "I guess that's up to you."
"I want to be fair. I wouldn't want to hurt her."
He said, "You can never be happy—never have anything that's worth while in the world without hurting someone."
"Let's not go through that again, darling. Please, not now—"
He kissed her and then he said, "Thanks, Linda—thanks for not telling me it's over when we both know it is."
"It's the only way," she said. "If we did anything else it would never be the same. We tried so hard, but all we have is another unsuccessful summer romance."
"No—no," he said. "It's more than that, my dearest. Who knows? Maybe we'll both be back next year."

It was evening. Service in the main dining room was moving at a slower and more leisurely pace. The guests, dressed in tweeds or heavy sweaters, light toppers or stoles, gazed out of the large plate-glass window. The sun was falling behind the mountains, but there was a chill and weight in the air that foretold the end of summer.

Mr. Mandheimer had adjusted the thermostat before the

dining room opened. He explained to Audrey that he'd be back to put it up higher when all the people were in.

Danny Rose was bussing two stations. Joe had come in, as soon as he was through in the children's dining room, to cover Al's station. Audrey Grier was helping him.

Audrey and Joe were on their way through the swinging door that led to the kitchen when she said, "That's a boiled chicken top for Hymowitz on number five."

"I've got it," Joe said. "His wife is having the boiled beef flanken."

"That chicken has got to be salt-free," Audrey said.

"Don't worry," Joe said. "Everything is under control."

"Thanks," Audrey said. "I really should be getting around to the rest of the dining room. Thank God for Labor Day."

"They're all over you, aren't they?" Joe said.

"Nothing is right after the fifteenth," Audrey said. "Don't forget those lamb chops for that kvetch on number four. If anybody else asks for them, tell them they have to be ordered twenty-four hours in advance."

"They know," Joe said. "Al has them well trained."

On their way to the hot stove, Audrey asked, "Did he leave yet? He didn't even say good-by."

Joe said, "He's in his room. He's just laying there."

When Mr. Mandheimer came in for the second time to readjust the thermostat, Audrey Grier spoke to him.

"I was wondering," she said, "with this Myron Blum affair and then the big Labor Day week end coming up—we're going to need experienced boys."

"Call the agency," Mr. Mandheimer said.

"Of course I'm going to do that," Audrey said. "But frankly, Mr. Mandheimer—it's none of my business. You have every right, after a fight like that—but Al Brodie is a much better than average waiter. And you know how these people are after the fifteenth."

"You'll call the agency—one day, two days—you'll get all the Al Brodies you can use. You think all the hotels aren't laying off experienced boys?"

"It's just that he does know the house," Audrey Grier said.

Mr. Mandheimer turned back to the thermostat. "He's gone—left," he said.

"Naturally, it's up to you," Audrey Grier said. "It's not for anybody else to tell you how to run your business. But I just do happen to know that he's still in his room."

Mr. Mandheimer turned toward the door. "Franklin Delano Roosevelt wasn't indispensable—the Sesame can do business without Al Brodie."

Al put his suitcase under the back steps leading to the rear entrance of the main building. The night was cold and his jacket collar was up tight around his neck. He could hear the noise from the kitchen below and the voice of Jerry Furman announcing the evening activity on the loudspeaker.

He walked up the steps quickly and when he came to the first floor, he kicked the screen door open with his foot. It slapped hard against the wall. He noticed the spring wasn't connected and he fixed it.

When he got to the door of Marsha Cooper's room, he heard Phillip laughing. He heard the voice of Marsha Cooper. She was chanting, "Tendala, tendala, tendala . . ."

He knocked once lightly on the door.

"Hey, Marsha. It's Al Brodie," he said. His voice was choked and heavy. "I'd like to talk to you."

She said, "Just a minute, Al. I'll put the baby to sleep."

He turned away from the door and toward the steps.

He heard Phillip cry and then Marsha said to the baby, "Only once more. I can't keep this up all night."

There was the sound of the baby laughing as Marsha began to recite "Tendala" again.

He stood for a moment listening, and then suddenly he ran down the back steps. He kept running until he was standing outside the kitchen.

The night was dark, with only the thin lights from inside the kitchen streaking across the narrow entrance way, the freezer box, and the garbage room.

He heard the voices of waiters calling out orders. They

blurred with the humming from the dishwashing machine and the clang of china.

The salad man shouted at a waiter, "No more coleslaw. I'm telling you, the last week in August and they want the house."

The chef called from behind the stove, "Shut up. Give them what they want. Payday you'll want your money."

Al Brodie turned toward the freezer. A small yellow bulb was lit, indicating that the inside light was on. The lock hung open on a latch to the side. He pulled against the big steel handle and it sprung open. The cold fumes spiraled into the night and he went in. He saw cases of vegetables stacked along the floor—some open, the cardboard wrappers hanging fringed with ice. There were cans of frozen orange juice and strawberries, and cakes half exposed, their paper wrappings loose but frozen.

On the shelves were the even rows of rib filets that he had picked up from Mr. Fleischer's butcher shop that night with Mr. Mandheimer. They were caked in flakes that looked like snow. What the hell did Mr. Mandheimer care for Al Brodie? He was a waiter who'd stepped out of line and been fired. Upstairs Marsha was singing tendala to her kid. They've all got something, he thought, but me.

He reached out and grabbed at a rib. He felt the cold sting his hands. He hugged the rib to his body and then lugged it off behind the garbage room, and threw it among the leaves and dirt and grass. When he returned, the freezer box was filled with a thick mist. He pulled two ribs out this time and ran with them, stumbling a few steps up the hill behind the kitchen. One rib slipped from his hand and fell, and he dropped the other one and went back for more.

Two were left at the far end of the shelf, wedged against the wall, held tight by ice. There was a deep impression in the middle of one and he pulled at it. The ice cut his fingers and stuck beneath his nails.

The freezer door was open and there was a whirling sound from the motor. He thought he heard someone call his name, but the sound was lost in the humming of the motor. He kept trying to get the rib.

He felt a chill as though an icicle had been dropped down his shirt. He shuddered, but pulled until finally the last two ribs came loose. As he left this time, he pushed the door shut with his foot.

He saw Marsha Mandheimer looking at him. Her expression was tender and confused. He held the ribs tight waiting for her to speak but she just stood there. For a moment he looked about wildly, almost as if trying to find a place to run, then he faced her and said, "What are you doing here? Spying on me?"

She didn't answer him, so he went on. "Go ahead, turn me in, for Chris' sake. I'm fired. The old man gave me the gate. I've got no right even being around the place. What the hell, I'm destroying their property." He pushed the ribs toward her. "They're yours. They belong to them and you. You want them back? Look at them. Look at the eye on them."

He came closer to her, still talking, and lightly she put her hand on top of one of his.

"You can get twenty steaks from a filet," he said. "Did you know that? And from a rib you get a couple pieces of flanken and the deckles for pot roast."

Still she said nothing.

"You know how I know that? Me, just a lousy waiter— I know everything there is to know about a rib. Sure, Mandheimer took me to the butcher's with him. The old guy was crazy about me."

Very quietly she said, "Don't, Al, stop. It isn't worth it."

He pulled away from her and forced a laugh. "What d'you mean stop it—it's the truth. The goddamn truth. The old man was taking me to the butcher's and the old lady was telling me how I looked just like the kid. And you and me—we were doing real good too, weren't we, Marsh? Me, Al Brodie, I come up here with only two bucks in my pocket and before I know it, I have the whole place made. What happened? What happened to it all? You know what I got now, Marsha? Absolutely nothing. A guy like me, I make one mistake and I'm out."

Marsha said, "Don't talk like that. It isn't even true. Why don't you sit down awhile, Al? You're cold. That meat must be heavy."

"One goddamn slip and I'm right back where I started," he said.

"Al, Al. It's only a job."

"That's where you're wrong," Al said. "It was a hell of a lot more than that. But now, for all Mandheimer cares, I can take off on the next bus."

"All right," Marsha Cooper said. "I heard you the first time. So what are you trying to prove? What good does it do throwing out their food?"

"What good does it do?" Al Brodie repeated. "I'll tell you—" He looked at Marsha, then down at the ribs as if seeing them for the first time. All at once his body sagged. "Yeah. Who the hell am I fooling?" he said. "It doesn't do any damn good at all." He let the ribs fall. "I must be nuts—tossing away good ribs, for Christ's sake."

"You were tearing up their checks," Marsha said. "It never helps. Nobody knows better than I do."

They both sat down on the freezer steps. "I don't know, Marsh. I don't know any more. It was just that everyone had something and me—I got nothing."

"I wouldn't say you've got nothing, Brodie," Marsha Cooper said. "It might not be much, but at least you've got me. That is, if you want me."

He kept his eyes on the ground. "Cut it out, Marsh. A hell of a lot good I'd be for you—me, just another guy without a job."

Marsha reached for his red, cold hand and brought it close against her thigh. She waited quietly. They could hear the sounds from the kitchen and the rasp of a cricket outside. When she spoke, her voice was soft but even. "You'll be a lot of good for me," she said. "I only hope I can be half as good for you."

Al Brodie just shook his head and looked away. He freed his hand from hers.

"You know, I had a talk with my parents," she said. "I don't think it helped very much as far as your job goes. I guess I could have got it for you, but I couldn't ask. I never could see things quite through to the end."

He turned to her. "You talked to them for me?"

"Well, I knew the job meant a lot to you."

"Now what did you want to do a thing like that for?" he said. "You didn't have to beg for my job. What the hell, I knew what I was doing. Mandheimer told me what would happen if I rocked the boat."

"But you did it anyway. You had the fight with Stan just the same—"

"I had all I could take from the Mong."

"That doesn't sound like the guy who could twist Stanley Macht around his little finger any day of the week," she said. "I don't believe you."

"Believe what you want."

"I will, Brodie honey."

She looked at his slumped shoulders. Then, suddenly, she jabbed him in the side playfully. "Oh, shit, Brodie, snap out of it."

He jumped up, surprised and angry. "Where the hell do you get off talking like that." He pulled her roughly to her feet. "Where do you get off talking that way? Let's get this straight right now," he said, "I don't ever want to hear my girl using language like that again. Understand?"

She bounced a small fist off his chest. "Tough guy."

He looked down at her, and then he smiled. There was a sureness in Marsha Cooper's eyes that he had never seen before.

In the office the switchboard was buzzing. Mr. Mandheimer picked up the phone and took down the information for a reservation.

"You know," he said to his wife, "that makes the second call for a third-floor room. Myron Blum could fill this house."

"For five hundred dollars, he shouldn't fill the house yet," Mrs. Mandheimer said.

"Hurricane and all—this wouldn't be a bad year," Mr. Mandheimer said.

"So we'll build a bigger casino," Mrs. Mandheimer said. "You'll listen to me, we'll put new furniture in the Annex."

"It's not a full house yet. It could rain before Thursday," Mr. Mandheimer said.

"Stop it already, Sam," Mrs. Mandheimer said. "I've never seen you so nervous. We'll have a full house. We won't have a full house."

"So—" Mr. Mandheimer said, and he let out a deep breath. "Before the phone rang you were telling me what Calvin was saying to you—"

"He was telling me," Mrs. Mandheimer went on, "how that Stanley Macht, he was no good. How the basketball, it was no good."

Mr. Mandheimer took a few steps toward the office door and then came back. "The bellhop is telling us already how to run the hotel. They work for you too long, it's no good."

"He was just talking," Mrs. Mandheimer said. "He hasn't got a right to talk? You're so excited, Sam. Everything today makes you so excited."

"I'm excited?" Mr. Mandheimer said. "Your bellhop, your hostess—everybody is telling you how to run your hotel. But me, I'm excited."

The switchboard rang and Mr. Mandheimer hurried to answer it. When he came back he said, "Julius Skulnick wants we should hold a room for him, second floor main house, for Labor Day."

"Labor Day already," Mrs. Mandheimer said. She went over to one of the small black desks and made a notation on the cardboard backing from a shirt.

"So what's that?" Mr. Mandheimer said. "A new system?"

"For the Labor Day reservations," Mrs. Mandheimer said. "I'll put up on the wall here, we shouldn't have to ask each other a million questions."

"One time you'll be in a hurry, you wouldn't write it down, so what good's your chart?"

"I wouldn't forget," Mrs. Mandheimer said.

Mr. Mandheimer looked over her shoulder. "Second floor. What are you writing third floor, Becky?"

"I don't know Skulnick?" she said. "He didn't eat my heart out when he came to pay his bill last year?"

"I promised him second floor," Mr. Mandheimer said.

"He doesn't like it, he can check in someplace else," Mrs. Mandheimer said.

"That's a way to run a business?" Mr. Mandheimer said. "I don't know, Becky. You was never this way."

Mrs. Mandheimer said, "I didn't have a daughter she should tell me she does me a favor she leaves my house."

"You think she meant what she was saying, Becky?"

Mrs. Mandheimer looked up from the room-chart. "You think maybe she doesn't, Sam?"

Mr. Mandheimer shrugged. "Who knows? Who can tell what's in their hearts?" He nodded his head, adjusted his coat, started to look over the room-chart. "You know, it's not a bad idea, Becky," he said. "We'll be busy, a chart like this, it could be a help."

"Listen, Sam," Mrs. Mandheimer said, "you ordered some more blankets? We'll get a cold spell for the Blum week end, we'll be in trouble."

"I ordered already by County Supply. You think I wait, it should be the last minute?"

"So maybe you'll call the agency, you'll order the help early too. We shouldn't get what's left."

"Why not?" Mr. Mandheimer said. "We'll have a full house, we'll need a big staff."

"This late," Mrs. Mandheimer said, "there's no use fooling yourself, you wouldn't get experienced waiters."

"So?" Mr. Mandheimer said.

"You'll go to his room," Mrs. Mandheimer said. "You'll talk to Allen, he'll stay. He'll work by us over the holiday."

Mr. Mandheimer looked toward his wife. "You think so? You think so, Becky?" Before she could answer he bobbed his head and shrugged his shoulders. "Why not? He's a smart boy. He catches on fast. His lesson, he's learned."